The Collected Supernatural and Weird Fiction of Mrs. J. H. Riddell Volume 3

The Collected Supernatural and Weird Fiction of Mrs. J. H. Riddell Volume 3

Including Two Novels "The Disappearance of Jeremiah Redworth," and "The Uninhabited House," Two Novelettes "Diarmid Chittock's Story," and "The Open Door," and Five Short Stories of the Strange and Unusual

Mrs. J. H. Riddell

LEONAUR

The Collected
Supernatural and Weird
Fiction of
Mrs. J. H. Riddell
Volume 3
Including Two Novels "The Disappearance of Jeremiah Redworth," and "The
Uninhabited House," Two Novelettes "Diarmid Chittock's Story," and "The Open
Door," and Five Short Stories of the Strange and Unusual
by Mrs. J. H. Riddell

FIRST EDITION

Leonaur is an imprint
of Oakpast Ltd

Copyright in this form © 2012 Oakpast Ltd

ISBN: 978-0-85706-998-6 (hardcover)
ISBN: 978-0-85706-999-3 (softcover)

http://www.leonaur.com

Publisher's Notes

Contents

The Disappearance of Mr Jeremiah Redworth

CHAPTER 1

MR. REDWORTH STARTS FOR CADLEBURY

On a fine July morning, in a certain year of grace, Mr. Jeremiah Redworth left his house, situated in Dorking Street, Ludham, with the intention of proceeding to Cadlebury, distant, as the crow flies, some eight miles.

As no road, however, in that part of Surrey, does follow the crow's flight, Cadlebury, to all practical intents and purposes, is a thirteen or fourteen miles' journey from Ludham.

A journey across country, too, impossible by rail, save by making a considerable detour, and by calculating with much nicety the arrival and departure of corresponding trains.

For a man of his years, the distance might have seemed excessive to those who did not know that Mr. Redworth boasted he could do his twenty miles a day with the youngest fellow in the parish.

Over his head time had passed lightly; life for him had held wonderfully little trouble. Never had it been necessary for him to work too hard, or think very much, or sorrow over deeply; nature, when she created him, omitted from his constitution keen susceptibilities, loving sympathies, quick impulses; and the circumstances of his career, so far from supplying natural deficiencies, tended to deepen and harden every original trait.

Misfortune had spared and sickness overlooked him; never

had it been necessary or indeed possible for him to mix freely among all sorts and conditions of men. From the small world of a government office he retired to the smaller world of a sluggish country town, where he occupied the late leisure of his existence by turning his money over to good account by making small investments, by interesting himself in local matters, and laying out plans for his own future and for the future of those who should come after him.

When a human being is so constituted that, practically, he scarcely understands the meaning of suffering, sorrowing, or repenting, the years as a matter of course deal gently with him, and at seventy, Mr. Redworth, who had scarcely known what it was to have a day's real sickness since his teens, did not look so old, and in many respects really was not so old, as men little more than two thirds his age.

In a district where rheumatism racked the bones of quite young people, Mr. Redworth never experienced ache nor pain. Bronchitis had no terrors for him, and the members of his household could not remember that he had ever suffered from a cold in his head.

He was rarely out of bed after eleven p.m., or in bed after half past seven a.m. Nothing could induce him to wear a top-coat, or a wrapper round his throat.

"Thick boots and plenty of exercise!" was his motto.

"If you wear thick boots and take plenty of exercise," he remarked, addressing society generally, "you need never be ill, and you may live almost as long as you like."

Ludham accepted this statement, as it accepted many other dogmatic observations uttered by the same gentleman, without contradiction, and it is not on record that anybody ever asked him what the poor wretches were to do who could not wear thick boots or take plenty of exercise.

Mr. Redworth was in the enviable position of not only being able to make his own laws, but follow them.

There were few theories he chose to advance, that if it pleased him he might not carry into practice. In his own way he was as absolute an autocrat as the *Czar* of all the Russias, and if he ruled his subjects gently and with a fair amount of generosity, such admirable results were certainly owing less to the system than to the man.

Standing on the pipe-clayed steps leading to his own Hall door, for instance, the morning when he left his house in Dorking Street for the last time, neither of the ladies who accompanied him to the threshold with the kindly desire of "seeing him off," ventured to ask when he might be expected home.

Long previously some unspoken law had been laid down that the head of the establishment was not to be questioned, and consequently the members composing his household, like good children, "waited to be told."

Concerning his goings and comings it is therefore to Mr. Redworth's credit that he made no secrets; and many persons will consider it to his praise that regarding his affairs he was silent as the grave.

Thus, although Miss Redworth, his daughter, and Miss Gower, second cousin of his "admirable and lamented wife," had been told overnight that, "if fine, he intended walking to Cadlebury the next day," they were utterly ignorant what he meant to do when he got there; and when standing in the morning sunshine, his hat well brushed, his coat free from speck or stain, his linen spotless, his boots brightly polished, and his umbrella tightly furled, Mr. Redworth said to his daughter—

"You need not expect to see me back much before nine. Amelia." Amelia had no more knowledge than the dead lying in Ludham Churchyard how her surviving parent meant to improve the fleeting hours of that summer's day.

Afterwards Miss Gower remembered that, contrary to his usual habit, Mr. Redworth lingered for a minute on the step before taking his departure.

At the time it did not strike her as anything extraordinary, that he should have stood smoothing the wrinkles out of his gloves, and looking up at the sky ere crossing the street, and walking in his gentlemanly manner out of the town, but subsequently she recollected he had done so.

"I think I shall go by the canal," he remarked, as he moved away irresolutely, and then paused once again.

"You will find it much cooler than the road across the heath," observed Miss Gower.

"Yes, much cooler," he agreed; "and pleasanter," he added, swinging his umbrella.

Having made that further observation, he looked down on the pavement, took another irresolute step, then quite suddenly, saying to daughter and niece—

"Goodbye, for the present, my dears," Mr. Redworth walked out of their sight for ever.

Chapter 2

An Excusable Weakness

Mr. Redworth had married before he was thirty, and there were now two of his sons settled in London—men verging towards middle age, men with grave faces and staid manners, possessed of wives and families.

The ex-government clerk had done well for them, given them good educations, placed them early in suitable situations, managed to get them subsequently into good business houses, and when the chance of desirable partnerships fell in their way. assisted them wisely and economically to the fulfilment of their wishes. When in due time the young men beheld young women sufficiently fair, and possessed of a little money in the present, and the chance of more in the future, Mr. Redworth once again came to the front, enabled them to buy a couple of houses in a convenient neighbourhood, helped them considerably in the matter of furniture, and, in a word, started them almost unweighted in the race of matrimony.

Both Trenhill and Gower were very good sons of a very good father; neither, it may be safely said, had given an hour's real anxiety in their younger days, and now, when they were no longer young, but men with assured positions in the mercantile world, men safely prosperous, and well able to provide for the families growing up about them, Mr. Redworth might have been excused had he referred to them in atone of conscious pride, and informed acquaintances, with a certain triumph, that Trenhill Redworth, partner in the house of Basing, Hull, and Redworth, bacon factors, Tooley Street, and Gower Redworth, junior in the firm of Morris and Redworth, bone crushers, Bermondsey, were his two eldest born.

But Mr. Redworth did nothing of the sort. Perhaps it would be going too far to say that in his later life Mr. Redworth felt ashamed of the bacon warehouse and the bone-crushing factory, but undoubtedly he never alluded to either with enthusiasm.

While he was struggling, while he felt, with all the economy he could practise, that there may be some difficulty in meeting rent and taxes, paying tradesmen's bills, providing for the proper education of a growing family, and making provision for those left behind in case of his premature death, Mr. Redworth, being unable to indulge the solitary weakness his nature knew, had, with laudable common sense, invested his sons, so to speak, in the stock most likely to return a sound and safe dividend.

Since they left school they had not really cost him a penny. While in situations they had received sufficient, if moderate salaries, and for all moneys afterwards advanced they paid him interest at the rate of five *per cent.*

He had been generous enough to give them a hundred pounds a-piece the day they were married, and the furniture he personally presented to the respective wives might perhaps have amounted to three hundred more; but these things had been of his own free will; and as his sons were always sending him parcels and hampers directed to Ludham station. South Western Railway, carriage paid, it may be assumed that even for that five hundred pounds he had an ample return.

And yet no one ever heard Mr. Redworth speak with effusion of those good citizens, Trenhill and Gower, any more than any man living had ever known him talk with softened voice and smiling face, of—

"My daughter Amelia."

Mr. Redworth, like each among us, had his weakness, and in his case it took the form of—birth.

It was a natural foible, no doubt, in a man who, having risen from nothing, had for years and years of his life been thrown in contact with people who owed everything to connection—who visited at houses, the doors of which were closed to him—who claimed relationship with Lord This and the Duke of That, who had the ways and the manners and the habits of the Upper Ten, and who looked down on trade and tradespeople with an ignorant contempt which to anyone capable of seeing and appreciating the humour of the position, would have been enjoyable in the extreme.

Mr. Redworth, unhappily, could not enjoy the joke, and suffered in consequence.

The nephew of a woollen-draper in a country town, foisted into a government office by the influence of a member of Parliament, "Society" to him meant something on the other side of a perpetually-closed door—Paradise—Heaven—if the readers have no objection to strong language.

This story has to deal so little with what the man was, that it is unnecessary to devote space which might be otherwise employed in telling how young Jeremiah modelled his manners upon those of young Tremaine, tied his cravats after the fashion of Gervais, modulated his voice like Howards, and endeavoured to walk like the Honourable Major Helleric, chief, in Redworth's calf-days, of his department.

Coming from the most humble stock, he worshipped rank, for which reason he ignored the city, and said as little as he could avoid about the sons who were earning their living honestly and hardly in Tooley Street and Bermondsey.

He had married his wife for the sake of her "family." Happily for him he never knew the ins and outs of that deceptive pedigree.

The real state of the case was this: once upon a time, a hardworking man of the name of Gower rented a farm within walking distance of a garrison and cathedral town in the far west of

England.

He had many fair daughters, and amongst them one fairer than all, called Amelia, who, attracting the notice of a certain Major Cartress, left her home, and was secretly married to the officer in question. Eventually a scandal arose about the business.

It was said, and with justice, that Miss Gower's husband had been guilty of bigamy—that she was not his first wife, and that if she liked to proceed to extremities, she could send him to prison.

All this occurred at a distance from Miss Gower's parental home, and close to the parental home of Major Cartress's first wife.

To the rescue came Jenkins, Mrs. Cartress's father, a gentleman accustomed to look upon everything from a pound-shilling-and-pence view.

"Now look here," he said to Mrs. Cartress number two, "we know the fellow is a scoundrel, and that he richly deserves prosecuting; but how will prosecuting him serve you? If he were snug in jail tomorrow you could not be more free to marry somebody else that you are now. As regards supporting you, even if he had any money—which he has not—you could not compel him to make you any allowance. Now I'll tell you what I am willing to do if you choose to keep yourself quiet. Leave the management of the affair to me, and I will write you a cheque for a hundred pounds, and pay you twenty-five pounds a year so long as you remain unmarried. You need not decide today. Perhaps you would like to consult your friends. At all events, take no step you cannot recall till after you have thought the matter over."

Miss Gower did think the matter over, and discovered that what Mr. Jenkins said was perfectly true. The business was a bad one, but an exposure could not mend it. To her it had been a great glory to call herself the lady of a major, but life with the major was not, after the honeymoon, destitute of troubles.

A very shrewd and a very sensible woman, she decided to accept Mr. Jenkins' offer if he would agree to change its terms.

"I think," she said, "I could make a boarding-house pay in London. Enable me to purchase or start one, and I will never ask you for another shilling."

"Very well," agreed Mr. Jenkins, after a minute's hesitation. And the same day she left Manchester for London.

Arrived there, she dressed in widow's weeds, and commenced her metropolitan career in the character of a lady whose husband was dead.

Ere long, in point of fact, Major Cartress did actually die, and none of her new friends ever suspected there had been anything awkward about the lady's marriage.

She experienced no difficulty in stating where the ceremony took place, and the name of the officiating clergyman. It was impossible for her dearest crony to hint at the existence of any mystery about her. Had it been necessary to show her "marriage lines," she could have taken them at once out of her desk, and with them the certificate of baptism of Amelia Laura, daughter of Major Frederick Cartress and Amelia his wife.

As years went on, she talked more and more of the "reduced circumstances" in which she had been left, and of the struggles she had been obliged to make in order to maintain herself and child.

About the same time she began to find it pay to allude frequently to "the Gowers," and to make constant mention of "Trenhill, my father's property."

Poor old Mr. Gower had gone to a world where anxieties about rent-days, and the failure of crops, harassed him no more, and there was, consequently, not the slightest fear of that stalwart farmer bringing his horrid fustian between the wind and her nobility.

Mrs. Cartress had been a beautiful girl, and as she developed into a very handsome woman, the friends of her later life, who heard references to "the Gowers," and were treated to many touching reminiscences of "Trenhill," were wont to declare that anyone could see the lady had come of distinguished people. "Her features are quite aristocratic," they never failed to add, "and her manners noble."

Eventually, there can be no doubt Mrs. Cartress herself came to believe she was in some way related to the members of a certain titled house.

Prints representing several of them graced her walls, and the widow often said, with a sigh, "It is heart-breaking to think how far the branches of good families sometimes droop."

"The anomaly of a Gower keeping a boarding-house," she often remarked, with what her admirers called "a queenly gesture."

"It is always those the best born who struggle most bravely against adversity," was another of her utterances. Indeed, in the course of years, she acquired a sufficient number of these sayings to enable her effectually to garnish her conversation with them.

As for the daughter, growing to womanhood, if the blood of all the rightful Gowers had flowed in her veins, she could not have been prouder of her pedigree. Trenhill, to her imagination, was a ducal residence, and her grandfather, she firmly believed, had been a fine old English gentleman.

"She takes after my poor husband in looks," Mrs. Cartress frequently observed. "She doesn't in the least resemble the Gowers."

Knowing a young fellow who boarded in the house of this reduced gentlewoman, Mr. Redworth was brought into contact with his future wife, and it is satisfactory to be able to state that, till the hour of his death, he was never disillusioned on the subject of Miss Cartress's ancestry.

If Miss Cartress had stepped across the threshold of Dunrobin Castle to become his bride, Mr. Redworth could not have felt more certain that she was a relative of the owner.

It was a harmless fancy, and one which tended greatly to his happiness, and as Mrs. Redworth kept herself a little aloof from general society, everyone who was thrown in contact with the lady, firmly believed Mr. Redworth's statement that she had come of very great people indeed.

After his two eldest sons were placed in those houses in which they eventually became partners, a great change took place in Mr. Redworth's circumstances.

The woollen-draper, then an old man, died intestate, and to the thousands he had put by, and to the goodwill of his business, Mr. Redworth, in default of any nearer relation, succeeded.

It is unnecessary perhaps to say that with all convenient speed the goodwill of the business was disposed of, and Mr. Redworth, banking the amount of the purchase money as well as the thousands already referred to, began to look about him for suitable investments.

At this time his family consisted of only four children; one had died in infancy, and two were carried off by fever in the teens.

Thus there was a gap often years intervening between Miss Redworth and her youngest brother John Morrison Redworth, whilst a still wider interval stretched between his "old" brothers and the "boy."

On this lad, this Benjamin, Mr. Redworth expended all the hope and pride of his nature.

As harassed mothers, to whom infants have come so fast that before one can walk another requires to be hushed and tended, say pathetically they have never been able to "enjoy" a baby, so Mr. Redworth, who had always kept up appearances and done his duty towards wife and children, and found both often a struggle, knew when his uncle's money rendered life quite easy to him, he had never got much pleasure out of any one of his sons till curly haired, blue-eyed John began to go to school and bring home his little prizes.

Hitherto everything connected with the Redworth family had of necessity been almost strictly useful, but John, his father determined, should be ornamental as well.

He inherited all his grandmother's beauty, he was quick, and bright, and clever, and he had cast back to some remote ancestor, perhaps to one of the remarkable Gowers, for a temper which seemed incapable of being ruffled—sunny, cheerful, and unselfish.

No greediness or grasping, no envy or jealously about that curly-pated little lad, no dangerous instincts lurking in the depths of his dark blue eyes—a good truthful merry boy full of noble and generous impulses, a boy of whom any father might have been fond and proud, a favourite with servants, and teachers, and visitors, and school fellows.

If his brothers were not quite so fond of him as other people, it was because they felt they too were possessed of admirable qualities, which the world should have been equally swift to recognise.

Naturally also they contrasted the Spartan severity of their training with the many indulgences granted to this Benjamin of the household.

"Our father will rue it all someday," they often said, shaking their prematurely old heads over their parent's folly; and yet, despite this jealousy, they sincerely loved the boy with a faithful brotherly love calculated to stand much wear and tear.

What projects that father built upon that son! All his own life had to him almost unconsciously lacked was to find fruition in the future of his youngest born.

John should be not merely a great man, but also a great gentleman. There was no height to which in imagination Mr. Redworth did not sometimes climb when considering John's possibilities.

Had not the boy been born with the typical spoon in his mouth?

Which of his other children found wealthy sponsors who gave costly gifts to the infant for whom they so solemnly renounced the world and a few other sinful items.

The silver mug, the silver knife, fork and spoon, the coral and bells—were not these things laid up as evidences of how fortune had smiled upon the lad's birth.

In itself, John Morrison might not, Mr. Redworth considered, be a desirable name, but when accompanied with many tips, and the prospect of a fine legacy, it became not merely bearable but poetical.

What puzzled Mr. Redworth most was the choice of a profession. To such a prodigy there were so many open.

To be Lord Chief Justice, for instance, was not a bad kind of thing. A Bishopric, too, presented an eminently desirable sort of opening. About the post of Prime Minister there was a certain instability, which to Mr. Redworth had its drawbacks; but still if his son made that goal his ambition, he would not object.

"So much," he was wont to remark, "depends upon the bent of a young man's mind," which indeed, so far as John Morrison Redworth was concerned, proved terribly true. Everything depended upon that, and yet while he was still in his teens, everyone except, perhaps, his father knew the lad's mind had no bent at all.

"If he had only been put to business early!" sighed his brothers, overlooking the fact that if he had been put to business from his nurse's arms, he never would have compassed the successes they achieved; that no matter what his training, nature must have proved too strong for art, and rendered him just as unfit to become a prosperous merchant as to grapple with the difficulties of statesmanship.

But his father considered him perfection, and believed all the shortcomings of his career were attributable to the scurvy treatment accorded him by that shocking old hypocrite his godfather.

"Always led us to suppose John should be his heir, always treated him like his own son, sir. Everyone believed him to be an old bachelor; but when he died there was a wife with half-a-dozen children ready to swallow up the property. Not a sixpence to John—he was not thought worth even the scrape of a pen."

Chapter 3

Miss Gower

The long summer day passed slowly away. Miss Redworth, who, since her mother's death, had presided over her father's establishment, looked after such household details as required her supervision, and then joined Miss Gower, who was engaged in

18

the harmless occupation of crocheting an elaborate antimacassar.

Miss Cower was a relation of the deceased Mrs. Redworth, and as such very dear indeed to the widower's heart. A certain James Gower, son of the Trenhill farmer, had at an early age gone to Canada to seek his fortune, and this Hilda Susannah, so skilful in all kinds of delicate needlework, was his granddaughter. A correspondence had always been maintained between James and his sister Mrs. Cartress, and that epistolary acquaintance, kept up after his death between the younger members of the family, was sufficient, when Hilda was left an orphan with only a moderate dot, to render her being consigned to England and the care of so respectable a gentleman as Mr. Redworth, as natural as under the circumstances it happened to be expedient.

Not handsome like her far-off relative Mrs. Cartress, or pretty like her own mother, or stately and dignified like Mrs. Redworth, Miss Gower nevertheless was possessed of charms which appealed to the tastes of most of the Redworth family.

Pallid of complexion, slight of figure, with features small and fairly well cut, she appeared to Mr. Redworth an eminently genteel and good-looking young woman.

She never became red with heat or blue with cold; her hair was always perfectly smooth and her dress eminently neat. Her collars, and cuffs, and gloves could not have been smoother or more free from crease or crumple if she had been a lay figure. Her jacket was never dusty, her feathers were never out of curl. When you had seen Miss Gower once you had seen her always. However fashions might change, and what the latest mode she affected, you felt she must have been similarly attired for years. There was never any novelty about her, or, for that matter, any antiquity either; a young old woman, with self-possessed manners; never excited, never very sorrowful, never very glad, never certainly lively, and never greatly depressed; dowered, as poor Mr. Redworth imagined, with that repose which "marks the line of Vere de Vere;" in the eyes of Miss Redworth and her brothers a very superior girl indeed, but who might, to persons accustomed to wider views of humanity, have seemed singularly self-contained and inscrutable.

Such as she was, Mr. Redworth destined her for his youngest son. Someday, it was quite understood—it had always been understood—that Miss Gower and John Redworth should, as the ex-government clerk tersely expressed the proceeding, "Make a match of it."

"A wife any man might be proud of," remarked Mr. Redworth; "fit to ride in her carriage; and who may ride in her carriage someday, who knows."

Of course no one could venture to prophesy what might occur when that vague someday arrived; but there were not wanting persons who said positively unless Mr. Redworth left his son very well off, that young gentleman would have to proceed through life in a somewhat more modest fashion.

Long before the world—the Redworth world I mean—had decided that John Morrison Redworth would never achieve greatness—that he was not very clever—that he was inclined to be extravagant—and that he had not a bit of industry in his nature. In this case the world's verdict was true, and Miss Gower knew it. And yet Miss Gower loved him. So far as it was in her nature to love anything, Miss Gower loved her handsome, good-tempered, debonair cousin with all her heart.

Someday also she believed he would love her, and meantime there was no one else; of that she felt quite certain. He was still fancy free, he cared for nobody; she was sure she had not a rival in the world!

The day wore on. After partaking of a seasonable repast, at which cold lamb, mint sauce, a cool salad, and some raspberry tarts occupied the chief places of honour, Miss Redworth and Miss Gower proceeded in the glowing heat of a July afternoon to pay visits. Then they had a little walk by the river, and strolled back across the town meadows to Dorking Street.

"John will be at home before us," remarked Miss Redworth, stifling a yawn.

"Yes, I heard his train come in some time since," answered Miss Gower. Never having discovered whether the bent of his mind inclined to the Episcopal Palace, or the leadership of the House of Commons, John Redworth had, pending the development of any decided taste, permitted himself to accept a "post under government."

In a word, he was at five-and-twenty a clerk, as his father had been before him; with this difference, that he did as little work as he could; that he was spending more than his salary; and that he had not the faintest idea of trying to do anything better in life than to lounge through it.

He was asked, however, to many parties. Young men of good family called him "Jack," and "Redworth," and, to a certain extent, made him free of their own rank, whatever value such freedom might confer.

Very different, indeed, was he from his brothers, the steady and respectable City merchants; and if his father chafed sometimes at his want of application, he exulted in the son, who, so far as appearance and manner went, "might have been heir to the Crown."

At Ludham the inhabitants knew very little indeed of the habits of courts, or the tastes and ways of princes, and Mr. Redworth's statement was therefore received without contradiction. Ludham, however, had got an inkling that Mr. John Redworth was going to the dogs, but it did not care to tell his father so.

When the two ladies reached home they were informed that Mr. John had not come back.

"He will be down by the next train," said Miss Redworth; "shall we wait tea, dear?"

"By all means," agreed Miss Gower, and so after she had taken off her bonnet and laid aside her jacket, and pulled out her gloves finger by finger, and smoothed her ever-smooth light hair, the young lady descended to the drawing-room, and resumed the manufacture of that antimacassar which day by day grew in size and beauty.

The "next train" had been in some time, and still John Redworth did not come.

"I think we had better have tea, dear," suggested Miss Redworth, consulting her watch,

"Just as you like," answered Miss Gower.

Miss Redworth did like, and so the ladies went into the dining-room, where there were a great many flies, and partook of tea, which was always set out in that dreary apartment.

Mr. Redworth had no patience with people "lolling about" at meals, and the tea-table was therefore invariably spread with mathematical accuracy, chairs being ranged round the festive board, as though the family were above to have a regular dinner.

Thus laid it was a somewhat dismal repast for two persons, and so apparently Miss Gower felt, for she sipped her tea indifferently, and crumbled a biscuit idly, whilst the flies came and went, and the noise of rattling conveyances sounded through the open windows as though carts and cabs were rushing through the room. Children at their play screamed and shouted on the side paths, and there did not seem a breath of fresh air stirring in all the land.

"I wonder where John can be," marvelled Miss Redworth.

"Gone to spend the evening with some friend, I dare say," said Miss Gower; "but it is strange he did not telegraph."

John Redworth had a way of telegraphing. It saved much trouble and prevented useless conjecture.

"Shall we go up to the drawing-room?" asked Miss Redworth, when the decorous meal was concluded.

"Yes," answered Miss Gower, and after having uttered that monosyllable she returned to her crochet work.

Almost in silence for some time the two ladies continued their respective employments.

In that establishment there was never much of the pleasant chatter which obtains in some families. Decorous, respectable, well-ordered, well-managed was the little household over which Miss Redworth presided, but lively—never.

Gaiety is not the distinguishing quality of some homes. Gaiety certainly was about the last sin which could be laid at the door of the Redworths.

"Papa will soon be back now," said Miss Redworth at length.

"It is past nine," said Miss Gower. "I suppose he meant to return by train. Hark! There he is."

But Miss Gower was wrong. The latch-key she heard thrust into the lock belonged not to Mr. Redworth, but to his son, who was greeted over the banisters by his sister—

"Why, John, is that you?"

"Yes, Amy. Late, am I not?"

"We thought perhaps you had gone off for the evening."

"No. I only went on to Cadlebury."

"To Cadlebury? Did you see anything of papa?"

"Nothing."

"How wearily you speak, John," remarked his sister. "Have you had tea?"

"I don't want any tea thank you."

"Should you like some supper now, or will you wait till papa returns?"

"Where is the governor?" asked the young man, coming up the staircase.

"Where? Why, he told you this morning he was going to Cadlebury."

"Did he? Oh, yes, I remember. Well, is he not back?"

"No—not yet."

"What on earth can he have found to occupy him all day at Cadlebury?"

"I don't know. He said we need not expect him before nine o'clock."

"Then he meant to return by the train which brought me. He can't be here now till half-past ten."

"Perhaps he is walking back," suggested Miss Gower. By this time they were all in the drawing-room together.

"I should think that would be too much of a good thing, even for him," said the young man, throwing himself into an easy-chair. "By Jove! How hot it is!"

"Won't you have a glass of wine?" asked his sister. "You seem quite knocked up. Why did you go on to Cadlebury?"

"Oh! I wanted to see a fellow down there, and I thought I

could have been home long ago. Yes, Amy, I should like a glass of wine, please. If you give me the keys I can get it for myself."

But already Miss Gower was at the door, and halfway down the stairs.

One of the delights of her life was to minister to this young man's wants. One of the greatest pleasures of her monotonous existence was to hear him say, "Thank you, Hilda," or, "You are far too good to me," or, "You really make me feel ashamed of my laziness." She brought up the wine and some biscuits, and, pouring out a glass of sherry, carried it to where he sat.

As she did so she tripped over a footstool, and, to save herself from falling, laid a hand upon his arm.

"Why, John," she exclaimed, "your sleeve is quite wet."

"Wet still, is it?" he said carelessly, and yet colouring a little as he spoke, "I thought it would have been dry long ago."

"What were you doing to get your sleeve wet?" asked his sister. If it were a rule of the house that Mr. Redworth's proceedings were beyond question, the same tolerance was not extended to the actions of any other member of the family.

"I was getting something out of the water," he answered.

"Why, John, how odd you are tonight," exclaimed Miss Redworth. "What was the something you were getting out of the water?"

"Ah! That is my secret," he replied, with an uneasy laugh. "Can't you let a fellow have some peace, when he comes home badgered and worried. Look here, do you want any money, either of you? for a wonder I have got a lot—behold!" and he pulled some gold out of his pocket, and let the sovereigns fall from one hand into the other, with a pleasant gliding melody.

"My dear John!" cried out his sister.

"How rich you are, all of a sudden," observed Miss Gower.

"Yes—for a wonder a horse I backed won, and this is the result. Now, girls, what shall I buy for you? Don't be modest, Amy. Speak up, and declare what your feminine soul most longs for."

"That my brother should be wise and give up betting, and save his money," said his sister, earnestly. "Oh, John! How I do wish—"

"Like a dear girl, don't begin preaching to me tonight. I'm tired to death. I have been running about all day. If you don't mind, I think I will go to bed. I suppose I ought to sit up to remonstrate with the governor about keeping such late hours—but I'll let him off for this once."

As the door closed behind the young man, the two women looked at each other.

"I wonder what is the matter with him," said Miss Redworth.

"I wonder why he went to Cadlebury," said Miss Gower.

Chapter 4

Missing

John Redworth had never achieved a reputation for early rising, or regularity of any sort. In a house where punctuality was the rule, he proved the exception. Housemaids had to tap several times at his door before he evinced the slightest intention of turning out of bed, and his sister never expected to see him till she was pouring out second cups of coffee.

For this reason Miss Redworth looked surprised when, on the morning succeeding his visit to Cadlebury, her youngest brother entered the breakfast-room even before the kettle was brought up. Such an event had not taken place since she assumed possession of the household keys, and naturally she felt a surprised astonishment at its occurrence.

"I went to bed last night as such an unearthly time," he explained, somewhat sheepishly, as though not being late for breakfast was a thing any man might feel ashamed of. "Is not the governor down yet? At what hour did he turn up last night?'

"He never turned up at all," answered his sister. "I wish, John, you would not call him 'governor;' it does sound to me so disrespectful."

"My dear girl, there you are quite wrong. 'Governor' is a term of the highest respect. And so he didn't come home? What little game can he have on hand? It won't do, Amy. We must not permit this sort of thing to continue. We shall hear of the dad getting into all sorts of scrapes. It will be necessary for me to speak to him seriously."

"I did not go to bed until nearly two o'clock," said Miss Redworth, a little complainingly.

"You look as if you hadn't been to bed at all," answered her brother, with fraternal frankness. "Eyelids heavy, cheeks pale, and that sort of thing. Sitting up o' nights does not agree with your style of beauty, Amy. And the fair Hilda Susannah, did she sit up also?"

"Yes, it was natural, considering papa's regular habits, we should feel a little uneasy."

"No doubt; when a gentleman of his age takes to evil courses, matters do look serious."

"John," said his sister—by command of Mr. Redworth the young man had been called John by his family since he was a baby, never Jack—"try not to be absurd for a minute—don't laugh at me. I want to ask you a question. Do you think any accident can have happened to papa?"

"Accident," repeated her brother, "what kind of accident could have happened to him?"

"That is what I cannot imagine."

Mr. John Redworth thrust his hands deep in his coat pockets, walked to the window, and then walked back again.

"If the train had smashed up we should have heard of it," he said, after a moment's reflection. "Father always goes about the world labelled like luggage. Card-case, pocket-book with name and address printed on it, linen marked, a few letters directed to Jeremiah Redworth, Esq., invariably upon his person. No, Amy, you need not be uneasy. Ill news, you know, travels fast, and ill news about the governor would have come home like a shot."

"And yet still, John, I cannot help feeling uneasy. I have a sensation of something being amiss, which I am unable to shake off. Last night, or rather this morning, when I went upstairs to bed, it seemed to me as if there was someone lying dead in the house. Do you know, I felt so nervous, I was almost afraid to go into his room as I passed, and while I lay awake—for I could not sleep—I could have declared I heard him walking about as he does when he is dressing, and opening and shutting the drawers. You will think me very foolish, but I cannot get over my fancy that something has gone wrong," and, as if to emphasize her statement, Miss Redworth covered her face, and sobbed aloud.

To do him justice, John Redworth looked sorry and sympathetic.

"Poor Amy," he said, kneeling on one knee beside his sister, and putting an arm affectionately round her neck, "you ought not to have sat up so late. What a brute I was to go to bed and leave you to do work you are so little used to. See how undesirable a virtue regularity is," he added, speaking in his usual tone. "Because, for once in his orderly life, the governor fails to return at the time appointed, you at once imagine something dreadful must have happened to him; whereas if I were to remain away for days, you would say, 'Oh, he's sure to come back all right. No need to be uneasy about him—one never can get rid of a bad shilling.' Moral—don't marry a punctual man, Amy. Ah! Hilda you're just in time to hear the pith of my sermon. If you desire to keep a quiet mind, and to live to a good old age, never select a husband like the governor. Here is Amy crying fit to break her heart because he did not come back last night at nine o'clock, for all the world as if he were housemaid in this strictly respectable establishment."

"It does not strike me as a laughing matter," answered Miss Gower, somewhat crossly. "Fifty things might have happened to your father."

"Of course they might, my dear," retorted the young man, "and one of these days the sky might fall, but I do not think that is likely."

"If you could be serious for a minute, John, I should like to ask what you consider we had better do," said Miss Redworth.

"Do!" repeated her brother, "what on earth do you mean?"

"About papa not coming home, of course."

"I should suggest employing the town crier," answered her brother. "How pleased the governor would be to hear, as he came along Market Street, old Williams ringing his bell, and shouting, 'Lost, stolen, or strayed—Jeremiah Redworth, Esquire.'"

"I suppose you think all this very funny, John," remarked Miss Gower, "but I confess your mirth strikes me as ill-timed. At your father's age so many accidents may occur."

"A good many accidents may occur to a man at any age," said Mr. John Redworth, dryly.

"I wish we could hear something about him, though," exclaimed Miss Redworth.

"Pooh! My dear," cried her brother, "you will have the governor marching in here directly, cool as a cucumber, and fresh as a daisy, after a fourteen miles' walk, and when you tell him you felt uneasy about his absence, he will say—

"'Business detained me,' or 'I met an old friend, and we partook of a simple dinner at the "White Stag," where I slept. You need never be uneasy about me, Amelia.'"

Having delivered himself of which imitation of his father's curt utterances and pompous tones, the young Redworth finished his breakfast in haste, though there was, for a wonder, abundance of time and to spare before his train started, and saying he thought he would be off, rose from the table and departed.

"He is like all men," commented Miss Redworth, "selfish and unfeeling."

Miss Gower answered nothing. Toying with food, to which she brought no appetite, her heart was singing a dull refrain—

"There is something the matter. Why did he go to Cadlebury, and what has happened to detain my uncle?"

Both questions were destined to be repeated by other people, besides Miss Gower, before many days had passed.

In the chain of circumstantial evidence so soon to entangle John Redworth's future life, that morning's restlessness formed no slight link. It had ever been his pleasant practice to reach the station breathless, to start running when the final bell rang, to dart into the first possible carriage—often as not into the guard's van after the train was in motion; but to be too soon, that never happened before in the experience of Ludham, and on the present occasion it proved once too often.

"Why, there's Jack Redworth. I must be off," said young Homer to his wife, leaving his breakfast almost untouched, and forgetting, in his hurry, to kiss the baby and to take his gloves.

"There's that John Redworth," remarked Mrs. Straitlace to her husband. "You will be late again, Mr. S.; I wonder how it is that you never can be induced to get up at a proper hour in the morning."

"What has come to our clock," exclaimed Mr. Harris; "I told you I thought we were all wrong last night, Mary. It is of no use trying to catch that train now."

"Then you may as well have another cup of tea, and make yourself comfortable," answered his sister, placidly.

As John Redworth passed along the high Street, Mr. Nunn, the chemist, stood in slippered ease at his shop door, exchanging some mild words of wisdom with his neighbour, Mr. Hazeldine, saddler.

"Good morning, Nunn—good morning, Hazeldine," said the young man in greeting as he approached.

"Good morning to you, sir. lively morning, ain't it?" severally replied the worthies addressed; then, as their eyes followed his retreating figure, Mr. Nunn observed to Mr. Hazeldine—

"Something must have happened in Dorking Street. It wants ten minutes to the hour yet, and the church clock is always striking the quarter after, when he passes to the train."

"Shouldn't wonder if the father and he have had a row. Sure to come some day. There are none so blind as those that won't see. If Old Redworth had not wilfully shut his eyes, he must have known long ago the pranks his hopeful son has been up to."

"It is a pity, too," observed Mr. Nunn; "for he is a fine young fellow."

"One of those fine fellows born with a capacity for bringing nobles to ninepences," said Mr. Hazeldine, who considered himself a bit of an orator, and had a reputation in the town for turning neat sentences.

Why that morning of all mornings John Redworth, so pro-verbial a sluggard, should have been unable to rest in his bed; why the preceding evening of all evenings he had gone to Cadlebury, were matters over which Ludham was puzzling its astute brains before the next new moon.

But as yet there was no thought of harm having come to Mr. Redworth; even the members of his own household, so far the only persons who knew of his absence, feared nothing worse than that an accident had happened—that a train had run off the rails—that he had been attacked by sudden illness—that he had met with some misfortune. It was in these and similar grooves that the thoughts of Miss Redworth and Miss Gower travelled, as they sat wondering what "could be detaining papa," or "when we shall her anything of uncle."

"Though papa is so active, still he is not very young," re-marked Miss Redworth; "and people do have fits and attacks of that kind away from home."

"You must not dwell upon such possibilities, dear," answered Miss Gower, smoothing the antimacassar over her lap, the better to catch the exquisite effect of the pattern. "Depend upon it, we shall either see him about dinner-time, or have a letter by the second post."

But the bright hours wore on—dinner-time came and passed the postman's knock echoed down the deserted street, and still nothing was seen of Mr. Redworth, neither did any letter arrive from him.

About three o'clock there came a double knock at the front door. "That's papa!" cried Miss Redworth, forgetting her parent was not wont to herald his advent in such fashion. "That's papa!" and she went on to the landing, and was halfway downstairs when she stopped disappointed. It was only someone asking for her father.

"No, sir, master is not at home," she heard the trim house-maid answer.

"Do you know when he will be home, my girl?" said a rich, jolly, well fed voice,

Miss Redworth recognised as belonging to a certain farmer, who owned a considerable amount of land lying high above Ludham in a lonely region known as "The Wastes."

"No, sir, I don't," replied the housemaid a little stiffly, for she did not care to be addressed as "my girl," by a visitor in the hall of her master's house.

Such amenities, in her opinion, should be confined to Sunday afternoons, and to the young men she honoured from time to time with her smiles.

"Well, I suppose there is somebody in the house who knows when he will be visible," insisted the visitor. "Just step up and ask your mistress, Mary, my dear."

"My name ain't Mary, sir."

"All right, Sally then. Step up and ask your mistress. Servant, ma'am," continued the speaker, breaking off his address to the obdurate fair, and turning to Miss Redworth, who at this juncture appeared on the staircase; "I am just taking the liberty of inquiring when you might be expecting Mr. Redworth. I have a sort of appointment with him, and if I could see him this afternoon, why I shouldn't have to make another journey into the town tomorrow. And that is how it is."

"I am very sorry, but I really do not know when papa will be home. He went to Cadlebury yesterday morning."

"Yes, I know he was at Cadlebury," interrupted Mr. Garland. "I passed him yesterday evening on my return journey (I go to Cadlebury twice a week, you understand), and offered to give him a lift as far as the 'Dolphin,' but he would not have it."

"You passed him last night did you say, Mr. Garland; about what time was that?" asked Miss Redworth; and it seemed to the poor lady as if a cold hand were laid upon her heart.

Yes, not without reason had she been afraid. All her apparently groundless alarm had been caused by a sure presentiment of evil.

"Well, I couldn't say to a few minutes," answered Mr. Garland, "but it must have been nigh upon nine, for I didn't start from 'The Three Fighting Cocks,'—that is where I mostly put up, you understand, miss—till after it had gone the half-hour. Oh! It must have been later than that. I met Dick Winterly on the bridge, and he hindered me awhile, and it would take me better than twenty minutes to drive to Saul's Wood Corner. It must have been after nine."

"Perhaps Mr. Garland would take a glass of sherry, Amy." It was Miss Gower who said this—Miss Gower, who, hearing voices in the hall, had come softly downstairs, and now touching her cousin" arm, looked with a quick, warning glance, first towards the kitchen and then in the direction of the dining-room. Miss Redworth accepted the hint at once. "How could I be so thoughtless as to keep you standing here, Mr. Garland," she exclaimed; "pray walk in and sit down; you must take a glass of wine."

"Well, thankee, miss," said Mr. Garland, whose normal condition was that of chronic thirst. "I did find it main warm driving over they Wastes; there is not a bit of shelter this time of day, the sun pours right down on every inch of the dusty road. If equally agreeable, miss, excuse me, but I see the spirits is there; wine always do turn sour on my stomach. Much obliged, I'll just put in the water for myself."

"Leave me to get out the things, Amy," said Miss Gower, gently pushing her cousin into an armchair; then, after placing brandy, water, biscuits, and a tumbler on the table, she took a seat herself and remarked—

"Mr. Garland, we are very uneasy about my uncle."

"Uneasy," he repeated, pausing in his employment of adding that modicum of water, which indeed, except as a matter of appearance, might as well have been omitted. "I am sorry to hear that; what has happened?"

"He never came home last night."

"Never came home! why, bless my soul, I passed him at Saul's Wood Corner on his way home."

"He has not returned, at any rate," said Miss Gower.

Mr. Garland took a draught of brandy and water, then he replaced the tumbler on the table, laid the palms of his hands flat on his knees, and remarked—

"Well, that's extraor'nary too."

"It is so extraordinary, Mr. Garland, that we do not know what to think of it." commented Miss Gower.

"Never come home, not at all!" said Mr. Garland, struggling to grasp the fact stated.

"We have never seen him since he started yesterday morning," put in Miss Redworth, speaking low and faint.

Mr Garland looked at her, and comprehension dawned upon him.

"No, no," he entreated, "don't you go for to be frightened like that. He'll be back soon, never doubt. Why, he was well enough when I left him, though he seemed a bit put out about something. There was nothing wrong with him, bless you. Take a glass of wine, miss. It'll do you good. She had better have a drop of something," he added, turning a look of helpless appeal, which but for the circumstances would have been ludicrous, towards Miss Gower.

"She had no sleep last night," explained that young lady, who knew all the wines in bond would not prove of much service at the moment to her cousin. "It was at Saul's Wood Corner, you say, you parted from my uncle? Three roads meet there, I think."

Mr. Garland nodded.

"Did you notice which he took?"

"Well, to tell you the truth, I did not. Miss," answered Mr Garland, helping himself uninvited to more brandy, and feeling that the exigencies of the position justified his doing so. "The upper road is not good for about a mile thereabouts, and the mare was fresh, and Mr. Redworth had put up my monkey a bit, and we parted a trifle short."

"Did you and papa quarrel then?" asked Miss Redworth.

"No, not by no means," explained Mr. Garland. "You see, miss, he was up in the stirrups, so to speak, rather on the high and mighty; and when a man makes another a civil offer of turning a good three mile out of his way to give that other a lift, why he don't take it kindly to have his nose snapped off, do he, ladies?"

"I daresay not," agreed Miss Gower; "but if you only would tell us exactly what passed, we should be so much obliged. We should know better what to think."

"For the matter of that, miss, there is not a lot to tell. I was driving along pretty sharp, for the mare she were fresh and keen to get home, and not thinking of seeing your governor—Mr. Redworth, I should say—along that road at that time of night, I had passed him before it occurred to me who it was. Well. I pulled up, and a job I had with the mare to make her stop, and I backed her a few yards, and your father came along stepping out brisk as he always does, and so I said to him—

"'You are out late. Mr. Redworth.'

"'No. sir, it's not particularly late so far as I am aware'

"He spoke quite nettled like, but I took no notice; I only said in a neighbourly way 'it is late, at any rate, for you to be ten mile from home. Jump up, and I'll give you a lift as far as the "Dolphin." I can just as well take the Trotterbeck Road home. The mare is not a bit tired, and we can talk over that small matter of business of ours as we go along.'

"'Sir', he said, 'you are very good, and mean well doubtless, but when I desire a conveyance I can afford to pay for one, and when I wish to talk with you on business, I shall select a more fitting time and place.'

"Well, this vexed me a trifle, ladies; I had not meant to offend him, and many as good a gentleman as your father has taken a lift and thanked me into the bargain, so I made the remark—

"'Something seems to have put you out, Mr. Redworth.'

"'Whether that be so or not, I apprehend'—yes that was the word he used, and it struck me at the time as queer, because I thought it meant something quite else—'I apprehend, sir, is no concern of yours.'

"That did cut me. It was more the way he said it than the words themselves. If I had been a beggar he could not have come more the tol-de-roy sort of manner over me; so I gathered up my reins and answered, short you know, in as 'good as I got' kind of way. you understand—

"'You are quite right there, whether you are tired or cross is no concern of mine, and I'm——(begging your pardon, ladies, for repeating the expression, but I was riled) 'if I make it mine. As regards that matter, however, in which I suppose I may venture to say I have some slight interest, I should like to get it settled one way or another, and I'd be obliged if you would name your fitting time and place for discussing it'

"'Tomorrow afternoon,' he said, 'at my house in Dorking Street; three o'clock will suit me very well.'

"'I'm glad to hear anything suits you,' I up and answered, for indeed, ladies, he stirred my bile.

"'That will do, sir' goodnight, sir,' he said, with a wave of his hand; and not to be left behind in politeness, I took my hat off and made him a bow. There you have, I believe, all that took place. I don't think another word passed between us."

"What can have become of him?" conjectured Miss Gower, uttering her thought aloud.

"That's the puzzle," said Mr. Garland oracularly.

"I—I must do something." cried Miss Redworth, rising and laying her hand on the table "I can bear this suspense no longer."

Miss Gower had risen too, and they both now stood looking down upon Mr. Garland, who sat gazing with an expression of profound wisdom into his brandy and water.

"Did he seem—did you notice if he had been at all—" and Miss Gower's glance falling upon Mr. Garland's tumbler, supplied a finish to the sentence.

"I know what you mean," said Mr. Garland, half closing one eye in a manner indicative of genial comprehension. "Bless you, no, not a sign of it on him. Sober as—"I was." Mr. Garland had intended to say, but a doubt of the fitness of the simile crossing his mind, he substituted—"the town pump."

"How could you ask such a question," remonstrated Miss Redworth, "when you know papa to be one of the most temperate of men?"

"Yes," answered Miss Gower, "and, as a rule, one of the most equable," which remark cut two ways.

"Look here, ladies," said Mr. Garland, who had at length eliminated an idea out of his tumbler, "would you like me to go to Cadlebury, and just take a look round?"

"You've only to speak the word," he went on, seeing that they looked at each other, "and here am I, and there's the mare, both at your service. She won't mind the run over, bless you, and I'd feel it an honour, and I may add a pleasure, to do either of you a service."

Having finished which sentence, Mr. Garland once again, as if in utter absence of mind, helped himself to the contents of the decanter.

Had he refrained from showing himself this final mark of attention, Miss Redworth, in her despair, would have accepted his help. As it was she said—

"Thank you, Mr. Garland; but I think I had better telegraph to my brother."

"Ah, yes!" answered Mr. Garland, speaking sapiently, if thickly. "Most like he'll understand all about it. No doubt it was hearing of some of his pranks upset the governor."

"What do you mean?" asked Miss Redworth, surprised out of her usual slow reticence of manner.

"Oh, not much," replied Mr. Garland, "only I heard Mr. Purslet say yesterday, if the chance offered, he would give the old gentleman—your respected father, you understand, miss—a hint of Master Jack's going on."

"Goings on?' repeated Miss Redworth. "How has my brother been goings on?"

"Oh, I don't want to say anything against your brother, I am sure, miss. A nice, free, affable young fellow as anybody need wish to meet. But nobody can deny he does go the pace a bit too fast to be always sure; and now Mr. Purslet says he's getting himself mixed up with a girl. Nothing wonderful about that, you think, and you're right. There always is a girl—I have often remarked the fact as curious, myself."

Mr. Garland was in so pleasant and communicative a frame

of mind that, much as the ladies desired to know all about this girl whom he mentioned, both felt afraid of leading him on to further revelations. As there was nothing, they felt satisfied, he would refrain from telling, it seemed all the more necessary they should refrain from asking.

Accordingly, they glanced at each other and remained silent, while Mr. Garland, misinterpreting such reticence, said, in a voice rendered genially husky by the weather, his potations, and his sympathy—

"Don't put any more questions, if you please. I should be loath to refuse you anything, but this is a matter I would rather not be mixed up in, if agreeable to present company. Mr. Redworth, supposing he sees fit, can tell you what Mr. Jack has been up to. But lor! young men will be young men, and I dare swear the governor himself had an eye for a pretty face and a neat ankle once upon a time. Only it's my belief it was hearing about that put your father's temper up last night. I have small doubt when I overtook him he had just come from Taunton Hall—been giving Black Dick a taste of his mind, most like, and a nasty taste, I expect, into the bargain."

"Black Dick?" said Miss Redworth, inquiringly.

"Taunton Hall? Where is Taunton Hall?" added Miss Gower, almost in the same moment.

"Why, Taunton Hall is that grim old house backing up against the canal between Saul's Corner and Cadlebury. It looks right over Wilderness Heath. And as for Black Dick, he's Squire Taunton—save the mark—and brother to the prettiest girl in Surrey, let that other be who she may—present company always excepted."

There came a change over Miss Gower as Mr. Garland finished his sentence. Always pale, she grew still paler; her lips, never red, became quite white; across her eyes there fell a shadow. Miss Redworth had not noticed it there ever before, and her voice seemed altered when she opened her mouth and said—

"Amy, if Mr. Garland will excuse us, I think we ought to telegraph to Trenhill." Broad as the hint was, Mr. Garland might have failed to take it, had not Miss Redworth, after the slightest inquiry as to whether he would like any more brandy, removed the decanter from the table and locked it up.

"I hope you will pardon our leaving you, Mr. Garland," she said, as she took the keys out of the sideboard. "I really feel very uneasy about my father."

"If I can do anything for you, ladies," remarked Mr. Garland, draining the last drop in his tumbler, "you have only to speak the word, There's me, and the mare, and the trap, quite at your service."

But Miss Redworth did not speak the word, and Mr. Garland departed, to spread the news through Ludham, and round and about The Wastes, that Old Redworth was missing;—"went to Cadlebury yesterday morning—has never turned up since, and there is the deuce and all to pay in Dorking Street."

CHAPTER 5
THE BEGINNING OF THE SEARCH

Mr. Trenhill Redworth, seated in the pleasant seclusion of a dark office at the back of his warehouse in Tooley Street, received, while engaged in writing letters for the evening post, this message from his sister:—

Something has happened about which I wish to speak to you. Come down by first train. Let nothing detain you.

Mechanically Mr. Trenhill counted the words of this telegram before devoting his mind to solving its meaning. To his business eye it seemed at first that his sister had needlessly exceeded the regulation shilling's worth. Satisfied on this point, he began to wonder what on earth Amelia could have to say to him.

She was not a woman of mystery, and if his father were dead, or stricken with paralysis, he believed no fear of shocking him would cause her to break the news in such a fashion as this.

"Get a South-Western time-table for July, and be quick about it," he said to one of his clerks; and, while the man ran off to do his bidding, he changed his office-coat for that he wore out-of-doors, brushed his hat, and marvelled "what was up."

38

"Surely my father cannot be going to marry again," he considered; and yet the idea took such hold of him, that when he looked at the time-table, and found that there was no train that he could catch to Cadlebury for another hour, he decided to drive to Somerset House on the chance of seeing his youngest brother, and ascertaining from him what was in the wind.

"Hallo! what brings you here—what has happened?" asked John Redworth, whom he met lounging out into the Strand.

"That is precisely what I want to know," answered the other, dismissing the cabman, and his remarks about the meanness of his fare, with a wave of his umbrella. "I have just had this message from Amy. Have you any idea what she means?"

John Redworth glanced at the paper. "I expect the governor has met with some accident," he answered. "He went to Cadlebury yesterday, and had not returned when I came off this morning. I was laughing about it before I left—laughing at the notion of his stopping out all night. I hope nothing serious has happened to the dear old chap."

"He has been a good father to you, John," said his brother, sententiously.

"Yes, he has, better than I deserve," agreed the young fellow, noticing, but not replying to the vague jealousy contained in the remark, "but don't let us stop here—don't let us even chance missing the next train. Amy might, I think, have been a little more explicit."

"You do not happen to know—that is, I suppose you have no reason to imagine he had any plan in his mind which might account for his absence?"

"I cannot imagine what you mean," was the reply.

"Well, coming along, and puzzling over Amelia's message, I began to wonder whether he was going to marry again, or anything of that sort."

"Governor marry again? That is a good joke," said the favourite son, laughing heartily at the notion. "What could put such an idea into your head, Trenhill?"

"I don't know. It occurred to me as possible, that's all. So you think there is nothing in it?"

"If the governor was up to any little game of that sort, he has kept it precious close. Still, there is never any telling what mischief a young elderly gentleman, with plenty of spare time on his hands, may fall into," and John Redworth laughed again at the expression of dismay on his brother's face. "If anything of that sort were to happen," he went on, "I suppose we would soon all get the route."

"It would fall hardest upon you," remarked Trenhill.

"Yes, I suppose it would," agreed his brother.

In the full blaze of the afternoon sun they travelled down to Ludham in a train which, having been carefully placed out in the heat to bake, with all the carriage windows shut, seemed red hot to the passengers.

"Pheugh! How warm it is," gasped John Redworth, letting in as much air as is ever to be obtained at the Waterloo Station. "If we were loaves, what fine ovens these compartments would make."

It was cooler by the time they reached Ludham, and in that pleasant little country town a gentle air, fragrant with the smell of hay, and the scents of roses and lilies, and clover and gillyflowers, came rustling through the trim clean streets, and met the passengers who had travelled down from the noise and dust of London to that rural spot, situated in the midst of green meadows, and surrounded by tranquilly flowing streams.

Somehow, after leaving the junction, both Trenhill Redworth and his brother grew more silent and more silent still. Something besides the calm quiet of the country fell across their hearts, and as the bustling little engine sped now across wide stretches of pasture land, and anon over bridges spanning sluggish rivers, and the canal fringed with reeds and grasses of a strange and vivid green, both men seemed disposed rather to look away towards distant points of the ever-changing landscape, than to engage in conversation.

At length talk between them ceased altogether, and in utter silence they left the train at Ludham Station, and walked out into the street leading up to the centre of the town.

As they paced along, many a curious glance and word of wisdom followed them.

"That's the eldest son," remarked Mr. Nunn, the chemist.

"They've heard something, most likely," answered Mr. Hazeldine.

"I wonder if Mr. Redworth has returned," said another.

"Very probably he has been up in London consulting his sons there."

In the faces of all the persons who greeted him as he passed, John Redworth might, had he noticed their expression, have seen a look of suppressed excitement, inquiry, and compassion. Everyone felt there must be something very wrong. Mr. Redworth had been away all night, and, so far as they knew, two whole days in addition, and now there was Mr. Trenhill Redworth come down in answer to a telegram from his sister—all Ludham knew of the telegram within half-an-hour after its despatch—and he and young Jack were walking up to Dorking Street, silent as Trappists, and grave-looking as mutes.

Miss Redworth saw them coming to the house, and opened the door before they could knock.

"Here I am, Amy, you see," said her eldest brother.

"Yes, Trenhill, I see," she answered, and immediately burst into tears.

"He has not come home, then," suggested John Redworth.

"Have you heard anything of him?" asked Trenhill, as she shook her head in reply.

"Nothing," she sobbed. "Mr. Garland saw him last night at Saul's Corner, and offered to give him a seat to the 'Dolphin,' but he would not accept it."

"What have you done?" asked Trenhill.

"I did not know what to do. I have left everything till I heard what you would advise."

By this time Miss Gower was in the hall, and had shaken hands silently and gravely with both brothers.

For a minute they all four stood quiet, no one uttering a

word.

Then Trenhill asked—

"Had he money about him?"

"We cannot tell," answered Miss Gower.

"Where was he going in Cadlebury?"

"We do not know," said Miss Redworth.

"He banked at Cadlebury, did he not?" inquired the eldest brother, practical and alert.

"Yes," replied John Redworth.

"'Then the first thing to do is to get over to Cadlebury with all speed," said Trenhill.

"We cannot manage it now by train," explained his brother, "so we must hire a conveyance;" which, however, proved easier said than done. In Ludham not a conveyance was to be had before the next morning. All the horses were out, or tired, or bespoke.

No butcher even, or grocer, or tradesman of any description could "oblige" Jack Redworth with the loan of a trap. In that primitive region people were not accustomed to emergencies, and had a general idea that emergencies, like most other things with which they had to deal, could wait their convenience.

"What is to be done now?" asked Trenhill, when his brother returned and reported the failure of his mission.

"I shall walk over," answered the younger man, "and take my chance of getting a conveyance back."

"I will walk with you," said the other, and without any further discussion they started off.

"We had better go by the canal," remarked John Redworth moodily, when they left the town behind. "He liked that way best, and we may hear something of him at the locks."

"Very well," agreed Trenhill, and accordingly they walked across the fields, stepping out briskly till they reached a lane, which conducted them straight to the canal bank.

Crossing the canal over a railway bridge, they got down on the towing-path, and set their faces due west towards Cadlebury.

The whole of that walk burnt itself into John Redworth's

memory. Never while he lives will he forget the glory of light which flooded the water, the trees bathed in the rich evening sunshine—the murmuring reeds standing out, thick though they grew, one by one with a marvellous individuality. It is often present with him how the shadow of the bridges fell athwart the canal—how deep the locks looked as they skirted their edges—how dark the pine woods appeared, blocking up the sky at Saul's Corner—how silent everything was; so silent that the flutter of a bird among the brushwood of the plantations, or the scurrying of a rabbit across some bit of heath land, startled the two men, and caused them to pause and ask, "What was that?"

No tidings of Mr. Redworth at any lock-house they passed—no news of him to be learned from any barge lying alongside the banks, or floating lazily down with the sluggish current.

Two lock-keepers had noticed the gentleman, whom they knew by sight, walking towards Cadlebury upon the previous morning, but they did not see him return. The bargemen could give no information at all.

One of their number was entreated if he heard any intelligence of the person Mr. Trenhill Redworth described, to communicate his news, good or bad, to Miss Redworth, in Dorking Street, Ludham.

"You will find half-a-crown waiting there for you," said Mr. Trenhill grandly, hearing which an old waterman seated in the bows, dressed in a blue jersey and wearing a sou'-wester, laughed out, and remarked—

"You must bid higher than that, master. If we see him a going down with the stream we wouldn't pick him out of the water for four times over half of a crown. For why d'ye see—t'ain't a pleasant job to begin with, and then there's a lot of bother arterwards, and a day, or may be two, or sometimes more, loss o'time over the crowner bisness. It don't pay, sir, and that's the fact; and a working man's time's his money, and that's where it is. Why, when young Mr. Leicester, the vicar's son at Allaton, was missing—a half-witted chap, you may have heard tell on him—his father had notices stuck about offering five shillings reward for news of him. He advertised him, too, in the papers, and first and last must have wasted a mort o' money over the lad. Well, at the time lots of us on the Thames knew well enough where he was; down with one tide, up with another; till at last when someone did fish him ashore he could only be identified by his clothes. Five shillings! If the vicar had only made it pounds, he could have been buried comfortably long enough before he got news of him. If you think of it, sir, five pounds ain't none too much."

"Come away; come on, for Heaven's sake. Trenhill," said John Redworth, looking quite sick and faint.

"Don't like it, sir," remarked the old sinner, with a grim smile; "why, that's just what it is; we don't like it neither, and two and six pence can't make us like it. However, we have seen nothing on the canal such as you enquired about; no gentleman with an umbrella—no hat a floating—no nothing. Thanking you, sir, and hoping you will find him safe and sound on dry land," and the man pocketed the money the younger Redworth flung him, and the sun wrapped the barge round with a golden glory, and illumined the old waterman's jersey and sou'-wester, as though he had been some rare missal adorned with a thousand varying tints and cunning devices.

Almost immediately after parting company with him, they reached a spot where the canal came to a sort of fork, one arm of which went straight through pleasant fields and smiling hamlets, whilst the other branched off into a dark and lonely region, bordered on one side by a wood of stunted oak trees, and on the other by pine plantations, reaching down to the water's edge.

"What a dreary place!" exclaimed Trenhill Redworth, as they crossed a narrow footbridge, and found themselves on a path evidently little used, where the branches of the oak trees brushed their hats, and the acorns and oak-apples of the previous autumn lay thick beneath their feet. "What a horribly dreary place. It might be a thousand miles from London, in an uninhabited land. It is like some picture I have seen of a deserted clearing in the far west. See how weird those felled trees stripped of their bark look, lying on the opposite bank. How white they are and ghostly, stretching up skeleton arms from the ground. And that little bay quite choked up with rushes! I never saw reeds in such rank luxuriance before. It is awfully lonely, John. Do you know, if you were not with me I should feel afraid."

Twenty-four hours previously John Redworth would have treated such a statement with boisterous derision, but a change had come over him, and the gloom of the silent pines and the mysterious desolation of the oak wood, the sullen darkness of the lonely canal, and the dense vegetation on the other side of the water, where reeds grew rank, and weeds and grasses tangled themselves in extricable confusion, affected even his spirits, and touched his soul with melancholy.

It was a place and hour for despondency; the sun had sunk below the horizon, and in lieu of purple, and gold, and crimson, sad grey lines streaked the darkening sky.

Around them there was utter silence, a silence which could be felt; about them everything saddest and gloomiest in nature seemed closing—in the distance, far along the path they were traversing, the woods on each side the water seemed to meet and close the way; stretching where the pines grew densest far beyond its original limits, the canal looked like a darkling lake.

Even in the noontide of a summer's day that lonely spot more resembles some pictured scene in the tropics, than a landscape in fair, pensive Surrey, and with the evening shadows drawing down over dark fir-trees and weird distorted oaks—over glades where mosses had grown tenderly and softly along the rotten trunks and branches of fallen trees—over broken locks through which no barge had passed for years, and bridges too rotten to bear even the weight of a child, the spot appeared so eerie and mysterious, so sympathetic with mystery and sorrow, or crime, that Mr. Trenhill Redworth, a man who had small appreciation of nature even in her most joyous moods, might well be excused the nervous tremor which found expression in the sentence repeated.

"It is a lonely place," agreed his brother, whose own associations with that stretching, watery highway were perhaps none of the pleasantest. "Like everything else, which having served its purpose is laid on the shelf, the canal looks dead; and, in fact, has been dead this many a year. The living branch we left behind us at Saul's Corner, the reeds and the weeds will choke this all up some fine day, and then we shall not be troubled any more with a canal once useful, which is useful no more. I never come here but I think of one of the main coach roads; there are plenty of them on the Middlesex side of the Thames, with the grass growing where the hoofs of four spanking horses used to make good music. What shall we have to put railways out of court, Trenhill? Here is what not very long ago was a very grand water highway, and look at it now. Just on the other side this wood to our left runs the South Western Railway. Hark, there goes an express to Portsmouth or Southampton! How will our great-grandchildren, or, for that matter, our grandchildren travel? An interesting question, if you believe that the progress of the future will be even as slow as the progress of the past."

"I care nothing about the future," answered Mr. Trenhill Redworth, irritably; "or, for that matter, the past either; the present is always quite sufficient for me. What on earth could induce my father to select such a road as this for walking in the middle of the night?"

"If that Garland man really did see him at Saul's Corner on his way home, he took the other side of the canal, and would not get on the bank till he crossed the bridge at Trotterbeck."

"Then, why on earth, did you select this confounded road?"

"I am sure I cannot tell you," answered his brother; "only," he went on, "it did not seem likely we should hear much of him on a lonely country road."

"Where, supposing him to have selected this cheerful way home, would he be most likely to touch the canal?"

"Just where we spoke to those fellows on the barge; this, you understand, would be the route he took in the morning. Supposing Garland to have been correct in his statement, which is doubtful, the man being, except as regards his business capacity, always more or less befuddled with drink, he had from Saul's

Corner the choice of two direct routes; he could go straight along the Trotterbeck Road; which would bring him out near Ludham Station; or he could, by crossing Trotterbeck Bridge, get on the canal bank, and so back to Dorking Street the way we have come. There is not much difference in the number of steps, only in the daytime the canal and the fields are the coolest."

"It is all most mysterious," said the elder brother.

"Awfully mysterious," answered the younger, shivering. "I hope we shall obtain some clue at Cadlebury."

"What could induce a man at my father's time of life to take such a walk as this?"

"Well, you see he was fond of walking, and after all, for one so light and active, it is not much of a distance."

"I know my legs are aching, at any rate," said the other.

"You are not accustomed to so many miles straight out," answered John.

He was singularly mild and conciliatory. Even at the time this change of manner struck the elder brother as curious. Hitherto this Benjamin of the Redworth household had been more prone to jeer that to excuse, to scoff than to sympathize, and it seemed remarkable to hear him reply in such measured and unobjectionable sentences.

"What is that strange-looking place across the water?" said Trenhill Redworth, after a pause, devoted to considering how nice John could be when he laid aside his "West End" manners; and as he spoke he paused, and pointed through the gathering twilight to a building on the opposite side of the canal. "Is it a church or a castle?"

"It is neither," replied his brother. "It is Taunton Hall."

"Why, that is where Amy said Mr. Garland thought my father must have called."

"It is not improbable."

"Then why did we not go that way, and make enquiry at the house?'

"You forget. Mr. Garland overtook him at Saul's Corner, which we have long passed."

"True; I had forgotten that. But why should he have called so late in the evening at Taunton Hall? Was he intimate with the owner?"

"No—certainly not."

"Then, I repeat, why should he call? The place looks a mansion. The people who live there are great swells, I suppose?"

"Quite the contrary. Dick Taunton, the present squire, is considered the black sheep of the county."

"And why?'

"I do not know. I know facts—I can't pretend to state causes. The place is in bad odour, and, by consequence, the people who live there. The last owner but one elected to be buried in his own garden, without help of sexton, clergyman, undertaker, or any of the conventional assistants; and ever since, even the children scurry past Taunton Hall and say it is haunted. Of course, a man who lives in a haunted house, with one of his progenitors planted out in the garden, must be a very bad man. At least, such is the opinion, of all the people who reside round and about this quarter. It is a queer old place. Might be made very beautiful and very imposing; but the present squire is letting it go to wreck and ruin."

"Why on earth should my father call there, instead of going back by train to Ludham?"

"The only reason I can imagine for his doing so, is that I know Dick Taunton, and very likely the governor called to tell him he would cut me off with a brass farthing, if the acquaintance were not discontinued."

"Is this Mr. Taunton a very disreputable person, then?" asked Trenhill Redworth.

"Most people think he is," was the reply.

"And what do you think?" persisted the other.

"He is a friend of mine, and, contrary to the custom of friends, I decline to abuse him."

"Then you cannot defend him?"

"Surely his bad or good qualities do not concern you?"

"Only so far as this, my boy," said Trenhill Redworth, laying an affectionate hand on his brother's shoulder, "if he be disreputable, we don't desire to see you associate with him."

"That is very kind of you, Trenhill, since there cannot be the slightest doubt that someday—say tomorrow—the governor will order me out of the house because I decline to dissever myself from Richard Taunton. Cheer up," he added, "there will be all the more left for you, and Gower, and Amy."

"What does all this mean, John?"

"It means that as every family must have its scapegrace, I propose to represent that character in ours. In each thousand, so many *per cent* go to the devil. I am one of the percentage, and I am going to the devil. I have been travelling that nice easy road for many a long day."

"I don't like this, John. You shouldn't talk so wildly."

"Do you suppose I like it?" was the fierce rejoinder. "Do you imagine there dawns a day when I fail to kick against the pricks, and wish—unavailingly—I could get rid of the bad Bohemian blood in me, which hates restraint, and rebels against the awful decorous—killingly decorous life in Dorking Street? I ought to have been a soldier, Trenhill. Some day, I suppose, I shall enlist. The old restless Viking blood will have its way, even in the midst of civilisation. Look, there are the dim religious lights of Cadlebury. Let us push on."

When they reached Cadlebury, they found the manager of the "All England," where Mr. Redworth banked, unbending his mind over a game of backgammon with his wife. It would be, perhaps, unfair to say he welcomed any interruption of this pastime; but most undoubtedly he greeted John Redworth with effusion, and when he heard the cause which had brought the two brothers so far from home at so late an hour, threw himself heart and soul into the business.

"Money about him" he repeated. "I should think he had, indeed. I will give you all particulars in a few minutes. Let me see!" And having by this time lit the gas, and produced some ponderous books, he opened them and ran his eye from one to another, in search of the information required.

"Yes," he said at last, speaking across to the two Redworths, who stood on the other side of the counter in the bank, which seemed strangely silent and empty. "Yes, I was right. Five hundred in notes, and a bill at sight on London for nine hundred more."

"Good heavens! He has been robbed and murdered." It was Trenhill Redworth who uttered this exclamation. John, leaning against the counter, and looking white and faint, spoke never a word.

"I would not fear the worst," said the manager, kindly. "The first thing to do is to ascertain where he went after leaving here."

"A Mr. Garland saw him last night, about nine o'clock, at a place called Saul's Corner, if you know where that is," answered Trenhill Redworth.

"Saul's Corner? Why, it's on the way to Ludham; and he distinctly told me he meant to return home by rail."

"At any rate, Mr. Garland says he overtook him at the point I have mentioned, and offered to give him a lift, which he declined."

"It looks awkward," remarked the manager, after a pause. "You had better set the police to work. Shall I send and ask the inspector to step down here?"

"No, we will go to the office. By-the-bye, you can give me the number of the notes of course?"

"Yes, they ought to be stopped."

"I will return to London tonight, and get to the bank as soon as it opens in the morning."

"There is an express at 10.5. You will have time to see the inspector, and take a bit of supper before starting. I will go up with you to the office, if agreeable."

All this time John Redworth never opened his lips. Like one dazed, he accompanied his brother and the manager to the police station, and when there he volunteered no statement, and started no conjecture as to the possible cause of his father's disappearance. All the talking he left to his companions, and it was not till the inspector addressed him that he uttered a word.

"You were at Cadlebury last evening, too, Mr. John," remarked the inspector.

"Yes," answered the young man.

"And at Taunton Hall," added Mr. Policeman, with a knowing look.

"Yes, I was at Taunton Hall."

"You did not see anything of Mr. Redworth on your way back here?"

"No, I did not come back here. I walked across to Malby, and took the train from that station"

"I see. Well, your father might have done the same thing."

"If he had he would have turned through the wood instead of going on to Saul's Corner; besides, I don't fancy he was acquainted with the short cut across Malby Mead."

"Mr. Garland might have been mistaken as to the exact place where he overtook him."

"Mr. Garland had an idea my father walked home in order to call at Taunton Hall," said Trenhill Redworth.

"What the——, ahem!" exclaimed the inspector, suddenly breaking out, and as suddenly checking himself.

"We had better ascertain whether Mr. Redworth did call there," he went on after a moment's pause. "He may have said something to the squire about where he was going. I think I will take a walk over to the Hall now."

"I will walk over with you," offered John Redworth, "it is all on my way home."

"Can't you get back to Ludham by train?" asked his brother.

"I would rather do it on foot," answered the young man.

It was a dreary walk out to Taunton Hall, and, as the inspector remarked afterwards, "Mr. Jack was not the liveliest of company."

In effect he scarcely opened his lips the whole way—a marvellous change for one who had ever been free of speech, and almost too ready of tongue.

"Seems as if everybody had gone to bed," observed the policeman, as they passed up to the back entrance—of late years the front hall door had never been opened—"there is not a light in any of the windows."

"Let us try, at any rate," said his companion, applying his hand to the bell pull, and ringing a loud peal, which seemed to echo through the lonely house. "Here comes someone," he added, as a light flickered across the hall, and the sound of heavy footsteps was heard tramping over the stone floor. A noise of bolts being withdrawn, and locks unfastened, and then the door was flung wide, and Squire Taunton, holding a lamp in his hand, peered out into the darkness.

"It is I, Dick," explained John Redworth. "Can we come in for a minute?"

"Surely, lad; but what's this—and what's the matter?"

"Matter enough," answered the inspector; "at least we are afraid there is—Mr. Jack's father is missing."

"Missing! What do you mean? Come in, and tell me what has happened."

As he spoke he led the way into a small room, poorly and even meanly furnished with old-fashioned chairs and tables, of almost obsolete design, and battered with the wear and tear of years. Though it was summer, a wood fire smouldered on the hearth, and quite evidently the squire had been drinking, for a decanter of spirits and a half-emptied tumbler stood upon the table.

"Sit down," he said, "and tell me what has gone wrong."

"Well, you see, squire, it is a very awkward-looking business. Here is a gentleman leaves Cadlebury with, as far as we know, a matter of fourteen hundred pounds about him—he is last seen on the road home at nine o'clock, or thereabouts, and from that time to this nobody has set eyes upon him."

"Where was he last seen?" asked Mr. Taunton.

"At Saul's Corner, by Mr. Garland, who offered to give him a lift, which he refused," said John Redworth, gloomily.

"And he has never been seen since?"

"Never, so far as we can learn," answered the inspector.

"What we came here to know, squire, was if he called on you last night, and whether he gave you any hint as to where he was going?"

"Call on me!" repeated Mr. Taunton. "What induced you to

imagine he should do such a thing? I know nothing of Mr. Redworth. I never spoke to him in my life."

"Mr. Garland thought he had called, at all events," said the inspector.

"Did he tell Garland he meant to do so?"

"No, it was only the old fellow's notion," answered John Redworth, quickly, and as he did so the superintendent looked at him with a certain curiosity.

"Then he did not call here, squire?" returned that functionary, after a pause so slight it seemed scarcely worth noticing.

"Not to my knowledge. I was away though all day at Fadesley, and did not get home till between eleven and twelve. If he had called though I should have been sure to hear of it. I will ask my sister, if you like, but I am positive he never came to this house. Help yourselves," he suggested, placing some more glasses on the table. "There is cold water in that jug, and hot in the kettle," after which exercise of hospitality, he left the room.

"Won't you have a drop of something, Mr. Jack," asked the inspector, drawing his own chair forward and turning to the young man, who sat with one elbow resting on his knee, and his head supported by his hand. "You look regular done up. Do, sir, have just a nip to pull you together and keep the night air out."

"Let me alone, will you," retorted Mr. John Redworth. "This is not a time for me to be drinking."

In his heart Mr. Inspector thought it was probably not a time for the young gentleman to be making merry. He had his own theory about the matter, and as it happened to be that Mr. Redworth's youngest son knew pretty well what had happened to his father, he did not feel much surprise at his refusal to partake of strong liquors.

"Wants to keep his head clear," though the astute officer. "He does not manage the sorrowful and downcast business badly either, though I dare say he feels a bit vexed too."

As he poured the rum in his own glass and added some cold water, he stole another glance at his companion.

"Ay, he could tell us all we ask to know," decided Mr. Inspector, taking a long pull at his rum-and-water, after which refreshment he drew a long breath, and said audibly, "Ah!"

"No, he did not call here," said Mr. Taunton, re-entering the room at this moment, and then he sat down and mixed for himself, and he and the inspector sat for a little while talking over the matter, discussing the pros and cons in true country gossiping fashion, till John Redworth interrupted the conversation.

"I can't stand this any longer," he remarked, getting up and looking about him with a dazed sort of uncertainty. "I must get home, and hear if they have any tidings there. Dick, can you spare me a trap of any kind? I begin to feel knocked up; I don't think I would walk to Ludham tonight. If you will let me have the dog-cart, it shall be sent back to you early in the morning."

"Never mind about that," said the squire heartily; "you can have the trap and welcome. Should you like me to drive you over? You don't look much fit to go alone."

"With your leave, Mr. Jack," interposed the inspector; "If you are going to drive to Ludham, I'll go along with you. It will be better for me to see some of our people over there at once. Too much time, to my thinking, has been lost already."

"Hold the light then while I put in the mare," suggested Mr. Taunton; and so saying, he thrust a lantern into the man's hand, and led the way across the yard to his stables.

"Seems to take it bad, don't he, squire?" remarked the inspector, nodding towards the house where John Redworth still remained.

"Yes, he does; and that is strange, too, since we can't tell for certain whether anything out of the way has happened to the old man or not."

"I fancy there ain't much room for doubt about that. When a gentleman of Mr. Redworth's habits disappears as if the earth had opened and swallowed him up and the money he was carrying up, I think there can't be any great ground for expecting that he'll show for breakfast, say at nine o'clock tomorrow morning."

Mr. Taunton shivered; he was putting on the mare's collar at the moment, and she feeling the unwonted tremor laid back her ears, and plunged nervously.

"Steady, steady!" exclaimed her master. "Stand clear of her heels, man. Perhaps, after all"—he went on pulling the mare's mane from underneath her head band—"perhaps after all Redworth had not any money about him; he may have paid it away in Cadlebury. There is a deuce of a while, you know, between the time the bank closes and nine o'clock at night, and he seems to have been at the bank early."

"There is; but when the mystery is cleared up I think you will find he had the money on him."

"They have stopped payment, I suppose?"

"The elder brother is going to do that first thing in the morning."

"Pity he had not done it first thing this morning," commented the squire.

"As I understand, he knew nothing about the matter till between four and five today."

"But Jack knew, why didn't he see to it?"

"Mr. Jack is a careless sort of young gentleman," was the sapient answer. "Altogether he has let a lot of valuable time slip through his fingers."

"Shall you be coming back this way?" asked Mr. Taunton, taking no apparent notice of the reflection on his friend's promptitude, and shoving the shafts of the dog-cart in the tugs as he spoke.

"Very likely I shall, sir, though I can't say for certain."

"If you do, call as you pass, and tell me if anything has been heard of the old gentleman. He might have fallen into the canal, you know."

"He might," agreed the inspector, dryly; "at any rate I suppose we shall know more about it before we are much older."

In which idea, however, Mr. Inspector chanced to be mistaken.

Chapter 6

Mr. Garland's Statement

By eleven o'clock the next morning it was known all over

Ludham that Mr. Trenhill Redworth had telegraphed to his sister the news of the notes having been changed on the previous day. At a very much earlier hour Ludham, waking from slumber, learned there was no news whatever of Mr. Redworth; not a trace of him could be found. If, to quote the policeman's words, the earth had opened and swallowed him up, his disappearance could not have been more complete or mysterious; and the population of Ludham stood about in groups wondering what could have become of him.

Throughout the day people strained their eyes across the fields, and idled along the banks of the town river and the more remote canal, vaguely expecting to see coming from some remote distance the body of Mr. Redworth—alive or dead. It seemed incredible to the mind of Ludham that so old a resident should never return to it. If it could bury him with every mark of respect, and have its curiosity satisfied as to the manner of his decease, the town might have been satisfied; but as matters stood, everything was so unsatisfactory that all the inhabitants seemed suddenly to grow demoralized. They neglected their business; people talked familiarly to those with whom they had only the slightest acquaintance, the dissenting minister compared notes with the priest, and the collector of poor rates fell into friendly conversation with the man he had summoned three days before.

To the surprise of the whole town, John Redworth had gone up to London that morning as usual.

"It was strange," Ludham said. "It would have seemed more natural for him to stay with his sister."

Not that his sister lacked company, it may be remarked. Directly after breakfast visitors began to wend their way towards the trim house in Dorking Street, and all day long callers came and went, exchanged greetings with each other on the staircase, and in the drawing-room exhorted Miss Redworth to "keep up."

The hours went by—the sunny, weary hours—and still there came no news of Mr. Redworth. Amongst all the visitors, that one most eagerly looked for, most anxiously expected, never arrived. Living or dead, Mr. Redworth never again crossed the threshold of his own house. He had left his home in the bright light of as fine a summer's morning as ever dawned, and no noon, or afternoon, or evening that afterwards shone for others saw him return. He came back no more; not a creature beheld him again walk down the street, or pace steadily from the railway station. His place in church was never filled again by him. He was gone, without the escort of kindly friends and mercenary mutes—without the conventional proprieties of nodding plumes and elaborate hat-bands and mourning coaches, and red-faced undertakers he had disappeared; and left nor sign nor token as to how and whither he was departed.

It is no exaggeration to say that the whole countryside was talking about the missing man, the mystery of whose disappearance deepened with every fresh fact elicited concerning him.

From the statement of the Bank of England people it seemed that an elderly gentleman, calling himself Jeremiah Redworth, and giving his address Dorking Street, Ludham, Surrey, had on the previous morning exchanged some notes for gold.

He came in a cab and went away in a cab, the driver of which being discovered, stated that he took up the gentleman in Lombard Street, and after a short delay at the bank, set him down at the London Bridge Terminus. Heard his fare inquire when there would be a train for Brighton.

The gentleman was stout built, but seemed old and feeble. Both he and a railway porter helped him out of the cab. He spoke in a low voice, as though tired or ill.

The notes thus changed, it seemed, were those obtained from Messrs. Williams, Deacon, and Co., who cashed the draft, payable at sight, over the counter. The person who presented it asked for the amount "short."

As for the other notes, gold was taken for them, both earlier in the day and later— in the one case the bearer gave the name of a gentleman residing in North Audley Street—in the other that of a builder at Bow.

When matters came subsequently to be fully investigated, it

turned out that by a singular coincidence the gentleman resident in North Audley Street was abroad, and the builder of Bow
lying ill of a fever at the time their names were used, and it was
therefore assumed that the addresses had been taken at random
from the directory.

Nothing seemed to connect either with the affair, and no
special attention had been given to the appearance of the persons who presented the notes.

But the circumstances surrounding the cashing of the draft
were different.

The signature was not a bad imitation of Mr. Redworth's
handwriting. His calligraphy had never been slovenly. Though
gentlemanlike, it was clear, sharp, neat, with a tiny flourish here
and there, at once old-fashioned and apologetic.

Experts, as usual, took different sides when their opinion on
the question came to be asked. One eminent gentleman declared positively it must be the signature of the missing man,
giving various cogent reasons for the conclusion he had formed;
while another gentleman, equally famous, urged several arguments why it could not be the handwriting of Mr. Redworth—
admitting, however, that it was a most admirable forgery.

Several friends who had been intimate with the late government clerk for years, said—

"That's Redworth's copperplate, right enough;" but the
manager of All England, and the clergyman of Ludham, said the
signature was a still and poor imitation of the original, while Mr.
Garland declared recklessly—

"He'd have known it to be a counterfeit half a mile off."

Still, the doubt added a fresh piquancy to the mystery. "Could
it be that the old gentleman had really levanted with his own
money?' was a question men began to put to each other, whilst
ladies, who looked with suspicion on the conduct of their own
husbands, shook their heads and remarked, there "was no telling."

Even Mr. Trenhill Redworth could not get that idea of a
second marriage out of his head, and for a time at least public

opinion set strongly in favour of the idea that Mr. Redworth had fallen into the hands of some designing woman, and that he would be heard of when all the money was spent.

"Because, if you think of it," said the representative Miss Gadabout, of Ludham, "why should the poor old gentleman have drawn out all that money, when he could just as easily have paid by cheque? Depend upon it, there is a woman at the bottom of the mystery, and I should not wonder at all myself if she turns out to be a widow."

That there was no known widow in the whole circle of Mr. Redworth's acquaintances likely to have wrought such ruin, only served to render this solution of the enigma more captivating.

Such a wide field was at once offered for idealism, that Ludham for a time literally lost its head in rambling about the pastures of conjecture, where imaginary widows roved at will and spirited away elderly gentlemen possessed of well-lined pocket-books.

It was whilst Ludham was still holding fast to this idea of a mysterious elopement, that Trenhill and Gower Redworth, laying their heads together, decided to offer a reward of £5 for information concerning the whereabouts of an elderly gentleman missing from his home in Ludham. Height, five feet ten inches; very spare in figure, upright, quick walker; thin face, grey eyes, aquiline nose, grey hair and whiskers; linen marked J. R. Was last seen at Saul's Corner. Any intelligence would be thankfully received by Miss Redworth, Dorking Street, Ludham; Trenhill Redworth, Tooley Street, London; Messrs. Smiler and Riler, Lincoln's Inn Fields; or the Police Inspector, Cadlebury, Surrey.

"You won't make much by that move, Gower," John Redworth was overheard to say at Ludham Station, as the two brothers paused to look at the poster just pasted up. "Much better to have offered a hundred pounds, or even more, at once."

"There is no use in wasting money," answered his more cautious elder. "It is easy to increase the reward if this brings us no intelligence. We will wait a little."

So Mr. Gower Redworth, and Ludham generally, waited, but of Mr. Redworth, senior, there came no tidings. Upon the solicitors in Lincoln's Inn Fields there called indeed a certain Mr. Blex, who stated he had been expecting to hear from Mr. Redworth concerning a farm that gentleman desired to purchase. The matter, it appeared, was so far advanced that on the Saturday subsequent to the date of his disappearance, Mr. Redworth was to have paid him, Mr. Blex, a deposit upon the transaction.

It was well known to Messrs. Smiler and Riler that their nominal client had a passion for conducting his own legal business, as far as possible, without the assistance of solicitors.

He never came to them till he wanted matters set what he called "a little to rights;" and, putting two and two together, the firm arrived, without difficulty, at the conclusion that Mr. Redworth intended to devote a considerable part of the proceeds of the bank post-bill to arranging preliminaries with Mr. Blex.

But then, what did he mean to do with the remainder, and with the notes? Mr. Garland could tell them that.

"I've as pretty a bit of land, sir, as you'd wish to see," he remarked to Mr. Smiler, who made a journey to Ludham with a view of reducing order out of the chaos reigning there, and who went about listening to the small-talk of the town, and "gathering facts" together which he could arrange methodically at his leisure—"as sweet a bit as you'd find between this and London, though I says it, as perhaps oughtn't. It lies just on the slope of the hill looking away towards Dangermere. I've got the mare here. She's standing at the inn round the corner. I can run you up to the very spot in half an hour, and if you'll let me take you round to my house, you can have whatever you like to put a name on, in the way of spirits. Come, let me persuade you."

"Thank you very much, Mr. Garland," said Mr. Smiler, quietly. "Some other time I may avail myself of your offer; but just now I am trying to get some light thrown on the mystery of our poor friend's disappearance, and I fear that going with you to see the charming place you mention would not greatly help forward our enquiry."

"There's a deal of truth in what you say, sir," agreed Mr. Garland, respectfully. "But it is a lovely piece of land, and lying dead on my hands now, in a manner of speaking. For over a year past Mr. Redworth has been very sweet upon it, casting sheep's eyes, as it were, every now and then over the fences. It does not greatly fit in with the rest of my freehold; for a three-sided field of Blex's cuts it most away from the other part, d'ye see?"

"I see," said Mr. Smiler, nodding.

"So one day, when Mr. Redworth says to me. 'Garland, if I was to take a fancy to that slice of land of yours, a-looking over Dangermere, would you sell it, and what would you want for it?' I made answer that as for selling it, I didn't care if I did, always providing I got its full value, or thereabouts. 'For,' I explained, I think I should have more than the bare price as earth. Some day, Mr. Redworth,'—this was how I put it—'when Mr. Blex is dead, them as comes after him will give a fancy figure for that bit o' frontage. Thrown all together, it would make a compact little estate. Anybody as gave his mind to it might build a nice genteel cottage orny there, as the saying is.' 'That is what I should do if I gave my mind to it,' he answers, and went away, and I heard nothing more about the matter for months—not indeed till a week or ten days before I saw him last, when he says, 'I wish you'd set a price on that there slice o'land, and give me the refusal of it for a month.'"

"And did you?" asked Mr. Smiler.

"Well, sir, to be straightforward, as such is always best, I did not. I was, as it happened, a trifle hard up at the time, and I thought he might as well settle his mind and mine about the matter at once; for which reason I fixed a price and said he might either take it or leave it within the fortnight. Directly I had done so, Blex comes to me, and he says, 'I want that outlying few acres of yours, farmer, looking down on Dangermere. They ain't o' no manner o' use to you, and I can work them in with my lot. What price do you set on them?' So I told him Mr. Redworth had the refusal of them, and he smiled, and said, 'Deep old file, that! Well, it don't make much difference.' Then I surmised Mr. Redworth was after his land too."

"You were right," remarked Mr. Smiler. "Go on."

"I thought it over, and jest shoved the mare into harness, and drove down to Dorking Street. Being hard up as it happened— bear that in mind, please, sir—I thought I would try and bring my gentleman to book. So I say to him—this is the remark I made—'Mr. Redworth, sir, Mr. Blex has been with me a-hankering arter that bit o'land, and I must ask you, please, to make up your mind for good about it before Saturday week, as arter that I'll let him or anybody else have the slice, as'll give me my price. The fact is,'—I did not hesitate to tell him this (there's no false shame about me, Mr. Smiler. Always paid my way honest, and always hope to do so; but the best of men may be cornered once in a way)—'The fact is, I've pressing need of a trifle of cash, and I expect the value of the mossil would put me a good bit to the right side.'"

"Very straightforward indeed," commented Mr. Smiler; "and what said Mr. Redworth?"

"Oh! he acted honourable too, I'll say that of him. He made me this answer—'I can't tell you for certain by the time you name whether I shall buy the land or not; but, whether I do or no, you shan't be stuck for a few hundreds. If I don't purchase I'll lend.'"

"Most extraordinary!" ejaculated the lawyer.

"Wasn't it, sir? I could scarce believe my ears. I felt quite amazed, in a manner; but I thanked him, and said I only wanted to get what I needed in a regular way, and that if he would but make up his mind one way or other, I could have all I wanted from my bankers, without fear or favour."

"And what was the upshot?'

"I could get nothing more from him than that he would manage it all—that I should not be ill-convenienced. He was quite agreeable, and let out he had a fancy for building a house up on The Wastes for the 'young couple. But I haven't quite decided yet, Garland,' he said, 'so don't you tell nothing to nobody. It is time Mr. John and my niece were thinking about settling,' he says, 'and I suppose I shall have to make them a wedding present. The first time you are in Ludham again, give me a call, and we can talk the matter over at our leisure.'

"I never saw Mr. Redworth after, if you believe me, sir, except when I overtook him at Saul's Corner, and he was then *that* snappish, and *that* disagreeable, I made sure he had been hearing some gossip about young Jack and Miss Lettie Taunton. We parted to say short, and I'm sorry for it now; I'm very sorry for it now."

"It might have been an awkward meeting for you, Mr. Garland," observed the lawyer.

"You mean because he had money on him, and I was hard up," answered the farmer, frankly. "Yes, I've been a good bit roasted about that already," he added good-humouredly. "Whenever the young fellows are in a mind to tease me, they say, 'Where have you hid Redworth, Garland? They are going to bring a fellow down from the Bank of England to identify you,' and such like; but, lor, I don't heed them. They don't mean no harm. I'm sure if I had thought of any evil coming to the old gentleman, I'd a brought him home right to his own door—that I would. The mare would a-done it, as soon as not, and never turned a hair."

"I quite believe it, Mr. Garland," said Mr. Smiler. "But now, what is *your* notion about the matter—confidentially, between you and me—what opinion have you formed on the subject?"

"I have no opinion." replied Mr. Garland, helplessly—"I am all at sea, if you understand."

"You don't suspect anybody, then?"

"Lor, no. Who is there to suspect?"

"Inspector Downing says he has a clue?"

"I don't believe a word of it—that is, begging your pardon, sir—I think he has only got hold of some cat's egg."

Mr. Smiler looked at the speaker, and remarked—

"You are satisfied there is nothing in it, then?"

"Nothing, I'd take my oath. It's a shame for Downing to think of such a thing, and for half a pin I'd punch his head for his pains. The lad's a wild lad, and has fallen into bad company, but he's right enough at heart, I'd stake my life on it."

"Thank you, Mr. Garland," said the lawyer, shaking hands very cordially with the last person who was known to have seen Mr. Redworth alive, and he made his way back to Dorking Street, refusing all the former's hospitable entreaties to put a "name on something" at the bar of the "Lion and Bear," just round the corner.

CHAPTER 7

READING THE WILL

It was not long in oozing out that Inspector Downing had his suspicions concerning John Redworth.

Putting two and two together, as he himself would have said, he did not indeed feel the slightest doubt but that the young man "knew all about it,"—knew where his father could be found, exactly how everything happened, and why Mr. Redworth never returned home.

For a long time previously the proceedings of the Dorking Street Benjamin had been matters of public notoriety; and at Cadlebury, more especially, the company he kept, the races he frequented, his liking for convivial entertainments, were subjects discussed in bar parlours, amongst the loungers always meeting and loitering upon the bridge, and talked over in second and third class carriages by persons who knew the Redworths by sight and reputation, and travelled constantly up and down the line.

Even to sleepy out-of-the-world Ludham, hints often came that Mr. John Redworth was not the immaculate young man his father believed.

"Lor! the old fellow don't know half his time where wild Jack really is. Some day won't there be a flare up."

It was thus the plebeian herd criticised the going and coming, the prospects mid the probable future misfortunes of Mr. Redworth's favourite son.

"If that Taunton girl's eyes don't get him into trouble," remarked Mr. Purslet, "I'll eat my own words. She'll be the bone of contention one day, contradict me who will."

But no one did will to contradict Mr. Purslet, for everybody who knew anything of the Tauntons, and of John Redworth's intimacy with them, shared that gentleman's opinion.

"He'll be taken in and done for," said Mr. Purslet to Mr. Garland, on the very day when Mr. Redworth disappeared "taken in and done for, if no hands is stretched out to stop him. 'Tain't my business, in course, but if I see the governor I'll give him a hint about Master Jack's goings on."

That this hint had been given, the inspector knew.

"I met him," said Mr. Purslet, in answer to a leading question, "on his way to the station. He had dined, but he was just as usual, as calm and precise as ever, and he told me he was sauntering up to the station, where he would have more than half an hour to wait.

"'I left The Grange,' he explained—you know his lofty indifferent sort of way, making believe he did not feel proud of having been over at Whittelbys, and yet determined I should know he had been—'I left The Grange too soon, as it turns out, but that is better than being too late. I cannot recollect having ever been too late in my life, Mr. Purslet.'"

"And then you told him, I suppose," suggested the inspector.

"Then I told him. I said, 'I hope you'll excuse me, Mr. Redworth, but I really do not feel it my duty, knowing what I cannot help knowing, to hold my tongue, and I must tell you Mr. John is mighty intimate at Taunton Hall.'

"That was the beginning of it. Before I had half finished telling him what a radical people considered Black Dick, and what a beauty his sister was held to be, he turned sharp on his heel.

"'I'll settle that matter tonight,' he says. 'I'm obliged to you, Mr. Purslet—yes, I'm truly obliged to you'; and then with a little gasping choking sound in his throat he went off."

Now the theory Downing built up for himself was this—

Having ascertained for a certainty that Squire Taunton was ten miles off about the time Mr. Redworth must have started for the Hall, his not improbable supposition was that the father and son met on the road, and exchanged some high words, after which Mr. Redworth proceeded on his way along, till overtaken by Mr. Garland.

The inspector's presumption was that the son left the high road in order to reach Malby, and that the pair, through some fatality, encountered each other once again, either in the woods or in the lonely meads it was necessary to cross before reaching the fifth-rate station, where, according to his own account, John Redworth took train for the Junction.

The hours, it is true, did not dovetail accurately, or indeed at all, but Downing decided that the young man did not return home by the time generally supposed.

"He is used to all sorts of dodges," reflected the inspector, "and he might even have got a lift on a stray engine or luggage train as far as the junction, and then he would be pretty sure to fall in with something or somebody who would give him a seat close into Ludham."

That the young fellow ever murdered his father in cold blood, Downing rationally rejected as an utterly absurd idea.

"But they came to words, I am positive," he thought, walking meditatively about Cadlebury, "and then likely to blows. The old man could be blusterous, I'll be bound, and the whole thing needn't have been the work of two minutes; and as for what he did with the body, why, there's holes enough in the old canal to bury a troop of horse, and weeds and dirt and mud enough to keep them down till Judgement-day. The notes are the unlikeliest part of the whole affair; but still in his first scare he would be pretty sure to try to make it appear his father had been robbed as well as murdered. Besides, he has been flush of cash ever since; I know that. He has been paying off heaps of small debts, and he is a changed and altered man.

"All the town over there," jerking his head in the direction of Ludham, "has noticed a difference in the chap ever since the night his father didn't come home, and I'm not so soft as to suppose he is breaking his heart only because the old man is missing. I wish anybody else had been in it, that I do; for though he was sometimes a cheeky young hound, I don't believe he had really any bad in him at bottom. He's worth a dozen of the other brothers; only to think of them offering a dirty five pounds for information concerning the whereabouts of their own lawful father. Blest if I should not a' felt ashamed to see the bills posted up. Well, they won't hear much about it from me for that money."

Which would have been a very judicious resolution on the part of Mr. Downing, had not other people chanced to be just as sharp, if not sharper than he was.

Long before he began his investigations Ludham entertained its suspicions, and every question the inspector asked only added fuel to the fire.

It might be all very well for old ladies of both sexes to imagine Mr. Redworth was absent of his own free choice, but the sterner portion of the population knew better.

The old gentleman had fallen a victim to foul play of some sort, and in the absence of any other person whom it was possible to suspect of having had a hand in his disappearance, the wiseacres of Ludham laid their heads together, and decided that matters looked bad as regarded John Redworth.

Ere long they were confirmed in this opinion; for within six weeks of Mr. Redworth's disappearance the family in Dorking Street received a very terrible shock, which, in due time, communicated itself to the whole population.

It came about in this wise—John Redworth wanted money—not an uncommon want with him; further, he said he needed it immediately.

Now the sum named, though in itself perhaps not large, sounded enormous in the ears of his more frugal brothers.

"Why, what can you want with a hundred pounds?" asked Trenhill Redworth. "You have your salary, and living has never cost you a penny, and—"

"Look here, Trenhill," interrupted the young man; "a hundred pounds now will be of more use to me than probably a thousand in the future. I suppose when matters are squared up there will be something coming to me under my father's will. Advance me what I ask for, and deduct any sum you choose from my inheritance hereafter, only don't torment me with questions, there's a good fellow."

That both Gower and Trenhill Redworth were good fellows there could be no question.

They were honest and kindly, upright, and, in some ways, generous; but they were prudent, and moreover human, and they had always been a little jealous of their father's favourite, and apt to consider themselves rather hardly done by in comparison.

As the coat of many colours stirred up the ire of Joseph's brethren to the pitch of final exasperation, so the story told by Mr. Garland and Mr. Blex concerning those two little properties on "The Wastes," excited the righteous indignation of John Redworth's brothers.

"What had the lad ever done," they asked each other, "that he should be so favoured? Wherein was he better than they, that the old man should buy and build for him, and scarcely take so much thought of their children as to send the future representative of the Toughly Street Bacon Warehouse and the Bermondsey Bone boiling business a sovereign upon each respective birthday.

"A gentleman forsooth." Were they not gentleman also. If their father had only indulged them in the same chances of making friends, with the same opportunities for elegant leisure, would they not have been far finer gentlemen than this idle brother?

They had always felt sore about the favour shown to John, and most undoubtedly it made them sorer still to hear their father had conceived such generous intentions towards the pair he designed for each other.

"It was not quite fair," Trenhill said to Gower, while Gower in reply remarked—"It was very unfair."

"And most likely he has left him the bulk of his property," observed Trenhill. "I have no doubt of it," agreed the other. Perhaps because they felt somewhat anxious to know exactly how matters did stand in the will, the two elder brothers had agreed

that no steps should be taken in order to prove it till the following July, unless meantime some tiding reached them concerning
their father's fate.

"Everything can remain just as it is," said Gower to his sister.

"We will provide such moneys as may be required for the
house here, and John has of course his salary. I do not exactly
know what provision the law makes for such a case, but however
that may be, I should not like us to appear in any unseemly haste
about the matter."

"Then you have quite given up all hope of ever seeing our
poor father again?"

"Alas, yes. It is possible hereafter some light may be thrown
upon his fate. Of course none of us can imagine for a moment,
if not dead, he would keep us in ignorance of his whereabouts."

"No, oh! no."

"Yet still, though I feel quite satisfied he has met his end by
foul play, I for one should never agree to probate being taken
out at present."

"You are quite right, Gower; I should not like it either."

"Because matters can, of course, go on just as they are."

But that happened to be precisely what matters could not
do. Theoretically it may appear an easy thing to permit a man's
affairs to remain in *status quo* for twelve months, but practically
the arrangement is full of difficulties.

Little obstacles were constantly presenting themselves, which,
though unimportant, required patience to overcome, and then
came the younger brother's demand for one hundred pounds,
which he entreated should at once be advanced to him.

"I assure you, Trenhill," he went on, seeing that his elder hesitated, and looked troubled, "I would not ask for a penny if I
were not in pressing need. Let me have that sum, and I promise
I won't trouble you for another sixpence till the year is up."

"I must talk to Gower about it," said Trenhill Redworth,
gravely. "We are neither of us rich, and of course we cannot deal
in any way with our father's property till the will is proved."

"Very well then, I suppose I must go to the Jews," retorted the other irritably. "The next thing I ask you for, Trenhill, I know you will refuse!"

"I don't refuse this," was the reply. "I only tell you I must discuss your request with Gower. I will do so this evening, and let you know tomorrow if we can anyhow arrange to let you have what you wish."

"I thank you," said John Redworth; but he spoke the words ungraciously. Evidently he wanted one hundred pounds there and then.

"As if," explained the elder brother, when speaking about the interview, "money were kept in tap, and to be had by running for it round the corner."

"We shall have a lot of trouble with him, I foresee that," observed Mr. Gower Redworth, oracularly.

"If we knew how much money he is to have, it would simplify matters a good deal."

"That is precisely what we ought to know," said Gower, "and I will go to Smiler and explain our difficulty to him."

The result of all of which was that Mr. Smiler said he would fix an early day for running down to Ludham and reading the will.

"Or perhaps," amended that gentleman, who possibly did not see his way to making a sufficiently good thing out of another journey to Dorking Street, "you could bring your sister up here tomorrow, and then the affair might be got over without further delay."

"I think, Miss Redworth," said the lawyer next morning, when, dressed in deep mourning, she, accompanied by her brothers, attended at Lincoln's Inn to hear how Mr. Redworth had left his property, "you told me you did look over your father's papers some time since'?"

"Directly we began to fear—there was something wrong, I opened his desk, in the hope of finding some clue—some—"

"Exactly so; I understand," finished Mr. Smiler briskly, "and in doing so you discovered, I believe, no trace of a will, or anything of that sort?"

"None."

"We may take it, I imagine, for granted, that there was no such thing, because, although the will I hold in my hand was made some few years since, the very arrangements we have been given to understand Mr. Redworth intended to carry out, were in accordance with the wishes expressed in this paper. As his property increased—and his investments were at once so judicious and so fortunate that it did increase greatly—Mr. Redworth was in the habit of altering his will in accordance with the change in his circumstances, and with one exception, which you shall presently hear, every legacy was in each will substantially the same, except in amount; that is to say, he did not change his intentions with regard to the disposal of his money—he merely varied or enlarged the various gifts. This will was drawn up immediately after the decease of his old friend Mr. Jace, who died intestate, and the bulk of whose properly went consequently to the son who, if his father had left a will, would certainly not have inherited it."

"I remember my father speaking about that," commented Gower. "That fact produced a great impression upon Mr. Redworth. He did speak about the matter, and said how grieved poor Jace would be if he could know Willoughby had come in for the freeholds. He said it behoved every man to arrange his affairs before his death, so that there could be no frustrating his intentions afterwards, and, in short, he gave me his instructions and executed this will, which I think there can be no doubt is the last, and which, if you please, I will now read to you."

Miss Redworth and her two eldest brothers simply inclined their heads in answer to Mr. Smiler's final statement. John Redworth took no notice of the lawyer's remark, but with his eyes devoured the paper as if he would fain have grasped its contents without tarrying for Mr. Smiler's slow utterance of them.

Mr. Smiler unfolded the will, softly smoothed out the folds with his plump right hand, cleared his throat, and began.

The faces of the three elder Redworths were gravely expectant—interested, as was natural, but not unduly so. That of the youngest, however, wore a look of eager and undisguised anxiety,

Mr. Smiler, glancing at him as he went on, wondered, but outwardly took no notice. Something was coming which he suspected would try the equanimity of the four.

Stripped of legal verbiage, the provisions of the will flowed on smoothly enough. The aforesaids and whereases, the hereby and the hereinbefore-mentioneds, delayed the course of the reading a little, but did not alter the fairness of the disposition.

The whole of the property of which Mr. Redworth died possessed was to be sold, and dealt with as follows:

> Four thousand pounds to his dear son Gower, four thousand pounds to his dear son Trenhill, four thousand pounds to his beloved daughter Amelia, free from the control of any husband she might marry. In the event of her dying unmarried, or without children, such sum of four thousand pounds was to be divided between her brothers Gower and Trenhill, their heirs, executors, and so forth.

At this point Mr. Smiler paused and took a pinch of snuff. "I am one of the few men now extant," he was wont to say, "who still take snuff." Gower and Trenhill drew a breath relieved. After all, he had not left everything to John, as they once feared he might. It was not a wholly unfair will—on the contrary.

But John Redworth's face never changed its expression of intense enquiry—never relaxed its look of eager anxiety.

Once again Mr. Smiler glanced at him, and then proceeded:

> The residue of my property (after the payment of the aforesaid legacies, one hundred pounds to each of my executors, fifty pounds to the poor of the parish of Ludham, and a like sum to the Dispensary at Cadlebury), I leave to my youngest son. John Morrison Redworth, subject to no condition whatever, save and except that within twelve calendar months from the date of my death, he shall marry my much loved and highly esteemed niece, Hilda Susannah Gower—

Mr. Smiler stopped suddenly, and looked up. "You spoke, I think," he said, addressing John Redworth, and his two brothers and his sister turned towards him as if in confirmation of the lawyer's words.

"No, I didn't speak," he answered. "Go on."

And in the event of the said John Morrison refusing to marry his said cousin, or of his dying before such marriage can be solemnized, it is my will that the whole of my property, always excepting such portion as is devoted to paying the legacies hereinbefore mentioned, shall be employed in building and endowing almshouses for twelve widows, to be called 'The Redworth Charity.' And that I may not embarrass my will with the details of a project only to be carried out in the event of a contingency which I trust may never arise, I leave the plans, specifications, and all other particulars necessary for the purpose named, in separate form for the guidance of my executors. On the other hand, should the said Hilda Susannah Gower refuse to marry her said cousin, or die before the marriage, a legacy similar in amount to that left to his brothers— namely, four thousand pounds—is to be paid to the said John Morrison Redworth, and the residue of my property is to be devoted to the purposes before mentioned, the number of almshouses to be reduced to six.

Then followed some directions about the testator's funeral, the names of the executors, a desire strongly expressed that Mr. Smiler. who was one of the executors, should conduct all the legal business connected with the estates, a couple of codicils relating to matters of no general interest, and the will ended.

Mr. Smiler laid his hand upon it tenderly, and looked at John Redworth, on whom also the eyes of his sister and brothers were fastened curiously.

For a moment there was a dead silence. Not one of those present uttered a word. Then John Redworth rose and walked across to the window, and, with his hands thrust into his pockets, stood there with his back to the company.

All at once he said hoarsely, and without turning his head towards the person he addressed—

"You may give out the contract for those almshouses at once, Mr. Smiler. I shall never come to you for any of that money."

"Now, now, now," began the lawyer.

"You have a year, at any rate, in which to consider the matter," said Trenhill Redworth.

"Your father always intended you to marry Hilda, so it is mere affectation pretending that this takes you by surprise," remarked Gower.

"That is true enough; but I did think he would have left me something—say a five-pound-note, for instance—with no condition hanging to it."

"But, John, you like Hilda, don't you?" here interrupted his sister, crossing to where he stood, and laying a persuasive hand on his arm.

"Like her? Of course I like her. Why shouldn't I?"

"That is just what I say."

"But my liking or disliking her has nothing to do with the matter," he persisted.

"It has everything to do with it," pleaded his sister. "If you like her you will marry her, and get all this money."

"I shall never marry Hilda Gower."

"And why not, in Heaven's name?" asked Trenhill Redworth, surprised out of the usual calm gravity which characterized his demeanour.

"For a very sufficient reason."

"Surely you can tell us what that reason is."

"Certainly,"—and he turned his back to the window and faced them all as he spoke—"it is a very simple one. I shall not marry Hilda Gower, because *I am married already.*"

"To Miss Taunton?" said Mr. Smiler, interrogatively.

"To Lettie Taunton," answered the young man. And having thus satisfied the curiosity of his family, John Redworth went out of the office, and shut the door after him.

CHAPTER 8

MISS GOWER'S NIGHT VIGIL

When Miss Redworth returned to Ludham, which she did by a train arriving at that town about seven o'clock, she went straight up to her bedroom. Terrible as the mystery of her father's disappearance had been, this certainty of her brother's marriage was worse. It involved so many questions, it created such a tangle of mental and family difficulty, it was likely to cause such a division of interests, that the poor lady felt disheartened. To her, as to her father, John had been an idol, and it was hard not merely to feel every hope cherished about him was destroyed, but that another trouble might be connected with his most unhappy choice, the length and depth of which no one belonging to John Redworth had courage to contemplate.

In ten minutes after her return, Miss Gower was in possession of the story. In broken sentences, interrupted by many sobs, Miss Redworth told her dear friend what had happened.

When she had quite finished. Miss Gower made no comment on the news. What she said was—

"Now, Amy, I will fetch you cup of tea, and you must try to keep quiet. All this has been too much for you."

Then, when her cousin, thoroughly worn out, had fallen into an uneasy slumber, she stole away down the stairs, and wandered about the lonely house, which seemed so silent and so desolate, that the dead might have come and taken possession of it.

She could not rest. She felt as if she never should wish to sleep again, livery hope, and plan, and wish of her life had been bound up in John Redworth; and now she was told the man she loved—the man she expected to marry was the husband of another woman.

"How shall I bear—how shall I bear it?" she moaned, as she paced the drawing-room, to-and-fro, to-and-fro. The servants were gone to bed. She was the only person stirring in the house; but still she kept treading the carpet with impatient feet, battling with her misery all alone.

She scarce knew what she was doing. As she thought she tore

her handkerchief into shreds. It was a dainty trifle; one she had embroidered for herself. But next morning she found it in her pocket rent to tatters—torn asunder almost thread by thread, and the lace, which had been old and beautiful, a mere ball of rags.

"I must have taken the news very badly," she said to herself, with a bitter smile. "Worse than I thought I did. Lucky I was quite alone."

She remembered somewhat of her agony—remembered drawing up the blind and looking out into the quiet street, longing to rush away and walk for miles and miles through the silent country. She recollected a mad desire to go down to the river and dip her head in the cool water. She knew she had imagined, if she could find rest anywhere, it would be in a particular little dell, shaded by great elm trees, where, in the springtime, grew early primroses and scented violets.

If she had yielded to the wild impulse which seemed to urge her out, she would have rushed away into the night and wandered through the fields and beside the murmuring streams, till fatigue overcame her.

"I was mad," she said, recalling these things, and then she repeated her former thanksgiving with a difference. "How fortunate there was no one to see me."

Long after midnight, when she was toiling with weary limbs up to her own room, she heard Miss Redworth calling her name faintly.

"Do you want me. Amy?" she asked, pushing open the door she had purposely left ajar.

"Dear Hilda, I thought I should never make you hear," was the answer. "Should you mind sleeping here for the remainder of the night? I am so frightened; I feel so nervous, you cannot think. I have that old fancy about there being someone moving in papa's room; did you hear that noise? As if the drawers were being opened and closed. I never can continue to live in this house. I must tell Trenhill so tomorrow."

"It is all fancy, dear," said Miss Gower; "there is no one in that room; to satisfy you and myself too, I will look into it, and come back to you in a minute."

And so saying, Miss Gower slipped into her own apartment, undressed hurriedly, put on a wrapper over her night-gown, thrust her feet into a pair of slippers, and then crossed the passage and opened the door of that room, which, living or dead, Mr. Redworth was never to re-enter.

The moon had risen, and each object that apartment contained was clearly visible in the bright light which flooded every corner.

There was the plain iron bedstead, with its snowy hangings and its smoothly-spread counterpane. There were ranged the boots the man would never require more—between the windows stood a bureau his hand should not again unlock—beside the bed was a chest of drawers, where his linen still lay ready for use. In the looking-glass Miss Gower caught a reflection of her own pale face, and for a moment shrunk back scared. In its loneliness and silence the room was terribly suggestive of the unsolved mystery; it would scarcely have seemed so dreadful had a corpse been lying in it, as it did with that aspect of waiting, in the trim orderliness of its arrangement. Everything there was ready for the coming of the man who had never returned home.

As the apartment looked on the evening he was expected back so it looked then.

No one had cared to change the order of the furniture, or to remove any of Mr. Redworth's belongings.

"Where is he?" each separate article seemed to say to the woman who looked around. "Is he in some depth of that long lonely canal—in some sedge-covered bay, half weed, half slime, beside that weird sheet of water bordered by a vegetation which is almost tropical in its rank luxuriance—is he lying in some ditch among the dark woods where last autumn's leaves have drifted thick and brown, or has he floated away through a broken lock along the river which flows into the Thames, and will he be brought back here someday battered and disfigured, recognizable only by such of his garments as the wash and the drift of the water have spared?'

Shivering, Miss Gower retreated from the room and closed the door. As she did so it seemed to her excited fancy that she heard a sound in the deserted chamber, something which was neither sob, nor moan, and yet was like a low wail of pain and sorrow.

She would have opened the door again, but her courage failed her. Overwrought, she stepped swiftly back into her cousin's room, and after shooting the bolts and turning the key, nestled down into the bed beside her.

But not to sleep. No—till after the servants had gone downstairs, and the stir and hum of awakening life was heard in the street, she never closed her eyes, and when at last she did fall into an uneasy slumber, utterly worn out by mental and physical exhaustion, it was only to be suddenly awakened by a cry from Miss Redworth, who, starting up, panted out—

"Oh! Hilda, I have had such an awful dream; such a horrible, horrible dream! I thought I was in a darksome cavern, the walls of which were dripping with water, and the floor with slime. There were dreadful creatures crawling about and sticking to the roof, and as I slipped, and put up my hand to save myself from falling, I touched filthy things that were cold and noisome. And at one end of this place, so far from me, that for a time I could scarce discern his features, I saw my father. He seemed struggling to rise, and stretched one arm out so imploringly, and turned such a beseeching face towards me, that I tried to rise and help him. But as I ran I stumbled and fell. I strove to save myself, and doing so touched some slimy animal that dropped from the roof to the ground. And then I woke, Hilda—I woke—but it all seems to me real even now."

CHAPTER 9

MISS GOWER DISAPPOINTS HER RELATIVES

Time went on, but Scotland Yard, and Mr. Downing, and the Ludham gossips made little progress in unravelling the mystery of Mr. Redworth's disappearance. The body was not found—

no clue could be discovered to the identity of the person who changed the notes. Ludham could not fasten the crime of patricide upon John Redworth, although it felt no manner of doubt that he had killed his father; and it is quite certain that even the young man's brothers believed him guilty.

At heart they were loyal and affectionate, however, and even when they felt most satisfied of his sin, they agreed to try and step between him and its consequences. They entertained no Spartan ideas of justice. He was of their blood, and they decided to do all men could to save him from the consequences of his crime.

Upon them there settled a sorrowful gravity, which in a few weeks aged them more than years, whilst Miss Redworth grew old and worn under the incubus of her apprehensions and her memories. She could not forget her brother's manner on the night when she and Miss Gower waited and watched for the return of the missing man. She recollected the jingle of those sovereigns, the sleeve soaked with water, the unwonted hour at which he had risen next morning; and her heart grew sick and faint as she thought all things seemed against him, that he was guilty, and that he alone understood the mystery of his father's fate.

Through all, however, Miss Gower remained apparently steadfast to her cousin. Whether she believed him innocent is open to doubt, but it is certain she maintained his cause.

To her very soul she felt the bitterness of his desertion; but she did not mean to let the world—her world—guess the length and depth of her despair.

When Miss Redworth elected to go to London, Miss Gower determined to remain in the neighbourhood of Ludham. She was free to choose her own path in life, and she decided upon following an extremely independent course. Her money, which Mr. Redworth had managed for her, and managed judiciously, could now, she felt, be expended in a manner likely to attract attention, and secure her a marked position in Ludham. There was no reason why she should not start as a lady of landed property on her own account. Mr. Redworth's programme could be carried out, minus the husband. Practically, what she proposed to herself was to do what nobody else seemed disposed to attempt.

"I will take John's part against every one. I will visit his wife. I will make myself a person of importance in the neighbourhood; and, for the rest, my day will come. All things are possible to him who can wait. I can wait. There is some secret about this marriage which I have to discover. John is not a happy husband, and it shall not be my fault if she is a happy wife."

Just as methodically as she might have traced a pattern out on muslin, Miss Gower arranged her plans for the discomfiture of Mrs. John Redworth.

"I daresay she is pretty," said Miss Gower, looking, the while, at her own rejected face in the glass. "I have no doubt, indeed, she is; but, before we are any of us much older, he will wish he had never seen her. I don't believe a man reared as he has been will be able to endure the social ostracism his connection with the Taunton Hall people must involve. But we shall see." And forthwith she stepped boldly into the breach which had opened between the bridegroom and his family, wrote a friendly letter to Mrs. John, and a congratulatory one to Mr. John; and, in fact, achieved an amount of politeness which poor Miss Redworth could not have compassed had anyone offered her a thousand a year for doing so.

And Miss Gower had her reward. From Paris, where the married couple were gone, after some little delay she received few gracefully-worded lines of affectionate thanks from Mrs. John Redworth, and a most grateful epistle from John. He wrote:

I shall never forget your kindness, Hilda. It was like water in the desert; and certainly, if anyone might have been supposed to possess a right to feel aggrieved at my conduct, you were that person. My dear cousin, highly as I have always esteemed you, I never thought so much of you as I do now.

And, after much more to the same effect, he ended by signing himself, "Yours affectionately, J.R."

With a certain set grimness of aspect. Miss Gower folded up this letter, after she had read it twice over, and put it carefully aside.

"Ah! My dear cousin," she mentally exclaimed, "the plot is thickening. I have a great deal still to learn about you and your beautiful wife. This letter is dated from Paris; but if you only knew I had seen you in Bloomsbury, the other evening, you might not feel quite so easy in your mind. What on earth could you be doing in Bloomsbury, when we all supposed you on the other side of the Channel?"

Inspector Downing could have told her, had she propounded the enquiry to him, for he, too, beheld the young man entering a lodging-house situated in one of those quiet streets that abound in the neighbourhood of Russell and Brunswick Squares.

The inspector, or one of his satellites, had never lost sight of John Redworth since the night after his father disappeared, and there could be no doubt but that, putting two and two together, the inspector understood the Bloomsbury lodging-house contained another strong motive for getting rid of Mr. Redworth.

That the young man had made away with the old man, Mr. Downing entertained no manner of doubt, and yet he could not fix the crime upon him. Not merely was he unable to trace anyone who had seen John Redworth returning home on that particular night in a suspicious and clandestine manner, but he had found several persons who could speak to the fact of having noticed him in the train which reached Ludham a little after nine o'clock.

In a word, at the time when Mr. Redworth was stated to have been at Saul's Corner, his son was seen at Ludham, which, of course, rendered it exceedingly difficult to connect him with the mystery.

The inspector never doubted his guilt, and, for that matter, Ludham also was quite satisfied young Redworth knew perfectly well what had become of his father. But still, the evidence necessary to secure a conviction had not been obtained, and Mr.

Downing went about in a dissatisfied manner, looking at the bills placarding the neighbourhood, which bills offered at last two hundred and fifty pounds for such information, *et cetera, et cetera*, the reward promised by the Redworth family being supplemented by another hundred from government.

It would be too much to say that the course of conduct Miss Gower elected to pursue met with any violent expressions of disapproval from her relatives; but Miss Redworth did admit that Hilda had disappointed them.

For a young woman to desert her family at such a crisis—to reject the shelter of respectable and well-ordered homes—to set herself up, as it were, above the Redworths, and refuse to be guided, as concerned her pecuniary affairs, by the advice of men who were up in all city matters, seemed to her cousins a very sad thing.

But what appeared sadder than all, was her selecting Mr. Garland's as a fit and proper house in which to take up her residence. "A vulgar, drunken old gossip," said Miss Redworth to Miss Gower, summing him up.

"Yes, dear, but *he* believes in John, and he has a nice motherly wife, and the air up on The Wastes is crisp and invigorating; and I think London would kill me—and, in short, I mean to remain with the Garlands for the present."

"I don't fancy she can be quite in her right senses," observed Gower Redworth, seeking about for an explanation of her conduct. "We know she was very fond of John, and I daresay the disappointment has turned her head a little. All the same, however, I do not think she ought to set our wishes so totally at defiance."

"It is a queer start," thought Inspector Downing. "If she had been his sister I could have understood it, but, as matters are, I confess I do not comprehend the meaning of this move. I'll know all about it someday, however, or my name is not Thomas Downing."

Wherein Mr. Downing chanced to be wrong. He never understood Miss Gower's little move, and his name remained Thomas Downing, as it had ever been.

There is nothing so hard to understand as the secret of a woman's actions, when they are prompted solely by pique. Whilst the inspector was puzzling himself over Miss Gower's motives, she felt all she then wanted was—if John Redworth were happy, to make him unhappy; if he were unhappy, to behold the misery himself had wrought.

She wanted to see him sorry, regretful, repentant. She desired to watch him tire of his wife's beauty, and contrast the life he might have led with her, Hilda Gower—the life of competence, respectability, peace, comfort with the poverty-stricken, disreputable existence he must drag on at Taunton Hall.

For she knew he was coming to live with his wife and brother-in-law, at the old house on the road to Cadlebury; and, from the hints thrown out by Mr. Downing, and the chatter of Mr. Garland, she understood what a prolonged residence there was likely to prove.

"Mr. Garland," she said one morning, in the fine September weather. "If you are going to Malby this afternoon, I wish you could take me with you as far as Trotterbeck. I can easily walk from there over to Taunton Hall. I want to enquire when my cousin and his wife really are expected back."

"You know the squire ain't at the Hall, miss?"

"It is not the squire I wish to see, just at present," answered Miss Gower. She was quite at home by this time with the Garland family, and found the homage and respect they paid her peculiarly gratifying She had her own rooms, and was waited upon as she had never been waited on in Dorking Street; "though I confess I have a curiosity to see both brother and sister; all I desire today is to learn for certain when my cousin means to return. I am afraid, very much afraid, Mr. Garland, his prolonged absence is doing him harm amongst his friends here."

"I don't think there is much in that," observed Mr. Garland, bluntly. "In my poor opinion, except you and me, and may be just one and another here and there, the poor fellow hasn't a friend left in Ludham. He might have lived down the notion of being concerned in that unfortunate business, but he will never live down his marriage with Miss Taunton. It was the worst day's work he ever took in hand, and so, I am afraid, he will find it."

"She is very beautiful, though, Mr. Garland, you say?"

"Very beautiful; but lor! what is beauty, when a man comes to have to look at it week in, week out, for the remainder of his life?"

"I should say it is a great deal," remarked Miss Gower, plucking a sprig of sweet-briar, and inhaling its peculiar perfume as she spoke. "But you have not answered my question yet—will you take me as far as Trotterbeck?"

"I'll take you to any place you like, miss. As I have told you before, there's me, and there's the mare, and we are both always at your service, day or night. The mare won't tire, and I am sure I won't. But as for dropping you at Trotterbeck, I can't hear of such a thing. We will go by Saul's Wood Corner, and, if you like, you can walk from there up to the Hall—that is not far, and if you choose to stroll about the heath or the canal for an hour or so, why, I will call for you at the Hall on my way back from Malby. There are some good gardens and shady walks at the Hall, only the whole place has been let to run wild. I used to go bird's-nesting there when I was a lad. It is a pity to see a property like it running to seed, as one may say. It might just as well be in chancery. If it were mine, I would dig up that old squire, will or no will, and bury him where all decent men ought to be buried—in the parish churchyard. I should not like to lie in bed o'nights and think of him being outside the window just at my elbow, as it were."

"His was a strange fancy, certainly," remarked Miss Gower.

"Yes, and if you notice, strange fancies are mostly at the beginning of every evil that happens in a family," said Mr. Garland, sententiously. "When folks commence being odd, they generally end by being beggars—that is what I have observed. Living up here on these Wastes, I can look down upon a vast of places that have changed hands, even within my memory, and nine times out often the trouble came through somebody who was different from his neighbours. Look at the Tauntons, for example. Ne'er one of them like anybody else, and going on each heir worse than the man that went before him."

"Till the evil culminated in the present squire," finished Miss Gower.

"You are right, there. But he never had much chance," said Mr. Garland, charitably; for all at once he remembered the Tauntons were now allied to the Redworths, and, in consequence, after a fashion, connected with the lady he addressed.

Chapter 10

Taunton Hall

About a mile from Saul's Corner, on the main road from Ludham to Cadlebury, there stands, fronting Wilderness Heath, a large redbrick mansion.

It lies well back from the highway, and is screened from the impertinent observation of passing travellers by high walls and a double line of fine old elms.

A place, once upon a time, of considerable pretension—a place which might, even in the time of the Black Squire, have been rendered fit for the habitation of any nobleman or gentleman. But it owned an evil reputation.

Ever since the period when the long avenue, leading right away from the house to Saul's Corner in one direction, and to Wilderness Heath on the other, was converted into a public road, Taunton Hall, shorn of its wild moorland avenue, and of its splendid approaches, shared the fate of human beings who go down in the world.

The high wall, reared by the occupier to shield his mansion from the gaze of the vulgar, at once assumed, to the rural mind, an air of sullen mystery. Had the then Squire Taunton been disposed so to humour the popular fancy as to allow his few neighbours to look through iron gates at the lawns and gardens his walls enclosed, people might have been satisfied; but he did nothing of the sort. Between himself, his grand cedar trees, his parterres, his smooth grass plots, his rare shrubs and beautiful flowers, and the prying herd, he interposed not merely high walls, but heavy wooden doors; and so still, so grim, so utterly silent the place always looked, that ere long the people said the squire was out of his mind, and then, improving upon that idea, that the place was haunted.

Stories were told of some great and purely imaginary crime which had been committed within the Hall. On special nights in the year, it was said, a figure dressed all in black would dart out on any passer-by, and keep beside him for a mile or more, no matter how fast he ran. When Squire Taunton died—the squire who sold the best part of his patrimony and built the walls—his widow at once went abroad, to "foreign parts," and the house was shut up till, the young heir dying, a distant relative succeeded to the property.

For generations after that, Taunton Hall never descended from father to son, and it was the popular belief that Taunton Hall never would so descend again.

"There is a curse upon the house and upon the owners," said those best informed about the matter. "Someday there will be no owner for the Hall, and then it will be pulled down, and a good riddance, too."

Originally the Taunton quivers must have held an extraordinary number of male arrows, for thus far, spite of the singular fact concerning the descent, or rather non-descent, from father to son, the Hall had never lacked an heir when the latest owner died.

As a rule, however, the owners did not much affect the place. Most of them had estates elsewhere, or houses in London, or palaces in "foreign parts." So long as they retained sufficient of their ancient prestige to marry heiresses, or to obtain good posts under government, no Taunton really resided at the Hall, which gradually went, not exactly to wreck and ruin, but was left to repair and embellish itself, as, by the aid of climbing ivy, or twining parasites, and wildly-spreading rose-trees, it managed to do not unsuccessfully.

Back to the Hall at length there came a certain Marmaduke Taunton, who, having in his mad youth inherited and scorned the place, returned to it in his sorrowful old age.

Haunted, then, the Hall was, no doubt, by memories of evil deeds, of sins that had sorrowfully come home at the nightfall, of hopes which had borne no fruit, of resolves abandoned almost as soon as formed. Weary, worn, disappointed, disenchanted, disillusioned, of all the bright dreams of his reckless manhood, the old squire came back, in the decline of his godless life, to bemoan his fate, and to say, with the wise foolish king, "All is vanity."

He resided at the Hall for years, living the life of a hermit, varying the routine of his existence only by a rare drive into Cadlebury, or a rarer journey to London, seeing no one, save, at distant intervals, his lawyer, who was also his agent; yet keeping up some remnant of his ancient state, being served and waited upon with all due ceremony, by aged domestics who were almost as recluse in their habits and reserved in their manners as the squire himself.

After about twenty years of this secluded life. Mr. Taunton died, and in dying dealt the last blow to all hope of rehabilitating the Hall.

It was not in his power to deal with the estate, which, after being docked of its magnificent avenues, was strictly entailed, but he possessed a considerable personality, and this he left to the next heir, upon condition that he, the testator, was buried in a mausoleum he had erected in the garden, without any ceremony of consecration or Christian rites being performed over his remains.

It was supposed and hoped that the new squire would either reject the legacy, and so get rid of the conditions imposed, or else find some legal loophole through which he might creep; but he accepted the burden laid upon him with the most perfect equanimity.

So long as "Old Marmydeuk"—it was thus he pronounced the name of his predecessor—"so long as Old Marmydeuk did not come to life again, he was welcome to rest in the garden, or anywhere else about the premises.

"I'd take a parish full o'corpses on the same terms," further explained Mr. Taunton; and thus, to the scandal of all the country side, the old squire was planted out amongst his shrubs and flowers, and the new squire took possession of the Hall, shut up all the best rooms, barred the Hall door, and set up his household gods in the kitchen.

There, in the evenings, he smoked his pipe and drank his beer, regardless of all the proprieties. He had come from the plough, and Taunton Hall, and the atmosphere of drawing-rooms, would have suffocated him. He said quite frankly that he could not a-bear fine gentlemen, adding, not very chivalrously, that "fine ladies sickened him."

He rose at four, and went to bed at eight. He liked fat bacon, and loved the odour of a farmyard. He had never been fond of society, and for that reason, certainly not from any apprehension of overstepping the conventionalities, did not frequent public-houses, or ask any neighbour to drop in and smoke and drink beer with him.

Week in, week out, he stood over his labourers in the fields, sometimes working as hard with them as though his living depended upon his exertions. A bear in his manners, an animal in his habits, in every respect a contrast to the refined cynic who lay quite quietly under the rustling trees, and never rose from his grave even when his successor filled the great Hall with wheat, and set his men to churn in the dining-room, under the very eyes of his ancestors, male and female, who, wigged, powdered, patched, laced, furbelowed, and clad in armour, frowned or simpered, or stared solidly from the walls.

He had vegetated in this manner for about ten years, knowing no variety in his life save that which was wrought by the advent of seedtime and harvest, the snows of winter and the drought of summer, when he met with a terrible accident.

While helping to build a rick, he overbalanced himself, and falling to the ground broke his thigh, also having the disaster to encounter in his descent the prongs of a pitchfork, which entered his side.

All that skill could do for him was done. The doctors saved his life, and patched him up as well as they were able, but the accident left him a cripple, and a peevish invalid to boot. Walking became a pain and a weariness. It was only slowly and with difficulty he could drag himself into the more distant fields. Every change of weather affected his health, and consequently his spirits and his temper. The house, as he said, with a certain unconscious pathos, "seemed like a prison to him" and the only thing he appeared really to enjoy was sitting on a low broken wall down by the deserted canal, watching the sluggish waters flowing slowly by, and looking at the fish swimming about in shoals, or making widening circles as they rose to the surface after flies.

What he thought about, or whether he thought of anything, no one ever knew, but there was something so sad and solitary about the appearance of the owner of Taunton Hall, as with sunken eyes he looked across the canal at the woods beyond, or let his glance wander over the giant rushes and the great masses of floating weeds, that most of the few men who passed by on the narrow watery highway stopped to exchange a greeting with him, sometimes bringing him news from the outer world, and frequently praying his acceptance of fish caught in the deeper and darker water further down, where the pine plantation stretched to the brink of the canal, and the alder-trees grew thick beside the woodland paths, leading off, one to Saul's Corner, and the other to Wilderness Heath.

It was then Mrs. Taunton's brother chanced to be asked to assist in managing the estate. The son of a village innkeeper—a man who had tried innkeeping, and various other ways of living, with an almost equal amount of non-success, it was quite in the ordinary course of events he should think himself competent to look after his brother-in-law's affairs.

As a first step, he began to breed cattle; and when he failed in that endeavour he tried his hand at growing flax. The latter attempt resulting in a loss, he next turned his attention to a more congenial occupation—that of dealing in horses—and making one lucky hit, he set that against years of misfortune, and season after season destitute of profit, and would suffer no one to have the best of the argument concerning his system of management.

It was this brother who insisted that his nephew and niece should be sent to school.

"Taking what his father was left, and the money I shall make for him," said that worthy, "Dick will one day have a fine fortune. It is time he was being educated and taught to behave like a gentleman."

As for his niece, in his opinion there was no position to which she might not aspire.

"With her good looks, and a handsome dot, she ought to marry a duke," he was wont to remark, pushing back an old sun bonnet off the girl's face. "You must not run about like a wild colt any longer, Lettie. What a gipsy it is. Ay, I warrant me you and your brother are true Tauntons—true chips of the old block. Anyone may see it who is not stone blind, and likes to compare you with those old dead-and-gones hanging in the house there. Be a good girl, and give your mind to your book. Learn how to *parlez vous*; don't let crotchets and quavers daunt you, and some day you'll see what you shall see, and then, maybe, when I am in my grave you'll remember what your poor old uncle prophesied about you."

And, accordingly, to school the boy and girl were sent. As a matter of form, the squire's opinion had been requested on the subject, but he declined to give it.

"Do as you like," he exclaimed, idly picking blades of grass as he spoke, and pitching them into the water. "I'm of no account—I am nowt and I am nobody now. Give them learning, an' ye please, but if learning do no more for them nor this fine place has done for me, then don't come and say it's my fault. We was all better and happier, I'm thinking, in the farm I'll never see more, than we've ever been at Taunton Hall."

Before his children had, to use his own expression, "got much learning" at the very third-rate school where they were being educated, Mr. Taunton died. He was not buried in the mausoleum with old Marmaduke, but carried down the back staircase he had elected to use in life, through the kitchen hall, across the farmyard, and out by the stable entrance to Cadlebury, where the service was read over his remains in orthodox form, and all the rites of the Church were complied with by his relatives on behalf of this English Heathen.

For years he had been a cipher in his own house, regarded by no member of the establishment, and interfering with nothing that was done. Nevertheless, it is possible his death proved a relief to wife and brother-in-law.

Whether looking gloomily into the canal, or nestling in the chimney corner, he had seemed a very skeleton at the feast of life to those still strong enough and hearty enough to enjoy the good things placed before them.

Thus at length the spell was broken, for Richard Taunton did succeed to his father's property, but if people had shaken their heads wisely before, they shook them still more wisely now.

There were evil days in store for Taunton Hall, so declared the oldest inhabitants. There would be wild doings when the young man came into his own. He had never been trained to manage a property. His one idea with regard to money was to spend it. He had every trait of the maddest and most thoughtless of the worst of the Tauntons, without one of their redeeming qualities; whilst as for the girl, she was handsome enough in all conscience, but would come to no good either. So prophesied the croakers and scandalmongers; whilst more charitable folks trusted the brother and sister might meet with some friend who would advise them for their good; and neutralize the evil influence of their silly vulgar mother, and harum-scarum, speculative, dissipated uncle.

Much company of a somewhat indifferent sort came to the Hall in those days.

Gentlemen who talked loudly about race-horses—ladies who dressed mighty fine and who drank a considerable amount of champagne, made up a society which Mrs. Taunton and her brother thought very desirable and fashionable indeed. The old place opened its doors most hospitably at that period; the back entrance, through which the late squire had been borne to his rest, was now only used by the servants of the house, and the grooms, valets and maids etc., of the grand folks who came driving their four-in-hands, their pairs of "slashing" bays, their horn-announced tandems, and their fast-trotting nags.

For these great personages the once jealously-closed gates now stood hospitably open. Quite in style the equipages whirled round the short carriage sweep on the Hall-door, the moss was scraped off the drive—the grass on the lawns was mown—the roses were cut in—the weeds were hacked down—the handsomest living rooms were swept and garnished, and the "best that could be bought in London," as Mrs. Taunton's brother was wont to aver, procured in the way of eating and drinking.

Once a real lord spent a night at Taunton Hall, and the wife, or rather a lady who had been the wife of a certain nobleman, but who was divorced from him by no wish of her own, spent three days with Mrs. Taunton; and when at eighteen Richard Taunton insisted upon leaving the Halls of learning, where he had spent three weary years, and returning home, he found himself the object of much interest to many very distinguished persons, several of whom, in the most amiable manner, promised to take him by the hand and show him life.

During the course of the next six years the young squire may indeed be said to have seen every sort of life, save that which was reputable; but at the end of that time he appeared suddenly one day at the Hall, there and then turned his uncle out of doors, dismissed every servant, save an old woman who had in succession nursed him and his sister, and without the slightest break in the process, relapsed into barbarism.

The primitive life lived by his father when he first succeeded to the property, had at least one element of safety—the man worked. His son, on the contrary, did not work. He led the life of a savage in the worst sense.

Quick and clever, he had learned enough to know better, to understand as his father had never done, that the mere fact of possessing property involves duties, of which the man who owns nothing is free.

Quite voluntarily he cut himself adrift, not merely from the companions who had exercised so disastrous an influence on his pecuniary prospects, but also from the slightest hope of every taking up a fair or decent position in life.

He had not the distaste for society which characterized his father, but he selected for his boon companions the lowest of the low—men who laughed at his poorest jokes and joked coarsely themselves in return—who lived like human swine, and who, even in outward appearance, seemed to have set the opinions of the better portion of the world as much at defiance as possible.

His mother did not long survive the changes instituted by her son. On her death-bed she gave voice to many utterances; but, like most of the utterances she had made in life, they were so little to the purpose, that her son might be excused for paying small attention to them.

In one respect he did fulfil her wishes. She had as grand a funeral as feathers and velvet could compass. No money was stinted over the affair, and if very few persons "followed," that was not the fault either of Dick or of the "baked meats" prepared for the occasion.

Her coffin was not carried out through the back door and across the farmyard. No, as might have befitted one of the ancient ladies whose portraits graced the interior of the Hall, Mrs. Taunton was carried by way of the great staircase to the front entrance, and thence to the hearse, which, with its attendant coaches, stood ready awaiting her.

Through the same portals the mourners returned to the house, and in like manner the few guests subsequently departed.

It was then Richard Taunton closed the massive oaken door, and shot the bolts which secured it—then he raised the long disused bar and dropped it into its place—then he padlocked the chain which for years had hung pendant, and, turning to his sister, said grimly—

"There has been no luck about the house since that door was opened by my uncle. I have closed it now, and we shall see what will happen before it is flung wide again."

Chapter 11

Saul's Wood

It was to this house, crossing a foot-bridge at Saul's Corner, Miss Gower made her way.

She believed Dick Taunton to be absent from home, but if she had not been certain of the fact, it would have made little difference in her course of action.

There was a mystery about John Redworth, which she imagined could be solved only at Taunton Hall, and as she meant to devote herself to unravelling that mystery, she had no intention of suffering such a trifle as the presence or absence of the master of the house to interfere with her design. Making his way over the canal at Trotterbeck, Mr. Garland, taking the least direct road to Malby, so managed as to set Miss Gower down at that precise spot where the scene assumed a character of utter loneliness and desolation.

Not easily impressed by any of nature's moods, the woman felt nevertheless impelled to stand for a moment on the narrow bridge, and take in every detail of the weird and solitary landscape. She was utterly alone; there did not seem another human being in the universe beside herself. At first in the distance she could hear the jingle of Mr. Garland's wheels, and the regular click, click, of his mare's hoofs; but these sounds grew fainter and fainter, and at length died utterly away, leaving her in the midst of a silence she could hear, of an isolation such as she had never before imagined.

The sombre pines—the dark canal—the murmuring reeds—the rustling rushes—the stunted oak-trees—the sorrowful sobbing of the water as it oozed through some broken lock-gates higher up the disused canal—all these things forced themselves upon her attention at once, and would take no denial about impressing themselves on her memory.

With that still unsolved mystery shadowing her spirits and oppressing her recollection, the gloom of the pine woods, seemed to deepen as she stood, the dark waters to look more treacherous, the bays where the stream lapped in upon the sward, and the sward encroached upon the water, more suggestive of what might be lying or have lain amongst the tangled grass and the oozing mud, and the dripping weeds and the rank luxuriance of the reeds and rushes.

Bah! with a shiver Miss Gower sped from the bridge, to plunge into the greater loneliness of the pine-woods. The air was full of that peculiar scent which comes only when the spines and the cones of the firs are falling—a scent which is not that of awaking life, as in the early spring, but of death. As she looked to right and left, she could see nothing but the regular lines of trees, light brown trunks standing in symmetrical order. There was not the sound of a woodman's axe, not even the distant murmur of children's voices; there were no songs or birds, nothing save the rustling of the dry, dead leaves, as some rabbit scurried away to its burrow.

Although every inch of this wood had been examined, and each pit and ditch searched, it seemed to Miss Gower that her relative must be lying in some nook which had escaped observation. Imagination was not her strong point; yet, as she hurried along, she thought she must next day ask Mr. Garland to return there with her, in order that they two might look for themselves, and get rid of the haunting visions that had begun to torment her of this missing man lying there all alone, through the solitary nights, and days; the pines shutting out the blue sky and the breeze of heaven, and keeping grim and gruesome guard over the secrets hidden amongst them.

With a gasp of relief she at length beheld the open country once again, and hurrying onward, soon found herself crossing the stretch of common-land which intervenes between Saul's Wood and Saul's Corner.

It was a nasty bit of ground, full, as anyone who had ever taken a short cut over the grass knew, of unexpected hillocks, deep drains, the gnarled roots of ancient thorn-trees, and inexplicable swampy spots, in which the unwary adventurer usually plunged over his ankles.

A charming place for children to disport themselves, had

there been any children near at hand to take advantage of such lavish opportunities for covering themselves with mud and running the risk of breaking their limbs; but there were few boys and girls resident at all near at hand. Such cottages as the neighbourhood boasted were perched away amongst the gorse and heather on Wilderness Heath, and there was not a human habitation of any sort of description nearer Saul's Corner than Taunton Hall.

It was with not a little curiosity that Miss Gower paused as she approached this house, and looked at so much of the edifice as could be seen from the highway. A great gloomy pile of red brick, festooned up to the very chimney pots with ivy—a mansion any man might have been proud to call his home—stately, mysterious, with a certain air of dignity, in spite of the decay and neglect visible upon it, which appealed to the best, if the weakest, part of Miss Gower's nature.

"What would I not give to own such a residence," she thought, and then she stepped aside from the main road to ask a passing labourer which was the entrance to Taunton Hall.

"You'd best go through the next gate and across the stable-yard and up to the door you'll see in the right-hand corner," he answered, in the lazy Surrey accent and laborious drawl to which years had rendered Miss Gower so familiar.

"But I do not want to go to the back door," she said, mounting immediately her high horse; "I wish to see some of the family."

"Well, it is all one," was the stolid reply. "Whoever you want to see, you'll have to inquire for them where I tell you. If the queen was to take it into her head to stop at the Hall, she'd have to go in at the back door, or else stay outside. The squire has sworn a great oath, they say, not to open the hall-door to man or woman. If he had shut it many a year ago, mayhap he'd a-bin richer today."

"A singular family this into which my cousin has married," thought Miss Gower, with a certain amount of satisfaction, as she picked her way up the back avenue, and across a large and old-fashioned stable-yard at the furthest corner of which, and quite overshadowed by a fine chestnut-tree, was the door at which John Redworth and Inspector Downing had entered on the night after Mr. Redworth's disappearance.

On this occasion the door stood wide open, showing the spacious Hall stone-flagged, and the numerous doors opening to right and left, which told of the ample domestic arrangements planned by the builders of the mansion, who never could have imagined the day would come when all the pomp and circumstances of a once-great family would be represented by a wild, impecunious, moody, daredevil squire, an imperfectly-educated and gipsy-like sister, and an old serving-woman—the most worthy individual of the three.

It was this person who at sight of Miss Gower came hurrying across from the dairy, a look of eager expectation on her face, which changed to one of despondency when she heard Miss Gower's first sentence.

"I called to inquire when Mr. and Mrs. Redworth are expected back."

"I beg your pardon, miss; I made sure you were one of the ladies from the Vicarage as have come new into Cadlebury, and were talking of taking their butter and eggs from here. I was just printing the pats when I saw you coming, and lovely butter it is."

"They sell to anybody who will buy then," mentally remarked Miss Gower; answering aloud—

"I shall be very glad to have some from you if you have any to spare. I did not know there was such a thing to be purchased here."

"Bless you, yes, miss. We sell everything but fruit, and that don't really pay for the picking. I might say bushels of strawberries rotted on the ground this summer. You were asking about Miss Lettie—or, as I should say, Mrs. Redworth. I had a letter this morning from Mr. Richard, where he says his sister had been very ill—some sort of fever; but he hoped they would soon be able to get her home again. He says she is pining like for the old place."

"It is a place anyone might be proud of," answered Miss Gower, graciously.

"Ay, poor thing; but it's little either of pleasure of comfort she has had in it," remarked the woman, with a sigh.

"Let us hope, then, the future may make amends for the past," said Miss Gower. "Her husband is one of the most amiable of human beings."

"You know him, miss?" asked the woman, curling up the corner of her apron with her fingers, and looking curiously at her visitor.

"Know him! Of course I do—he is my cousin."

"Well, miss; if you'll excuse the liberty, I must make so bold as to say I am very glad to see you. It will be like new life to Miss Lettie to hear anybody belonging to Mr. John has been over. She used to take on because she was afraid none of his friends would be agreeable to the match."

"You seem to be very much attached to your mistress," remarked Miss Gower.

"No one could be off being attached to her that knew her," was the answer. "She hasn't a fault, except that she is at times a bit quick in her temper; but then it's off almost before you could say it had been on. But I am sure I humbly ask your pardon, miss; here I have been letting you stand, and never asking you in, or if you would please to take any refreshment. You must be tired, miss, if you walked from Cadlebury."

"No, I drove over; that is, a friend left me at Saul's Corner, and he is to call for me as he returns. If I should not be disturbing you, I should like to wander a little about the place. I have so often noticed it as we passed; you must have fine gardens, have you not?"

"Ay. no finer in the county, once upon a time, but they are gone to wreck and ruin. Still you can see what they have been, and there is some good fruit yet on the trees, if you have a fancy for any, and I could make you a cup of tea, miss, in about a quarter of an hour, when I have finished printing the butter."

"Oh! by the bye, the butter." exclaimed Miss Gower. "If you

could spare me three pounds, and some eggs, and lend me a basket. I should be so much obliged. No, I will not have any tea, thank you; but after I have been through the gardens, perhaps you would give me a glass of milk. You are quite certain I shall not be intruding if I walk round the place?"

"Intruding!" repealed the old woman. "The squire would be only too proud to think you had come over, and I can tell you. Miss Lettie will be so pleased she won't know what to do."

"They are in Paris, I think you said."

"Yes, miss. The squire sent me an envelope with the address on, for he knows I am no great scholar. Here it is," she added pulling some papers out on an inner pocket, "and his letter too, if you would care to look at it, miss. They both write to me as free as if I was their mother, which, indeed, I might be, having known them ever since they were born."

Chapter 12

What Miss Gower Beheld in the Porch

Through an arched doorway leading out of the stable-yard, Miss Gower passed into the shrubberies, so wild and neglected in some parts, that the laurels had grown completely over the walks, and made a roof of greenery which shut out even the light of day.

On the lawn the grass grew rank. It had not been mowed all the summer, and the thunder showers and the autumn rains had beaten it down level with the ground. Underneath the trees the dead leaves of the dead years were lying rotting. Every weed of its kind seemed to grow in that place and to multiply exceedingly. Nettles, docks, and bindweed contested the ground with rare shrubs and exquisite plants, but nothing seemed to be cared for; creepers trailed untrained, the roses had flung long branches across the walks—honeysuckles lay prone on the ground, and the jessamine sprays were wildly searching about for something against which to lean.

With that instinctive sense of order and fitness, which was part and parcel of her nature. Miss Gower, as she walked along, employed her deft fingers in finding supports for the creepers, and lifting the roses from the untrimmed box edgings.

Quite as much a matter of course it seemed to her to try to put things straight, as it had evidently been to the Tauntons to leave everything to go awry.

Such a wilderness of a kitchen-garden! Miss Gower, as she pushed open the door leading into it, stood for a moment appalled. Plantations of Jerusalem artichokes, cabbages all run to seed, towering lettuces—turnips showing yellow flower—convolvulus smothering the raspberry canes—bindweed climbing up the espaliers—shoots wildly flying wide from the trees once trained against the walls—ruddy-cheeked apples guarded by a growth of noble nettles—mellow pears, which could only be gathered after a wrestle with briers and thistles.

"Oh! What can these people be?" she cried, almost aloud. "If I had such a home there should not be a weed on the beds, or a bramble across the walks."

She passed on to the fields beyond, where an evident attempt to farm well had been made; but the old story of carelessness and lack of method could be read in the broken fences and the dilapidated gates—in the reeds rotting in the canal—and the mud silted up amongst the rushes.

"Want of money—want of method—want of self-respect—want of respect for the opinion of others—this is the story he who runs may read here, and John has thrown his lot in with such people, and will reap his reward. As he has sown he must gather."

Thus soliloquizing, Miss Gower walked back towards the house, this time taking a different route, which brought her at length close to Squire Marmaduke's last resting-place.

She had heard of this mausoleum before, and now paused to read, with some curiosity, the only words graven on the marble—"*Do not pity me, I sleep sound.*"

She stood and thought about it. Stood and wondered about the dead, with no echo from the outer world breaking the terrible stillness. What could have been his story? What had he done with his life? How all alone in that great house did he occupy those evening hours of existence which preceded this long sleep? She could not feel surprise at the place having an evil reputation. She was not sure herself that she should care to rise morning after morning and look out upon that solitary grave, with its silent iteration of a fact no one would ever have dreamed of disputing.

Had he lain, when living, through long nights awake? had he tossed warily, seeking for rest and finding none? had he in the hours of darkness beheld, as in a vision, the desolation coming upon his house? had he indeed gone down to his grave hoping nothing, fearing nothing?

The influence of the scene and the hour was upon her, while she walked slowly away, pondering sadly. Was this, indeed, all wealth and rank had been able to do for a man? Was this all the world and its pleasures could give in the way of happiness? The greatest good, to sleep sound—the highest bliss, to lie quite quiet with closed eyes and folded hands.

If this were so—

She had reached this point in her meditations when, lifting her eyes, she saw something that caused every nerve in her body to thrill with expectancy, astonishment, and delight.

She had reached a point from which she could distinctly see the Hall door.

The branches of a great cedar tree shaded her eyes from the glare of the setting sun, but the light fell perfectly distinct upon the porticoed porch, the old-fashioned windows that flanked the door, the steps, and the figure of a man standing upon them.

It was her uncle! She could not be mistaken. At last—at last, quite safe and sound, erect as ever, umbrella in hand, waiting to be admitted. Miss Gower was not in the habit of running, but she did run then—through the long tangled grass she sped, unmindful of bramble or mound, or moisture, or a pain which shot through her left side.

"Uncle! Uncle!" she cried, as she reached the edge of the gravel sweep, but he never answered her call.

His silence did not surprise her, for she heard that her voice was hoarse, and knew that the sound of it could not carry far.

Just for an instant she paused to draw breath, and to ease that dragging pain in her side, then she ran forward once again.

It was Mr. Redworth—there could not be the slightest doubt about that.

It was he as had left his home more than two months previously, wearing the same clothes, holding the same umbrella; neither leaner nor fatter—changed in no one single respect.

In the rapture of seeing him once more, she forgot to marvel at the singularity of the coincidence—at the extraordinary chance of herself and Mr. Redworth visiting Taunton Hall on the same day and at the same time.

"Uncle! Uncle!" she screamed at the very pitch of her voice, forgetful for once of the proprieties and of all possible listeners and spectators. "Uncle!" but he never stirred.

"Uncle," she repeated, and there crept over her a subtle and intangible dread. "Uncle, it is I, Hilda!" but still he never turned.

By this time she had grown sick with an inexplicable fear; but she was no coward, this pale-faced, sleek-haired, careful-handed woman—quite the contrary—and for this reason she pressed on and drew closer to the tops, and said again, "Uncle!"

Then all at once her heart seemed to drop out of her body, and she clutched at the pillars of the porch to support her.

For no living being stood there.

She could see the steps covered with untrodden mosses, the straggling hop vine wreathed across the entrance, the door Squire Taunton had closed so resolutely against all comers—but of the familiar figure she had beheld, no sign, no token! Before her there was utter vacancy.

On each side of the porch beneath the high long windows of the Hall stood a very old and curiously-carved stone seat, and it was upon one of these Miss Gower found herself when at length she could again see the light of day, the neglected lawn, the gloomy cedars, and the great sweep of drive in front of the lonely house.

Very slowly memory gave her back a thorough recollection of what had occurred. "I did not dream it," she considered. "I did see him—fancy played no trick with me then. What does it mean? What can it mean? Have I gone mad, or—"

"I have been a' most all over the place looking for you, miss," here interposed the Tauntons' only domestic. "I could not think where you had got to, till Dan told me he see a lady walking round by the tomb. I've brewed you a cup of tea, miss, hoping you would excuse the liberty; but whatever, miss, is the matter with you? Have you been taken with a faintness? You are as white as if you had seen a ghost."

"I don't know about that," answered Miss Gower, slowly; "but I know what I have seen. You have heard about Mr. Redworth's disappearance?"

"Surely, miss—everybody has heard of that."

"Well, of course I scarcely expect you to believe me; but, as truly as I speak, I saw Mr. Redworth standing at that door not ten minutes ago."

"For any sake, miss, don't say that—oh! for any sake, don't think that," and the woman wrung her hands as she spoke.

"I tell you I saw him as plainly as I see you now, I ran across the lawn to speak to him. I called him when I was standing there, and again and again till I came quite close to the steps. The whole of that time I saw him, and then all in a minute he disappeared."

"You fancied it, miss—you just fancied it all. How could it be; here one minute and away the next? What would he be doing here at a door that has not been opened for years? Look at it—at the green mould on the steps, at the hops growing right across from one side to the other—oh! miss, whatever you do, don't go away with a notion like that. It would fairly kill Miss Lettie if she were to hear such a thing spoken of."

"Well, I saw him at any rate," persisted Miss Gower. "Fifty Miss Letties, and a thousand hop-plants, and the accumulated moss of centuries cannot alter that face. With my own eyes I saw Mr. Redworth standing upon the doorstep; and what makes this all the stranger, is that it was not far from here he was seen last alive."

"Well, miss, it is not for me to contradict you, but if it was Mr. Redworth you saw standing here, where is he now?"

"That is just what I would give anything to know," answered Miss Gower; "and what I mean to know," she added, under her breath, as she rose, and, accompanied by the old woman, slowly retraced her way to the house, where that cup of tea was still being brewed to death.

CHAPTER 13

MR. GARLAND'S REVELATION

For a wonder, Miss Gower felt disposed to be frank and confidential with Mr. Garland, as they drove behind that gentleman's mettlesome mare back to The Wastes; but she restrained her impulse, and, in consequence, lapsed into reverie.

"You seem a bit low, miss," suggested Mr. Garland, when he felt he could endure his companion's silence no longer. "Heard no bad news over yonder, I hope?"

"No, oh, no," she replied, rousing herself. "Only it's a depressing place, I think."

"Well, as for that, any place would be depressing that hadn't made the acquaintance of a good scythe and a sharp pruning-knife for years and years. What the Hall wants, inside and outside, is, what you might call a good spring cleaning. It's a bother while it's about, but lor! How sweet and clean everything do seem afterwards, to be sure! Yes, I take it, all the Hall needs is to be turned, in a manner of speaking, out of windows. It wants a thorough whitewashing, and painting, and scrubbing—all the spiders and their webs swept away, all the corners looked after, the walks gravelled and the grass mowed, and the ricks let stand a year before they are sold. It is a shame to see a fine place let go to ruin, as that is doing. There is not a better bit of land in the neighbourhood.

"Why, in those meadows by the canal, you should be able to see stock fatten while you are looking on. The squire ought now to turn over a new leaf, clean and clear up, and try to get before the world a little. I believe he could do it, too, if he would only dig up old Marmaduke, and take him over to Cadlebury Churchyard. 'Tain't right, in Christian times, to have a corpse forming the centre ornament of a pleasure-ground. It is no wonder, I am sure, that folks say the Hall is haunted."

"No, I do not think it is," answered Miss Gower, with a shiver. "It is an eerie sort of place, Mr. Garland."

"Come, come," said Mr. Garland, with rough kindness. "You must not let yourself down like this. Why, I shall begin to think you have seen Mr. Redworth. People do say, you know, he walks about there."

"Say my uncle walks about the Hall'?"

"Well, about Saul's Wood, and the Hall, and such like. But lor! what won't people say?"

Miss Gower clutched the rail of the dog-cart, and looked straight between the mare's ears, which were laid amiably flat back on her neck, while she thought over this statement. Then she asked:

"Mr. Garland, do you think my uncle is really dead?'

"Think?' he repeated, surprised. "I am sure of it, miss. Wherever he may be, and that's most like only known to his Maker, himself, and the man as made away with him, he'll never turn up again in Ludham alive. Often when I heard the old ladies talk about his having levanted with some slut of a girl or schemer of a widow, I laughed to myself at the notion of a man of his sort exchanging his comforts for the company of any woman on earth. No, miss, that notion won't hold water, or we ain't driving home to The Wastes tonight."

"You mistake," remarked Miss Gower, who had listened quite patiently to the foregoing sentence. "What I meant was, do you think it possible he may be kept anywhere, locked up?"

"In a madhouse, or such like," suggested Mr. Garland, as she paused. "No, miss, I don't. Because, why, how would his being locked up benefit anybody? People don't run the risk of getting themselves into trouble, nowadays, for the mere pleasure of the thing. Wherever Mr. Redworth may be, he is dead enough; and so you need not fret yourself by supposing to the contrary."

Had it all, then, been an optical delusion? Miss Gower understood there were such things—nay, had experienced deceptions of the kind when, in her girlhood, she fell into a low state of health. The form they then assumed was that of black spots, and things like morsels of cobwebs floating before her eyes—black spots which appeared to her perfectly real—cobwebs she often lifted her hand to brush away.

She had not thought of these things for years, but now they recurred to her with a curious sense of satisfaction. Far too sensible to try to terrify herself by dwelling upon the figure, which appeared so real, she gladly seized on any idea likely to account for the phenomenon.

Seated beside homely, practical, matter-of-fact Mr. Garland, Miss Gower found that, with every stride of the vaunted mare homeward towards The Wastes, she felt more inclined to disbelieve the evidence of her senses.

The keen fresh air which blew across the hills was less favourable to the tricks of fancy than the damp dull air that hung around Taunton Hall.

There was a mystery, but Miss Gower began to reject the extremity of such a mystery as the appearance of her uncle standing at the door of Taunton Hall suggested.

"I think," she said to Mr. Garland, "when I visit Taunton Hall again, I shall not go by way of Saul's Corner. Its worst enemy could not describe that route as cheerful."

"Cheerful," repeated her companion with a laugh, "my word, no. That bit by the water, where the reeds grow is so thick, and the path to match through the wood, is as ugly a piece of country as anybody need desire to see. I can tell you I did not half like leaving you there today, but you would not be said. A wilful woman must have her way."

"What could be my uncle's fancy for choosing such dreary roads?" marvelled Miss Gower; but Mr. Garland only shook his head in reply, and intimated that some higher power alone could understand that puzzle.

"For myself," added Mr. Garland, playfully touching up the mare, who at once broke into a canter, "I am quite free to say I never did understand the governor, and I never expect to do so now. There was ways in him I never could make head nor tail of, and that I don't believe anybody else ever made head or tail or either, and so far as I am concerned, miss, I just wish you could put him clean out of your head, and never go a-nigh Taunton Hall no more. It's a nice enough place, and I dare say they are nice enough people for them as likes such a lot, but I don't believe either one or t'other will suit you, miss. There's a breeze for you!" proceeded Mr. Garland, sniffing up the air which came from moors where the heather and the gorse grew thick. "No churchyard smell about that, no dead leaves and rotting rushes— clear and sweet and wholesome."

And Mr. Garland, radiant with natural pride and pleasure in residing so far above his neighbours, drove up to his own door, and commended Miss Gower to the especial care of Mrs. Garland, with the words—

"She's a bit low, like."

Not a week later, however, Mr. Garland himself returned from Cadlebury not merely a "bit" low, but very low indeed.

That he had partaken freely of stimulants was quite evident, yet he immediately called for more.

"Hot and strong!" he roared, and when the desired mixture was brought, he astonished every one by draining off the contents of his glass, and then asking for his prayer-book.

"Now whatever can he want with that, and Sunday three days off," audibly conjectured Mrs. Garland.

"Never you mind, Mrs. G.," answered her husband, "make yourself quite easy, it ain't the order for Holy Matrimony I want to look up, you may be sure. Once was enough of that sort of thing. No, I remember, it ain't here at all. Miss Gower, would you be so good as to turn down a leaf for me in your Bible, if it is handy, where there is that story about the Witch of Endor."

"Certainly," answered Miss Gower, and she found the chapter

he referred to without comment, only looking at him curiously as she laid the book beside his elbow.

"My eyes are a trifle weak," remarked Mr. Garland, after he had vainly tried to steady his sight sufficiently to decipher the small type. "Driving over The Wastes is trying after night, more particularly when there is a north wind blowing in one's teeth, and a weakly moon dodging in and out, and playing at bo-peep among the clouds. Would you mind," he added, with an appealing look to Miss Gower, "just reading me out that piece—you know."

Very clearly and distinctly Miss Gower read out the whole of the chapter, Mr. Garland indicating the points which affected him most deeply by striking the palm of his hand on the table.

"You see there were such things then," he remarked huskily, when she had finished. "It seems strange that a man should be able to eat after seeing such a sight."

And Mr. Garland's tone indicated that something in the shape of a stimulant might have been preferable.

At that minute the youngest of the house of Garland entered, holding on to his mother's skirts, and chattering as he ran along.

He had been over to Cadlebury with his father, and was full of the day's adventures.

"And oh! ma," he was saying when his utterances first reached Miss Gower's ear. "Part of the way there was a man walked so fast beside us. Though pa made the mare gallop, he was able to keep up. I never did see anybody walk so quick before; and pa has got a cold, ma, he has been shaking and shivering for ever so long."

"Now," interposed Mr. Garland, hastily, "is that child going to bed tonight, mother, or is he not—because, when I was young, little boys was not let sit up to interfere with the comfort of their elders. There, run along, sonny, that's a fine little man; and, Miss Gower, my dear, would you just mix me the least drop more spirits, my hand is a bit shaky tonight. I have got a cold driving by those damp meadows. Tomorrow," he added, mysteriously, as Mrs. Garland bore her child off to bed—having previously made a statement to the effect that if "some people would go there themselves it might be better for other people"—"Tomorrow— quietly, you know—by that fallen tree on the corner of the path overlooking Dangermere—I have got something to tell you— just by yourself—you understand; but mum's the word now, and indeed I think it may be as well to follow the missus's advice, and go to bed while I can."

"Let me assist you to the door," said Miss Gower, amiably, and she helped him to his feet and guided him across the carpet, and placed his hand on the banisters with a dexterity and an appreciation of the position which would have made Miss Redworth stare.

By this time Miss Gower was quite at home with the Garland family. She had her own private sitting-room, it is true, but she rarely occupied it, preferring the appreciative friendliness of the farmer's circle to the solitary stateliness of her select apartment.

At The Wastes she was made more of than she had ever been, even in Dorking Street. There Mr. Redworth was the prominent figure in the household, but amongst the Garlands Miss Gower was queen. And that she liked the position, there was no denying.

Next morning Mr. Garland was sober and sad. Mrs. Garland had not been agreeable in many of her remarks, and besides, his head was, as he stated confidentially to Miss Gower, "fit to fly into a thousand pieces."

"Sit you down there, miss," he said, indicating the smoothest portion of the fallen tree, "and I'll take a rest at the same time myself. I fancy I must have had a drop too much last night, I feel so queer and shaky. You mixed that finishing up tumbler pretty stiff, didn't you now? You were a trifle liberal with the liquor; but then, lor, tain't that as is the matter with me," added Mr. Garland magnanimously, "and there is no use telling lies about it, though mind you, if I hadn't have let slip what I did when I was all upset, I'd have kept it close and snug, even from you, I would."

"I don't think you would, Mr. Garland," answered Miss Gower, "not from me, at any rate."

"Well, perhaps you're right, and it may be right for you to know it, seeing how things was between him and you. Now, mind, miss, you're not to consider what I am going to tell you was the outcome of liquor, for it wasn't, though I don't deny I had drank a decent lot at Cadlebury. I might have thought this morning I had imagined it, but the child was with me, and you heard what the child said last night."

"Yes, I heard." answered Miss Gower.

"I suppose you know there has always been tales concerning something that haunts the Hall. It is an old story now, and most folks as have not to go past there after dark thinks an idle story, too."

"It is said a figure follows people. I recollect hearing it talked about."

"Well, I've driven past the place often enough after dark, and in the noonday, with the sun shining, and the rain pelting, but I never saw anything worse nor myself till—"

"Last night," supplied his auditor, as he paused.

Mr. Garland took off his hat and wiped his forehead, though the season was autumn, and the day not warm.

"I don't think I am a coward," he said. "I hope I ain't; but, I declare, I shall always take the other road to Cadlebury, though it is a matter of three miles further."

"Tell me what you saw, Mr. Garland," entreated Miss Gower. "If it concerns my uncle, I have, as you say, a right to know, and we may be interrupted."

"That's true, miss, well, here goes. I had met a few friends in Cadlebury, and taken as much as was good for me, though, mind you, maybe I might have taken a tumbler more if it had not been for the child. But I did not want to keep him out very late, so the ostler at the 'Three Fighting Cocks' put the mare in, and I took the reins, and off we went at a good round pace, for the mare she was fresh, and the oats at the 'Cock' are good, and she knew her nose was turned to her own stable, and there! she did spank along.

"I left it pretty well to her, for, lor! she don't need no driving, she don't. I'd back her to thread her way in and out among the traffic of Cheapside as well as I could guide her.

"We had done the distance from Cadlebury in quick time, and were just passing what used to be, in old Marmaduke's time, the main entrance to the Hall, when bang my lady gives a shy that nearly upset the trap, and then off she went like the very devil begging your pardon for using such an expression.

"She had never shied before to my knowledge, and what with surprise and being well nigh pitched out of the dog-cart myself (the rug was strapped round the child), and trying to pull her up, I did not at first notice what had frightened her, till suddenly I saw on the grass by the roadside a man keeping up with us. If you believe me, miss, walking and keeping up easily, though the mare was tearing along the road at a mad gallop.

"It was all I could do to hold her. We went down to Saul's Corner like a flash of lightning, and then, of her own will, for she was, I may say, beyond my control, she slackened her speed, and stopped dead.

"I could feel her trembling. It shook the trap, and at her head, miss—you may believe me or not as you like—was the same figure I had seen. *It had kept pace with us all the way.*

"Either of her own accord, or because he told her, most like because he did, the mare turned slowly round—I'll swear I never pulled the reins—turned slowly round and began trotting feebly like back to Cadlebury. I could not have hindered her if my life had depended on it, and on the grass by the roadside the figure still held foot with her.

"I could see him plainly in the moon's sickly light. There was the pines of Saul's Wood, there was the bit of common with its tufts of heather, and its holes and pitfalls, there was Wilderness Heath, and *there was he.*

"'Father, father,' says Willie, 'doesn't that man walk fast—did you ever see a man walk so fast before?' The lad, you understand, thought it was a man, and did not feel frightened like me and the mare.

"At the sound of a human voice, even though it was but a

child's, the mare gathers courage, pricks up her ears, and makes another dash for it. The noise of her own hoofs seemed to give her spirit, and maybe she thought she was leaving it behind, for she broke from a trot into a canter, and from a canter into a gallop. And I sat holding the reins without a bit of strength in my hands or body.

"When we neared the gates again, just the same thing happened as had occurred at Saul's Corner, the mare, of her own accord, slackened speed and slopped dead.

"Then I saw the figure once more standing at her head."

Mr. Garland paused and drew a long breath, and stared straight away over Dangermere, as if he beheld something very far off indeed.

Miss Gower, her hands clasped, her fingers locked together, watched him as she had watched him from the beginning of his narrative.

"Was that all?' she asked, finding her companion began to pull the bark off the tree, and made no effort to continue.

"That's not all," he answered, "though in my humble opinion it is more than enough. I was just trying to speak, I had opened my mouth and wetted my lips, and meant to get out some word, when the figure turned and walked quite leisurely through the closed gates. It went straight up to them and disappeared. The mare she tried to follow, there seemed a spell laid on her, you understand, but it waved its hand, and she stopped obedient.

"I do not know how long I had sat there stunned—not long, I dare say—when I felt Willie pulling at my sleeve, and asking if we were going home. He was not a bit frightened, bless you, he did not understand. For myself alone, I don't think I could have done it, but for the sake of the child I tried to draw myself together, and spoke to the mare, and touched her with the whip to waken her up and get her round. If she had been turned into stone she could not have minded me less, no, miss, she could not. She stood there, under the shade of those black old tress, with her head down and her knees bent under her, trembling like a Christian."

"How soon did she move?" asked Miss Gower.

"She never moved at all; if I had left her to herself she would have been there till now. I screwed up my courage at last and got down, and took her by the head, and in a manner of speaking forced her away from the gate. The creature was all in a lather. When I laid my hand on her I might have dipped it in water, it was so wet.

"I had to lead her every step of the way to Saul's Corner. I don't expect you to credit it, but she would scarce put one foot before the other, and I was compelled, as I may say, to drag her along.

"It was the longest mile I ever walked, and the moon she kept blinking in and out, and the wind it howled and howled across Wilderness Heath, and then went sobbing and moaning among the pines, and the mare she did nothing but stumble, stumble, and slip about as if she was drunk or travelling over ice. I had to keep a hold of her till we got to Trotterbeck Bridge. I came home that way, for though she stepped out freer after we left Saul's Corner behind, she made as if to stop every now and then, but at the ferry-house there I got her a quart of ale and put a dash of spirits in it—they are licensed, you know—and she didn't lose much time after that I can tell you. Right glad was I to get up on The Wastes again though the wind blew fit to blow a fellow's eyes out; and now I think that is all I have to tell you."

"No; you have to tell me something more. Did you see the face—did you recognize the—?" and Miss Gower paused expressively.

"I did, miss, I did; it was himself, none other."

"You remember a question I asked you the other day," said Miss Gower. "Do you know why I asked it?'

"I have been turning the matter over in my mind," answered Mr. Garland, slowly. "and I expect you saw him too."

She nodded in answer.

"I suppose," he went on, "you don't feel disposed to say no more about it?"

"There is not much to say," was her reply. "Either he was

standing at the Hall door that afternoon I went over there, or I fancied so. When I got across the lawn and gravel sweep, however, he was gone."

"Aye, aye," commented Mr. Garland, "I thought as much."

"That," she continued, "was why I asked if you conceived it possible he was kept away by anyone. Do you still hold to your opinion that he is not?"

"Firmer than ever," he answered. "I'd be glad to think he was staying away of his own accord, or kept away, or out of his head, or anything except what I must think—I would indeed. But it is out of the question. What you saw at the Hall door might have been him or anybody else for that matter, but what I saw could neither have been him nor anybody else in the flesh. For it was not even as if the thing had run, though the smartest young fellow would have found his work cut out to keep up with the mare. It did not run, it did not seem to hurry; it kept beside us as a shadow does, without seeming trouble or even movement. It was just there always alongside—gliding, gliding on. And then, though it was his face it was not his face."

There ensued silence for a moment, dead silence, during the continuance of which Mr. Garland picked away industriously at the bark of the fallen tree, and Miss Gower let her eyes travel over The Wastes to far-off Dangermere.

Suddenly she said—

"What do you think of it all, Mr. Garland? What is your reading of the mystery?"

Mr. Garland paused before he answered—looked all around him as if suspicious of eavesdroppers, drew closer to his companion—so close that she could hear his voice, though subdued to a mere whisper. Then he began—

"Look here, miss, this is between you and me, ain't it, between you and me only?"

"Of course," she murmured.

"John did not treat you well, everybody knows that; and for my part I can't understand why he should have gone past you for the sake of the handsomest woman that ever lived; but still

114

he was blind and he did choose Miss Taunton, we can't get over that."

Miss Gower winced as if she had received a blow.

"Yet still," proceeded Mr. Garland, "such is the loveliness of your nature, that, instead of being angry with him, as indeed most might, and saying this, that, and the other about his wife, you stand by him, and go over to Taunton Hall and make little of your own slight, and, in a word, to cut it short, act more like an angel than a woman."

The angel so addressed made no verbal reply. She only raised her hand as deprecating further laudation.

"Such being the case," went on Mr. Garland, "I can speak free—I must speak free. I like the young man myself—I always did like him, and I stood up for him, you know that, but when you ask me what I think of these events—these signs and to-kens—omens, as indeed they may well be considered, I can only answer you straightforward. I believe John Redworth was the cause of his father's death. I believe the old gentleman met with his death at Taunton Hall or Saul's Corner, or some place between the two. I believe there is great trouble in store for John if he stays about these parts, and that the poor dead father, who was main fond of his favourite son, has come back from his grave to ask you and me, who he knows are faithful friends, to try and persuade him to leave England entirely and go away before worse comes of it."

On the side of Mr. Redworth senior this seemed to be such an entirely preposterous proceeding that Miss Gower looked at Mr. Garland amazed, and was about to express her dissent from his conclusions; but she saw he was so much in earnest, that he felt the power of his argument so completely, that she altered her intention and said—

"It may be so. No one can understand the length and breadth of a parent's affection, and Mr. Redworth loved John very dearly. All I suppose, however, we can do for the present is to wait and watch and see. I tell you candidly that, unless John be very much changed, it would be worse than useless to endeavour to influence him with any account of what we have seen. He would think, perhaps, we were trying to entice him into some admission; or if he did not do that, he would be quite certain to suggest that I had been dreaming, and that you—"

"Had taken a drop too much," finished Mr. Garland, so naively that Miss Gower smiled, in spite of herself. "I thought of that. He was always a trifle given to jeering and scoffing, and mocking, not ill-naturedly, but in a good-humoured sort of way. Still, I can't fancy he'd make a jest of this. You see, if his conscience ain't clear, and I'm afraid it can't be, the image of the old man must always be rising before him—always. Upon the other hand, he may be as innocent as our Willie, and then it would be hard to name such a thing to him. There, I must leave it to you, miss—you that are fond of him, and that know him so well, can manage to give him a hint better than a stranger. With your good leave I'll wash my hands of the matter, only if you want my help tell me. There's me, and there's the mare, but, lor! I'm afraid she won't be much use at Taunton Hall very soon again. She had a scare last night, poor beast. At any rate, there's my hand, I'll help you by night or day if you will only tell me how, and I'll keep the secret of what I saw close as wax."

Having delivered himself of which peroration, Mr. Garland rose from the tree and walked away, only to return after he had gone a few yards to say, in a tragic whisper, "Oh! I had nearly forgotten to tell you—they are coming home tomorrow, all of 'em, Mr. and Mrs. John Redworth, and the squire."

CHAPTER 14

Miss Gower shows her Colours

Drear December! very drear, very raw, and very depressing, that year, was far spent, when one morning Miss Gower drove by the long route, over The Wastes and across Wilderness Heath, to Taunton Hall.

Much as she desired to understand the mystery of Mr. Redworth's death, thoroughly determined though she was to pierce and peer and pry till she should be able to fasten the guilt of his father's murder upon John Redworth, and so bring that faithless lover "to his knees," Miss Gower, nevertheless, could not conquer the aversion she entertained to passing Saul's Corner. That dismal bit of road, with its attendant memories of sullen canal and desolate bays, thick with now decaying reeds, of lonely pine woods and neglected common, filled her soul with a sense of fear she felt powerless to overcome. Taunton Hall she could manage, more especially if she kept well away from the front entrance, and from the disused portions of the house, but not that gloomy wood, which looked more terrible than Avernus.

During her many visits to Taunton Hall her resentment and her desire for revenge had both been stimulated to the highest degree by the sight of beautiful Lettie Redworth, *nee* Taunton, and the spectacle of John Redworth's anxious devotion to his young wife.

Here was a change indeed. John, who had always been a sort of grand *sultan* in his father's house, with a couple of women ever ready to anticipate his wants, now seemed to find no peace or pleasure save in waiting upon a mistress as hard to satisfy as she had been easy to win.

Not a thing seemed really to gratify her. Peevish, affectionate, exacting, demonstrative, all by turn, she tried, and yet retained her slave, by exhibitions of temper, and endless caprices that might well have alienated him from her.

But John's love never changed. The moment after she had irritably bidden him leave her, he was ready to do her lightest bidding; when serving her his feet never grew weary; to try and give her pleasure he would have coined his heart into gold if he had only known how.

Miss Gower looked on and marvelled. "She knows his secret," she would decide one hour.

"He is afraid of her knowing it," she decided the next, and then her smile grew brighter and her step more light.

"Someday," she thought, "I will destroy his paradise. His couch is not all roses now, but at no remote period he shall find it all thorns."

By tacit consent she and Mr. Garland avoided all mention of Taunton Hall and the missing man.

"I have washed my hands of the concern," he repeated more than once, when he saw Miss Gower bent on solving the still unsolved mystery. "I know nothing, and I want to know nothing. I am trying to forget, and succeeding, I am thankful to say, fairly. Perhaps I did take a drop too much at Cadlebury that night, anyhow it ain't no concern of mine and if I was you, miss, I'd just drop it. No matter what he has done, he's sorry enough I'll be bound, and maybe it'd be best for nobody to mell or meddle."

"I do not wish to do either," answered Miss Gower with dignity. "All I want is to show my cousin he is not quite deserted, and his wife, she has at least one female friend."

"It is very noble of you," commented Mr. Garland, "but I hope, I do hope, you won't come anigh any harm over there. You have got a neat little fortune, you must remember, if you'll excuse me for making so free as to mention it, and the squire, all the world knows, stands in need of money, and he has ways with him when he chooses as would wile the bird off her bush, and, oh! miss, whatever you do, don't marry Black Dick. If the old gentleman never rose from his grave for anything else, he'd rise to prevent that, and with reason, too."

"Why, Mr. Garland," answered Miss Gower coquettishly, "the squire is most agreeable. I call him a delightful man."

With a sign and a groan Mr. Garland turned aside in despair. He did not now offer his own services or those of the mare so freely as formerly, for he felt that, to use his own expression, Miss Gower had gone a "step beyond him."

"She's lost her head over the reckless scoundrel," he soliloquized; "or maybe she thinks she'd like to be mistress of the Hall. Well, there's no understanding women, and I am sure nobody need want to try and understand them."

So there was silence between Mr. Garland and the young lady, only he groaned when he saw the fat dumpling of a pony Richard Taunton had selected for her, harnessed in what the farmer contemptuously called an old clothes'-basket.

"Aye, she'll drive over there once too often," decided Mr. Garland, and Inspector Downing was of his mind.

"She's got the clue," said that gentleman to himself, in strict confidence, "but among them they'll hush it up. I see how it will be. She'll marry the brother and try to queen it at the Hall, and Dick and she will manage to persuade Jack to leave the country—that is what the plan is, as far as I can see, at present."

All of which only proved that Mr. Downing, like many another of his class, was the victim of a theory—one portion of that theory being that Miss Gower was deeply in love with handsome, unscrupulous Richard Taunton.

And, indeed, the squire and his brother-in-law were both of the same opinion.

It was only Lettie who dissented from it—Lettie, who in those moments when she could throw aside her mask and appear the wretched woman she actually was, would lay her hand on Black Dick's shoulder and say—

"Oh! my dear, my dear, don't let that Delilah deceive you. She is here for no good. She hates us all. When I first saw her face I trembled and turned cold. See, Dick, I tremble and turn cold now as I speak of her."

But when did man ever listen to the wisdom of woman if its utterances were directed against one of her own sex.

"You do not like Hilda, sweet," remarked John Redworth, one day, "and I am sorry; for, indeed, I who know her thoroughly, can assure you she is very very good."

"You are jealous of her, Lettie, that is about the fact of the matter," said the squire, complacently; and so poor vehement Lettie, rebuffed on all sides, finding even her old nurse had nothing but words of praise for the fair-spoken lady, who was always so beautifully dressed, and ready with her money, and full of pleasant words, relapsed into silence, relinquished all remonstrance.

Indeed she was too ill to have much energy left either for warfare or argument.

She had come home weakly, and, day by day, she felt her strength failing.

When her husband was away, she sat for hours looking out listlessly at the mournful canal, at the gloomy trees, at the wet sodden earth; just as her father had done after his accident, so did Lettie now she seemed to have gained the one good she ever desired— John Redworth for her husband.

Thus it chanced one dreary day in December, when Miss Gower drove over from The Wastes, Mrs. Redworth was very low both in health and spirits. The hand Miss Gower took in hers felt cold and clammy, while the cheek presented reluctantly for her to kiss was hot and feverish.

"I am afraid you are not so well today, dear," remarked Miss Gower.

"I am never well," was the answer.

"We must try to make you better."

"I do not know how you are to set about it then," retorted Mrs. Redworth.

"As a beginning," said Mrs. Gower, softly, while, uninvited, she took off her bonnet and gloves, and removed her fur-jacket, "I should earnestly recommend you, Lettie, not to brood so constantly over the past."

"Perhaps you will be kind enough to mention what portion of the past you would recommend me to erase from my memory."

"There must be several," replied Miss Gower, with amiable candour, "upon which it cannot be pleasant for you to dwell— the mystery of Mr. Redworth's death—the circumstances connected with your hurried and private marriage—John's disinheritance—all these you should discard from recollection. You ought to remember that seeing you so constantly low and ailing must be most wearing to your husband. He is devoted to you, of course, as no one can know better than yourself, but his very love makes his anxiety all the keener. His life in itself cannot be pleasant, on remembering what he must remember, and—"
She stopped; there was a look on Mrs. Redworth's face which

daunted even her.

"How dare you speak to me in such a manner!" exclaimed the sick woman. "In what way can my husband's affairs concern you, what business is it of yours when or where I was married, or whether I ever was married at all? I wish you would leave the house, and never enter it again. Directly John returns home I shall ask him whether it is by his wish you come here making life intolerable to me. If you are to remain here constantly, I will go away. I would rather be away. I wish we had never re-entered the Hall."

"I don't wonder at that," returned Miss Gower, "if you have seen in it what I have seen."

"What have you seen?'

"Mr. *Redworth. John's murdered father,'*" was the answer.

With a moan, John Redworth's wife repeated the words, then tottering to her feet, she raised her arms above her head, and, before Miss Gower could reach her, fell heavily to the floor.

"She knows, but he thinks she does not know," decided that lady as she rang the bell violently, and raised Lettie's head upon her knee, and wiped the blood from her mouth.

"Send someone for a doctor at once," she cried, as Black Dick, followed by the servant, rushed into the room, "your sister is dangerously ill."

CHAPTER 15

THROUGH THE OPEN DOOR

Mrs. Redworth was dangerously ill. So ill that there seemed small likelihood of her ever being better.

"How long has this been going on?" asked the Cadlebury doctor, who was fetched by Dick Taunton, in wild haste.

"She was never very strong, and she caught cold on her wedding trip," explained the squire, but he said it doggedly, as one who, having reluctantly learned a lesson, repeats it with unwilling lips.

If Miss Gower had never been considered an angel before, she must have proved her right to that character then.

"Do not grieve so bitterly," she said to Black Dick, who sat with arms crossed upon the table and his head resting upon them, "We will all do our best for her. I will not leave here till she is better," and she laid her hand, her soft deft hand, on his shoulder with a caressing assurance as she spoke.

The man did not answer by words, but he lifted his head a little and pressed his lips to her hand in mute acknowledgement.

"There is nothing," went on Miss Gower, "I would not do for John, or your sister, or—you."

Ay, truly, nothing. As she spoke her thoughts sped back to the night when she paced her room in an agony of disappointment and mortification, and felt herself a woman slighted!

Before an hour had elapsed the pony carriage was on its way back to The Wastes, without Miss Gower. The lad she had constituted her attendant bore a very touching and affectionate note to Mrs. Garland, which note next morning brought Mr. Garland and the mare, and a profusion of such homely delicacies as their larder boasted, to the Hall.

In the goodness and fullness of his heart. Mr. Garland placed even at the disposal of Dick Taunton the services of himself and the mare.

"Any time, day or night," he said, "there's me and there's the mare, and you, squire, as is a judge of horseflesh—though I can't say the pony you chose for Miss Gower did your taste much credit—come out and look at my nag. There ain't a better nor a willinger in the whole countryside. She is sound to the backbone; true, and able, like Miss Gower. Ay, there's a woman, if you please; a friend in need a friend indeed, a woman in ten thousand."

"I quite agree with you, Mr. Garland," said Black Dick, wringing the farmer's hand, for Miss Gower's devotion to his sister had touched him sensibly.

"That is right, that is well spoken," remarked Mr. Garland, tossing off the tumbler Mr. Taunton had considerately presented, "a woman in ten thousand, that is what she is," which, if Mr. Garland had known everything, might be regarded as fortunate.

Never was there a more attentive nurse. "I had better stay with her entirely, John," suggested his cousin, "she talks of things the knowledge of which it would be as well to keep in the family."

Whereupon poor John, who was only too well aware that there were things upon Lettie's mind the outside world ought not know, thanked Miss Gower even with tears in his eyes, and invoked blessings that it is humbly to be hoped never bore fruit.

The poor young thing rambled as she lay, wandered from topic to topic, from misery to misery. She was always creating for herself imaginary terrors, and shrinking from them; always pursued by some haunting horror which she tried vainly to elude.

She was so weak—she was so incoherent—she was always in such an agony of fear, it could only be regarded as marvellous that Miss Gower managed to piece together so much as she did—out of so little to weave so great a whole.

Yes, Miss Gower began to understand it all; in fact, she believed she did understand it all, except how Mr. Redworth was murdered, and the precise spot where he lay. That his grave was somewhere in the vicinity of the Hall she felt convinced, but that was a matter of merely minor importance; as regarded all great details, she had now the ball at her feet, and could afford to play with and indulge her victims as an angler humours a trout.

How good she was, and how kind, how untiring in her attention to Lettie, how punctual in her administration of food and medicine—how watchful of her repose!

"We ought, John, to have further advice," she said one day. "if money is the impediment, let me be your banker; I, you know, have enough and to spare."

"If you have," interrupted the squire, who overheard what was said, "I wish you would let some of it come this way. I stand in sore need of filthy lucre."

"Really and truly?" questioned Miss Gower.

"Really and truly, young lady," answered Mr. Taunton.

"Then why not have some of mine?" she suggested. "It does not matter to me where it is, except that of course I should prefer a friend had the use of it. I may just as well take a mortgage over Taunton Hall as any other Hall or Court in England—better if my doing so will be of the slightest service to you. But, perhaps, all I have would not be enough. How much do you want?"

For reply the squire, looking more curiously and earnestly at her than he had ever done before in their acquaintance, said he did not want any, he had been only joking; in spite of which statement, however, he went two days running to his solicitors, and put together a few articles such as might prove useful in a hurried journey. Further, he sold some cattle, and did not bank the proceeds in the All England at Cadlebury.

Whilst he was engaged in these proceedings, a great London doctor arrived to see his sister.

It was quite late in the afternoon before he drove up the principal entrance to Taunton Hall, the gates of which were set wide.

No one knew then who had unfastened the bolts; but the flyman, finding them hospitably open, turned in and set down his fare at the Hall door, and rang a peal fit to bring the house about his ears.

It was Miss Gower in person who answered the summons— Miss Gower, graceful and self-possessed as ever.

She had spent a considerable amount of time that morning in oiling the locks and unfastening the chains, and as she opened the door she said softly to the doctor—

"I am so thankful to see you," and then stopped—surprised by a sudden horror.

For, pushing in front of the doctor, though unseen by him, there entered the figure of a tall spare man, arrayed in clothes free from speck of dust, carrying in his hand a trim umbrella.

Stricken for the moment dumb. Miss Gower watched this newcomer flit across the hall and up the staircase.

"I am going mad," she murmured to herself, as the great physician said—

"I trust I may be able to be of some service, madam," and so recalled her to the common affairs of life.

When the doctor saw his patient, he looked very grave indeed. She was sitting up in bed, her long black hair streaming about her shoulders, her eyes bright with a strained and unnatural light, her cheeks flushed with excitement.

"Someone," she began, "has opened the Hall door—that door—Dick fastened up so securely—which I did not open even on the night when——Who shot back the locks and turned the keys'?" she asked suddenly and wildly.

"I did," said Miss Gower, in her gentlest tones.

"And who gave you permission to open any door my brother ordered to be kept shut. You did it on purpose. You did it to let *him* in. He came straight up here and looked at me with that unchangeable face. He is hidden in some corner now," and she covered her eyes with a cry of indescribable agony and fear.

"This is very bad," remarked the doctor, as he advanced and laid his hand on her forehead; "poor young thing! there, there don't look so frightened. I have only come to do you good. Lie down quietly, I won't disturb you."

"Make her go away," said the patient.

Surprised, the doctor turned towards Miss Gower, but she was equal to the occasion.

"Do you want poor Hilda to leave you, dear?" she cooed, "surely you would not be so cruel."

"Yes I would," snapped Mrs. Redworth. "I hate the sight of you, stealing and crawling about me, and you had no right to open that door. Oh! Dear—oh! dear, dear me!"

Miss Gower directed a swift and meaning glance at the doctor, and then stole out of the room.

"You had better go up," she suggested to the regular medical attendant, whom she met in the passage, "the London physician is here. Mrs. Redworth is frightfully restless and unmanageable."

And then Miss Gower did an extraordinary thing—a thing unprecedented. She went to the cupboard in the squire's especial sitting-room, where spirits of some kind were always to be found, and, selecting a bottle which contained brandy, poured herself out half a wine-glassful and drank off the contents as if they had been water.

"I wonder if that will make me tipsy," she marvelled, as she looked in surprise at the deed she had done.

"Hey day," cried Mr. Taunton, entering the room at the moment, "how is this, Miss Gower? It can't be possible you have been converted and are taking to my good ways." And he laughed out genially.

"Your sister has frightened me," answered Miss Gower coldly. "She was angry at my having opened the hall door, as if one could invite a physician of eminence to enter the house through a dirty farmyard."

"You opened the hall door?" he said, inquiringly.

"Yes, I did," she answered, defiantly, replying to his tone rather than his words, "as there was no one else to do it for me."

For a moment the squire pondered over this utterance, then he strode up to the cupboard, and in his turn pouring out brandy—a bumper this time—emptied it as he muttered audibly—

"By——, Lettie was right after all."

"Master!" at this juncture cried out a shrill voice, "master, where are you?" and thinking his sister was worse, the squire set down the decanter and rushed into the passage, followed by Miss Gower.

It was old Deborah who had called—old Deborah standing there, her cap awry, her grey hair disordered, her face distorted with terror.

"Master, someone has set the front door wide, and he is standing there on the step. Go to him quick before anybody else sees. He is standing as he did that night when—"

"*Will* you hold your tongue, you fool?" demanded the squire, savagely, but he made no step forward into the hall.

"The door stands wide, master," frantically persisted the woman, wild with affright, "and he is there waiting. I dare not go anigh him myself, but—"

"*I* am not afraid, I will go" exclaimed Miss Gower, recklessly, and she darted past both of them, and was at the foot of the principal staircase before Mr. Taunton could seize her. Then, with an awful oath, he bade her mind her own business, and, pushing her on one side, strode towards the door.

It was fast. There were the locks and bolts and chains as they had been before Miss Gower undid them, but the man's blood was up and his fear gone, and he shot back the locks and undid the bolts, and dropped the chains with a great rattle and flung open the door.

There was not a creature on the step, not a living being to be seen, and yet he and his companions all felt that something had crossed the threshold and was lurking in the shadows beyond.

"What was that?" Mr. Taunton asked, but Miss Gower could not answer him.

For reply all he heard was old Deborah's hail of "master, master, oh! my poor young lady," and then he rushed out into the night, banging the heavy door behind.

CHAPTER 16
WIDE OF THE MARK

That same evening Mr. Garland chancing—no unusual occurrence for him—to loiter into the bar of "The Three Fighting Cocks" while the ostler was harnessing his mare, heard three pieces of intelligence.

First, a great London doctor had been down to see Mrs. Redworth; second, he and the local authority agreed that she could never be better, and that she would not be much longer ill; and third, Dick Taunton had passed up the main street apparently either mad or drunk.

Popular opinion inclined to adopt the former suggestion. To gentleman in the very act of imbibing more than their better halves consider good for them, a certain disagreeable personality seems to attach even to the mildest form of inebriation.

"Ah! Poor fellow," said Mr. Purslet, "enough to drive him mad. He was fond of his sister whatever his other faults."

"And surely it was a bad job for her taking up with that Jack Redworth," added a second.

"It is now said,"—whispered Mr. Purslet, but, at this juncture the heads drew so close and the words of wisdom were spoken so low, that no one outside the charmed circle could catch their sound.

But they meant something pitiful, so much was clear, since Mr. Garland remarked, "Poor little lass! And she motherless;" and someone else observed, "That Miss Gower had a lucky escape;" and another remarked, "He never knew a father or a mother's favourite turn out well."

"Black Dick was well-nigh distraught," capped the fortunate individual who had seen the owner of Taunton Hall; "they say he broke away from the doctors when they told him the news, and took leave of his senses there and then. All I know for certain is, he had no hat on when I met him."

Hearing which, the collective wisdom of "The Fighting Cocks" shook its head, and said "that looked very bad."

"Tell you what, gentlemen," remarked Mr. Garland, buttoning up his coat and winding a muffle handkerchief round his neck preparatory to wrestling with the night air, "as I go home I'll take a look in at the Hall. Of late I have gone the other road, not being, to tell you the truth, over and above partial to Saul's Corner; but duty is duty, and I could not sleep in my bed if I was to fail in asking how it is faring with that poor sick lass, and with my young lady, who has acted noble—I can't say more nor less—noble."

The first event which marked the progress of Mr. Garland's homeward journey was a struggle between himself and the redoubtable mare after they crossed Cadlebury Bridge. He wanted to take the road to Saul's Corner, and she wished to follow that across Wilderness Heath. Upon the mare's mind (it at the time having been perfectly clear) there was no doubt evidently as to the reality of the vision she had one night beheld outstripping even her speed across the stretch of common land, and she laid her ears flat back and twisted her body into a semicircle, and pranced and plunged, and absolutely refused to heed the bidding of either whip or bit.

"I don't want to thrash you, and if I did I don't suppose it would do much good," observed Mr. Garland out loud as he put his whip in its socket, and tied his reins to the dashboard, and resignedly got down to lead the creature along the road he wished her to go.

But she refused to travel it for leading either. She whinnied and tossed her head and put her feet straight out, and lifted the sides of her lips and showed all her teeth, and made, in fine, such a trouble and disturbance, that Mr. Garland was fain at length to leave her and his trap behind at a convenient smithy, and pursue his way to the Hall on foot.

He was passing the great gates when, perceiving they were open, he turned up the front avenue, to save himself, as he afterwards stated, "a good few steps."

"Lor, what a dismal place it is," he thought, when he got well under the shade of the trees, and beneath the gloom of the cedars, and thought of old Marmaduke lying there all alone with never another dead man near to keep him company. "I wonder if what I saw that night was real eyesight or Scotch whiskey. I wonder whether the place is uncanny, and Redworth will someday be found hid away among those unwholesome shrubberies. Bless my soul! What is that?'

He might well ask. In the glimmering light he could just discern a something clad all in white rushing towards him. Then a cold hand touched his, and a wild hollow voice exclaimed—

"Oh! Dick, turn back, turn back; she knows all; she is telling him—I always feared her—she has put the puzzle together, I crawled out of bed and listened—and *he*—he is in the house too tonight. I saw him clearly, Dick, as I have so often seen him in my dreams, with his poor broken arm and his ghastly face. He came close up beside my pillow, and I—I—"

He had her in his strong grasp even while she swayed and tottered; before she could fall he lifted her. This was no ghost, but the lightest load of flesh and blood man ever carried.

On along the drive, past the darkly-silent windows—up the steps—under the porch—through the door standing so hospitably open into the great unlighted hall he bore his burden.

Arrived there he did not know which way to carry her, and paused irresolute, till seeing a door in the distance standing ajar and hearing the sound of voices, he strode towards it. He was about to enter the apartment when a sentence he heard stopped him. It was this—

"God in heaven! Hilda! You don't mean to say you think *I murdered my father?*"

"I do not think—I am sure," was the answer, spoken in an accent of shrill and vindictive triumph. "I am neither blind nor deaf, John, and I know all the very good reasons you had for wanting him out the way. You were short of money, and he had money about him. You were not aware of the tenor of his will, and you fancied you would have your share to play with. Do you think I am ignorant that when you went ostensibly on your wedding tour, you travelled no further than London, where your child was born two days after your marriage? I know where that child is buried.

"I have talked with the nurse who attended your wife. I have heard Lettie raving about the dead man, and his broken arm, and his dishevelled grey hair. You thought, no doubt, when you deserted me for her, you did a fine thing, and that I would sit down patiently under the slight, and never lift a finger to avenge myself. But you were mistaken, John Redworth. I loved you with all my heart; and now I hate you with all my heart, and I will never know one night's sound sleep till I see you in the dock, on your trial for wilful murder."

"That is at least a pleasure I can deny you," said Richard Taunton, mockingly, as, pushing open an inner door, he crossed the room to where John Redworth and his accuser stood. "If there were murder in question, I was the murderer. I am the man, madam, and he you have accused is innocent of all knowledge, as he is of any crime."

"Here's your wife, John Redworth," said Mr. Garland, at this juncture pushing into the apartment, and, red and panting, carrying the light figure as if it were some terrible weight. "I met

130

her down the avenue. Herself and One Above alone knows how she managed to get there. She was flying to warn you, squire, not knowing that miss here had got on the wrong scent. And if you'll be advised by me, you'll just forget what you said this minute, and make a bolt for it. To my thinking there has been mischief enough already; for all the justice and all the confessing in the world won't bring the dead back to life."

But his words were unheeded. Already John Redworth had his wife in his arms, and was carrying her off to her own chamber. Richard Taunton was alternately ringing the bell and imploring Mr. Garland to go for the doctor, while Miss Gower remained immovable, her eyes fastened on the wall opposite to the chair into which she had dropped, repeating some sentences inaudible to the two men, wildly waiting for something to happen, they scarce knew what.

Suddenly, through the stillness of the house, there rang out a terrible cry. It seemed to rend the stillness of the solemn night, and cleave a way after the soul departed.

"Poor lass—poor young thing," said Mr. Garland, drawing the back of his hand across his eyes. "She won't know trouble any more—never any more."

CHAPTER 17

HOW IT HAPPENED

At the smithy the mare stood waiting for her master till, in despair, the farrier put her up and went to bed himself.

It was blackest morning—a cold, bleak morning, with a biting wind, before Mr. Garland reappeared to claim his refractory quadruped, and then he was not alone.

Miss Gower stood beside him. She had played out her game, and lost, and now she was going away from Taunton Hall, and the dead woman, and her revenge, feeling herself beaten. She had heard the whole story told. The mystery of Mr. Redworth's disappearance was solved at last; but it no longer possessed the slightest interest for her.

Driving over those dreary Wastes in the coldest hour in all

the twenty-four, the hour before dawn, she recalled the words of Richard Taunton's confession as she might the sentences of some tale, with which she had no manner of connection, read in the years gone by.

"You're shivering, miss, keep the wraps well about you," advised Mr. Garland, but his tone was no longer what it had been.

As he drove, his thoughts were not with the vindictive hypocritical woman beside him, but with the sinner he had heard confess his guilt—the "poor girl" knowledge of that guilt had killed.

In half-a-dozen sentences Richard Taunton told his story.

"There's not much to tell," he had said, standing before the three of them, his sister lying dead above, the murdered man's son looking at him through eyes blinded with tears.

"Yes, he did come to the Hall that night," explained the squire, "but I was away from home. He came to the front door, through which no one had been admitted since I locked it up after my mother's funeral. Lettie happened to be at that side of the house, outside, you understand, and saw him, and he said some bitter things to her, that were true enough, no doubt, but hard for a woman to bear.

"He did not stay long, and then she, low and out of spirits before, on account of what had passed between you and her Jack, down by the canal side went into the house and cried till she could cry no longer.

"Deborah, it appears, saw Mr. Redworth also, but I did not know that till quite recently.

"It was late before I got to Saul's Corner that night. Coming along, and singing a verse or two of a foolish song I had stopped to hear at Trotterbeck bridge, it struck me all at once that I heard an unusual sound, so I pulled up and listened. There was a feeble cry of 'Help.' I could not see anything, but I could distinguish that one word, and horribly eerie it seemed to me, floating about in that lonely place, with the dark pines to my left hand, and the desolate heath stretching away to my right.

"'Who calls?' I shouted out, and for answer there came the

merest whisper of a cry—

""'Here, help.'

"It was some time before I could find him. He had tripped up in one of those holes that abound on the common, and there he was lying, with a broken arm, and something the matter with his ribs, his head cut, and injuries in all directions. I put my flask to his mouth, and tried to get him to walk, but he could not do it, so I had to bring the trap up us close as I was able, and lift him into it. Shall I go on?

"I got him home," he proceeded, after John Redworth had silently signified a wish for the story to be finished "got him home and carried him into the house. Deb had gone to bed, and there was no one up but Lettie. We did what we could for him, though we felt almost frightened at having brought him to the Hall, fearing if anything happened, the blame would be laid on us, after the words he had spoken to Lettie; but still we did help him—remember that, Jack; I am telling you the simple truth, Mr. Garland, and we went on doing what we could, till even Lettie began to fear it was of no use, that he would die before sunrise.

"I don't know how it happened, but accidentally, in moving his coat his pocket-book dropped out. I opened it, and saw the money, and then the devil took possession of me.

"I had got notice, if I did not pay up the back interest on my mortgages, the mortgagees would foreclose. I was at my wits' end, and as I turned over the notes I thought of all those notes could do for me, of the freedom they might compass.

"As I thought this I lifted up my eyes, and met his glance. It dropped in a minute, but—must I finish. Can't you guess the rest?"

"I want to know how he died," said John Redworth with a forced and terrible calmness.

"I had some laudanum in the cupboard, and I poured it down his throat. Lettie was not in the room, she had gone out to make him a cup of coffee, and when she came back he was dead, or seemed dead, and there could be no return along the road I had travelled. I made away with the body. I placed it, as I thought, out of my own sight and the sight of all men for ever; but I tell you he has been at bed and at board with me ever since from that night, he has sat opposite me at table, and walked with me through the woods. It killed Lettie. She was dying by inches when you—turning to Miss Gower came among us, but the pace quickened after that, for she never imagined but you were following on the right track, it never occurred to her you were trying to fasten the crime on John. She has gone now, and no disgrace or grief of mine can trouble her in the future, so do what you like. The words I have spoken tonight I promise to repeat when and where you will."

But both John Redworth and Mr. Garland shook their heads.

"The best thing you can do," said the farmer, "for the sake of the living and the dead, is to let the mystery of Mr. Redworth's disappearance stay a mystery to the end; and as for Miss here, I'll just take her back with me presently. She will be better up at The Wastes. I always said the air down here did not suit her, and I say so still. If I could do anything for you, Mr. John, be sure and let me know," he went on, turning to the younger man. "Is there anything, think you, I can do for you now?"

For answer John Redworth covered his face with his hands; what could any man do for him, or woman either?

"Thank you," he said, after a moment's pause, "but you can do nothing; leave me alone, please, will you?"

So they went away and left him alone with his grief. He had had his life and he spoiled it. His chance had been given him and he missed it; in the joyous spring-time he had planted thistles, and he could never now hope to gather figs.

The Uninhabited House

MISS BLAKE—FROM MEMORY

If ever a residence, "suitable in every respect for a family of position," haunted a lawyer's offices, the "Uninhabited House," about which I have a story to tell, haunted those of Messrs. Craven and Son, No. 200, Buckingham Street, Strand.

It did not matter in the least whether it happened to be let or unlet: in either case, it never allowed Mr. Craven or his clerks, of whom I was one, to forget its existence.

When let, we were in perpetual hot water with the tenant; when unlet, we had to endeavour to find some tenant to take that unlucky house.

Happy were we when we could get an agreement signed for a couple of years—although we always had misgivings that the war waged with the last occupant would probably have to be renewed with his successor.

Still, when we were able to let the desirable residence to a solvent individual, even for twelve months, Mr. Craven rejoiced.

He knew how to proceed with the tenants who came blustering, or threatening, or complaining, or bemoaning; but he did not know what to do with Miss Blake and her letters, when no person was liable for the rent.

All lawyers—I am one myself, and can speak from a long and varied experience—all lawyers, even the very hardest, have one client, at all events, towards whom they exhibit much forbearance, for whom they feel a certain sympathy, and in whose

135

interests they take a vast deal of trouble for very little pecuniary profit.

A client of this kind favours me with his business—he has favoured me with it for many years past. Each first of January I register a vow he shall cost me no more time or money. On each last day of December I find he is deeper in my debt than he was on the same date a twelvemonth previous.

I often wonder how this is—why we, so fierce to one human being, possibly honest and well-meaning enough, should be as wax in the hand of the moulder, when another individual, perhaps utterly disreputable, refuses to take "No" for an answer.

Do we purchase our indulgences in this way? Do we square our accounts with our own consciences by remembering that, if we have been as stone to Dick, Tom, and Harry, we have melted at the first appeal of Jack?

My principal, Mr. Craven—than whom a better man never breathed—had an unprofitable client, for whom he entertained feelings of the profoundest pity, whom he treated with a rare courtesy. That lady was Miss Blake; and when the old house on the Thames stood tenantless, Mr. Craven's bed did not prove one of roses.

In our firm there was no son—Mr. Craven had been the son; but the old father was dead, and our chief's wife had brought him only daughters.

Still the title of the firm remained the same, and Mr. Craven's own signature also.

He had been junior for such a number of years, that, when Death sent a royal invitation to his senior, he was so accustomed to the old form, that he, and all in his employment, tacitly agreed it was only fitting he should remain junior to the end.

A good man, I, of all human beings, have reason to speak well of him. Even putting the undoubted fact of all lawyers keeping one unprofitable client into the scales, if he had not been very good he must have washed his hands of Miss Blake and her niece's house long before the period at which this story opens.

The house did not belong to Miss Blake. It was the property

of her niece, a certain Miss Helena Elmsdale, of whom Mr. Craven always spoke as that "poor child."

She was not of age, and Miss Blake managed her few pecuniary affairs.

Besides the "desirable residence, suitable," *etcetera*, aunt and niece had property producing about sixty-five pounds a year. When we could let the desirable residence, handsomely furnished, and with every convenience that could be named in the space of a half-guinea advertisement, to a family from the country, or an officer just returned from India, or to an invalid who desired a beautiful and quiet abode within an easy drive of the West End—when we could do this, I say, the income of aunt and niece rose to two hundred and sixty-five pounds a year, which made a very material difference to Miss Blake.

When we could not let the house, or when the payment of the rent was in dispute, Mr. Craven advanced the lady various five and ten pound notes, which, it is to be hoped, were entered duly to his credit in the Eternal Books. In the mundane records kept in our offices, they always appeared as debits to William Craven's private account.

As for the young men about our establishment, of whom I was one, we anathematised that house. I do not intend to reproduce the language we used concerning it at one period of our experience, because eventually the evil wore itself out, as most evils do, and at last we came to look upon the desirable residence as an institution of our firm—as a sort of *cause célèbre*, with which it was creditable to be associated—as a species of remarkable criminal always on its trial, and always certain to be defended by Messrs. Craven and Son.

In fact, the Uninhabited House—for uninhabited it usually was, whether anyone was answerable for the rent or not—finally became an object of as keen interest to all Mr. Craven's clerks as it became a source of annoyance to him.

So the beam goes up and down. While Mr. Craven poohpoohed the complaints of tenants, and laughed at the idea of a man being afraid of a ghost, we did not laugh, but swore. When, however, Mr. Craven began to look serious about the matter, and hoped some evil-disposed persons were not trying to keep the place tenantless, our interest in the old house became absorbing. And as our interest in the residence grew, so, likewise, did our appreciation of Miss Blake.

We missed her when she went abroad—which she always did the day a fresh agreement was signed—and we welcomed her return to England and our offices with effusion. Safely I can say no millionaire ever received such an ovation as fell to the lot of Miss Blake when, after a foreign tour, she returned to those lodgings near Brunswick Square, which her residence ought, I think, to have rendered classic.

She never lost an hour in coming to us. With the dust of travel upon her, with the heat and burden of quarrels with railway porters, and encounters with cabmen, visible to anyone who chose to read the signs of the times, Miss Blake came pounding up our stairs, wanting to see Mr. Craven.

If that gentleman was engaged, she would sit down in the general office, and relate her latest grievance to a posse of sympathising clerks.

"And he says he won't pay the rent," was always the refrain of these lamentations.

"It is in Ireland he thinks he is, poor soul!" she was wont to declare.

"We'll teach him different, Miss Blake," the spokesman of the party would declare; whilst another ostentatiously mended a pen, and a third brought down a ream of foolscap and laid it with a thump before him on the desk.

"And, indeed, you're all decent lads, though full of your tricks," Miss Blake would sometimes remark, in a tone of gentle reproof. "But if you had a niece just dying with grief, and a house nobody will live in on your hands, you would not have as much heart for fun, I can tell you that."

Hearing which, the young rascals tried to look sorrowful, and failed.

In the way of my profession I have met with many singular

persons, but I can safely declare I never met with any person so singular as Miss Blake.

She was—I speak of her in the past tense, not because she is dead, but because times and circumstances have changed since the period when we both had to do with the Uninhabited House, and she has altered in consequence—one of the most original people who ever crossed my path.

Born in the north of Ireland, the child of a Scottish-Ulster mother and a Connaught father, she had ingeniously contrived to combine in her own person the vices of two distinct races, and exclude the virtues of both.

Her accent was the most fearful which could be imagined. She had the brogue of the West grafted on the accent of the North. And yet there was a variety about her even in this re-spect. One never could tell, from visit to visit, whether she pro-posed to pronounce "written" as "wrutten" or "wretten"; (The wife of a celebrated Indian officer stated that she once, in the north of Ireland, heard Job's utterance thus rendered—"Oh! that my words were wrutten, that they were prented in a buke.") whether she would elect to style her parents, to whom she made frequent reference, her "pawpaw and mawmaw," or her "pepai and memai."

It all depended with whom Miss Blake had lately been most intimate. If she had been "hand and glove" with a "nob" from her own country—she was in no way reticent about thus styling her grander acquaintances, only she wrote the word "knob"—who thought to conceal his nationality by "awing" and "hawing," she spoke about people being "morried" and wearing "sockcloth and oshes." If, on the contrary, she had been thrown into the society of a lady who so far honoured England as to talk as some people do in England, we had every A turned into E, and every U into O, while she minced her words as if she had been saying "niminy piminy" since she first began to talk, and honestly be-lieved no human being could ever have told she had been born west of St. George's Channel.

But not merely in accent did Miss Blake evidence the fact

that her birth had been the result of an injudicious cross; the more one knew of her, the more clearly one saw the wrong points she threw out.

Extravagant to a fault, like her Connaught father, she was in no respect generous, either from impulse or calculation.

Mean about minor details, a turn of character probably inherited from the Ulster mother, she was utterly destitute of that careful and honest economy which is an admirable trait in the natives of the north of Ireland, and which enables them so frequently, after being strictly just, to be much more than liberal.

Honest, Miss Blake was not—or, for that matter, honourable either. Her indebtedness to our firm could not be considered other than a matter of honour, and yet she never dreamt of paying her debt to Mr. Craven.

Indeed, to do Miss Blake strict justice, she never thought of paying the debts she owed to anyone, unless she was obliged to do so.

Nowadays, I fear it would fare hard with her were she to try her old tactics with the British tradesman; but, in the time of which I am writing, co-operative societies were not, and then the British tradesman had no objection, I fancy, to be gulled.

Perhaps, like the lawyer and the unprofitable client, he set-off being gulled on one side his ledger against being fleeced on the other.

Be this as it may, we were always compounding some liability for Miss Blake, as well as letting her house and fighting with the tenants.

At first, as I have said, we found Miss Blake an awful bore, but we generally ended by deciding we could better spare a better man. Indeed, the months when she did not come to our office seemed to want flavour.

Of gratitude—popularly supposed to be essentially characteristic of the Irish—Miss Blake was utterly destitute. I never did know—I have never known since, so ungrateful a woman.

Not merely did she take everything Mr. Craven did for her as a right, but she absolutely turned the tables, and brought him in her debtor.

Once, only once, that I can remember, he ventured to ask when it would be convenient for her to repay some of the money he had from time to time advanced.

Miss Blake was taken by surprise, but she rose equal to the occasion.

"You are joking, Mr. Craven," she said. "You mean, when will I want to ask you to give me a share of the profits you have made out of the estate of my poor sister's husband. Why, that house has been as good as an annuity to you. For six long years it has stood empty, or next to empty, and never been out of law all the time."

"But, you know, Miss Blake, that not a shilling of profit has accrued to me from the house being in law," he pleaded. "I have always been too glad to get the rent for you, to insist upon my costs, and, really—."

"Now, do not try to impose upon me," she interrupted, "because it is of no use. Didn't you make thousands off the dead man, and now haven't you got the house? Why, if you never had a penny of costs, instead of all you have pocketed, that house and the name it has brought to you, and the fame which has spread abroad in consequence, can't be reckoned as less than hundreds a year to your firm. And yet you ask me for the return of a trumpery four or five sovereigns—I am ashamed of you! But I won't imitate your bad example. Let me have five more today, and you can stop ten out of the colonel's first payment."

"I am very sorry," said my employer, "but I really have not five pounds to spare."

"Hear him," remarked Miss Blake, turning towards me. "Young man"—Miss Blake steadily refused to recognise the possibility of any clerk being even by accident a gentleman—"will you hand me over the newspaper?"

I had not the faintest idea what she wanted with the newspaper, and neither had Mr. Craven, till she sat down again deliberately—the latter part of this conversation having taken place after she rose, preparatory to saying farewell—opened the sheet out to its full width, and commenced to read the debates.

"My dear Miss Blake," began Mr. Craven, after a minute's pause, "you know my time, when it is mine, is always at your disposal, but at the present moment several clients are waiting to see me, and—"

"Let them wait," said Miss Blake, as he hesitated a little. "Your time and their time is no more valuable than mine, and I mean to stay *here*," emphasising the word, "till you let me have that five pounds. Why, look, now, that house is taken on a two years' agreement, and you won't see me again for that time—likely as not, never; for who can tell what may happen to anybody in foreign parts? Only one charge I lay upon you, Mr. Craven: don't let me be buried in a strange country. It is bad enough to be so far as this from my father and my mother's remains, but I daresay I'll manage to rest in the same grave as my sister, though Robert Elmsdale lies between. He separated us in life—not that she ever cared for him; but it won't matter much when we are all bones and dust together—"

"If I let you have that five pounds," here broke in Mr. Craven, "do I clearly understand that I am to recoup myself out of Colonel Morris' first payment?"

"I said so as plain as I could speak," agreed Miss Blake; and her speech was very plain indeed.

Mr. Craven lifted his eyebrows and shrugged his shoulders, while he drew his cheque-book towards him.

"How is Helena?" he asked, as he wrote the final legendary flourish after Craven and Son.

"Helena is but middling, poor dear," answered Miss Blake—on that occasion she called her niece Hallana. "She frets, the creature, as is natural; but she will get better when we leave England. England is a hard country for anyone who is all nairves like Halana."

"Why do you never bring her to see me?" asked Mr. Craven, folding up the cheque.

"Bring her to be stared at by a parcel of clerks!" exclaimed Miss Blake, in a tone which really caused my hair to bristle. "Well-mannered, decent young fellows in their own rank, no doubt, but not fit to look at my sister's child. Now, now, Mr. Craven, ought Kathleen Blake's—or, rather, Kathleen Elmsdale's daughter to serve as a fifth of November guy for London lads? You know she is handsome enough to be a duchess, like her mother."

"Yes, yes, I know," agreed Mr. Craven, and handed over the cheque.

After I had held the door open for Miss Blake to pass out, and closed it securely and resumed my seat, Miss Blake turned the handle and treated us to another sight of her bonnet.

"Goodbye, William Craven, for two years at any rate; and if I never see you again, God bless you, for you've been a true friend to me and that poor child who has nobody else to look to," and then, before Mr. Craven could cross the room, she was gone.

"I wonder," said I, "if it will be two years before we see her again?"

"No, nor the fourth of two years," answered my employer. "There is something queer about that house."

"You don't think it is haunted, sir, do you?" I ventured.

"Of course not," said Mr. Craven, irritably; "but I do think someone wants to keep the place vacant, and is succeeding admirably."

The question I next put seemed irrelevant, but really resulted from a long train of thought. This was it:

"Is Miss Elmsdale very handsome, sir?"

"She is very beautiful," was the answer; "but not so beautiful as her mother was."

Ah me! two old, old stories in a sentence. He had loved the mother, and he did not love the daughter. He had seen the mother in his bright, hopeful youth, and there was no light of morning left for him in which he could behold the child.

To other eyes she might, in her bright spring-time, seem lovely as an angel from heaven, but to him no more such visions were to be vouchsafed.

If beauty really went on decaying, as the ancients say, by this time there could be no beauty left. But oh! greybeard, the beauty remains, though our eyes may be too dim to see it; the beauty, the grace, the rippling laughter, and the saucy smiles, which once had power to stir to their very depths our hearts, friend—our hearts, yours and mine, comrade, feeble, and cold, and pulseless now.

CHAPTER 2
THE CORONER'S INQUEST

The story was told to me afterwards, but I may as well weave it in with mine at this juncture.

From the maternal ancestress, the Demoiselles Blake inherited a certain amount of money. It was through no fault of the paternal Blake—through no want of endeavours on his part to make ducks and drakes of all fortune which came in his way, that their small inheritance remained intact; but the fortune was so willed that neither the girls nor he could divert the peaceful tenure of its half-yearly dividends.

The mother died first, and the father followed her ere long, and then the young ladies found themselves orphans, and the possessors of a fixed income of one hundred and thirty pounds a year.

A modest income, and yet, as I have been given to understand, they might have married well for the money.

In those days, particularly in Ireland, men went very cheap, and the Misses Blake, one and both, could, before they left off mourning, have wedded, respectively, a curate, a doctor, a constabulary officer, and the captain of a government schooner.

The Misses Blake looked higher, however, and came to England, where rich husbands are presumably procurable. Came, but missed their market. Miss Kathleen found only one lover, William Craven, whose honest affection she flouted; and Miss Susannah found no lover at all.

Miss Kathleen wanted a duke, or an earl—a prince of the blood royal being about that time unprocurable; and an attorney, to her Irish ideas, seemed a very poor sort of substitute. For which reason she rejected the attorney with scorn, and remained single, while the dukes and earls were marrying and intermarrying with their peers or their inferiors.

Then suddenly there came a frightful day when Kathleen and Susannah learned they were penniless, when they understood their trustee had robbed them, as he had robbed others, and had been paying their interest out of what was left of their principal.

They tried teaching, but they really had nothing to teach. They tried letting lodgings. Even lodgers rebelled against their untidiness and want of punctuality.

The eldest was very energetic and very determined, and the youngest very pretty and very conciliatory. Nevertheless, business is business, and lodgings are lodgings, and the Misses Blake were on the verge of beggary, when Mr. Elmsdale proposed for Miss Kathleen and was accepted.

Mr. Craven, by that time a family man, gave the bride away, and secured Mr. Elmsdale's business.

Possibly, had Mrs. Elmsdale's marriage proved happy, Mr. Craven might have soon lost sight of his former love. In matrimony, as in other matters, we are rarely so sympathetic with fulfilment as with disappointment. The pretty Miss Blake was a disappointed woman after she had secured Mr. Elmsdale. She then understood that the best life could offer her was something very different indeed from the ideal duke her beauty should have won, and she did not take much trouble to conceal her dissatisfaction with the arrangements of Providence.

Mr. Craven, seeing what Mr. Elmsdale was towards men, pitied her. Perhaps, had he seen what Mrs. Elmsdale was towards her husband, he might have pitied him; but, then, he did not see, for women are wonderful dissemblers.

There was Elmsdale, bluff in manner, short in person, red in the face, cumbersome in figure, addicted to naughty words, not nice about driving fearfully hard bargains, a man whom men hated, not undeservedly; and yet, nevertheless, a man capable of loving a woman with all the veins of his heart, and who might, had any woman been found to love him, have compassed earthly salvation.

There were those who said he never could compass eternal; but they chanced to be his debtors—and, after all, that question lay between himself and God. The other lay between himself and his wife, and it must be confessed, except so far as his passionate, disinterested love for an utterly selfish woman tended to redeem and humanise his nature, she never helped him one step along the better path.

But, then, the world could not know this, and Mr. Craven, of whom I am speaking at the moment, was likely, naturally, to think Mr. Elmsdale all in the wrong.

On the one hand he saw the man as he appeared to men: on the other he saw the woman as she appeared to men, beautiful to the last; fragile, with the low voice, so beautiful in any woman, so more especially beautiful in an Irish woman; with a languid face which insured compassion while never asking for it; with the appearance of a martyr, and the tone and the manner of a suffering saint.

Everyone who beheld the pair together, remarked, "What a pity it was such a sweet creature should be married to such a bear!" but Mr. Elmsdale was no bear to his wife: he adored her. The selfishness, the discontent, the ill-health, as much the consequence of a peevish, petted temper, as of disease, which might well have exhausted the patience and tired out the love of a different man, only endeared her the more to him.

She made him feel how inferior he was to her in all respects; how tremendously she had condescended, when she agreed to become his wife; and he quietly accepted her estimation of him, and said with a humility which was touching from its simplicity:

"I know I am not worthy of you, Kathleen, but I do my best to make you happy."

For her sake, not being a liberal man, he spent money freely; for her sake he endured Miss Blake; for her sake he bought the place which afterwards caused us so much trouble; for her sake, he, who had always scoffed at the folly of people turning their houses into stores for "useless timber," as he styled the upholsterer's greatest triumphs, furnished his rooms with a lavish disregard of cost; for her sake, he, who hated society, smiled on visitors, and entertained the guests she invited, with no grudging hospitality. For her sake he dressed well, and did many other things which were equally antagonistic to his original nature; and he might just as well have gone his own way, and pleased himself only, for all the pleasure he gave her, or all the thanks she gave him.

If Mr. Elmsdale had come home drunk five evenings a week, and beaten his wife, and denied her the necessaries of life, and kept her purse in a chronic state of emptiness, she might very possibly have been extremely grateful for an occasional kind word or smile; but, as matters stood, Mrs. Elmsdale was not in the least grateful for a devotion, as beautiful as it was extraordinary, and posed herself on the domestic sofa in the character of a martyr.

Most people accepted the representation as true, and pitied her. Miss Blake, blissfully forgetful of that state of impecuniosity from which Mr. Elmsdale's proposal had extricated herself and her sister, never wearied of stating that "Katty had thrown herself away, and that Mr. Elmsdale was not fit to tie her shoe-string."

She generously admitted the poor creature did his best; but, according to Blake, the poor creature's best was very bad indeed.

"It's not his fault, but his misfortune," the lady was wont to remark, "that he's like dirt beside her. He can't help his birth, and his dragging-up, and his disreputable trade, or business, or whatever he likes to call it; he can't help never having had a father nor mother to speak of, and not a lady or gentleman belonging to the family since it came into existence. I'm not blaming him, but it is hard for Kathleen, and she reared as she was, and accustomed to the best society in Ireland,—which is very different, let me tell you, from the best anybody ever saw in England."

There were some who thought, if Mrs. Elmsdale could tolerate her sister's company, she might without difficulty have condoned her husband's want of acquaintance with some points of grammar and etiquette; and who said, amongst themselves, that whereas he only maltreated, Miss Blake mangled every letter in the alphabet; but these carping critics were in the minority.

Mrs. Elmsdale was a beauty, and a martyr; Mr. Elmsdale a rough beast, who had no capacity of ever developing into a prince. Miss Blake was a model of sisterly affection, and if eccentric in her manner, and bewildering in the vagaries of her accent, well, most Irish people, the highest in rank not excepted, were the same. Why, there was Lord So-and-so, who stated at a public meeting that "roight and moight were not always convartible tarms"; and accepted the cheers and laughter which greeted his utterance as evidence that he had said something rather neat.

Miss Blake's accent was a very different affair indeed from those wrestles with his foe in which her brother-in-law always came off worsted. He endured agonies in trying to call himself Elmsdale, and rarely succeeded in styling his wife anything except Mrs. H.E. I am told Miss Blake's mimicry of this peculiarity was delicious: but I never was privileged to hear her delineation, for, long before the period when this story opens, Mr. Elmsdale had departed to that land where no confusion of tongues can much signify, and where Helmsdale no doubt served his purpose just as well as Miss Blake's more refined pronunciation of his name.

Further, Miss Helena Elmsdale would not allow a word in depreciation of her father to be uttered when she was near, and as Miss Helena could on occasion develop a very pretty little temper, as well as considerable power of satire, Miss Blake dropped out of the habit of ridiculing Mr. Elmsdale's sins of omission and commission, and contented herself by generally asserting that, as his manner of living had broken her poor sister's heart, so his manner of dying had broken her—Miss Blake's—heart.

"It is only for the sake of the orphan child I am able to hold up at all," she would tell us. "I would not have blamed him so much for leaving us poor, but it was hard and cruel to leave us disgraced into the bargain"; and then Miss Blake would weep, and the wag of the office would take out his handkerchief and ostentatiously wipe his eyes.

She often threatened to complain of that boy—a merry, mischievous young imp—to Mr. Craven; but she never did so. Perhaps because the clerks always gave her rapt attention; and an interested audience was very pleasant to Miss Blake.

Considering the nature of Mr. Elmsdale's profession, Miss Blake had possibly some reason to complain of the extremely unprofitable manner in which he cut up. He was what the lady described as "a dirty money-lender."

Heaven only knows how he drifted into his occupation; few men, I imagine, select such a trade, though it is one which seems to exercise an enormous fascination for those who have adopted it.

The only son of a very small builder who managed to leave a few hundred pounds behind him for the benefit of Elmsdale, then clerk in a contractor's office, he had seen enough of the anxieties connected with his father's business to wash his hands of bricks and mortar.

Experience, perhaps, had taught him also that people who advanced money to builders made a very nice little income out of the capital so employed; and it is quite possible that some of his father's acquaintances, always in want of ready cash, as speculative folks usually are, offered such terms for temporary accommodation as tempted him to enter into the business of which Miss Blake spoke so contemptuously.

Be this as it may, one thing is certain—by the time Elmsdale was thirty he had established a very nice little connection amongst needy men: whole streets were mortgaged to him; terraces, nominally the property of some well-to-do builder, were virtually his, since he only waited the well-to-do builder's inevitable bankruptcy to enter into possession. He was not a sixty *per cent* man, always requiring some very much better security than "a name" before parting with his money; but still even twenty *per cent*, usually means ruin, and, as a matter of course, most of Mr. Elmsdale's clients reached that pleasant goal.

They could have managed to do so, no doubt, had Mr. Elmsdale never existed; but as he was in existence, he served the purpose for which it seemed his mother had borne him; and sooner or later—as a rule, sooner than later—assumed the shape of Nemesis to most of those who "did business" with him.

There were exceptions, of course. Some men, by the help of exceptional good fortune, roguery, or genius, managed to get out of Mr. Elmsdale's hands by other paths than those leading through Basinghall or Portugal Streets; but they merely proved the rule.

Notably amongst these fortunate persons may be mentioned a Mr. Harrison and a Mr. Harringford—'Arrison and 'Arringford, as Mr. Elmsdale called them, when he did not refer to them as the two Haitches.

Of these, the first-named, after a few transactions, shook the dust of Mr. Elmsdale's office off his shoes, sent him the money he owed by his lawyer, and ever after referred to Mr. Elmsdale as "that thief," "that scoundrel," that "swindling old vagabond," and so forth; but, then, hard words break no bones, and Mr. Harrison was not very well thought of himself.

His remarks, therefore, did Mr. Elmsdale very little harm—a money-lender is not usually spoken of in much pleasanter terms by those who once have been thankful enough for his cheque; and the world in general does not attach a vast amount of importance to the opinions of a former borrower. Mr. Harrison did not, therefore, hurt or benefit his quondam friend to any appreciable extent; but with Mr. Harringford the case was different.

He and Elmsdale had been doing business together for years, "everything he possessed in the world," he stated to an admiring coroner's jury summoned to sit on Mr. Elmsdale's body and inquire into the cause of that gentleman's death—"everything he possessed in the world, he owed to the deceased. Some people spoke hardly of him, but his experience of Mr. Elmsdale enabled him to say that a kinder-hearted, juster, honester, or better-principled man never existed. He charged high interest, certainly, and he expected to be paid his rate; but, then, there was no deception about the matter: if it was worth a borrower's while to take money at twenty *per cent,* why, there was an end of the matter. Business men are not children," remarked Mr. Harringford, "and ought not to borrow money at twenty *per cent,* unless they can make thirty *per cent,* out of it." Personally, he had never paid Mr. Elmsdale more than twelve and a half or fifteen *per cent.*; but, then, their transactions were on a large scale. Only the day before Mr. Elmsdale's death—he hesitated a little over that word, and became, as the reporters said, "affected"—he had paid him twenty thousand pounds. The deceased told him he had urgent need of the money, and at considerable inconvenience he raised the amount. If the question were pressed as to whether he guessed for what purpose that sum was so urgently needed, he would answer it, of course; but he suggested that it should not be pressed, as likely to give pain to those who were already in terrible affliction.

Hearing which, the jury pricked up their ears, and the coroner's curiosity became so intense that he experienced some difficulty in saying, calmly, that, "as the object of his sitting there was to elicit the truth, however much he should regret causing distress to anyone, he must request that Mr. Harringford, whose scruples did him honour, would keep back no fact tending to throw light upon so sad an affair."

Having no alternative after this but to unburden himself of his secret, Mr. Harringford stated that he feared the deceased had been a heavy loser at Ascot. Mr. Harringford, having gone to that place with some friends, met Mr. Elmsdale on the racecourse. Expressing astonishment at meeting him there, Mr. Elmsdale stated he had run down to look after a client of his who he feared was going wrong. He said he did not much care to do business with a betting man. In the course of subsequent conversation, however, he told the witness he had some money on the favourite.

As frequently proves the case, the favourite failed to come in first: that was all Mr. Harringford knew about the matter. Mr. Elmsdale never mentioned how much he had lost—in fact, he never referred again, except in general terms, to their meeting. He stated, however, that he must have money, and that immediately; if not the whole amount, half, at all events. The witness found, however, he could more easily raise the larger than the smaller sum. There had been a little unpleasantness between him and Mr. Elmsdale with reference to the demand for money made so suddenly and so peremptorily, and he bitterly regretted having even for a moment forgotten what was due to so kind a friend.

He knew of no reason in the world why Mr. Elmsdale should have committed suicide. He was, in business, eminently a cautious man, and Mr. Harringford had always supposed him to be wealthy; in fact, he believed him to be a man of large property. Since the death of his wife, he had, however, noticed a change in him; but still it never crossed the witness's mind that his brain was in any way affected.

Miss Blake, who had to this point postponed giving her evidence, on account of the "way she was upset," was now able to tell a sympathetic jury and a polite coroner all she knew of the matter.

"Indeed," she began, "Robert Elmsdale had never been the same man since her poor sister's death; he mooned about, and would sit for half an hour at a time, doing nothing but looking at a faded bit of the dining-room carpet."

He took no interest in anything; if he was asked any questions about the garden, he would say, "What does it matter? *she* cannot see it now."

"Indeed, my lord," said Miss Blake, in her agitation probably confounding the coroner with the chief justice, "it was just pitiful to see the creature; I am sure his ways got to be heart-breaking."

"After my sister's death," Miss Blake resumed, after a pause, devoted by herself, the jury, and the coroner to sentiment, "Robert Elmsdale gave up his office in London, and brought his business home. I do not know why he did this. He would not, had she been living, because he always kept his trade well out of her sight, poor man. Being what she was, she could not endure the name of it, naturally. It was not my place to say he shouldn't do what he liked in his own house, and I thought the excitement of building a new room, and quarrelling with the builder, and swearing at the men, was good for him. He made a fireproof place for his papers, and he fitted up the office like a library, and bought a beautiful large table, covered with leather; and nobody to have gone in would have thought the room was used for business. He had a Turkey carpet on the floor, and chairs that slipped about on castors; and he planned a covered way out into the road, with a separate entrance for itself, so that none of us ever knew who went out or who came in. He kept his affairs secret as the grave."

"No," in answer to the coroner, who began to think Miss Blake's narrative would never come to an end. "I heard no shot: none of us did: we all slept away from that part of the house; but I was restless that night, and could not sleep, and I got up and looked out at the river, and saw a flare of light on it. I thought it odd he was not gone to bed, but took little notice of the matter for a couple of hours more, when it was just getting gray in the morning, and I looked out again, and still seeing the light, slipped on a dressing-wrapper and my slippers, and ran down-stairs to tell him he would ruin his health if he did not go to his bed.

"When I opened the door I could see nothing; the table stood between me and him; but the gas was flaring away, and as I went round to put it out, I came across him lying on the floor. It never occurred to me he was dead; I thought he was in a fit, and knelt down to unloose his cravat, then I found he had gone.

"The pistol lay on the carpet beside him—and that," finished Miss Blake, "is all I have to tell."

When asked if she had ever known of his losing money by betting, she answered it was not likely he would tell her anything of that kind.

"He always kept his business to himself," she affirmed, "as is the way of most men."

In answer to other questions, she stated she never heard of any losses in business; there was plenty of money always to be had for the asking. He was liberal enough, though perhaps not so liberal latterly, as before his wife's death; she didn't know anything of the state of his affairs. Likely, Mr. Craven could tell them all about that.

Mr. Craven, however, proved unable to do so. To the best of his belief, Mr. Elmsdale was in very easy circumstances. He had transacted a large amount of business for him, but never any involving pecuniary loss or anxiety; he should have thought him the last man in the world to run into such folly as betting; he had no doubt Mrs. Elmsdale's death had affected him disastrously. He said more than once to witness, if it were not for the sake of his child, he should not care if he died that night.

All of which, justifying the jury in returning a verdict of "suicide while of unsound mind," they expressed their unanimous opinion to that effect—thus "saving the family the condemnation of *felo de se*" remarked Miss Blake.

The dead man was buried, the church service read over his remains, the household was put into mourning, the blinds were drawn up, the windows flung open, and the business of life taken up once more by the survivors.

CHAPTER 3

OUR LAST TENANT

It is quite competent for a person so to manage his affairs, that, whilst understanding all about them himself, another finds it next to impossible to make head or tail of his position.

Mr. Craven found that Mr. Elmsdale had effected this feat; entries there were in his books, intelligible enough, perhaps, to the man who made them, but as so much Hebrew to a stranger.

He had never kept a business banking account; he had no regular journal or ledger; he seemed to have depended on memoranda, and vague and uncertain writings in his diary, both for memory and accuracy; and as most of his business had been conducted *viva voce*, there were few letters to assist in throwing the slightest light on his transactions.

Even from the receipts, however, one thing was clear, *viz.*, that he had, since his marriage, spent a very large sum of money; spent it lavishly, not to say foolishly. Indeed, the more closely Mr. Craven looked into affairs, the more satisfied he felt that Mr. Elmsdale had committed suicide simply because he was well-nigh ruined.

Mortgage-deeds Mr. Craven himself had drawn up, were nowhere to be found; neither could one sovereign of the money Mr. Harringford paid be discovered.

Miss Blake said she believed "that Harringford had never paid at all"; but this was clearly proved to be an error of judgment on the part of that impulsive lady. Not merely did Harringford hold the receipt for the money and the mortgage-deeds cancelled, but the cheque he had given to the mortgagee bore the endorsement—"Robert Elmsdale"; while the clerk who cashed it stated that Mr. Elmsdale presented the order in person, and that to him he handed the notes.

Whatever he had done with the money, no notes were to be found; a diligent search of the strong room produced nothing more important than the discovery of a cash-box containing three hundred pounds; the title-deeds of River Hall—such being the modest name by which Mr. Elmsdale had elected to have his residence distinguished; the leases relating to some small cottages near Barnes; all the letters his wife had ever written to him; two locks of her hair, one given before marriage, the other cut after her death; a curl severed from the head of my "baby daughter"; quantities of receipts—and nothing more.

"I wonder he can rest in his grave," said Miss Blake, when at last she began to realize, in a dim sort of way, the position of affairs.

According to the River Hall servants' version, Mr. Elmsdale did anything rather than rest in his grave. About the time the new mourning had been altered to fit perfectly, a nervous housemaid, who began perhaps to find the house dull, mooted the question as to whether "master walked."

Within a fortnight it was decided in solemn conclave that master did; and further, that the place was not what it had been; and moreover, that in the future it was likely to be still less like what it had been.

There is a wonderful instinct in the lower classes, which enables them to comprehend, without actual knowledge, when misfortune is coming upon a house: and in this instance that instinct was not at fault.

Long before Mr. Craven had satisfied himself that his client's estate was a very poor one, the River Hall servants, one after another, had given notice to leave—indeed, to speak more accurately, they did not give notice, for they left; and before they left they took care to baptize the house with such an exceedingly bad name, that neither for love nor money could Miss Blake get a fresh "help" to stay in it for more than twenty-four hours.

First one housemaid was taken with "the shivers"; then the cook had "the trembles"; then the coachman was prepared to take his solemn affidavit, that, one night long after everyone in the house to his knowledge was in bed, he "see from his room above the stables, a light a-shining on the Thames, and the figures of one or more a passing and a repassing across the blind." More than this, a new page-boy declared that, on a certain evening, before he had been told there was anything strange about the house, he heard the door of the passage leading from the library into the side-road slam violently, and looking to see who had gone out by that unused entrance, failed to perceive sign of man, woman, or child, by the bright moonlight.

Moved by some feeling which he professed himself unable to "put a name on," he proceeded to the door in question, and found it barred, chained, and bolted. While he was standing wondering what it meant, he noticed the light as of gas shining from underneath the library door; but when he softly turned the handle and peeped in, the room was dark as the grave, and "like cold water seemed running down his back."

Further, he averred, as he stole away into the hall, there was a sound followed him as between a groan and a cry. Hearing which statement, an impressionable charwoman went into hysterics, and had to be recalled to her senses by a dose of gin, suggested and taken strictly as a medicine.

But no supply of spirituous liquors, even had Miss Blake been disposed to distribute anything of the sort, could induce servants after a time to remain in, or charwomen to come to, the house. It had received a bad name, and that goes even further in disfavour of a residence than it does against a man or woman.

Finally, Miss Blake's establishment was limited to an old creature almost doting and totally deaf, the advantages of whose presence might have been considered problematical; but, then, as Miss Blake remarked, "she was somebody."

"And now she has taken fright," proceeded the lady. "How anyone could make her hear their story, the Lord in heaven alone knows; and if there was anything to see, I am sure she is far too blind to see it; but she says she daren't stay. She does not want to see poor master again till she is dead herself."

"I have got a tenant for the house the moment you like to say you will leave it," said Mr. Craven, in reply. "He cares for no ghost that ever was manufactured. He has a wife with a splendid digestion, and several grown-up sons and daughters. They will soon clear out the shadows; and their father is willing to pay two hundred and fifty pounds a year."

"And you think there is really nothing more of any use amongst the papers?"

"I am afraid not—I am afraid you must face the worst."

"And my sister's child left no better off than a street beggar," suggested Miss Blake.

"Come, come," remonstrated Mr. Craven; "matters are not so bad as all that comes to. Upon three hundred a year, you can live very comfortable on the Continent; and—"

"We'll go," interrupted Miss Blake; "but it is hard lines—not that anything better could have been expected from Robert Elmsdale."

"Ah! dear Miss Blake, the poor fellow is dead. Remember only his virtues, and let his faults rest."

"I sha'n't have much to burden my memory with, then," retorted Miss Blake, and departed.

Her next letter to my principal was dated from Rouen; but before that reached Buckingham Street, our troubles had begun.

For some reason best known to himself, Mr. Treseby, the good-natured country squire possessed of a wife with an excellent digestion, at the end of two months handed us half a year's rent, and requested we should try to let the house for the remainder of his term, he, in case of our failure, continuing amenable for the rent. In the course of the three years we secured eight tenants, and as from each a profit in the way of forfeit accrued, we had not to trouble Mr. Treseby for any more money, and were also enabled to remit some small bonuses— which came to her, Miss Blake assured us, as godsends—to the Continent.

After that the place stood vacant for a time. Various caretakers were eager to obtain the charge of it, but I only remember one who was not eager to leave.

That was a night-watchman, who never went home except in the daytime, and then to sleep, and he failed to understand why his wife, who was a pretty, delicate little creature, and the mother of four small children, should quarrel with her bread and butter, and want to leave so fine a place.

He argued the matter with her in so practical a fashion, that the nearest magistrate had to be elected umpire between them.

The whole story of the place was repeated in court, and the night-watchman's wife, who sobbed during the entire time she stood in the witness-box, made light of her black eye and numerous bruises, but said, "Not if Tim murdered her, could she stay alone in the house another night."

To prevent him murdering her, he was sent to gaol for two months, and Mr. Craven allowed her eight shillings a week till Tim was once more a free man, when he absconded, leaving wife and children chargeable to the parish.

"A poor, nervous creature," said Mr. Craven, who would not believe that where gas was, any house could be ghost-ridden.

"We must really try to let the house in earnest."

And we did try, and we did let, over, and over, and over again, always with a like result, till at length Mr. Craven said to me: "Do you know, Patterson, I really am growing very uneasy about that house on the Thames. I am afraid some evil-disposed person is trying to keep it vacant."

"It certainly is very strange," was the only remark I felt capable of making.

We had joked so much about the house amongst ourselves, and ridiculed Miss Blake and her troubles to such an extent, that the matter bore no serious aspect for any of us juniors.

"If we are not soon able to let it," went on Mr. Craven, "I shall advise Miss Blake to auction off the furniture and sell the place. We must not always have an uninhabited house haunting our offices, Patterson."

I shook my head in grave assent, but all the time I was thinking the day when that house ceased to haunt our offices, would be a very dreary one for the wags amongst our clerks. "Yes, I certainly shall advise Miss Blake to sell," repeated Mr. Craven, slowly.

Although a hard-working man, he was eminently slow in his ideas and actions.

There was nothing express about our dear governor; upon no special mental train did he go careering through life. Eminently he preferred the parliamentary pace: and I am bound to say the life-journey so performed was beautiful exceedingly, with waits not devoid of interest at little stations utterly outside his profession, with kindly talk to little children, and timid women, and feeble men; with a pleasant smile for most with whom he came in contact, and time for words of kindly advice which did not fall perpetually on stony ground, but which sometimes grew to maturity, and produced rich grain of which himself beheld the garnering.

Nevertheless, to my younger and quicker nature, he did seem often very tardy.

"Why not advise her now?" I asked.

"Ah! my boy," he answered, "life is very short, yet it is long enough to have no need in it for hurry."

The same day, Colonel Morris appeared in our office. Within a fortnight, that gallant officer was our tenant; within a month, Mrs. Morris, an exceedingly fine lady, with grown-up children, with very young children also, with *ayahs*, with native servants, with English servants, with a list of acquaintances such as one may read of in the papers the day after a queen's drawing-room, took possession of the Uninhabited House, and, for about three months, peace reigned in our dominions.

Buckingham Street, as represented by us, stank in the nostrils of no human being.

So far we were innocent of offence, we were simply ordinary solicitors and clerks, doing as fully and truly as we knew how, an extremely good business at rates which yielded a very fair return to our principal.

The colonel was delighted with the place, he kindly called to say; so was Mrs. Morris; so were the grown-up sons and daughters of Colonel and Mrs. Morris; and so, it is to be presumed, were the infant branches of the family.

The native servants liked the place because Mr. Elmsdale, in view of his wife's delicate health, had made the house "like an oven," to quote Miss Blake. "It was bad for her, I know," proceeded that lady, "but she would have her own way, poor soul, and he—well, he'd have had the top brick of the chimney of a ten-story house off, if she had taken a fancy for that article."

Those stoves and pipes were a great bait to Colonel Morris, as well as a source of physical enjoyment to his servants.

He, too, had married a woman who was not always easy to please; but River Hall did please her, as was natural, with its luxuries of heat, ease, convenience, large rooms opening one out of another, wide verandahs overlooking the Thames, staircases easy of ascent; baths, hot, cold, and shower; a sweet, pretty garden, conservatory with a door leading into it from the spacious hall, all exceedingly cheap at two hundred pounds a year.

Accordingly, at first, the colonel was delighted with the place, and not the less so because Mrs. Morris was delighted with it, and because it was also so far from town, that he had a remarkably good excuse for frequently visiting his club.

Before the newcomers, local tradesmen bowed down and did worship.

Visitors came and visitors went, carriages appeared in shoals, and double-knocks were plentiful as blackberries. A fresh leaf had evidently been turned over at River Hall, and the place meant to give no more trouble for ever to Miss Blake, or Mr. Craven, or anybody. So, as I have said, three months passed. We had got well into the dog-days by that time; there was very little to do in the office. Mr. Craven had left for his annual holiday, which he always took in the company of his wife and daughters—a correct, but possibly a depressing, way of spending a vacation which must have been intended to furnish some social variety in a man's life; and we were all very idle, and all very much inclined to grumble at the heat, and length, and general slowness of the days, when one morning, as I was going out in order to send a parcel off to Mrs. Craven, who should I meet coming panting up the stairs but Miss Blake!

"Is that you, Patterson?" she gasped. I assured her it was I in the flesh, and intimated my astonishment at seeing her in hers.

"Why, I thought you were in France, Miss Blake," I suggested.

"That's where I have just come from," she said. "Is Mr. Craven in?" I told her he was out of town.

"Ay—that's where everybody can be but me," she remarked, plaintively. "They can go out and stay out, while I am at the beck and call of all the scum of the earth. Well, well, I suppose there will be quiet for me sometime, if only in my coffin."

As I failed to see that any consolatory answer was possible, I made no reply. I only asked:

"Won't you walk into Mr. Craven's office, Miss Blake?"

"Now, I wonder," she said, "what good you think walking into his office will do me!"

Nevertheless, she accepted the invitation. I have, in the course of years, seen many persons suffering from heat, but I never did see any human being in such a state as Miss Blake was that day.

Her face was a pure, rich red, from temple to chin; it resembled nothing so much as a brick which had been out for a long time, first in the sun and the wind, and then in a succession of heavy showers of rain. She looked weather-beaten, and sunburnt, and sprayed with salt-water, all at once. Her eyes were a lighter blue than I previously thought eyes could be. Her cheekbones stood out more prominently than I had thought cheekbones capable of doing. Her mouth—not quite a bad one, by the way—opened wider than any within my experience; and her teeth, white and exposed, were suggestive of a set of tombstones planted outside a stonemason's shop, or an upper and lower set exhibited at the entrance to a dentist's operating-room. Poor dear Miss Blake, she and those pronounced teeth parted company long ago, and a much more becoming set—which she got exceedingly cheap, by agreeing with the maker to "send the whole of the city of London to her, if he liked"—now occupy their place.

But on that especial morning they were very prominent. Everything, in fact, about the lady, or belonging to her, seemed exaggerated, as if the heat of the weather had induced a tropical growth of her mental and bodily peculiarities. Her bonnet was crooked beyond even the ordinary capacity of Miss Blake's head-gear; the strings were rolled up till they looked like ropes which had been knotted under her chin. A veil, as large and black as a pirate's flag, floated down her back; her shawl was at sixes and sevens; one side of her dress had got torn from the bodice, and trailed on the ground leaving a broadly-marked line of dust on the carpet. She looked as if she had no petticoats on; and her boots—those were the days ere side-springs and buttons obtained—were one laced unevenly, and the other tied on with a piece of ribbon.

As for her gloves, they were in the state we always beheld them; if she ever bought a new pair (which I do not believe), she never treated us to a sight of them till they had been long past decent service. They never were buttoned, to begin with;

they had a wrinkled and haggard appearance, as if from extreme old age. If their colour had originally been lavender, they were always black with dirt; if black, they were white with wear.

As a bad job, she had, apparently, years before, given up putting a stitch in the ends of the fingers, when a stitch gave way; and the consequence was that we were perfectly familiar with Miss Blake's nails—and those nails looked as if, at an early period of her life, a hammer had been brought heavily down upon them. Mrs. Elmsdale might well be a beauty, for she had taken not only her own share of the good looks of the family, but her sister's also.

We used often, at the office, to marvel why Miss Blake ever wore a collar, or a tucker, or a frill, or a pair of cuffs. So far as clean linen was concerned, she would have appeared infinitely brighter and fresher had she and female frippery at once parted company. Her laces were always in tatters, her collars soiled, her cuffs torn, and her frills limp. I wonder what the natives thought of her in France! In London, we decided—and accurately, I believe—that Miss Blake, in the solitude of her own chamber, washed and got-up her cambrics and fine linen—and it was a "get-up" and a "put-on" as well.

Had any other woman, dressed like Miss Blake, come to our office, I fear the clerks would not have been over-civil to her. But Miss Blake was our own, our very own. She had grown to be as our very flesh and blood. We did not love her, but she was associated with us by the closest ties that can subsist between lawyer and client. Had anything happened to Miss Blake, we should, in the event of her death, have gone in a body to her funeral, and felt a want in our lives for ever after.

But Miss Blake had not the slightest intention of dying: we were not afraid of that calamity. The only thing we really did dread was that some day she might insist upon laying the blame of River Hall remaining uninhabited on our shoulders, and demand that Mr. Craven should pay her the rent out of his own pocket.

We knew if she took that, or any other pecuniary matter,

seriously in hand, she would carry it through; and, between jest and earnest, we were wont to speculate whether, in the end, it might not prove cheaper to our firm if Mr. Craven were to farm that place, and pay Miss Blake's niece an annuity of say one hundred a year.

Ultimately we decided that it would, but that such a scheme was impracticable, because Miss Blake would always think we were making a fortune out of River Hall, and give us no peace till she had a share of the profit.

For a time, Miss Blake—after unfastening her bonnet-strings, and taking out her brooch and throwing back her shawl—sat fanning herself with a dilapidated glove, and saying, "Oh dear! oh dear! what is to become of me I cannot imagine." But, at length, finding I was not to be betrayed into questioning, she observed:

"If William Craven knew the distress I am in, he would not be out of town enjoying himself, I'll be bound."

"I am quite certain he would not," I answered, boldly. "But as he is away, is there nothing we can do for you?"

She shook her head mournfully. "You're all a parcel of boys and children together," was her comprehensive answer.

"But there is our manager, Mr. Taylor," I suggested.

"Him!" she exclaimed. "Now, if you don't want me to walk out of the office and never set foot in it again, don't talk to me about Taylor."

"Has Mr. Taylor offended you?" I ventured to inquire.

"Lads of your age should not ask too many questions," she replied. "What I have against Taylor is nothing to you; only don't make me desperate by mentioning his name."

I hastened to assure her that it should never be uttered by me again in her presence, and there ensued a pause, which she filled by looking round the office and taking a mental inventory of everything it contained.

Eventually, her survey ended in this remark, "And he can go out of town as well, and keep a brougham for his wife, and draw them daughters of his out like figures in a fashion-book, and my poor sister's child living in a two-pair lodging."

"I fear, Miss Blake," I ventured, "that something is the matter at River Hall."

"You fear, do you, young man?" she returned. "You ought to get a first prize for guessing. As if anything else could ever bring me back to London."

"Can I be of no service to you in the matter?"

"I don't think you can, but you may as well see his letter." And diving into the depths of her pocket, she produced Colonel Morris' communication, which was very short, but very much to the purpose.

"Not wishing," he said, "to behave in any unhandsome manner, I send you herewith" (herewith meant the keys of River Hall and his letter) "a cheque for one half-year's rent. You must know that, had I been aware of the antecedents of the place, I should never have become your tenant; and I must say, considering I have a wife in delicate health, and young children, the deception practised by your lawyers in concealing the fact that no previous occupant has been able to remain in the house, seems most unpardonable. I am a soldier, and, to me, these trade tricks appear dishonourable. Still, as I understand your position is an exceptional one, I am willing to forgive the wrong which has been done, and to pay six months' rent for a house I shall no longer occupy. In the event of these concessions appearing insufficient, I beg to enclose the names of my solicitors, and have the honour, madam, to remain

"Your most obedient servant,

"Hercules Morris."

In order to gain time, I read this letter twice over; then, diplomatically, as I thought, I said:

"What are you going to do, Miss Blake?"

"What are *you* going to do, is much nearer the point, I am thinking!" retorted that lady. "Do you imagine there is so much pleasure or profit in keeping a lawyer, that people want to do lawyer's work for themselves?"

Which really was hard upon us all, considering that so long as she could do her work for herself, Miss Blake ignored both Mr. Craven and his clerks.

Not a shilling of money would she ever, if she could help it, permit to pass through our hands—not the slightest chance did she ever voluntarily give Mr. Craven of recouping himself those costs or loans in which her acquaintance involved her sister's former suitor.

Had he felt any inclination—which I am quite certain he never did—to deduct Miss Helena's indebtedness, as represented by her aunt, out of Miss Helena's income, he could not have done it. The tenant's money usually went straight into Miss Blake's hands.

What she did with it, Heaven only knows. I know she did not buy herself gloves!

Twirling the colonel's letter about, I thought the position over.

"What, then," I asked, "do you wish us to do?"

Habited as I have attempted to describe, Miss Blake sat at one side of a library-table. In, I flatter myself, a decent suit of clothes, washed, brushed, shaved, I sat on the other. To ordinary observers, I know I must have seemed much the best man of the two—yet Miss Blake got the better of me.

She, that dilapidated, red-hot, crumpled-collared, fingerless-gloved woman, looked me over from head to foot, as I conceived, though my boots were hidden away under the table, and I declare—I swear—she put me out of countenance. I felt small under the stare of a person with whom I would not then have walked through Hyde Park in the afternoon for almost any amount of money which could have been offered to me.

"Though you are only a clerk," she said at length, apparently quite unconscious of the effect she had produced, "you seem a very decent sort of young man. As Mr. Craven is out of the way, suppose you go and see that Morris man, and ask him what he means by his impudent letter."

I rose to the bait. Being in Mr. Craven's employment, it is unnecessary to say I, in common with every other person about the place, thought I could manage his business for him very much better than he could manage it for himself; and it had always been my own personal conviction that if the letting of the Uninhabited House were entrusted to me, the place would not stand long empty.

Miss Blake's proposition was, therefore, most agreeable; but still, I did not at once swallow her hook. Mr. Craven, I felt, might scarcely approve of my taking it upon myself to call upon Colonel Morris while Mr. Taylor was able and willing to venture upon such a step, and I therefore suggested to our client the advisability of first asking Mr. Craven's opinion about the affair.

"And keep me in suspense while you are writing and answering and running up a bill as long as Midsummer Day," she retorted. "No, thank you. If you don't think my business worth your attention, I'll go to somebody that may be glad of it." And she began tying her strings and feeling after her shawl in a manner which looked very much indeed like carrying out her threat.

At that moment I made up my mind to consult Taylor as to what ought to be done. So I appeased Miss Blake by assuring her, in a diplomatic manner, that Colonel Morris should be visited, and promising to communicate the result of the interview by letter.

"That you won't," she answered. "I'll be here tomorrow to know what he has to say for himself. He is just tired of the house, like the rest of them, and wants to be rid of his bargain."

"I am not quite sure of that," I said, remembering my principal's suggestion. "It is strange, if there really is nothing objectionable about the house, that *no one* can be found to stay in it. Mr. Craven has hinted that he fancies some evil-disposed person must be playing tricks, in order to frighten tenants away."

"It is likely enough," she agreed. "Robert Elmsdale had plenty of enemies and few friends; but that is no reason why we should starve, is it?"

I failed to see the logical sequence of Miss Blake's remark, nevertheless I did not dare to tell her so; and agreed it was no reason why she and her niece should be driven into that workhouse which she frequently declared they "must come to."

"Remember," were her parting words, "I shall be here tomorrow morning early, and expect you to have good news for me."

Inwardly resolving not to be in the way, I said I hoped there would be good news for her, and went in search of Taylor.

"Miss Blake has been here," I began. "THE HOUSE is empty again. Colonel Morris has sent her half a year's rent, the keys, and the address of his solicitors. He says we have acted disgracefully in the matter, and she wants me to go and see him, and declares she will be back here first thing tomorrow morning to know what he has to say for himself. What ought I to do?"

Before Mr. Taylor answered my question, he delivered himself of a comprehensive anathema which included Miss Blake, River Hall, the late owner, and ourselves. He further wished he might be essentially *etceteraed* if he believed there was another solicitor, besides Mr. Craven, in London who would allow such a hag to haunt his offices.

"Talk about River Hall being haunted," he finished; "it is we who are witch-ridden, I call it, by that old Irishwoman. She ought to be burnt at Smithfield. I'd be at the expense of the faggots!"

"What have you and Miss Blake quarrelled about?" I inquired. "You say she is a witch, and she has made me take a solemn oath never to mention your name again in her presence."

"I'd keep her presence out of these offices, if I was Mr. Craven," he answered. "She has cost us more than the whole freehold of River Hall is worth."

Something in his manner, more than in his words, made me comprehend that Miss Blake had borrowed money from him, and not repaid it, so I did not press for further explanation, but only asked him once again what I ought to do about calling upon Colonel Morris.

"Call, and be hanged, if you like!" was the reply; and as Mr.

Taylor was not usually a man given to violent language, I understood that Miss Blake's name acted upon his temper with the same magical effect as a red rag does upon that of a turkey-cock.

4. Myself and Miss Blake

Colonel Morris, after leaving River Hall, had migrated temporarily to a fashionable West End hotel, and was, when I called to see him, partaking of *tiffin* in the bosom of his family, instead of at his club.

As it was notorious that he and Mrs. Morris failed to lead the most harmonious of lives, I did not feel surprised to find him in an extremely bad temper.

In person, short, dapper, wiry, thin, and precise, his manner matched his appearance. He had martinet written on every square foot of his figure. His moustache was fiercely waxed, his shirt-collar inflexible, his backbone stiff, while his shoulder-blades met flat and even behind. He held his chin a little up in the air, and his walk was less a march than a strut.

He came into the room where I had been waiting for him, as I fancied he might have come on a wet, cold morning to meet an awkward-squad. He held the card I sent for his inspection in his hand, and referred to it, after he had looked me over with a supercilious glance.

"Mr. Patterson, from Messrs. Craven and Son," he read slowly out loud, and then added:

"May I inquire what Mr. Patterson from Messrs. Craven and Son wants with me?"

"I come from Miss Blake, sir," I remarked.

"It is here written that you come from Messrs. Craven and Son," he said.

"So I do, sir—upon Miss Blake's business. She is a client of ours, as you may remember."

"I do remember. Go on."

He would not sit down himself or ask me to be seated, so we stood throughout the interview. I with my hat in my hand, he twirling his moustache or scrutinising his nails while he talked.

"Miss Blake has received a letter from you, sir, and has requested me to ask you for an explanation of it."

"I have no further explanation to give," he replied.

"But as you took the house for two years, we cannot advise Miss Blake to allow you to relinquish possession in consideration of your having paid her six months' rent."

"Very well. Then you can advise her to fight the matter, as I suppose you will. I am prepared to fight it."

"We never like fighting, if a matter can be arranged amicably," I answered. "Mr. Craven is at present out of town; but I know I am only speaking his words, when I say we shall be glad to advise Miss Blake to accept any reasonable proposition which you may feel inclined to make."

"I have sent her half a year's rent," was his reply; "and I have refrained from prosecuting you all for conspiracy, as I am told I might have done. Lawyers, I am aware, admit they have no consciences, and I can make some allowance for a person in Miss Blake's position, otherwise."

"Yes, sir?" I said, interrogatively.

"I should never have paid one penny. It has, I find, been a well-known fact to Mr. Craven, as well as to Miss Blake, that no tenant can remain in River Hall. When my wife was first taken ill there—in consequence of the frightful shock she received—I sent for the nearest medical man, and he refused to come; absolutely sent me a note, saying, 'he was very sorry, but he must decline to attend Mrs. Morris. Doubtless, she had her own physician, who would be happy to devote himself to the case.'"

"And what did you do?" I asked, my pulses tingling with awakened curiosity.

"Do!" he repeated, pleased, perhaps, to find so appreciative a listener. "I sent, of course, for the best advice to be had in London, and I went to the local doctor—a man who keeps a surgery and dispenses medicines—myself, to ask what he meant by returning such an insolent message in answer to my summons. And what do you suppose he said by way of apology?"

"I cannot imagine," I replied.

"He said he would not for ten times over the value of all the River Hall patients, attend a case in the house again. 'No person can live in it,' he went on, 'and keep his, her, or its health. Whether it is the river, or the drains, or the late owner, or the devil, I have not an idea. I can only tell you no one has been able to remain in it since Mr. Elmsdale's death, and if I attend a case there, of course I say, Get out of this at once. Then comes Miss Blake and threatens me with assault and battery—swears she will bring an action against me for libelling the place; declares I wish to drive her and her niece to the workhouse, and asserts I am in league with someone who wants to keep the house vacant, and I am sick of it. Get what doctor you choose, but don't send for me.'"

"Well, sir?" I suggested.

"Well! I don't consider it well at all. Here am I, a man returning to his native country—and a beastly country it is!—after nearly thirty years' absence, and the first transaction upon which I engage proves a swindle. Yes, a swindle, Mr. Patterson. I went to you in all good faith, took that house at your own rent, thought I had got a desirable home, and believed I was dealing with respectable people, and now I find I was utterly deceived, both as regards the place and your probity. You knew the house was uninhabitable, and yet you let it to me."

"I give you my word," I said, "that we really do not know yet in what way the house is uninhabitable. It is a good house, as you know; it is well furnished; the drainage is perfect; so far as we are concerned, we do not believe a fault can be found with the place. Still, it has been a fact that tenants will not stay in it, and we were therefore glad to let it to a gentleman like yourself, who would, we expected, prove above subscribing to that which can only be a vulgar prejudice."

"What is a vulgar prejudice?" he asked.

"The idea that River Hall is haunted," I replied.

"River Hall is haunted, young man," he said, solemnly.

"By what?" I asked.

"By someone who cannot rest in his grave," was the answer.

171

"Colonel Morris," I said, "someone *must* be playing tricks in the house."

"If so, that someone does not belong to this world," he remarked.

"Do you mean really and seriously to tell me you believe in ghosts?" I asked, perhaps a little scornfully.

"I do, and if you had lived in River Hall, you would believe in them too," he replied. "I will tell you," he went on, "what I saw in the house myself. You know the library?"

I nodded in assent. We did know the library. There our trouble seemed to have taken up its abode.

"Are you aware lights have frequently been reflected from that room, when no light has actually been in it?"

I could only admit this had occasionally proved a ground of what we considered unreasonable complaint.

"One evening," went on the colonel, "I determined to test the matter for myself. Long before dusk I entered the room and examined it thoroughly—saw to the fastenings of the windows, drew up the blinds, locked the door, and put the key in my pocket. After dinner I took a cigar and walked up and down the grass path beside the river, until dark. There was no light—not a sign of light of any kind, as I turned once more and walked up the path again; but as I was retracing my steps I saw that the room was brilliantly illuminated. I rushed to the nearest window and looked in. The gas was all ablaze, the door of the strong room open, the table strewed with papers, while in an office-chair drawn close up to the largest drawer, a man was seated counting over bank-notes. He had a pile of them before him, and I distinctly saw that he wetted his fingers in order to separate them."

"Most extraordinary!" I exclaimed. I could not decently have said anything less; but I confess that I had in my recollection the fact of Colonel Morris having dined.

"The most extraordinary part of the story is still to come," he remarked. "I hurried at once into the house, unlocked the door, found the library in pitch darkness, and when I lit the gas the strong room was closed; there was no office-chair in the room, no papers were on the table—everything, in fact, was precisely in the same condition as I had left it a few hours before. Now, no person in the flesh could have performed such a feat as that."

"I cannot agree with you there," I ventured. "It seems to me less difficult to believe the whole thing a trick, than to attribute the occurrence to supernatural agency. In fact, while I do not say it is impossible for ghosts to be, I cannot accept the fact of their existence."

"Well, I can, then," retorted the colonel. "Why, sir, once at the Cape of Good Hope—" but there he paused. Apparently he recollected just in time that the Cape of Good Hope was a long way from River Hall.

"And Mrs. Morris," I suggested, leading him back to the banks of the Thames. "You mentioned some shock—"

"Yes," he said, frankly. "She met the same person on the staircase I saw in the library. He carried in one hand a lighted candle, and in the other a bundle of bank-notes. He never looked at her as he passed—never turned his head to the spot where she stood gazing after him in a perfect access of terror, but walked quietly downstairs, crossed the hall, and went straight into the library without opening the door. She fainted dead away, and has never known an hour's good health since."

"According to all accounts, she had not before, or good temper either," I thought; but I only said, "You had told Mrs. Morris, I presume, of your adventure in the library?"

"No," he answered; "I had not; I did not mention it to anyone except a brother officer, who dined with me the next evening."

"Your conversation with him might have been overheard, I suppose," I urged.

"It is possible, but scarcely probable," he replied. "At all events, I am quite certain it never reached my wife's ears, or she would not have stayed another night in the house."

I stood for a few moments irresolute, but then I spoke. I told him how much we—meaning Messrs. Craven and Son—his manager and his cashier, and his clerks, regretted the inconvenience to which he had been put; delicately I touched upon the concern we felt at hearing of Mrs. Morris' illness. But, I added, I feared his explanation, courteous and ample as it had been, would not satisfy Miss Blake, and trusted he might, upon consideration, feel disposed to compromise the matter.

"We," I added, "will be only too happy to recommend our client to accept any reasonable proposal you may think it well to make."

Whereupon it suddenly dawned upon the colonel that he had been showing me all his hand, and forthwith he adopted a very natural course. He ordered me to leave the room and the hotel, and not to show my face before him again at my peril. And I obeyed his instructions to the letter.

On the same evening of that day I took a long walk round by the Uninhabited House.

There it was, just as I had seen it last, with high brick walls dividing it from the road; with its belt of forest-trees separating it from the next residence, with its long frontage to the river, with its closed gates and shuttered postern-door.

The entrance to it was not from the main highway, but from a lane which led right down to the Thames; and I went to the very bottom of that lane and swung myself by means of a post right over the river, so that I might get a view of the windows of the room with which so ghostly a character was associated. The blinds were all down and the whole place looked innocent enough.

The strong, sweet, subtle smell of mignonette came wafted to my senses, the odours of jessamine, roses, and myrtle floated to me on the evening breeze. I could just catch a glimpse of the flower-gardens, radiant with colour, full of leaf and bloom.

"No haunted look there," I thought. "The house is right enough, but someone must have determined to keep it empty." And then I swung myself back into the lane again, and the shadow of the high brick wall projected itself across my mind as it did across my body.

"Is this place to let again, do you know?" said a voice in my ear, as I stood looking at the private door which gave a separate entrance to that evil-reputed library.

The question was a natural one, and the voice not unpleasant, yet I started, having noticed no one near me.

"I beg your pardon," said the owner of the voice. "Nervous, I fear!"

"No, not at all, only my thoughts were wandering. I beg your pardon—I do not know whether the place is to let or not."

"A good house?" This might have been interrogative, or uttered as an assertion, but I took it as the former, and answered accordingly.

"Yes, a good house—a very good house, indeed," I said.

"It is often vacant, though," he said, with a light laugh.

"Through no fault of the house," I added.

"Oh! it is the fault of the tenants, is it?" he remarked, laughing once more. "The owners, I should think, must be rather tired of their property by this time."

"I do not know that," I replied. "They live in hope of finding a good and sensible tenant willing to take it."

"And equally willing to keep it, eh?" he remarked. "Well, I, perhaps, am not much of a judge in the matter, but I should say they will have to wait a long time first."

"You know something about the house?" I said, interrogatively.

"Yes," he answered, "most people about here do, I fancy—but least said soonest mended"; and as by this time we had reached the top of the lane, he bade me a civil good-evening, and struck off in a westerly direction.

Though the light of the setting sun shone full in my face, and I had to shade my eyes in order to enable me to see at all, moved by some feeling impossible to analyse, I stood watching that retreating figure. Afterwards I could have sworn to the man among ten thousand.

A man of about fifty, well and plainly dressed, who did not appear to be in ill-health, yet whose complexion had a blanched look, like forced sea-kale; a man of under, rather than over middle height, not of slight make, but lean as if the flesh had been all worn off his bones; a man with sad, anxious, outlooking, abstracted eyes, with a nose slightly hooked, without a trace of whisker, with hair thin and straight and flaked with white, active and lithe in his movements, a swift walker, though he had a slight halt. While looking at him thrown up in relief against the glowing western sky, I noticed, what had previously escaped my attention, that he was a little deformed. His right shoulder was rather higher than the other. A man with a story in his memory, I imagined; a man who had been jilted by the girl he loved, or who had lost her by death, or whose wife had proved faithless; whose life, at all events, had been marred by a great trouble. So, in my folly, I decided; for I was young then, and romantic, and had experienced some sorrow myself connected with pecuniary matters.

For the latter reason, it never perhaps occurred to me to associate the trouble of my new acquaintance, if he could be so called, with money annoyances. I knew, or thought I knew, at all events, the expression loss of fortune stamps on a man's face; and the look which haunted me for days after had nothing in it of discontent, or self-assertion, or struggling gentility, or vehement protest against the decrees of fortune. Still less was it submissive. As I have said, it haunted me for days, then the memory grew less vivid, then I forgot the man altogether. Indeed, we shortly became so absorbed in the fight between Miss Blake and Colonel Morris, that we had little time to devote to the consideration of other matters.

True to her promise, Miss Blake appeared next morning in Buckingham Street. Without bestowing upon me even the courtesy of "good morning," she plunged into the subject next her heart.

"Did you see him?" she asked.

I told her I had. I repeated much of what he said; I assured her he was determined to fight the matter, and that although I did really not think any jury would give a verdict in his favour, still I believed, if the matter came into court, it would prevent our ever letting the house again.

"I should strongly recommend you, Miss Blake," I finished, "to keep what he offers, and let us try and find another tenant."

"And who asked you to recommend anything, you fast young man?" she demanded. "I am sure I did not, and I am very sure Mr. Craven would not be best pleased to know his clerks were setting themselves up higher than their master. You would never find William Craven giving himself airs such as you young whipper-snappers think make you seem of some consequence. I just tell him what I want done, and he does it, and you will please to do the same, and serve a writ on that villain without an hour's delay."

I asked on what grounds we were to serve the writ. I pointed out that Colonel Morris did not owe her a penny, and would not owe her a penny for some months to come; and in reply she said she would merely inquire if I meant that she and her poor niece were to go to the workhouse.

To this I answered that the amount already remitted by Colonel Morris would prevent such a calamity, but she stopped my attempt at consolation by telling me not to talk about things I did not understand.

"Give me William Craven's address," she added, "and I will write to him direct. I wonder what he means by leaving a parcel of ignorant boys to attend to his clients while he is away enjoying himself! Give me his address, and some paper and an envelope, and I can write my letter here."

I handed her the paper and the envelope, and placed pen and ink conveniently before her, but I declined to give her Mr. Craven's address. We would forward the letter, I said; but when Mr. Craven went away for his holiday, he was naturally anxious to leave business behind as much as possible.

Then Miss Blake took steady aim, and fired at me. Broadside after broadside did she pour into my unprotected ears; she opened the vials of her wrath and overwhelmed me with reproaches; she raked up all the grievances she had for years been cherishing against England, and by some sort of verbal legerdemain made me responsible for every evil she could recollect as ever having happened to her. Her sister's marriage, her death, Mr. Elmsdale's suicide, the unsatisfactory state of his affairs, the prejudice against River Hall, the defection of Colonel Morris— all these things she laid at my door, and insisted on making me responsible for them.

"And now," she finished, pushing back her bonnet and pulling off her gloves, "I'll just write my opinion of you to Mr. Craven, and I'll wait till you direct the envelope, and I'll go with you to the post, and I'll see you put the letter in the box. If you and your fine Colonel Morris think you can frighten or flatter me, you are both much mistaken, I can tell you that!"

I did not answer her. I was too greatly affronted to express what I felt in words. I sat on the other side of the table—for I would not leave her alone in Mr. Craven's office—sulking, while she wrote her letter, which she did in a great, fat, splashing sort of hand, with every other word underlined; and when she had done, and tossed the missive over to me, I directed it, took my hat, and prepared to accompany her to the Charing Cross office.

We went down the staircase together in silence, up Buckingham Street, across the Strand, and so to Charing Cross, where she saw me drop the letter into the box. All this time we did not exchange a syllable, but when, after raising my hat, I was about to turn away, she seized hold of my arm, and said, "Don't let us part in bad blood. Though you are only a clerk, you have got your feelings, no doubt, and if in my temper I hurt them, I am sorry. Can I say more? You are a decent lad enough, as times go in England, and my bark is worse than my bite. I didn't write a word about you to William Craven. Shake hands, and don't bear malice to a poor lonely woman."

Thus exhorted, I took her hand and shook it, and then, in token of entire amity, she told me she had forgotten to bring her purse with her and could I let her have a sovereign. She would pay me, she declared solemnly, the first day she came again to the office.

This of course I did not believe in the least, nevertheless I gave her what she required—and Heaven knows, sovereigns were scarce enough with me then—thankfully, and felt sincerely obliged to her for making herself my debtor. Miss Blake did sometimes ruffle one's feathers most confoundedly, and yet I knew it would have grieved me had we parted in enmity.

Sometimes, now, when I look upon her quiet and utterly respectable old age—when I contemplate her pathetic grey hair and conventional lace cap—when I view her clothed like other people and in her right mind, I am very glad indeed to remember I had no second thought about that sovereign, but gave it to her—with all the veins of my heart, as she would have emphasised the proceeding.

"Though you have no name to speak of," observed Miss Blake as she pocketed the coin, "I think there must be some sort of blood in you. I knew Pattersons once who were connected by marriage with a great duke in the west of Ireland. Can you say if by chance you can trace relationship to any of them?"

"I can say most certainly not, Miss Blake," I replied. "We are Pattersons of nowhere and relations of no one."

"Well, well," remarked the lady, pityingly, "you can't help that, poor lad. And if you attend to your duties, you may yet be a rich City alderman."

With which comfort she left me, and wended her homeward way through St. Martin's Lane and the Seven Dials.

Chapter 5

The Trial

Next day but one Mr. Craven astonished us all by walking into the office about ten o'clock. He looked stout and well, sunburnt to a degree, and all the better physically for his trip to the seaside. We were unfeignedly glad to see him. Given a good employer, and it must be an extremely bad *employé* who rejoices in his absence. If we were not saints, we were none of us very black sheep, and accordingly, from the porter to the managing clerk, our faces brightened at sight of our principal.

But after the first genial "how are you" and "good morning,"

Mr. Craven's face told tales: he had come back out of sorts. He was vexed about Miss Blake's letter, and, astonishing to relate, he was angry with me for having called upon Colonel Morris.

"You take too much upon you, Patterson," he remarked. "It is a growing habit with you, and you must try to check it."

I did not answer him by a word; my heart seemed in my mouth; I felt as if I was choking. I only inclined my head in token that I heard and understood, and assented; then, having, fortunately, work to attend to out of doors, I seized an early opportunity of slipping down the staircase and walking off to Chancery Lane. When I returned, after hours, to Buckingham Street, one of the small boys in the outer office told me I was to go to Mr. Craven's room directly.

"You'll catch it," remarked the young fiend. "He has asked for you a dozen times, at least."

"What can be wrong now?" I thought, as I walked straight along the passage to Mr. Craven's office.

"Patterson," he said, as I announced my return.

"Yes, sir?"

"I spoke hastily to you this morning, and I regret having done so."

"Oh! sir," I cried. And that was all. We were better friends than ever. Do you wonder that I liked my principal? If so, it is only because I am unable to portray him as he really was. The age of chivalry is past; but still it is no exaggeration to say I would have died cheerfully if my dying could have served Mr. Craven.

Life holds me now by many and many a nearer and dearer tie than was the case in those days so far and far away; nevertheless, I would run any risk, encounter any peril, if by so doing I could serve the man who in my youth treated me with a kindness far beyond my deserts.

He did not, when he came suddenly to town in this manner, stop at his own house, which was, on such occasions, given over to charwomen and tradespeople of all descriptions; but he put up at an old-fashioned family hotel where, on that especial evening, he asked me to dine with him.

Over dessert he opened his mind to me on the subject of the "Uninhabited House." He said the evil was becoming one of serious magnitude. He declared he could not imagine what the result might prove. "With all the will in the world," he said, "to assist Miss Blake and that poor child, I cannot undertake to provide for them. Something must be done in the affair, and I am sure I cannot see what that something is to be. Since Mr. Elmsdale bought the place, the neighbourhood has gone down. If we sold the freehold as it stands, I fear we should not get more than a thousand pounds for it, and a thousand pounds would not last Miss Blake three years; as for supposing she could live on the interest, that is out of the question. The ground might be cut up and let for business purposes, of course, but that would be a work of time. I confess, I do not know what to think about the matter or how to act in it."

"Do you suppose the place really is haunted?" I ventured to inquire.

"Haunted?—pooh! nonsense," answered Mr. Craven, pettishly. "Do I suppose this room is haunted; do I believe my offices are haunted? No sane man has faith in any folly of the kind; but the place has got a bad name; I suspect it is unhealthy, and the tenants, when they find that out, seize on the first excuse which offers. It is known we have compromised a good many tenancies, and I am afraid we shall have to fight this case, if only to show we do not intend being patient forever. Besides, we shall exhaust the matter: we shall hear what the ghost-seers have to say for themselves on oath. There is little doubt of our getting a verdict, for the British juryman is, as a rule, not imaginative."

"I think we shall get a verdict," I agreed; "but I fancy we shall never get another tenant."

"There are surely as good fish in the sea as ever came out of it," he answered, with a smile; "and we shall come across some worthy country squire, possessed of pretty daughters, who will be delighted to find so cheap and sweet a nest for his birds, when they want to be near London."

"I wish sir," I said, "you would see Colonel Morris yourself. I am quite certain that every statement he made to me is true in his belief. I do not say, I believe him; I only say, what he told me justifies the inference that someone is playing a clever game in River Hall," and then I repeated in detail all the circumstances Colonel Morris had communicated to me, not excepting the wonderful phenomenon witnessed by Mr. Morris, of a man walking through a closed door.

Mr. Craven listened to me in silence, then he said, "I will not see Colonel Morris. What you tell me only confirms my opinion that we must fight this question. If he and his witnesses adhere to the story you repeat, on oath, I shall then have some tangible ground upon which to stand with Miss Blake. If they do not—and, personally, I feel satisfied no one who told such a tale could stand the test of cross-examination—we shall then have defeated the hidden enemy who, as I believe, lurks behind all this. Miss Blake is right in what she said to you: Robert Elmsdale must have had many a good hater. Whether he ever inspired that different sort of dislike which leads a man to carry on a war in secret, and try to injure this opponent's family after death, I have no means of knowing. But we must test the matter now, Patterson, and I think you had better call upon Colonel Morris and tell him so."

This service, however, to Mr. Craven's intense astonishment, I utterly declined.

I told him—respectfully, of course: under no possible conditions of life could I have spoken other than respectfully to a master I loved so well—that if a message were to be delivered *viva voce* from our office, it could not be so delivered by me.

I mentioned the fact that I felt no desire to be kicked downstairs. I declared that I should consider it an unseemly thing for me to engage in personal conflict with a gentleman of Colonel Morris's years and social position, and, as a final argument, I stated solemnly that I believed no number of interviews would change the opinions of our late tenant or induce him to alter his determination.

"He says he will fight," I remarked, as a finish to my speech, "and I am confident he will till he drops."

"Well, well," said Mr. Craven, "I suppose he must do so then; but meantime it is all very hard upon me."

And, indeed, so it proved; what with Miss Blake, who, of course, required frequent advances to sustain her strength during the approaching ordeal; what with policemen, who could not "undertake to be always a-watching River Hall"; what with watchmen, who kept their vigils in the nearest public-house as long as it was open, and then peacefully returned home to sleep; what with possible tenants, who came to us imagining the place was to let, and whom we referred to Colonel Morris, who dismissed them, each and all, with a tale which disenchanted them with the "desirable residence"—it was all exceeding hard upon Mr. Craven and his clerks till the quarter turned when we could take action about the matter.

Before the new year was well commenced, we were in the heat of the battle. We had written to Colonel Morris, applying for one quarter's rent of River Hall. A disreputable blackguard of a solicitor would have served him with a writ; but we were eminently respectable: not at the bidding of Her most gracious Majesty, whose name we invoked on many and many of our papers, would Mr. Craven have dispensed with the preliminary letter; and I feel bound to say I follow in his footsteps in that respect.

To this notice, Colonel Morris replied, referring us to his solicitors.

We wrote to them, eliciting a reply to the effect that they would receive service of a writ. We served that writ, and then, as Colonel Morris intended to fight, instructed counsel.

Meanwhile the "Uninhabited House," and the furniture it contained, was, as Mr. Taylor tersely expressed the matter, "Going to the devil."

We could not help that, however—war was put upon us, and go to war we felt we must.

Which was all extremely hard upon Mr. Craven. To my

183

knowledge, he had already, in three months, advanced thirty pounds to Miss Blake, besides allowing her to get into his debt for counsel's fees, and costs out of pocket, and cab hire, and Heaven knows what besides—with a problematical result also. Colonel Morris' solicitors were sparing no expenses to crush us. Clearly they, in a blessed vision, beheld an enormous bill, paid without difficulty or question. Fifty guineas here or there did not signify to their client, whilst to us—well, really, let a lawyer be as kind and disinterested as he will, fifty guineas disbursed upon the suit of an utterly insolvent, or persistently insolvent, client means something eminently disagreeable to him.

Nevertheless, we were all heartily glad to know the day of war was come. Body and soul, we all went in for Miss Blake, and Helena, and the "Uninhabited House." Even Mr. Taylor relented, and was to be seen rushing about with papers in hand relating to the impending suit of Blake *v.* Morris.

"She is a blank, blank woman," he remarked to me; "but still the case is interesting. I don't think ghosts have ever before come into court in my experience."

And we were all of the same mind. We girt up our loins for the fight. Each of us, I think, on the strength of her celebrity, lent Miss Blake a few shillings, and one or two of our number franked her to luncheon.

She patronized us all, I know, and said she should like to tell our mothers they had reason to be proud of their sons. And then came a dreadfully solemn morning, when we went to Westminster and championed Miss Blake.

Never in our memory of the lady had she appeared to such advantage as when we met her in Edward the Confessor's Hall. She looked a little paler than usual, and we felt her general get-up was a credit to our establishment. She wore an immense fur tippet, which, though then of an obsolete fashion, made her look like a three-*per-cent.* annuitant going to receive her dividends. Her throat was covered with a fine white lawn handkerchief; her dress was mercifully long enough to conceal her boots; her bonnet was perfectly straight, and the strings tied by someone who understood that bows should be pulled out and otherwise fancifully manipulated. As she carried a muff as large as a big drum, she had conceived the happy idea of dispensing altogether with gloves, and I saw that one of the fingers she gave me to shake was adorned with a diamond ring.

"Miss Elmsdale's," whispered Taylor to me. "It belonged to her mother."

Hearing which, I understood Helena had superintended her aunt's toilet.

"Did you ever see Miss Elmsdale?" I inquired of our manager.

"Not for years," was the answer. "She bade fair to be pretty."

"Why does not Miss Blake bring her out with her sometimes?" I asked.

"I believe she is expecting the queen to give her assent to her marrying the Prince of Wales," explained Taylor, "and she does not wish her to appear much in public until after the wedding."

The court was crammed. Somehow it had got into the papers—probably through Colonel Morris' gossips at the club—that ours was likely to prove a very interesting case, and though the morning was damp and wretched, ladies and gentlemen had turned out into the fog and drizzle, as ladies and gentlemen will when there seems the least chance of a new sensation being provided for them.

Further, there were lots of reporters.

"It will be in every paper throughout the kingdom," groaned Taylor. "We had better by far have left the colonel alone."

That had always been my opinion, but I only said, "Well, it is of no use looking back now."

I glanced at Mr. Craven, and saw he was ill at ease. We had considerable faith in ourselves, our case, and our counsel; but, then, we could not be blind to the fact that Colonel Morris' counsel were men very much better known than our men—that a cloud of witnesses, thirsting to avenge themselves for the rent we had compelled them to pay for an uninhabitable house, were hovering about the court—(had we not seen and recognized them in the Hall?)—that, in fact, there were two very distinct sides to the question, one represented by Colonel Morris and his party, and the other by Miss Blake and ourselves.

Of course our case lay in a nutshell. We had let the place, and Colonel Morris had agreed to take it. Colonel Morris now wanted to be rid of his bargain, and we were determined to keep him to it. Colonel Morris said the house was haunted, and that no one could live in it. We said the house was not haunted, and that anybody could live in it; that River Hall was "in every respect suited for the residence of a family of position"—see advertisements in *Times* and *Morning Post*.

Now, if the reader will kindly consider the matter, it must be an extremely difficult thing to prove, in a court of law, that a house, by reason solely of being haunted, is unsuitable for the residence of a gentleman of position.

Smells, bad drainage, impure water, unhealthiness of situation, dampness, the absence of advantages mentioned, the presence of small game—more odious to tenants of furnished houses than ground game to farmers—all these things had, we knew, been made pretexts for repudiation of contracts, and often successfully, but we could find no precedent for ghosts being held as just pleas upon which to relinquish a tenancy; and we made sure of a favourable verdict accordingly.

To this day, I believe that our hopes would have been justified by the result, had some demon of mischief not put it into the head of Taylor—who had the management of the case—that it would be a good thing to get Miss Blake into the witness-box.

"She will amuse the jury," he said, "and juries have always a kindly feeling for any person who can amuse them."

Which was all very well, and might be very true in a general way, but Miss Blake proved the exception to his rule.

Of course she amused the jury, in fact, she amused everyone. To get her to give a straightforward answer to any question was simply impossible.

Over and over again the judge explained to her that "yes" or "no" would be amply sufficient; but all in vain. She launched out at large in reply to our counsel, who, nevertheless, when he sat down, had gained his point.

Miss Blake declared upon oath she had never seen anything worse than herself at River Hall, and did not believe anybody else ever had.

She had never been there during Colonel Morris' tenancy, or she must certainly have seen something worse than a ghost, a man ready and anxious to "rob the orphan," and she was going to add the "widow" when peals of laughter stopped her utterance. Miss Blake had no faith in ghosts resident at River Hall, and if anybody was playing tricks about the house, she should have thought a "fighting gentleman by profession" capable of getting rid of them.

"Unless he was afraid," added Miss Blake, with withering irony.

Then up rose the opposition counsel, who approached her in an easy, conversational manner.

"And so you do not believe in ghosts, Miss Blake?" he began.

"Indeed and I don't," she answered.

"But if we have not ghosts, what is to become of the literature of your country?" he inquired.

"I don't know what you mean, by talking about my country," said Miss Blake, who was always proclaiming her nationality, and quarrelling with those who discovered it without such proclamation.

"I mean," he explained, "that all the fanciful legends and beautiful stories for which Ireland is celebrated have their origin in the supernatural. There are, for instance, several old families who have their traditional banshee."

"For that matter, we have one ourselves," agreed Miss Blake, with conscious pride.

At this junction our counsel interposed with a suggestion that there was no insinuation about any banshee residing at River Hall.

"No, the question is about a ghost, and I am coming to that. Different countries have different usages. In Ireland, as Miss Blake admits, there exists a very ladylike spirit, who announces the coming death of any member of certain families. In England, we have ghosts, who appear after the death of some members of some families. Now, Miss Blake, I want you to exercise your memory. Do you remember a night in the November after Mr. Elmsdale's death?"

"I remember many nights in many months that I passed broken-hearted in that house," she answered, composedly; but she grew very pale; and feeling there was something unexpected behind both question and answer, our counsel looked at us, and we looked back at him, dismayed.

"Your niece, being nervous, slept in the same room as that occupied by you?" continued the learned gentleman.

"She did," said Miss Blake. Her answer was short enough, and direct enough, at last.

"Now, on the particular November night to which I refer, do you recollect being awakened by Miss Elmsdale?"

"She wakened me many a time," answered Miss Blake, and I noticed that she looked away from her questioner, and towards the gallery.

"Exactly so; but on one especial night she woke you, saying, her father was walking along the passage; that she knew his step, and that she heard his keys strike against the wall?"

"Yes, I remember that," said Miss Blake, with suspicious alacrity. "She kept me up till daybreak. She was always thinking about him, poor child."

"Very natural indeed," commented our adversary. "And you told her not to be foolish, I daresay, and very probably tried to reassure her by saying one of the servants must have passed; and no doubt, being a lady possessed of energy and courage, you opened your bedroom door, and looked up and down the corridor?"

"Certainly I did," agreed Miss Blake.

"And saw nothing—and no one?"

"I saw nothing."

"And then, possibly, in order to convince Miss Elmsdale of the full extent of her delusion, you lit a candle, and went downstairs."

"Of course—why wouldn't I?" said Miss Blake, defiantly.

"Why not, indeed?" repeated the learned gentleman, pensively. "Why not?—Miss Blake being brave as she is witty. Well, you went downstairs, and, as was the admirable custom of the house—a custom worthy of all commendation—you found the doors opening from the hall bolted and locked?"

"I did."

"And no sign of a human being about?"

"Except myself," supplemented Miss Blake.

"And rather wishing to find that some human being besides yourself was about, you retraced your steps, and visited the servants' apartments?"

"You might have been with me," said Miss Blake, with an angry sneer.

"I wish I had," he answered. "I can never sufficiently deplore the fact of my absence. And you found the servants asleep?"

"Well, they seemed asleep," said the lady; "but that does not prove that they were so."

"Doubtless," he agreed. "Nevertheless, so far as you could judge, none of them looked as if they had been wandering up and down the corridors?"

"I could not judge one way or another," said Miss Blake: "for the tricks of English servants, it is impossible for anyone to be up to."

"Still, it did not occur to you at the time that any of them was feigning slumber?"

"I can't say it did. You see, I am naturally unsuspicious," explained Miss Blake, naively.

"Precisely so. And thus it happened that you were unable to confute Miss Elmsdale's fancy?"

"I told her she must have been dreaming," retorted Miss Blake. "People who wake all of a sudden often confound dreams with realities."

"And people who are not in the habit of awaking suddenly often do the same thing," agreed her questioner; "and so, Miss

Blake, we will pass out of dreamland, and into daylight—or rather foglight. Do you recollect a particularly foggy day, when your niece, hearing a favourite dog moaning piteously, opened the door of the room where her father died, in order to let it out?"

Miss Blake set her lips tight, and looked up at the gallery. There was a little stir in that part of the court, a shuffling of feet, and suppressed whispering. In vain the crier shouted, "Silence! silence, there!" The bustle continued for about a minute, and then all became quiet again. A policeman stated "a female had fainted," and our curiosity being satisfied, we all with one accord turned towards our learned friend, who, one hand under his gown, holding it back, and the other raised to emphasise his question, had stood in this picturesque attitude during the time occupied in carrying the female out, as if done in stone.

"Miss Blake, will you kindly answer my question?" he said, when order once again reigned in court.

"You're worse than a heathen," remarked the lady, irrelevantly.

"I am sorry you do not like me," he replied, "for I admire you very much; but my imperfections are beside the matter in point. What I want you to tell us is, did Miss Elmsdale open that door?"

"She did—the creature, she did," was the answer; "her heart was always tender to dumb brutes."

"I have no doubt the young lady's heart was everything it ought to be," was the reply; "and for that reason, though she had an intense repugnance to enter the room, she opened the door to let the dog out."

"She said so: I was not there," answered Miss Blake.

Whereupon ensued a brisk skirmish between counsel as to whether Miss Blake could give evidence about a matter of mere hearsay. And after they had fought for ten minutes over the legal bone, our adversary said he would put the question differently, which he did, thus:

"You were sitting in the dining-room, when you were startled by hearing a piercing shriek."

"I heard a screech—you can call it what you like," said Miss

Blake, feeling an utter contempt for English phraseology.

"I stand corrected; thank you, Miss Blake. You heard a screech, in short, and you hurried across the hall, and found Miss Elmsdale in a fainting condition, on the floor of the library. Was that so?"

"She often fainted: she is all nairves," explained poor Miss Blake.

"No doubt. And when she regained consciousness, she entreated to be taken out of that dreadful room."

"She never liked the room after her father's death: it was natural, poor child."

"Quite natural. And so you took her into the dining-room, and there, curled upon the hearthrug, fast asleep, was the little dog she fancied she heard whining in the library."

"Yes, he had been away for two or three days, and came home hungry and sleepy."

"Exactly. And you have, therefore, no reason to believe he was shamming slumber."

"I believe I am getting very tired of your questions and cross-questions," she said, irritably.

"Now, what a pity!" remarked her tormentor; "for I could never tire of your answers. At all events, Miss Elmsdale could not have heard him whining in the library—so called."

"She might have heard some other dog," said Miss Blake.

"As a matter of fact, however, she stated to you there was no dog in the room."

"She did. But I don't think she knew whether there was or not."

"In any case, she did not see a dog; you did not see one; and the servants did not."

"I did not," replied Miss Blake; "as to the servants, I would not believe them on their oath."

"Hush! hush! Miss Blake," entreated our opponent. "I am afraid you must not be quite so frank. Now to return to business. When Miss Elmsdale recovered consciousness, which she did in that very comfortable easy-chair in the dining-room—what did she tell you?"

"Do you think I am going to repeat her half-silly words?" demanded Miss Blake, angrily. "Poor dear, she was out of her mind half the time, after her father's death."

"No doubt; but still, I must just ask you to tell us what passed. Was it anything like this? Did she say, 'I have seen my father. He was coming out of the strong-room when I lifted my head after looking for Juan, and he was wringing his hands, and seemed in some terrible distress'?"

"God forgive them that told you her words," remarked Miss Blake; "but she did say just those, and I hope they'll do you and her as played eavesdropper all the good I wish."

"Really, Miss Blake," interposed the judge.

"I have no more questions to ask, my lord," said Colonel Morris' counsel, serenely triumphant. "Miss Blake can go down now."

And Miss Blake did go down; and Taylor whispered in my ear:

"She had done for us."

CHAPTER 6

WE AGREE TO COMPROMISE

Colonel Morris' side of the case was now to be heard, and heads were bending eagerly forward to catch each word of wisdom that should fall from the lips of Serjeant Playfire, when I felt a hand, cold as ice, laid on mine, and turning, beheld Miss Blake at my elbow.

She was as white as the nature of her complexion would permit, and her voice shook as she whispered:

"Take me away from this place, will you?"

I cleared a way for her out of the court, and when we reached Westminster Hall, seeing how upset she seemed, asked if I could get anything for her—"a glass of water, or wine," I suggested, in my extremity.

"Neither water nor wine will mend a broken heart," she answered, solemnly; "and mine has been broken in there"—with a nod she indicated the court we had just left.

Not remembering at the moment an approved recipe for the cure of such a fracture, I was cudgelling my brains to think of some form of reply not likely to give offence, when, to my unspeakable relief, Mr. Craven came up to where we stood.

"I will take charge of Miss Blake now, Patterson," he said, gravely—very gravely; and accepting this as an intimation that he desired my absence, I was turning away, when I heard Miss Blake say:

"Where is she—the creature? What have they done with her at all?"

"I have sent her home," was Mr. Craven's reply. "How could you be so foolish as to mislead me as you have done?"

"Come," thought I, smelling the battle afar off, "we shall soon have Craven *v.* Blake tried privately in our office." I knew Mr. Craven pretty well, and understood he would not readily forgive Miss Blake for having kept Miss Helena's experiences a secret from him.

Over and over I had heard Miss Blake state there was not a thing really against the house, and that Helena, poor dear, only hated the place because she had there lost her father.

"Not much of a loss either, if she could be brought to think so," finished Miss Blake, sometimes.

Consequently, to Mr. Craven, as well as to all the rest of those connected with the firm, the facts elicited by Serjeant Playfire were new as unwelcome.

If the daughter of the house dreamed dreams and beheld visions, why should strangers be denied a like privilege? If Miss Elmsdale believed her father could not rest in his grave, how were we to compel belief as to calm repose on the part of yearly tenants?

"Playfire has been pitching into us pretty strong," remarked Taylor, when I at length elbowed my way back to where our manager sat. "Where is Mr. Craven?"

"I left him with Miss Blake."

"It is just as well he has not heard all the civil remarks Playfire made about our connection with the business. Hush! he is going to call his witnesses. No, the court is about to adjourn for luncheon."

Once again I went out into Westminster Hall, and was sauntering idly up and down over its stones when Mr. Craven joined me.

"A bad business this, Patterson," he remarked.

"We shall never get another tenant for that house," I answered.

"Certainly no tenant will ever again be got through me," he said, irritably; and then Taylor came to him, all in a hurry, and explaining he was wanted, carried him away.

"They are going to compromise," I thought, and followed slowly in the direction taken by my principal.

How I knew they were thinking of anything of the kind, I cannot say, but intuitively I understood the course events were taking.

Our counsel had mentally decided that, although the jury might feel inclined to uphold contracts and to repudiate ghosts, still, it would be impossible for them to overlook the fact that Colonel Morris had rented the place in utter ignorance of its antecedents, and that we had, so far, taken a perhaps undue advantage of him; moreover, the gallant officer had witnesses in court able to prove, and desirous of proving, that we had over and over again compromised matters with dissatisfied tenants, and cancelled agreements, not once or twice, but many, times; further, on no single occasion had Miss Blake and her niece ever slept a single night in the uninhabited house from the day when they left it; no matter how scarce of money they chanced to be, they went into lodgings rather than reside at River Hall. This was beyond dispute and Miss Blake's evidence supplied the reason for conduct so extraordinary.

For some reason the house was uninhabitable. The very owners could not live in it; and yet—so in imagination we heard Serjeant Playfire declaim—"The lady from whom the TRUTH had that day been reluctantly wrung had the audacity to insist

194

that delicate women and tender children should continue to inhabit a dwelling over which a CURSE seemed brooding—a dwelling where the dead were always striving for mastery with the living; or else pay Miss Blake a sum of money which should enable her and the daughter of the suicide to live in ease and luxury on the profits of DECEPTION."

And looking at the matter candidly, our counsel did not believe the jury could return a verdict. He felt satisfied, he said, there was not a landlord in the box, that they were all tenants, who would consider the three months' rent paid over and above the actual occupation rent, ample, and more than ample, remuneration.

On the other hand, Serjeant Playfire, whose experience of juries was large, and calculated to make him feel some contempt for the judgment of "twelve honest men" in any case from pocket-picking to manslaughter, had a prevision that, when the judge had explained to Mr. Foreman and gentlemen of the jury, the nature of a contract, and told them supernatural appearances, however disagreeable, were not recognized in law as a sufficient cause for breaking an agreement, a verdict would be found for Miss Blake.

"There must be one landlord amongst them," he considered; "and if there is, he will wind the rest round his finger. Besides, they will take the side of the women, naturally; and Miss Blake made them laugh, and the way she spoke of her niece touched them; while, as for the colonel, he won't like cross-examination, and I can see my learned friend means to make him appear ridiculous. Enough has been done for honour—let us think of safety."

"For my part," said Colonel Morris, when the question was referred to him, "I am not a vindictive man, nor, I hope, an ungenerous foe; I do not like to be victimized, and I have vindicated my principles. The victory was mine in fact, if not in law, when that old Irishwoman's confession was wrung out of her. So, therefore, gentlemen, settle the matter as you please—I shall be satisfied."

And all the time he was inwardly praying some arrangement might be come to. He was brave enough in his own way, but it is one thing to go into battle, and another to stand legal fire without the chance of sending a single bullet in return. Ridicule is the vulnerable spot in the heel of many a modern Achilles; and while the rest of the court was "convulsed with laughter" over Miss Blake's cross-examination, the gallant colonel felt himself alternately turning hot and cold when he thought that through even such an ordeal he might have to pass. And, accordingly, to cut short this part of my story, amongst them the lawyers agreed to compromise the matter thus—

Colonel Morris to give Miss Blake a third quarter's rent—in other words, fifty pounds more, and each side to pay its own costs.

When this decision was finally arrived at, Mr. Craven's face was a study. Full well he knew on whom would fall the costs of one side. He saw in prophetic vision the fifty pounds passing out of his hands into those of Miss Blake, but no revelation was vouchsafed on the subject of loans unpaid, of costs out of pocket, or costs at all. After we left court he employed himself, I fancy, for the remainder of the afternoon in making mental calculations of how much poorer a man Mrs. Elmsdale's memory, and the Uninhabited House had left him; and, upon the whole, the arithmetical problem could not have proved satisfactory when solved.

The judge complimented everyone upon the compromise effected. It was honourable in every way, and creditable to all parties concerned, but the jury evidently were somewhat dissatisfied at the turn affairs had taken, while the witnesses were like to rend Colonel Morris asunder.

"They had come, at great inconvenience to themselves, to expose the tactics of that Blake woman and her solicitor," so they said; "and they thought the affair ought not to have been hushed up."

As for the audience, they murmured openly. They received the statement that the case was over, with groans, hisses, and other marks of disapproval, and we heard comments on the matter uttered by disappointed spectators all the way up Parliament Street, till we arrived at that point where we left the main thoroughfare, in order to strike across to Buckingham Street.

There—where Pepys once lived—we betook ourselves to our books and papers, with a sense of unusual depression in the atmosphere. It was a gray, dull, cheerless afternoon, and more than one of us, looking out at the mud bank, which, at low water, then occupied the space now laid out as gardens, wondered how River Hall, desolate, tenantless, uninhabited, looked under that sullen sky, with the murky river flowing onward, day and night, day and night, leaving, unheeding, an unsolved mystery on its banks.

For a week we saw nothing of Miss Blake, but at the end of that time, in consequence of a somewhat imperative summons from Mr. Craven, she called at the office late one afternoon. We comprehended she had selected that, for her, unusual time of day for a visit, hoping our principal might have left ere she arrived; but in this hope she was disappointed: Mr. Craven was in, at leisure, and anxious to see her.

I shall never forget that interview. Miss Blake arrived about five o'clock, when it was quite dark out of doors, and when, in all our offices except Mr. Craven's, the gas was flaring away triumphantly. In his apartment he kept the light always subdued, but between the fire and the lamp there was plenty of light to see that Miss Blake looked ill and depressed, and that Mr. Craven had assumed a peculiar expression, which, to those who knew him best, implied he had made up his mind to pursue a particular course of action, and meant to adhere to his determination.

"You wanted to see me," said our client, breaking the ice.

"Yes; I wanted to tell you that our connection with the River Hall property must be considered at an end."

"Well, well, that is the way of men, I suppose—in England."

"I do not think any man, whether in England or Ireland, could have done more for a client than I have tried to do for you, Miss Blake," was the offended answer.

"I am sure I have never found fault with you," remarked Miss Blake, deprecatingly.

"And I do not think," continued Mr. Craven, unheeding her remark, "any lawyer ever met with a worse return for all his trouble than I have received from you."

"Dear, dear," said Miss Blake, with comic disbelief in her tone, "that is very bad."

"There are two classes of men who ought to be treated with entire confidence," persisted Mr. Craven, "lawyers and doctors. It is as foolish to keep back anything from one as from another."

"I daresay," argued Miss Blake; "but we are not all wise alike, you know."

"No," remarked my principal, who was indeed no match for the lady, "or you would never have allowed me to take your case into court in ignorance of Helena having seen her father."

"Come, come," retorted Miss Blake; "you do not mean to say you believe she ever did see her father since he was buried, and had the stone-work put all right and neat again, about him? And, indeed, it went to my heart to have a man who had fallen into such bad ways laid in the same grave with my dear sister, but I thought it would be unchristian——"

"We need not go over all that ground once more, surely," interrupted Mr. Craven. "I have heard your opinions concerning Mr. Elmsdale frequently expressed ere now. That which I never did hear, however, until it proved too late, was the fact of Helena having fancied she saw her father after his death."

"And what good would it have done you, if I had repeated all the child's foolish notions?"

"This, that I should not have tried to let a house believed by the owner herself to be uninhabitable."

"And so you would have kept us without bread to put in our mouths, or a roof over our heads."

"I should have asked you to do at first what I must ask you to do at last. If you decline to sell the place, or let it unfurnished, on a long lease, to someone willing to take it, spite of its bad character, I must say the house will never again be let through my instrumentality, and I must beg you to advertise River Hall yourself, or place it in the hands of an agent."

"Do you mean to say, William Craven," asked Miss Blake, solemnly, "that you believe that house to be haunted?"

"I do not," he answered. "I do not believe in ghosts, but I believe the place has somehow got a bad name—perhaps through Helena's fancies, and that people imagine it is haunted, and get frightened probably at sight of their own shadows. Come, Miss Blake, I see a way out of this difficulty; you go and take up your abode at River Hall for six months, and at the end of that time the evil charm will be broken."

"And Helena dead," she observed.

"You need not take Helena with you."

"Nor anybody else, I suppose you mean," she remarked. "Thank you, Mr. Craven; but though my life is none too happy, I should like to die a natural death, and God only knows whether those who have been peeping and spying about the place might not murder me in my bed, if I ever went to bed in the house; that is—"

"Then, in a word, you do believe the place is haunted."

"I do nothing of the kind," she answered, angrily; "but though I have courage enough, thank Heaven, I should not like to stay all alone in any house, and I know there is not a servant in England would stay there with me, unless she meant to take my life. But I tell you what, William Craven, there are lots of poor creatures in the world even poorer than we are—tutors and starved curates, and the like. Get one of them to stay at the Hall till he finds out where the trick is, and I won't mind saying he shall have fifty pounds down for his pains; that is, I mean, of course, when he has discovered the secret of all these strange lights, and suchlike."

And feeling she had by this proposition struck Mr. Craven under the fifth rib, Miss Blake rose to depart.

"You will kindly think over what I have said," observed Mr. Craven.

"I'll do that if you will kindly think over what I have said," she retorted, with the utmost composure; and then, after a curt good-evening, she passed through the door I held open, nodding to me, as though she would have remarked, "I'm more than a match for your master still, young man."

"What a woman that is!" exclaimed Mr. Craven, as I resumed my seat.

"Do you think she really means what she says about the fifty pounds?" I inquired.

"I do not know," he answered, "but I know I would cheerfully pay that sum to anyone who could unravel the mystery of River Hall."

"Are you in earnest, sir?" I asked, in some surprise.

"Certainly I am," he replied.

"Then let me go and stay at River Hall," I said. "I will undertake to run the ghost to earth for half the money."

Chapter 7

My Own Story

It is necessary now that I should tell the readers something about my own antecedents.

Aware of how uninteresting the subject must prove, I shall make that something as short as possible.

Already it will have been clearly understood, both from my own hints, and from Miss Blake's far from reticent remarks on my position, that I was a clerk at a salary in Mr. Craven's office.

But this had not always been the case. When I went first to Buckingham Street, I was duly articled to Mr. Craven, and my mother and sister, who were of aspiring dispositions, lamented that my choice of a profession had fallen on law rather than soldiering.

They would have been proud of a young fellow in uniform; but they did not feel at all elated at the idea of being so closely connected with a "musty attorney."

As for my father, he told me to make my own choice, and found the money to enable me to do so. He was an easy-going soul, who was in the miserable position of having a sufficient income to live on without exerting either mind or body; and yet whose income was insufficient to enable him to have superior hobbies, or to gratify any particular taste. We resided in the country, and belonged to the middle class of comfortable, well-to-do English people. In our way, we were somewhat exclusive as to our associates—and as the Hall and Castle residents were, in their way, exclusive also, we lived almost out of society.

Indeed, we were very intimate with only one family in our neighbourhood; and I think it was the example of the son of that house which first induced me to think of leading a different existence from that in which my father had grown as green and mossy as a felled tree.

Ned Munro, the eldest hope of a proud but reduced stock, elected to study for the medical profession.

"The life here," he remarked, vaguely indicating the distant houses occupied by our respective sires, "may suit the old folks, but it does not suit me." And he went out into the wilderness of the world.

After his departure I found that the life at home did not suit me either, and so I followed his lead, and went, duly articled, to Mr. Craven, of Buckingham Street, Strand. Mr. Craven and my father were old friends. To this hour I thank Heaven for giving my father such a friend.

After I had been for a considerable time with Mr. Craven, there came a dreadful day, when tidings arrived that my father was ruined, and my immediate presence required at home. What followed was that which is usual enough in all such cases, with this difference—the loss of his fortune killed my father.

From what I have seen since, I believe when he took to his bed and quietly gave up living altogether, he did the wisest and best thing possible under the circumstances. Dear, simple, kindly old man, I cannot fancy how his feeble nature might have endured the years which followed; filled by my mother and sister with lamentations, though we knew no actual want—thanks to Mr. Craven.

My father had been dabbling in shares, and when the natural consequence—ruin, utter ruin, came to our pretty country home, Mr. Craven returned me the money paid to him, and offered me a salary.

Think of what this kindness was, and we penniless; while all the time relations stood aloof, holding out nor hand nor purse, till they saw whether we could weather the storm without their help.

Amongst those relations chanced to be a certain Admiral Patterson, an uncle of my father. When we were well-to-do he had not disdained to visit us in our quiet home, but when poverty came he tied up his purse-strings and ignored our existence, till at length, hearing by a mere chance that I was supporting my mother and sister by my own exertions (always helped by Mr. Craven's goodness), he said, audibly, that the "young jackanapes must have more in him than he thought," and wrote to beg that I would spend my next holiday at his house.

I was anxious to accept the invitation, as a friend told me he felt certain the old gentleman would forward my views; but I did not choose to visit my relative in shabby clothes and with empty pockets; therefore, it fell out that I jumped at Miss Blake's suggestion, and closed with Mr. Craven's offer on the spot.

Half fifty—twenty-five—pounds would replenish my wardrobe, pay my travelling expenses, and leave me with money in my pocket, as well.

I told Mr. Craven all this in a breath. When I had done so he laughed, and said:

"You have worked hard, Patterson. Here is ten pounds. Go and see your uncle; but leave River Hall alone."

Then, almost with tears, I entreated him not to baulk my purpose. If I could rid River Hall of its ghost, I would take money from him, not otherwise. I told him I had set my heart on unravelling the mystery attached to that place, and I could have told him another mystery at the same time, had shame not tied my tongue. I was in love—for the first time in my life— hopelessly, senselessly, with a face of which I thought all day and dreamed all night, that had made itself in a moment part and parcel of my story, thus:

I had been at Kentish Town to see one of our clients, and having finished my business, walked on as far as Camden Town, intending to take an omnibus which might set me down somewhere near Chancery Lane.

Whilst standing at the top of College Street, under shelter of my umbrella, a drizzling rain falling and rendering the pavement dirty and slippery, I noticed a young lady waiting to cross the road—a young lady with, to my mind, the sweetest, fairest, most lovable face on which my eyes had ever rested. I could look at her without causing annoyance, because she was so completely occupied in watching lumbering vans, fast carts, crawling cabs, and various other vehicles, which chanced at that moment to be crowding the thoroughfare, that she had no leisure to bestow even a glance on any pedestrian.

A governess, I decided: for her dress, though neat, and even elegant, was by no means costly; moreover, there was an expression of settled melancholy about her features, and further, she carried a roll, which looked like music, in her hand. In less time than it has taken me to write this paragraph, I had settled all about her to my own satisfaction.

Father bankrupt. Mother delicate. Young brothers and sisters, probably, all crying aloud for the pittance she was able to earn by giving lessons at so much an hour.

She had not been long at her present occupation, I felt satisfied, for she was evidently unaccustomed to being out in the streets alone on a wet day.

I would have offered to see her across the road, but for two reasons: one, because I felt shy about proffering my services; the other, because I was exceedingly doubtful whether I might not give offence by speaking.

After the fashion of so many of her sex, she made about half a dozen false starts, advancing as some friendly cabby made signs for her to venture the passage, retreating as she caught sight of some coming vehicle still yards distant.

At last, imagining the way clear, she made a sudden rush, and had just got well off the curb, when a mail phaeton turned the corner, and in one second she was down in the middle of the road, and I struggling with the horses and swearing at the driver, who, in his turn, very heartily anathematized me.

I do not remember all I said to the portly, well-fed, swaggering cockney upstart; but there was so much in it uncomplimentary to himself and his driving, that the crowd already assembled cheered, as all crowds will cheer profane and personal language; and he was glad enough to gather up his reins and touch his horses, and trot off, without having first gone through the ceremony of asking whether the girl he had so nearly driven over was living or dead.

Meantime she had been carried into the nearest shop, whither I followed her.

I do not know why all the people standing about imagined me to be her brother, but they certainly did so, and, under that impression, made way for me to enter the parlour behind the shop, where I found my poor beauty sitting, faint and frightened and draggled, whilst the woman of the house was trying to wipe the mud off her dress, and endeavouring to persuade her to swallow some wine-and-water.

As I entered, she lifted her eyes to mine, and said, "Thank you, sir. I trust you have not got hurt yourself," so frankly and so sweetly that the small amount of heart her face had left me passed into her keeping at once.

"Are you much hurt?" I replied by asking.

"My arm is, a little," she answered. "If I could only get home! Oh! I wish I were at home."

I went out and fetched a cab, and assisted her into it. Then I asked her where the man should drive, and she gave me the name of the street which Miss Blake, when in England, honoured by making her abode. Miss Blake's number was 110. My charmer's number was 15. Having obtained this information, I closed the cab-door, and taking my seat beside the driver, we rattled off in the direction of Brunswick Square.

Arrived at the house, I helped her—when, in answer to my

knock, an elderly woman appeared, to ask my business—into the narrow hall of a dreary house. Oh! how my heart ached when I beheld her surroundings! She did not bid me goodbye; but asking me into the parlour, went, as I understood, to get money to pay the cabman.

Seizing my opportunity, I told the woman, who still stood near the door, that I was in a hurry, and leaving the house, bade the driver take me to the top of Chancery Lane.

On the next Sunday I watched No. 15, till I beheld my la-dy-fair come forth, veiled, furred, dressed all in her dainty best, prayer-book in hand, going alone to St. Pancras Church—not the old, but the new—whither I followed her.

By some freak of fortune, the verger put me into the same pew as that in which he had just placed her.

When she saw me her face flushed crimson, and then she gave a little smile of recognition.

I fear I did not much heed the service on that particular Sunday; but I still felt shy, so shy that, after I had held the door open for her to pass out, I allowed others to come between us, and did not dare to follow and ask how she was.

During the course of the next week came Miss Blake and Mr. Craven's remark about the fifty pounds; and within four-and-twenty hours something still more astounding occurred—a visit from Miss Blake and her niece, who wanted "a good talking-to"—so Miss Blake stated.

It was a dull, foggy day, and when my eyes rested on the younger lady, I drew back closer into my accustomed corner, frightened and amazed.

"You were in such a passion yesterday," began Miss Blake, coming into the office, dragging her blushing niece after her, "that you put it out of my head to tell you three things—one, that we have moved from our old lodgings; the next, that I have not a penny to go on with; and the third, that Helena here has gone out of her mind. She won't have River Hall let again, if you please. She intends to go out as a governess—what do you think of that?—and nothing I can say makes any impression upon her.

I should have thought she had had enough of governessing the first day she went out to give a lesson: she got herself run over and nearly killed; was brought back in a cab by some gentleman, who had the decency to take the cab away again: for how we should have paid the fare, I don't know, I am sure. So I have just brought her to you to know if her mother's old friend thinks it is a right thing for Kathleen Elmsdale's daughter to put herself under the feet of a parcel of ignorant, purse-proud snobs?"

Mr. Craven looked at the girl kindly. "My dear," he said, "I think, I believe, there will be no necessity for you to do anything of that kind. We have found a person—have we not, Patterson?—willing to devote himself to solving the River Hall mystery. So, for the present at all events, Helena—"

He paused, for Helena had risen from her seat and crossed the room to where I sat.

"Aunt, aunt," she said, "this is the gentleman who stopped the horses," and before I could speak a word she held my hand in hers, and was thanking me once again with her beautiful eyes.

Miss Blake turned and glared upon me. "Oh! it was you, was it?" she said, ungraciously. "Well, it is just what I might have expected, and me hoping all the time it was a lord or a baronet, at the least."

We all laughed—even Miss Elmsdale laughed at this frank confession; but when the ladies were gone, Mr. Craven, looking at me pityingly, remarked:

"This is a most unfortunate business, Patterson. I hope—I do hope, you will not be so foolish as to fall in love with Miss Elmsdale."

To which I made no reply. The evil, if evil it were, was done. I had fallen in love with Miss Blake's niece ere those words of wisdom dropped from my employer's lips.

CHAPTER 8

MY FIRST NIGHT AT RIVER HALL

It was with a feeling of depression for which I could in no way account that, one cold evening, towards the end of February, I left Buckingham Street and wended my way to the Uninhabited House. I had been eager to engage in the enterprise; first, for the sake of the fifty pounds reward; and secondly, and much more, for the sake of Helena Elmsdale. I had tormented Mr. Craven until he gave a reluctant consent to my desire. I had brooded over the matter until I became eager to commence my investigations, as a young soldier may be to face the enemy; and yet, when the evening came, and darkness with it; when I set my back to the more crowded thoroughfares, and found myself plodding along a lonely suburban road, with a keen wind lashing my face, and a suspicion of rain at intervals wetting my cheeks, I confess I had no feeling of enjoyment in my self-imposed task.

After all, talking about a haunted house in broad daylight to one's fellow-clerks, in a large London office, is a very different thing from taking up one's residence in the same house, all alone, on a bleak winter's night, with never a soul within shouting distance. I had made up my mind to go through with the matter, and no amount of mental depression, no wintry blasts, no cheerless roads, no desolate goal, should daunt me; but still I did not like the adventure, and at every step I felt I liked it less.

Before leaving town I had fortified my inner man with a good dinner and some excellent wine, but by the time I reached River Hall I might have fasted for a week, so faint and spiritless did I feel.

"Come, this will never do," I thought, as I turned the key in the door, and crossed the threshold of the Uninhabited House. "I must not begin with being chicken-hearted, or I may as well give up the investigation at once."

The fires I had caused to be kindled in the morning, though almost out by the time I reached River Hall, had diffused a grateful warmth throughout the house; and when I put a match to the paper and wood laid ready in the grate of the room I meant to occupy, and lit the gas, in the hall, on the landing, and in my sleeping-apartment, I began to think things did not look so cheerless, after all.

The seals which, for precaution's sake, I had placed on the

various locks, remained intact. I looked to the fastenings of the hall-door, examined the screws by which the bolts were attached to the wood, and having satisfied myself that everything of that kind was secure, went up to my room, where the fire was now crackling and blazing famously, put the kettle on the hob, drew a chair up close to the hearth, exchanged my boots for slippers, lit a pipe, pulled out my law-books, and began to read.

How long I had read, I cannot say; the kettle on the hob was boiling, at any rate, and the coals had burned themselves into a red-hot mass of glowing cinders, when my attention was attracted—or rather, I should say, distracted—by the sound of tapping outside the window-pane. First I listened, and read on, then I laid down my book and listened more attentively. It was exactly the noise which a person would make tapping upon glass with one finger.

The wind had risen almost to a tempest, but, in the interval between each blast, I could hear the tapping as distinctly as if it had been inside my own skull—*tap, tap,* imperatively; t*ap, tap, tap,* impatiently; and when I rose to approach the casement, it seemed as if three more fingers had joined in the summons, and were rapping for bare life.

"They have begun betimes," I thought; and taking my re-volver in one hand, with the other I opened the shutters, and put aside the blind.

As I did so, it seemed as if some dark body occupied one side of the sash, while the tapping continued as madly as before.

It is as well to confess at once that I was for the moment frightened. Subsequently I saw many wonderful sights, and had some terrible experiences in the Uninhabited House; but I can honestly say, no sight or experience so completely cowed me for the time being, as that dull blackness to which I could assign no shape, that spirit-like rapping of fleshless fingers, which seemed to increase in vehemence as I obeyed its summons.

Doctors say it is not possible for the heart to stand still and a human being live, and, as I am not a doctor, I do not like to contradict their dogma, otherwise I could positively declare my heart did cease beating as I listened, looking out into the night with the shadow of that darkness projecting itself upon my mind, to the impatient tapping, which was now distinctly audible even above the raging of the storm.

How I gathered sufficient courage to do it, I cannot tell; but I put my face close to the glass, thus shutting out the gas and fire-light, and saw that the dark object which alarmed me was a mass of ivy the wind had detached from the wall, and that the invisible fingers were young branches straying from the main body of the plant, which, tossed by the air-king, kept striking the window incessantly, now one, now two, now three, t*ap, tap, tap; tap, tap; tap, tap*; and sometimes, after a long silence, all together, *tap-p-p*, like the sound of clamming bells.

I stood for a minute or two, listening to the noise, so as to satisfy myself as to its cause, then I laid down the revolver, took out my pocket-knife, and opened the window. As I did so, a tremendous blast swept into the room, extinguishing the gas, causing the glowing coals to turn, for a moment, black on one side and to fiercest blaze on the other, scattering the dust lying on the hearth over the carpet, and dashing the ivy-sprays against my face with a force which caused my cheeks to smart and tingle long afterwards.

Taking my revenge, I cut them as far back as I could, and then, without closing the window, and keeping my breath as well as I could, I looked out across the garden over the Thames, away to the opposite bank, where a few lights glimmered at long intervals. "An eerie, lonely place for a fellow to be in all by himself," I continued; "and yet, if the rest of the ghosts, bodiless or clothed with flesh, which frequent this house prove to be as readily laid as those ivy-twigs, I shall earn my money—and—my—thanks, easily enough."

So considering, I relit the gas, replenished the fire, refilled my pipe, reseated myself by the hearth, and with feet stretched out towards the genial blaze, attempted to resume my reading.

All in vain: I could not fix my attention on the page; I could not connect one sentence with another. When my mind ought to have concentrated its energies upon Justice That, and Vice-Chancellor This, and Lord Somebody Else, I felt it wandering away, trying to fit together all the odds and ends of evidence worthy or unworthy concerning the Uninhabited House. Which really was, as we had always stated, a good house, a remarkably good house, well furnished, suitable in every respect, &c.

Had I been a "family of respectability," or a gentleman of position, with a large number of servants, a nice wife, and a few children sprinkled about the domestic picture, I doubt not I should have enjoyed the contemplation of that glowing fire, and rejoiced in the idea of finding myself located in so desirable a residence, within an easy distance of the West End; but, as matters stood, I felt anything rather than elated.

In that large house there was no human inmate save myself, and I had an attack of nervousness upon me for which I found it impossible to account. Here was I, at length, under the very roof where my mistress had passed all her childish days, bound to solve the mystery which was making such havoc with her young life, permitted to essay a task, the accomplishment of which should cover me with glory, and perhaps restore peace and happiness to her heart; and yet I was *afraid*. I did not hesitate to utter that word to my own soul then, any more than I hesitate to write it now for those who list to read: for I can truly say I think there are few men whose courage such an adventure would not try were they to attempt it; and I am sure, had any one of those to whom I tell this story been half as much afraid as I, he would have left River Hall there and then, and allowed the ghosts said to be resident, to haunt it undisturbed for evermore.

If I could only have kept memory from running here and there in quest of evidence *pro* and *con* the house being haunted, I should have fared better: but I could not do this.

Let me try as I would to give my attention to those legal studies that ought to have engrossed my attention, I could not succeed in doing so: my thoughts, without any volition on my part, kept continually on the move; now with Miss Blake in Buckingham Street, again with Colonel Morris on the river walk, once more with Miss Elmsdale in the library; and went constantly flitting hither and thither, recalling the experiences of a frightened lad, or the terror of an ignorant woman; yet withal I had a feeling that in some way memory was playing me false, as if, when ostentatiously bringing out all her stores for me to make or mar as I could, she had really hidden away, in one of her remotest corners, some link, great or little as the case might be, but still, whether great or little, necessary to connect the unsatisfactory narratives together.

Till late in the night I sat trying to piece my puzzle together, but without success. There was a flaw in the story, a missing point in it, somewhere, I felt certain. I often imagined I was about to touch it, when, heigh! presto! it eluded my grasp.

"The whole affair will resolve itself into ivy-boughs," I finally, if not truthfully, decided. "I am satisfied it is all—ivy," and I went to bed.

Now, whether it was that I had thought too much of the ghostly narratives associated with River Hall, the storminess of the night, the fact of sleeping in a strange room, or the strength of a tumbler of brandy-and-water, in which brandy took an undue lead, I cannot tell; but during the morning hours I dreamed a dream which filled me with an unspeakable horror, from which I awoke struggling for breath, bathed in a cold perspiration, and with a dread upon me such as I never felt in any waking moment of my life.

I dreamt I was lying asleep in the room I actually occupied, when I was aroused from a profound slumber by the noise produced by someone tapping at the window-pane. On rising to ascertain the cause of this summons, I saw Colonel Morris standing outside and beckoning me to join him. With that disregard of space, time, distance, and attire which obtains in dreams, I at once stepped out into the garden. It was a pitch-dark night, and bitterly cold, and I shivered, I know, as I heard the sullen flow of the river, and listened to the moaning of the wind among the trees.

We walked on for some minutes in silence, then my companion asked me if I felt afraid, or if I would go on with him.

"I will go where you go," I answered.

Then suddenly he disappeared, and Playfire, who had been his counsel at the time of the trial, took my hand and led me onwards.

We passed through a doorway, and, still in darkness, utter darkness, began to descend some steps. We went down—down—hundreds of steps as it seemed to me, and in my sleep, I still remembered the old idea of its being unlucky to dream of going downstairs. But at length we came to the bottom, and then began winding along interminable passages, now so narrow only one could walk abreast, and again so low that we had to stoop our heads in order to avoid striking the roof.

After we had been walking along these for hours, as time reckons in such cases, we commenced ascending flight after flight of steep stone-steps. I laboured after Playfire till my limbs ached and grew weary, till, scarcely able to drag my feet from stair to stair, I entreated him to stop; but he only laughed and held on his course the more rapidly, while I, hurrying after, often stumbled and recovered myself, then stumbled again and lay prone.

The night air blew cold and chill upon me as I crawled out into an unaccustomed place and felt my way over heaps of uneven earth and stones that obstructed my progress in every direction. I called out for Playfire, but the wind alone answered me; I shouted for Colonel Morris; I entreated someone to tell me where I was; and in answer there was a dead and terrible silence. The wind died away; not a breath of air disturbed the heavy stillness which had fallen so suddenly around me. Instead of the veil of merciful blackness which had hidden everything hitherto from view, a gray light spread slowly over the objects around, revealing a burial-ground, with an old church standing in the midst—a burial-ground where grew rank nettles and coarse, tall grass; where brambles trailed over the graves, and weeds and decay consorted with the dead.

Moved by some impulse which I could not resist, I still held on my course, over mounds of earth, between rows of head-stones, till I reached the other side of the church, under the shadow of which yawned an open pit. To the bottom of it I peered, and there beheld an empty coffin; the lid was laid against the side of the grave, and on a headstone, displaced from its upright position, sat the late occupant of the grave, looking at me with wistful, eager eyes. A stream of light from within the church fell across that one empty grave, that one dead watcher.

"So you have come at last," he said; and then the spell was broken, and I would have fled, but that, holding me with his left hand, he pointed with his right away to a shadowy distance, where the gray sky merged into deepest black.

I strained my eyes to discover the object he strove to indicate, but I failed to do so. I could just discern something flitting away into the darkness, but I could give it no shape or substance.

"Look—look!" the dead man said, rising, in his excitement, and clutching me more firmly with his clay-cold fingers.

I tried to fly, but I could not; my feet were chained to the spot. I fought to rid myself of the clasp of the skeleton hand, and then we fell together over the edge of the pit, and I awoke.

CHAPTER 9

A TEMPORARY PEACE

It was scarcely light when I jumped out of bed, and mur-muring, "Thank God it was only a dream," dressed myself with all speed, and flinging open the window, looked out on a calm morning after the previous night's storm.

Muddily and angrily the Thames rolled onward to the sea. On the opposite side of the river I could see stretches of green, with here and there a house dotting the banks.

A fleet of barges lay waiting the turn of the tide to proceed to their destination. The voices of the men shouting to each other, and blaspheming for no particular reason, came quite clear and distinct over the water. The garden was strewed with twigs and branches blown off the trees during the night; amongst them the sprigs of ivy I had myself cut off.

An hour and a scene not calculated to encourage superstitious fancies, it may be, but still not likely to enliven any man's spirits—a quiet, dull, gray, listless, dispiriting morning, and, being country-bred, I felt its influence.

"I will walk into town, and ask Ned Munro to give me some breakfast," I thought, and found comfort in the idea.

Ned Munro was a doctor, but not a struggling doctor. He was not rich, but he "made enough for a beginner": so he said. He worked hard for little pay; "but I mean some day to have high pay, and take the world easy," he explained. He was blessed with great hopes and good courage; he had high spirits, and a splendid constitution. He neither starved himself nor his friends; his landlady "loved him as her son;" and there were several good-looking girls who were very fond of him, not as a brother.

But Ned had no notion of marrying, yet awhile. "Time enough for that," he told me once, "when I can furnish a good house, and set up a brougham, and choose my patients, and have a few hundreds lying idle in the bank."

Meantime, as no one of these items had yet been realized, he lived in lodgings, ate toasted haddocks with his morning coffee, and smoked and read novels far into the night.

Yes, I could go and breakfast with Munro. Just then it occurred to me that the gas I had left lighted when I went to bed was out; that the door I had left locked was open.

Straight downstairs I went. The gas in the hall was out, and every door I had myself closed and locked the previous morning stood ajar, with the seal, however, remaining intact.

I had borne as much as I could: my nerves were utterly unhinged. Snatching my hat and coat, I left the house, and fled, rather than walked, towards London.

With every step I took towards town came renewed courage; and when I reached Ned's lodgings, I felt ashamed of my pusillanimity.

"I have been sleep-walking, that is what it is," I decided. "I have opened the doors and turned off the gas myself, and been frightened at the work of my own hands. I will ask Munro what

214

is the best thing to insure a quiet night."

Which I did accordingly, receiving for answer—

"Keep a quiet mind."

"Yes, but if one cannot keep a quiet mind; if one is anxious and excited, and——"

"In love," he finished, as I hesitated.

"Well, no; I did not mean that," I said; "though, of course, that might enter into the case also. Suppose one is uneasy about a certain amount of money, for instance?"

"Are you?" he asked, ignoring the general suggestiveness of my remark.

"Well, yes; I want to make some if I can."

"Don't want, then," he advised. "Take my word for it, no amount of money is worth the loss of a night's rest; and you have been tossing about all night, I can see. Come, Patterson, if it's forgery or embezzlement, out with it, man, and I will help you if I am able."

"If it were either one or the other, I should go to Mr. Craven," I answered, laughing.

"Then it must be love," remarked my host; "and you will want to take me into your confidence some day. The old story, I suppose: beautiful girl, stern parents, wealthy suitor, poor lover. I wonder if we could interest her in a case of small-pox. If she took it badly, you might have a chance; but I have a presentiment that she has been vaccinated."

"Ned," was my protest, "I shall certainly fling a plate at your head."

"All right, if you think the exertion would do you good," he answered. "Give me your hand, Patterson"; and before I knew what he wanted with it, he had his fingers on my wrist.

"Look here, old fellow," he said; "you will be laid up, if you don't take care of yourself. I thought so when you came in, and I am sure of it now. What have you been doing?"

"Nothing wrong, Munro," I answered, smiling in spite of myself. "I have not been picking, or stealing, or abducting any young woman, or courting my neighbour's wife; but I am wor-

215

ried and perplexed. When I sleep I have dreadful dreams—horrible dreams," I added, shuddering.

"Can you tell me what is worrying and perplexing you?" he asked, kindly, after a moment's thought.

"Not yet, Ned," I answered; "though I expect I shall have to tell you soon. Give me something to make me sleep quietly: that is all I want now."

"Can't you go out of town?" he inquired.

"I do not want to go out of town," I answered.

"I will make you up something to strengthen your nerves," he said, after a pause; "but if you are not better—well, before the end of the week, take my advice, and run down to Brighton over Sunday. Now, you ought to give me a guinea for that," he added, laughing. "I assure you, all the gold-headed cane, all the wonderful chronometer doctors who pocket thousands *per annum* at the West End, could make no more of your case than I have done."

"I am sure they could not," I said, gratefully; "and when I have the guinea to spare, be sure I shall not forget your fee."

Whether it was owing to his medicine, or his advice, or his cheery, health-giving manner, I have no idea; but that night, when I walked towards the Uninhabited House, I felt a different being.

On my way I called at a small corn-chandler's, and bought a quartern of flour done up in a thin and utterly insufficient bag. I told the man the wrapper would not bear its contents, and he said he could not help that.

I asked him if he had no stronger bags. He answered that he had, but he could not afford to give them away.

I laid down twopence extra, and inquired if that would cover the expense of a sheet of brown paper.

Ashamed, he turned aside and produced a substantial bag, into which he put the flour in its envelope of curling-tissue.

I thanked him, and pushed the twopence across the counter. With a grunt, he thrust the money back. I said goodnight, leaving current coin of the realm to the amount indicated behind me.

Through the night he shouted, "Hi! sir, you've forgotten your change."

Through the night I shouted back, "Give your next customer its value in civility."

All of which did me good. Squabbling with flesh and blood is not a bad preliminary to entering a ghost-haunted house.

Once again I was at River Hall. Looking up at its cheerless portal, I was amazed at first to see the outside lamp flaring away in the darkness. Then I remembered that all the other gas being out, of course this, which I had not turned off, would blaze more brightly.

Purposely I had left my return till rather late. I had gone to one of the theatres, and remained until a third through the principal piece. Then I called at a supper-room, had half a dozen oysters and some stout; after which, like a giant refreshed, I wended my way westward.

Utterly false would it be for me to say I liked the idea of entering the Uninhabited House; but still, I meant to do it, and I did.

No law-books for me that night; no seductive fire; no shining lights all over the house. Like a householder of twenty years' standing, I struck a match, and turned the gas on to a single hall-lamp. I did not trouble myself even about shutting the doors opening into the hall; I only strewed flour copiously over the marble pavement, and on the first flight of stairs, and then, by the servant's passages, crept into the upper story, and so to bed.

That night I slept dreamlessly. I awoke in broad daylight, wondering why I had not been called sooner, and then remembered there was no one to call, and that if I required hot water, I must boil it for myself.

With that light heart which comes after a good night's rest, I put on some part of my clothing, and was commencing to descend the principal staircase, when my proceedings of the previous night flashed across my mind; and pausing, I looked down into the hall. No sign of a foot on the flour. The white powder lay there innocent of human pressure as the untrodden snow; and yet, and yet, was I dreaming—could I have been drunk without my own knowledge, before I went to bed? The gas was ablaze in the hall and on the staircase, and every door left open overnight was close shut.

Curiously enough, at that moment fear fell from me like a garment which has served its turn, and in the strength of my manhood, I felt able to face anything the Uninhabited House might have to show.

Over the latter part of that week, as being utterly unimportant in its events or consequences, I pass rapidly, only saying that, when Saturday came, I followed Munro's advice, and ran down to Brighton, under the idea that by so doing I should thoroughly strengthen myself for the next five days' ordeal. But the idea was a mistaken one. The Uninhabited House took its ticket for Brighton by the same express; it got into the compartment with me; it sat beside me at dinner; it hob-nobbed to me over my own wine; uninvited it came out to walk with me; and when I stood still, listening to the band, it stood still too. It went with me to the pier, and when the wind blew, as the wind did, it said, "We were quite as well off on the Thames."

When I woke, through the night, it seemed to shout, "Are you any better off here?" And when I went to church the next day it crept close up to me in the pew, and said, "Come, now, it is all very well to say you are a Christian; but if you were really one you would not be afraid of the place you and I wot of."

Finally, I was so goaded and maddened that I shook my fist at the sea, and started off by the evening train for the Uninhabited House.

This time I travelled alone. The Uninhabited House preceded me.

There, in its old position, looking gloomy and mysterious in the shadows of night, I found it on my return to town; and, as if tired of playing tricks with one who had become indifferent to their vagaries, all the doors remained precisely as I had left them; and if there were ghosts in the house that night, they did not interfere with me or the chamber I occupied.

Next morning, while I was dressing, a most remarkable thing occurred; a thing for which I was in no wise prepared. Spirits, and sights and sounds supposed appropriate to spirithood, I had expected; but for a modest knock at the front door I was not prepared.

When, after hurriedly completing my toilet, I undrew the bolts and undid the chain, and opened the door wide, there came rushing into the house a keen easterly wind, behind which I beheld a sad-faced woman, dressed in black, who dropped me a curtsey, and said:

"If you please, sir—I suppose you are the gentleman?"

Now, I could make nothing out of this, so I asked her to be good enough to explain.

Then it all came out: "Did I want a person to char?"

This was remarkable—very. Her question amazed me to such an extent that I had to ask her in, and request her to seat herself on one of the hall chairs, and go upstairs myself, and think the matter over before I answered her.

It had been so impressed upon me that no one in the neighbourhood would come near River Hall, that I should as soon have thought of Victoria by the grace of God paying me a friendly visit, as of being waited on by a charwoman.

I went downstairs again.

At sight of me my new acquaintance rose from her seat, and began curling up the corner of her apron.

"Do you know," I said, "that this house bears the reputation of being haunted?"

"I have heard people say it is, sir," she answered.

"And do you know that servants will not stay in it—that tenants will not occupy it?"

"I have heard so, sir," she answered once again.

"Then what do you mean by offering to come?" I inquired.

She looked up into my face, and I saw the tears come softly stealing into her eyes, and her mouth began to pucker, ere, drooping her head, she replied:

"Sir, just three months ago, come the twentieth, I was a happy woman. I had a good husband and a tidy home. There was not a lady in the land I would have changed places with. But that night, my man, coming home in a fog, fell into the river and was drowned. It was a week before they found him, and all the time—while I had been hoping to hear his step every minute in the day—I was a widow."

"Poor soul!" I said, involuntarily.

"Well, sir, when a man goes, all goes. I have done my best, but still I have not been able to feed my children—his children— properly, and the sight of their poor pinched faces breaks my heart, it do, sir," and she burst out sobbing.

"And so, I suppose," I remarked, "you thought you would face this house rather than poverty?"

"Yes, sir. I heard the neighbours talking about this place, and you, sir, and I made up my mind to come and ask if I mightn't tidy up things a bit for you, sir. I was a servant, sir, before I married, and I'd be so thankful."

Well, to cut the affair shorter for the reader than I was able to do for myself, I gave her half a crown, and told her I would think over her proposal, and let her hear from me—which I did. I told her she might come for a couple of hours each morning, and a couple each evening, and she could bring one of the children with her if she thought she was likely to find the place lonely.

I would not let her come in the daytime, because, in the quest I had set myself, it was needful I should feel assured no person could have an opportunity of elaborating any scheme for frightening me, on the premises.

"Real ghosts," said I to Mr. Craven, "I do not mind; but the physical agencies which may produce ghosts, I would rather avoid." Acting on which principle I always remained in the house while Mrs. Stott—my charwoman was so named—cleaned, and cooked, and boiled, and put things straight.

No one can imagine what a revolution this woman effected in my ways and habits, and in the ways and habits of the Uninhabited House.

Tradesmen called for orders. The butcher's boy came whistling down the lane to deliver the rump-steak or mutton-chop I had decided on for dinner; the greengrocer delivered his vegetables; the cheesemonger took solemn affidavit concerning the freshness of his stale eggs and the superior quality of a curious article which he called country butter, and declared came from a particular dairy famed for the excellence of its produce; the milkman's yahoo sounded cheerfully in the morning hours; and the letter-box was filled with cards from all sorts and descriptions of people—from laundresses to wine merchants, from gardeners to undertakers.

The doors now never shut nor opened of their own accord. A great peace seemed to have settled over River Hall.

It was all too peaceful, in fact. I had gone to the place to hunt a ghost, and not even the ghost of a ghost seemed inclined to reveal itself to me.

CHAPTER 10

THE WATCHER IS WATCHED

I have never been able exactly to satisfy my own mind as to the precise period during my occupation of the Uninhabited House when it occurred to me that I was being watched. Hazily I must have had some consciousness of the fact long before I began seriously to entertain the idea.

I felt, even when I was walking through London, that I was being often kept in sight by some person. I had that vague notion of a stranger being interested in my movements which it is so impossible to define to a friend, and which one is chary of seriously discussing with oneself. Frequently, when the corner of a street was reached, I found myself involuntarily turning to look back; and, prompted by instinct, I suppose, for there was no reason about the matter, I varied my route to and from the Uninhabited House, as much as the nature of the roads permitted. Further, I ceased to be punctual as to my hours of business, sometimes arriving at the office late, and, if Mr. Craven had anything for me to do Cityward, returning direct from thence to River Hall without touching Buckingham Street.

By this time February had drawn to a close, and better weather might therefore have been expected; instead of which, one evening as I paced westward, snow began to fall, and continued coming down till somewhere about midnight.

Next morning Mrs. Stott drew my attention to certain footmarks on the walks, and beneath the library and drawing-room windows—the footmarks, evidently, of a man whose feet were not a pair. With the keenest interest, I examined these traces of a human pursuer. Clearly the footprints had been made by only one person, and that person deformed in some way. Not merely was the right foot-track different from that of the left, but the way in which its owner put it to the ground must have been different also. The one mark was clear and distinct, cut out in the snow with a firm tread, while the other left a little broken bank at its right edge, and scarcely any impression of the heel.

"Slightly lame," I decided. "Eases his right foot, and has his boots made to order."

"It is very odd," I remarked aloud to Mrs. Stott.

"That it is, sir," she answered; adding, "I hope to gracious none of them mobsmen are going to come burglaring here!"

"Pooh!" I replied; "there is nothing for them to steal, except chairs and tables, and I don't think one man could carry many of them away."

The whole of that day I found my thoughts reverting to those foot-marks in the snow. What purpose anyone proposed to serve by prowling about River Hall I could not imagine. Before taking up my residence in the Uninhabited House, I had a theory that some malicious person or persons was trying to keep the place unoccupied—nay, further, imagination suggested the idea that, owing to its proximity to the river, Mr. Elmsdale's Hall might have taken the fancy of a gang of smugglers, who had provided for themselves means of ingress and egress unknown to the outside world. But all notions of this kind now seemed preposterous.

Slowly, but surely, the conviction had been gaining upon me

that, let the mystery of River Hall be what it would, no ordinary explanation could account for the phenomena which it had presented to tenant after tenant; and my own experiences in the house, slight though they were, tended to satisfy me there was something beyond malice or interest at work about the place.

The very peace vouchsafed to me seemed another element of mystery, since it would certainly have been natural for any evil-disposed person to inaugurate a series of ghostly spectacles for the benefit of an investigator like myself; and yet, somehow, the absence of supernatural appearances, and the presence of that shadowy human being who thought it worthwhile to track my movements, and who had at last left tangible proof of his reality behind him in the snow, linked themselves together in my mind.

"If there is really anyone watching me," I finally decided, "there must be a deeper mystery attached to River Hall than has yet been suspected. Now, the first thing is to make sure that someone is watching me, and the next to guard against danger from him."

In the course of the day, I made a, for me, curious purchase. In a little shop, situated in a back street, I bought half a dozen reels of black sewing-cotton.

This cotton, on my return home, I attached to the trellis-work outside the drawing-room window, and wound across the walk and round such trees and shrubs as grew in positions convenient for my purpose.

"If these threads are broken tomorrow morning, I shall know I have a flesh-and-blood foe to encounter," I thought.

Next morning I found all the threads fastened across the walks leading round by the library and drawing-room snapped in two.

It was, then, flesh and blood I had come out to fight, and I decided that night to keep watch.

As usual, I went up to my bedroom, and, after keeping the gas burning for about the time I ordinarily spent in undressing, put out the light, softly turned the handle of the door, stole, still

223

silently, along the passage, and so into a large apartment with windows which overlooked both the library and drawing-room.

It was here, I knew, that Miss Elmsdale must have heard her father walking past the door, and I am obliged to confess that, as I stepped across the room, a nervous chill seemed for the moment to take my courage captive.

If any reader will consider the matter, mine was not an enviable position. Alone in a desolate house, reputed to be haunted, watching for someone who had sufficient interest in the place to watch it and me closely.

It was still early—not later than half-past ten. I had concluded to keep my vigil until after midnight, and tried to while away the time with thoughts foreign to the matter in hand.

All in vain, however. Let me force what subject I pleased upon my mind, it reverted persistently to Mr. Elmsdale and the circumstances of his death.

"Why did he commit suicide?" I speculated. "If he had lost money, was that any reason why he should shoot himself?"

People had done so, I was aware; and people, probably, would continue to do so; but not hard-headed, hard-hearted men, such as Robert Elmsdale was reputed to have been. He was not so old that the achievement of a second success should have seemed impossible. His credit was good, his actual position unsuspected. River Hall, unhaunted, was not a bad property, and in those days he could have sold it advantageously.

I could not understand the motive of his suicide, unless, indeed, he was mad or drunk at the time. And then I began to wonder whether anything about his life had come out on the inquest—anything concerning habits, associates, and connections. Had there been any other undercurrent, besides betting, in his life brought out in evidence, which might help me to a solution of the mystery?

"I will ask Mr. Craven tomorrow," I thought, "whether he has a copy of the *Times*, containing a report of the inquest. Perhaps—"

What possibility I was about to suggest to my own mind

I shall never now know, for at that moment there flamed out upon the garden a broad, strong flame of light—a flame which came so swiftly and suddenly, that a man, creeping along the River Walk, had not time to step out of its influence before I had caught full sight of him. There was not much to see, however. A man about the middle height, muffled in a cloak, wearing a cap, the peak of which was drawn down over his forehead: that was all I could discern, ere, cowering back from the light, he stole away into the darkness.

Had I yielded to my first impulse, I should have rushed after him in pursuit; but an instant's reflection told me how worse than futile such a wild-goose chase must prove. Cunning must be met with cunning, watching with watching.

If I could discover who he was, I should have taken the first step towards solving the mystery of River Hall; but I should never do so by putting him on his guard. The immediate business lying at that moment to my hand was to discover whence came the flare of light which, streaming across the walk, had revealed the intruder's presence to me. For that business I can truthfully say I felt little inclination.

Nevertheless, it had to be undertaken. So, walking downstairs, I unlocked and opened the library-door, and found, as I anticipated, the room in utter darkness. I examined the fastenings of the shutters—they were secure as I had left them; I looked into the strong-room—not even a rat lay concealed there; I turned the cocks of the gas lights—but no gas whistled through the pipes, for the service to the library was separate from that of the rest of the house, and capable of being shut off at pleasure. I, mindful of the lights said to have been seen emanating from that room, had taken away the key from the internal tap, so that gas could not be used without my knowledge or the possession of a second key. Therefore, as I have said, it was no surprise to me to find the library in darkness. Nor could I say the fact of the light flaring, apparently, from a closely-shut-up room surprised me either. For a long time I had been expecting to see this phe-nomenon: now, when I did see it, I involuntarily connected the light, the apartment, and the stranger together.

For he was no ghost. Ghosts do not leave footmarks behind them in the snow. Ghosts do not break threads of cotton. It was a man I had seen in the garden, and it was my business to trace out the connection between him and the appearances at River Hall.

Thinking thus, I left the library, extinguished the candle by the aid of which I had made the investigations stated above, and after lowering the gaslight I always kept burning in the hall, began ascending the broad, handsome staircase, when I was met by the figure of a man descending the steps. I say advisedly, the figure; because, to all external appearance, he was as much a living man as myself.

And yet I knew the thing which came towards me was not flesh and blood. Knew it when I stood still, too much stupefied to feel afraid. Knew it, as the figure descended swiftly, noiselessly. Knew it, as, for one instant, we were side by side. Knew it, when I put out my hand to stop its progress, and my hand, encountering nothing, passed through the phantom as through air. Knew, it, when I saw the figure pass through the door I had just locked, and which opened to admit the ghostly visitor—opened wide, and then closed again, without the help of mortal hand.

After that I knew nothing more till I came to my senses again and found myself half lying, half sitting on the staircase, with my head resting against the banisters. I had fainted; but if any man thinks I saw in a vision what I have described, let him wait till he reaches the end of this story before expressing too positive an opinion about the matter.

How I passed the remainder of that night, I could scarcely tell. Towards morning, however, I fell asleep, and it was quite late when I awoke: so late, in fact, that Mrs. Stott had rung for admittance before I was out of bed.

That morning two curious things occurred: one, the postman brought a letter for the late owner of River Hall, and dropped it in the box; another, Mrs. Stott asked me if I would allow her and two of the children to take up their residence at the Uninhabited House. She could not manage to pay her rent, she explained, and some kind friends had offered to maintain the elder children if she could keep the two youngest.

"And I thought, sir, seeing how many spare rooms there are here, and the furniture wanting cleaning, and the windows opening when the sun is out, that perhaps you would not object to my staying here altogether. I should not want any more wages, sir, and I would do my best to give satisfaction."

For about five minutes I considered this proposition, made to me whilst sitting at breakfast, and decided in favour of granting her request. I felt satisfied she was not in league with the person or persons engaged in watching my movements; it would be well to have someone in care of the premises during my absence, and it would clearly be to her interest to keep her place at River Hall, if possible.

Accordingly, when she brought in my boots, I told her she could remove at once if she liked.

"Only remember one thing, Mrs. Stott," I said. "If you find any ghosts in the dark corners, you must not come to me with any complaints."

"I sleep sound, sir," she answered, "and I don't think any ghosts will trouble me in the daytime. So thank you, sir; I will bring over a few things and stay here, if you please."

"Very good; here is the key of the back door," I answered; and in five minutes more I was trudging Londonward.

As I walked along I decided not to say anything to Mr. Craven concerning the previous night's adventures; first, because I felt reluctant to mention the apparition, and secondly, because instinct told me I should do better to keep my own counsel, and confide in no one, till I had obtained some clue to the mystery of that midnight watcher.

"Now here's a very curious thing!" said Mr. Craven, after he had opened and read the letter left at River Hall that morning. "This is from a man who has evidently not heard of Mr. Elmsdale's death, and who writes to say how much he regrets having been obliged to leave England without paying his I O U held by my client. To show that, though he may have seemed dishonest, he never meant to cheat Mr. Elmsdale, he encloses a draft on London for the principal and interest of the amount due."

"Very creditable to him," I remarked. "What is the amount, sir?"

"Oh! the total is under a hundred pounds," answered Mr. Craven; "but what I meant by saying the affair seemed curious is this: amongst Mr. Elmsdale's papers there was not an I O U of any description."

"Well, that is singular," I observed; then asked, "Do you think Mr. Elmsdale had any other office besides the library at River Hall?"

"No," was the reply, "none whatever. When he gave up his offices in town, he moved every one of his papers to River Hall. He was a reserved, but not a secret man; not a man, for instance, at all likely to lead a double life of any sort."

"And yet he betted," I suggested.

"Certainly that does puzzle me," said Mr. Craven. "And it is all against my statement, for I am certain no human being, unless it might be Mr. Harringford, who knew him in business, was aware of the fact."

"And what is your theory about the absence of all-important documents?" I inquired.

"I think he must have raised money on them," answered Mr. Craven.

"Are you aware whether anyone else ever produced them?" I asked.

"I am not; I never heard of their being produced: but, then, I should not have been likely to hear." Which was very true, but very unsatisfactory. Could we succeed in tracing even one of those papers, a clue might be found to the mystery of Mr. Elmsdale's suicide.

That afternoon I repaired to the house of one of our clients, who had, I knew, a file of the *Times* newspapers, and asked him to allow me to look at it.

I could, of course, have seen a file at many places in the city, but I preferred pursuing my investigations where no one was likely to watch the proceeding.

"*Times!* bless my soul, yes; only too happy to be able to oblige Mr. Craven. Walk into the study, there is a good fire, make yourself quite at home, I beg, and let me send you a glass of wine."

All of which I did, greatly to the satisfaction of the dear old gentleman.

Turning over the file for the especial year in which Mr. Elmsdale had elected to put a pistol to his head, I found at last the account of the inquest, which I copied out in shorthand, to be able to digest it more fully at leisure; and as it was growing dusk, wended my way back to Buckingham Street.

As I was walking slowly down one side of the street, I noticed a man standing within the open door of a house near Buckingham Gate.

At any other time I should not have given the fact a second thought, but life at River Hall seemed to have endowed me with the power of making mountains out of molehills, of regarding the commonest actions of my fellows with distrust and suspicion; and I was determined to know more of the gentleman who stood back in the shadow, peering out into the darkening twilight.

With this object I ran upstairs to the clerk's office, and then passed into Mr. Craven's room. He had gone, but his lamp was still burning, and I took care to move between it and the window, so as to show myself to any person who might be watching outside; then, without removing hat or top-coat, I left the room, and proceeded to Taylor's office, which I found in utter darkness. This was what I wanted; I wished to see without being seen; and across the way, standing now on the pavement, was the man I had noticed, looking up at our offices.

"All right," thought I, and running downstairs, I went out again, and walked steadily up Buckingham Street, along John Street, up Adam Street, as though *en route* to the Strand. Before, however, I reached that thoroughfare, I paused, hesitated, and then immediately and suddenly wheeled round and retraced my steps, meeting, as I did so, a man walking a few yards behind me and at about the same pace.

I did not slacken my speed for a moment as we came face to face; I did not turn to look back after him; I retraced my steps to the office; affected to look out some paper, and once again pursued my former route, this time without meeting or being followed by anyone, and made my way into the City, where I really had business to transact.

I could have wished for a longer and a better look at the man who honoured me so far as to feel interested in my movements; but I did not wish to arouse his suspicions.

I had scored one trick; I had met him full, and seen his face distinctly—so distinctly that I was able to feel certain I had seen it before, but where, at the moment, I could not remember.

"Never mind," I continued: "that memory will come in due time; meanwhile the ground of inquiry narrows, and the plot begins to thicken."

CHAPTER 11

MISS BLAKE ONCE MORE

Upon my return to River Hall I found in the letter-box an envelope addressed to —— Patterson, Esq.

Thinking it probably contained some circular, I did not break the seal until after dinner; whereas, had I only known from whom the note came, should I not have devoured its contents before satisfying the pangs of physical hunger!

Thus ran the epistle:—

Dear Sir,—

Until half an hour ago I was ignorant that you were the person who had undertaken to reside at River Hall. If you would add another obligation to that already conferred upon me, *leave that terrible house at once*. What I have seen in it, you know; what may happen to you, if you persist in remaining there, I tremble to think. For the sake of your widowed mother and only sister, you ought not to expose yourself to a risk which is *worse than useless*. I never wish to hear of River Hall being let again. Immediately I come of age, I shall sell the place; and if anything could give me happiness in this world, it would be to hear the house was razed to the ground. Pray! pray! listen to a warning, which, believe me, is not idly given, and leave a place which has already been the cause of so much misery to yours, gratefully and sincerely,

Helena Elmsdale.

It is no part of this story to tell the rapture with which I gazed upon the writing of my "lady-love." Once I had heard Miss Blake remark, when Mr. Craven was remonstrating with her on her hieroglyphics, that "Halana wrote an 'unmaning hand,' like all the rest of the English," and, to tell the truth, there was nothing particularly original or characteristic about Miss Elmsdale's calligraphy.

But what did that signify to me? If she had strung pearls together, I should not have valued them one-half so much as I did the dear words which revealed her interest in me.

Over and over I read the note, at first rapturously, afterwards with a second feeling mingling with my joy. How did she know it was I who had taken up my residence at River Hall? Not a soul I knew in London, besides Mr. Craven, was aware of the fact, and he had promised faithfully to keep my secret.

Where, then, had Miss Elmsdale obtained her information? from whom had she learned that I was bent on solving the mystery of the "Uninhabited House"?

I puzzled myself over these questions till my brain grew uneasy with vain conjectures.

Let me imagine what I would—let me force my thoughts into what grooves I might—the moment the mental pressure was removed, my suspicions fluttered back to the man whose face seemed not unfamiliar.

"I am confident he wants to keep that house vacant," I decided. "Once let me discover who he is, and the mystery of the 'Uninhabited House' shall not long remain a mystery."

But then the trouble chanced to be how to find out who he was. I could not watch and be watched at the same time, and I did not wish to take anyone into my confidence, least of all a professional detective.

So far fortune had stood my friend; I had learnt something suspected by no one else, and I made up my mind to trust to the chapter of accidents for further information on the subject of my unknown friend.

When Mr. Craven and I were seated at our respective tables, I said to him:

"Could you make any excuse to send me to Miss Blake's today, sir?"

Mr. Craven looked up in utter amazement. "To Miss Blake's!" he repeated. "Why do you want to go there?"

"I want to see Miss Elmsdale," I answered, quietly enough, though I felt the colour rising in my face as I spoke.

"You had better put all that nonsense on one side, Patterson," he remarked. "What you have to do is to make your way in the world, and you will not do that so long as your head is running upon pretty girls. Helena Elmsdale is a good girl; but she would no more be a suitable wife for you, than you would be a suitable husband for her. Stick to law, my lad, for the present, and leave love for those who have nothing more important to think of."

"I did not want to see Miss Elmsdale for the purpose you imply," I said, smiling at the vehemence of Mr. Craven's advice. "I only wish to ask her one question."

"What is the question?"

"From whom she learned that I was in residence at River Hall," I answered, after a moment's hesitation.

"What makes you think she is aware of that fact?" he inquired.

"I received a note from her last night, entreating me to leave the place, and intimating that some vague peril menaced me if I persisted in remaining there."

"Poor child! poor Helena!" said Mr. Craven, thoughtfully; then spreading a sheet of note-paper on his blotting-pad, and drawing his cheque-book towards him, he proceeded:

"Now remember, Patterson, I trust to your honour implicitly.

You must not make love to that girl; I think a man can scarcely act more dishonourably towards a woman, than to induce her to enter into what must be, under the best circumstances, a very long engagement."

"You may trust me, sir," I answered, earnestly. "Not," I added, "that I think it would be a very easy matter to make love to anyone with Miss Blake sitting by."

Mr. Craven laughed; he could not help doing so at the idea I had suggested. Then he said, "I had a letter from Miss Blake this morning asking me for money."

"And you are going to let her have some of that hundred pounds you intended yesterday to place against her indebtedness to you," I suggested.

"That is so," he replied. "Of course, when Miss Helena comes of age, we must turn over a new leaf—we really must."

To this I made no reply. It would be a most extraordinary leaf, I considered, in which Miss Blake did not appear as debtor to my employer but it scarcely fell within my province to influence Mr. Craven's actions.

"You had better ask Miss Blake to acknowledge receipt of this," said my principal, holding up a cheque for ten pounds as he spoke. "I am afraid I have not kept the account as I ought to have done."

Which was undeniably true, seeing we had never taken a receipt from her at all, and that loans had been debited to his private account instead of to that of Miss Blake. But true as it was, I only answered that I would get her acknowledgment; and taking my hat, I walked off to Hunter Street.

Arrived there, I found, to my unspeakable joy, that Miss Blake was out, and Miss Elmsdale at home.

When I entered the shabby sitting-room where her beauty was so grievously lodged, she rose and greeted me with kindly words, and sweet smiles, and vivid blushes.

"You have come to tell me you are not going ever again to that dreadful house," she said, after the first greeting and inquiries for Miss Blake were over. "You cannot tell the horror with which the mere mention of River Hall now fills me."

"I hope it will never be mentioned to you again till I have solved the mystery attached to it," I answered.

"Then you will not do what I ask," she cried, almost despairingly.

"I cannot," was my reply. "Miss Elmsdale, you would not have a soldier turn back from the battle. I have undertaken to find out the secret attached to your old home, and, please God, I shall succeed in my endeavours."

"But you are exposing yourself to danger, to—"

"I must take my chance of that. I cannot, if I would, turn back now, and I would not if I could. But I have come to you for information. How did you know it was I who had gone to River Hall?"

The colour flamed up in her face as I put the question.

"I—I was told so," she stammered out.

"May I ask by whom?"

"No, Mr. Patterson, you may not," she replied. "A—a friend— a kind friend, informed me of the fact, and spoke of the perils to which you were exposing yourself—living there all alone—all alone," she repeated. "I would not pass a night in the house again if the whole parish were there to keep me company, and what must it be to stay in that terrible, terrible place alone! You are here, perhaps, because you do not believe—because you have not seen."

"I do believe," I interrupted, "because I have seen; and yet I mean to go through with the matter to the end. Have you a likeness of your father in your possession, Miss Elmsdale?" I asked.

"I have a miniature copied from his portrait, which was of course too large to carry from place to place," she answered. "Why do you wish to know?"

"If you let me see it, I will reply to your question," I said.

Round her dear throat she wore a thin gold chain. Unfastening this, she handed to me the necklet, to which was attached a locket enamelled in black. It is no exaggeration to say, as I took

234

this piece of personal property, my hand trembled so much that I could not open the case.

True love is always bashful, and I loved the girl, whose slender neck the chain had caressed, so madly and senselessly, if you will, that I felt as if the trinket were a living thing, a part and parcel of herself.

"Let me unfasten it," she said, unconscious that aught save awkwardness affected my manipulation of the spring. And she took the locket and handed it back to me open, wet with tears—her tears.

Judge how hard it was for me then to keep my promise to Mr. Craven and myself—how hard it was to refrain from telling her all my reasons for having ever undertaken to fight the dragon installed at River Hall.

I thank God I did refrain. Had I spoken then, had I presumed upon her sorrow and her simplicity, I should have lost something which constitutes the sweetest memory of my life.

But that is in the future of this story, and meantime I was looking at the face of her father.

I looked at it long and earnestly; then I closed the locket, softly pressing down the spring as I did so, and gave back miniature and chain into her hand.

"Well, Mr. Patterson?" she said, inquiringly.

"Can you bear what I have to tell?" I asked.

"I can, whatever it may be," she answered.

"I have seen that face at River Hall."

She threw up her arms with a gesture of despair.

"And," I went on, "I may be wrong, but I think I am destined to solve the mystery of its appearance."

She covered her eyes, and there was silence between us for a minute, when I said:

"Can you give me the name of the person who told you I was at River Hall?"

"I cannot," she repeated. "I promised not to mention it."

"He said I was in danger."

"Yes, living there all alone."

"And he wished you to warn me."

"No; he asked my aunt to do so, and she refused; and so I—I thought I would write to you without mentioning the matter to her."

"You have done me an incalculable service," I remarked, "and in return I will tell you something."

"What is that?" she asked.

"From tonight I shall not be alone in the house."

"Oh! how thankful I am!" she exclaimed; then instantly added, "Here is my aunt."

I rose as Miss Blake entered, and bowed.

"Oh! it is you, is it?" said the lady. "The girl told me some one was waiting."

Hot and swift ran the colour to my adored one's cheeks.

"Aunt," she observed, "I think you forget this gentleman comes from Mr. Craven."

"Oh, no! my dear, I don't forget Mr. Craven, or his clerks either," responded Miss Blake, as, still cloaked and bonneted, she tore open Mr. Craven's envelope.

"I am to take back an answer, I think," said I.

"You are, I see," she answered. "He's getting mighty particular, is William Craven. I suppose he thinks I am going to cheat him out of his paltry ten pounds. Ten pounds, indeed! and what is that, I should like to know, to us in our present straits! Why, I had more than twice ten yesterday from a man on whom we have no claim—none whatever—who, without asking, offered it in our need."

"Aunt," said Miss Elmsdale, warningly.

"If you will kindly give me your acknowledgment, Miss Blake, I should like to be getting back to Buckingham Street," I said. "Mr. Craven will wonder at my absence."

"Not a bit of it," retorted Miss Blake. "You and Mr. Craven understand each other, or I am very much mistaken; but here is the receipt, and good day to you."

I should have merely bowed my farewell, but that Miss Elmsdale stood up valiantly.

236

"Goodbye, Mr. Patterson," she said, holding out her dainty hand, and letting it lie in mine while she spoke. "I am very much obliged to you. I can never forget what you have done and dared in our interests."

And I went out of the room, and descended the stairs, and opened the front door, she looking graciously over the balusters the while, happy, ay, and more than happy.

What would I not have done and dared at that moment for Helena Elmsdale? Ah! ye lovers, answer!

CHAPTER 12

HELP

"There has been a gentleman to look at the house, sir, this afternoon," said Mrs. Stott to me, when, wet and tired, I arrived, a few evenings after my interview with Miss Elmsdale, at River Hall.

"To look at the house!" I repeated. "Why, it is not to let."

"I know that, sir, but he brought an order from Mr. Craven's office to allow him to see over the place, and to show him all about. For a widow lady from the country, he said he wanted it. A very nice gentleman, sir; only he did ask a lot of questions, surely—"

"What sort of questions?" I inquired.

"Oh! as to why the tenants did not stop here, and if I thought there was anything queer about the place; and he asked how you liked it, and how long you were going to stay; and if you had ever seen aught strange in the house.

"He spoke about you, sir, as if he knew you quite well, and said you must be stout-hearted to come and fight the ghosts all by yourself. A mighty civil, talkative gentleman—asked me if I felt afraid of living here, and whether I had ever met any spirits walking about the stairs and passages by themselves."

"Did he leave the order you spoke of just now behind him?"

"Yes, sir. He wanted me to give it back to him; but I said I must keep it for you to see. So then he laughed, and made the remark that he supposed, if he brought the lady to see the place,

I would let him in again. A pleasant-spoken gentleman, sir— gave me a shilling, though I told him I did not require it."

Meantime I was reading the order, written by Taylor, and dated two years back.

"What sort of looking man was he?" I asked.

"Well, sir, there was not anything particular about him in any way. Not a tall gentleman, not near so tall as you, sir; getting into years, but still very active and light-footed, though with some-thing of a halt in his way of walking. I could not rightly make out what it was; nor what it was that caused him to look a little crooked when you saw him from behind.

"Very lean, sir; looked as if the dinners he had eaten done him no good. Seemed as if, for all his pleasant ways, he must have seen trouble, his face was so worn-like."

"Did he say if he thought the house would suit?" I inquired.

"He said it was a very nice house, sir, and that he imagined anybody not afraid of ghosts might spend two thousand a year in it very comfortably. He said he should bring the lady to see the place, and asked me particularly if I was always at hand, in case he should come tolerably early in the morning."

"Oh!" was my comment, and I walked into the dining-room, wondering what the meaning of this new move might be; for Mrs. Stott had described, to the best of her ability, the man who stood watching our offices in London; and—good heavens!— yes, the man I had encountered in the lane leading to River Hall, when I went to the Uninhabited House, after Colonel Morris' departure.

"That is the man," thought I, "and he has some close, and deep, and secret interest in the mystery associated with this place, the origin of which I must discover."

Having arrived at this conclusion, I went to bed, for I had caught a bad cold, and was aching from head to foot, and had been sleeping ill, and hoped to secure a good night's rest.

I slept, it is true, but as for rest, I might as well, or better, have been awake. I fell from one dream into another; found myself wandering through impossible places; started in an agony of fear, and then dozed again, only to plunge into some deeper quagmire of trouble; and through all there was a vague feeling I was pursuing a person who eluded all my efforts to find him; playing a terrible game of hide-and-seek with a man who always slipped away from my touch, panting up mountains and running down declivities after one who had better wind and faster legs than I; peering out into the darkness, to catch a sight of a vague figure standing somewhere in the shadow, and looking, with the sun streaming into my eyes and blinding me, adown long white roads filled with a multitude of people, straining my sight to catch a sight of the coming traveller, who yet never came.

When I awoke thoroughly, as I did long and long before daybreak, I knew I was ill. I had a bad sore throat and an oppression at my chest which made me feel as if I was breathing through a sponge. My limbs ached more than had been the case on the previous evening whilst my head felt heavier than a log of teak.

"What should I do if I were to have a bad illness in that house?" I wondered to myself, and for a few minutes I pondered over the expediency of returning home; but this idea was soon set aside.

Where could I go that the Uninhabited House would not be a haunting presence? I had tried running away from it once before, and found it more real to me in the King's Road, Brighton, than on the banks of the Thames. No!—ill or well, I would stay on; the very first night of my absence might be the night of possible explanation.

Having so decided, I dressed and proceeded to the office, remaining there, however, only long enough to write a note to Mr. Craven, saying I had a very bad cold, and begging him to excuse my attendance.

After that I turned my steps to Munro's lodgings. If it were possible to avert an illness, I had no desire to become invalided in Mr. Elmsdale's Hall.

Fortunately, Munro was at home and at dinner. "Just come in time, old fellow," he said, cheerily. "It is not one day in a dozen you would have found me here at this hour. Sit down, and have some steak. Can't eat—why, what's the matter, man? You don't mean to say you have got another nervous attack. If you have, I declare I shall lodge a complaint against you with Mr. Craven."

"I am not nervous," I answered; "but I have caught cold, and I want you to put me to rights."

"Wait till I have finished my dinner," he replied; and then he proceeded to cut himself another piece of steak—having demolished which, and seen cheese placed on the table, he said:

"Now, Harry, we'll get to business, if you please. Where is this cold you were talking about?"

I explained as well as I could, and he listened to me without interruption. When I had quite finished, he said:

"Hal Patterson, you are either becoming a hypochondriac, or you are treating me to half confidences. Your cold is not worth speaking about. Go home, and get to bed, and take a basin of gruel, or a glass of something hot, after you are in bed, and your cold will be well in the morning. But there is something more than a cold the matter with you. What has come to you, to make a few rheumatic pains and a slight sore throat seem of consequence in your eyes?"

"I am afraid of being ill," I answered.

"Why are you afraid of being ill? why do you imagine you are going to be ill? why should you fall ill any more than anybody else?"

I sat silent for a minute, then I said, "Ned, if I tell you, will you promise upon your honour not to laugh at me?"

"I won't, if I can help it. I don't fancy I shall feel inclined to laugh," he replied.

"And unless I give you permission, you will not repeat what I am going to tell you to anyone?"

"That I can safely promise," he said. "Go on."

And I went on. I began at the beginning and recited all the events chronicled in the preceding pages; and he listened, asking no questions, interposing no remark.

When I ceased speaking, he rose and said he must think over the statements I had made.

"I will come and look you up tonight, Patterson," he observed. "Go home to River Hall, and keep yourself quiet. Don't mention that you feel ill. Let matters go on as usual. I will be with you about nine. I have an appointment now that I must keep."

Before nine Munro appeared, hearty, healthy, vigorous as usual.

"If this place were in Russell Square," he said, after a hasty glance round the drawing-room, "I should not mind taking a twenty-one years' lease of it at forty pounds a year, even if ghosts were included in the fixtures."

"I see you place no credence in my story," I said, a little stiffly.

"I place every credence in your story," was the reply. "I believe you believe it, and that is saying more than most people could say nowadays about their friends' stories if they spoke the truth."

It was of no use for me to express any further opinion upon the matter. I felt if I talked for a thousand years I should still fail to convince my listener there was anything supernatural in the appearances beheld at River Hall. It is so easy to pooh-pooh another man's tale; it is pleasant to explain every phenomenon that the speaker has never witnessed; it is so hard to credit that anything absolutely unaccountable on natural grounds has been witnessed by your dearest friend, that, knowing my only chance of keeping my temper and preventing Munro gaining a victory over me was to maintain a discreet silence, I let him talk on and strive to account for the appearances I had witnessed in his own way.

"Your acquaintance of the halting gait and high shoulder may or might have some hand in the affair," he finished. "My own opinion is he has not. The notion that you are being watched, is, if my view of the matter be correct, only a further development of the nervous excitement which has played you all sort of fantastic tricks since you came to this house. If anyone does wander through the gardens, I should set him down as a monomaniac or an intending burglar, and in any case the very best thing you can do is to pack up your traps and leave River Hall to its fate."

I did not answer; indeed, I felt too sick at heart to do so. What he said was what other people would say. If I could not evolve some clearer theory than I had yet been able to hit on, I should be compelled to leave the mystery of River Hall just as I had found it. Miss Blake had, I knew, written to Mr. Craven that the house had better be let again, as there "was no use in his keeping a clerk there in free lodgings forever": and now came Ned Munro, with his worldly wisdom, to assure me mine was a wild-goose chase, and that the only sensible course for me to pursue was to abandon it altogether. For the first time, I felt disheartened about the business, and I suppose I showed my disappointment, for Munro, drawing his chair nearer to me, laid a friendly hand on my shoulder and said:

"Cheer up, Harry! never look so downhearted because your nervous system has been playing you false. It was a plucky thing to do, and to carry out; but you have suffered enough for honour, and I should not continue the experiment of trying how much you can suffer, were I in your shoes."

"You are very kind, Munro," I answered; "but I cannot give up. If I had all the wish in the world to leave here tonight, a will stronger than my own would bring me back here tomorrow. The place haunts me. Believe me, I suffer less from its influence, seated in this room, than when I am in the office or walking along the Strand."

"Upon the same principle, I suppose, that a murderer always carries the memory of his victim's face about with him; though he may have felt callously indifferent whilst the body was an actual presence."

"Precisely," I agreed.

"But then, my dear fellow, you are not a murderer in any sense of the word. You did not create the ghosts supposed to be resident here."

"No; but I feel bound to find out who did," I answered.

"That is, if you can, I suppose?" he suggested.

"I feel certain I shall," was the answer. "I have an idea in my mind, but it wants shape. There is a mystery, I am convinced, to solve which, only the merest hint is needed."

"There are a good many things in this world in the same position, I should say," answered Munro. "However, Patterson, we won't argue about the matter; only there is one thing upon which I am determined—after this evening, I will come and stay here every night. I can say I am going to sleep out of town. Then, if there are ghosts, we can hunt them together; if there are none, we shall rest all the better. Do you agree to that?" and he held out his hand, which I clasped in mine, with a feeling of gratitude and relief impossible to describe.

As he said, I had done enough for honour; but still I could not give up, and here was the support and help I required so urgently, ready for my need.

"I am so much obliged," I said at last.

"Pooh! nonsense!" he answered. "You would do as much or more for me any day. There, don't let us get sentimental. You must not come out, but, following the example of your gallant Colonel Morris, I will, if you please, smoke a cigar in the garden. The moon must be up by this time."

I drew back the curtains and unfastened the shutter, which offered egress to the grounds, then, having rung for Mrs. Stott to remove the supper-tray, I sat down by the fire to await Munro's return, and began musing concerning the hopelessness of my position, the gulf of poverty and prejudice and struggle that lay between Helena and myself.

I was determined to win her; but the prize seemed unattainable as the Lord Mayor's robes must have appeared to Whittington, when he stood at the foot of Highgate Hill; and, prostrated as I was by that subtle malady to which as yet Munro had given no name, the difficulties grew into mountains, the chances of success dwarfed themselves into molehills.

Whilst thus thinking vaguely, purposelessly, but still most miserably, I was aroused from reverie by the noise of a door being shut cautiously and carefully—an outer door, and yet one with the sound of which I was unacquainted.

Hurrying across the hall, I flung the hall-door wide, and looked out into the night. There was sufficient moonlight to have enabled me to discern any object moving up or down the lane, but not a creature was in sight, not a cat or dog even traversed the weird whiteness of that lonely thoroughfare.

Despite Munro's *dictum*, I passed out into the night air, and went down to the very banks of the Thames. There was not a boat within hail. The nearest barge lay a couple of hundred yards from the shore.

As I retraced my steps, I paused involuntarily beside the door, which led by a separate entrance to the library.

"That is the door which shut," I said to myself, pressing my hand gently along the lintel, and sweeping the hitherto unbroken cobwebs away as I did so. "If my nerves are playing me false this time, the sooner their tricks are stopped the better, for no human being opened this door, no living creature has passed through it."

Having made up my mind on which points, I re-entered the house, and walked into the drawing-room, where Munro, pale as death, stood draining a glass of neat brandy.

"What is the matter?" I cried, hurriedly. "What have you seen, what—"

"Let me alone for awhile," he interrupted, speaking in a thick, hoarse whisper; then immediately asked, "Is that the library with the windows nearest the river?"

"Yes," I answered.

"I want to go into that room," he said, still in the same tone.

"Not now," I entreated. "Sit down and compose yourself; we will go into it, if you like, before you leave."

"Now, now—this minute," he persisted. "I tell you, Patterson, I must see what is in it."

Attempting no further opposition, I lit a couple of candles, and giving one into his hand, led the way to the door of the library, which I unlocked and flung wide open.

To one particular part Munro directed his steps, casting the light from his candle on the carpet, peering around in search of something he hoped, and yet still feared, to see. Then he went to the shutters and examined the fastenings, and finding all well secured, made a sign for me to precede him out of the room. At the door he paused, and took one more look into the darkness of the apartment, after which he waited while I turned the key in the lock, accompanying me back across the hall.

When we were once more in the drawing-room, I renewed my inquiry as to what he had seen; but he bade me let him alone, and sat mopping great beads of perspiration off his forehead, till, unable to endure the mystery any longer, I said:

"Munro, whatever it may be that you have seen, tell me all, I entreat. Any certainty will be better than the possibilities I shall be conjuring up for myself."

He looked at me wearily, and then drawing his hand across his eyes, as if trying to clear his vision, he answered, with an uneasy laugh:

"It was nonsense, of course. I did not think I was so imaginative, but I declare I fancied I saw, looking through the windows of that now utterly dark room, a man lying dead on the floor."

"Did you hear a door shut?" I inquired.

"Distinctly," he answered; "and what is more, I saw a shadow flitting through the other door leading out of the library, which we found, if you remember, bolted on the inside."

"And what inference do you draw from all this?"

"Either that someone is, in a to me unintelligible way, playing a very clever game at River Hall, or else that I am mad."

"You are no more mad than other people who have lived in this house," I answered.

"I don't know how you have done it, Patterson," he went on, unheeding my remark. "I don't, upon my soul, know how you managed to stay on here. It would have driven many a fellow out of his mind. I do not like leaving you. I wish I had told my landlady I should not be back. I will, after this time; but tonight I am afraid some patient may be wanting me."

"My dear fellow," I answered, "the affair is new to you, but it is not new to me. I would rather sleep alone in the haunted house, than in a mansion filled from basement to garret, with the unsolved mystery of this place haunting me."

"I wish you had never heard of, nor seen, nor come near it," he exclaimed, bitterly; "but, however, let matters turn out as they will, I mean to stick to you, Patterson. There's my hand on it."

And he gave me his hand, which was cold as ice—cold as that of one dead.

"I am going to have some punch, Ned," I remarked. "That is, if you will stop and have some."

"All right," he answered. "Something 'hot and strong' will hurt neither of us, but you ought to have yours in bed. May I give it to you there?"

"Nonsense!" I exclaimed, and we drew our chairs close to the fire, and, under the influence of a decoction which Ned insisted upon making himself, and at making which, indeed, he was much more of an adept than I, we talked valiantly about ghosts and their doings, and about how our credit and happiness were bound up in finding out the reason why the Uninhabited House was haunted.

"Depend upon it, Hal," said Munro, putting on his coat and hat, preparatory to taking his departure, "depend upon it that unfortunate Robert Elmsdale must have been badly cheated by someone, and sorely exercised in spirit, before he blew out his brains."

To this remark, which, remembering what he had said in the middle of the day, showed the wonderful difference that exists between theory and practice, I made no reply.

Unconsciously, almost, a theory had been forming in my own mind, but I felt much corroboration of its possibility must be obtained before I dare give it expression.

Nevertheless, it had taken such hold of me that I could not shake off the impression, which was surely, though slowly, gaining ground, even against the dictates of my better judgement.

"I will just read over the account of the inquest once again," I decided, as I bolted and barred the chain after Munro's departure; and so, by way of ending the night pleasantly, I took out the report, and studied it till two, chiming from a neighbouring church, reminded me that the fire was out, that I had a bad cold, and that I ought to have been between the blankets and asleep hours previously.

CHAPTER 13

LIGHT AT LAST

Now, whether it was owing to having gone out the evening before from a very warm room into the night air, and, afterwards, into that chilly library, or to having sat reading the report given about Mr. Elmsdale's death till I grew chilled to my very marrow, I cannot say, all I know is, that when I awoke next morning I felt very ill, and welcomed, with rejoicing of spirit, Ned Munro, who arrived about midday, and at once declared he had come to spend a fortnight with me in the Uninhabited House.

"I have arranged it all. Got a friend to take charge of my patients; stated that I am going to pay a visit in the country, and so forth. And now, how are you?"

I told him, very truthfully, that I did not feel at all well.

"Then you will have to get well, or else we shall never be able to fathom this business," he said. "The first thing, consequently, I shall do, is to write a prescription, and get it made up. After that, I mean to take a survey of the house and grounds."

"Do precisely what you like," I answered. "This is Liberty Hall to the living as well as to the dead," and I laid my head on the back of the easy-chair, and went off to sleep.

All that day Munro seemed to feel little need of my society. He examined every room in the house, and every square inch about the premises. He took short walks round the adjacent neighbourhood, and made, to his own satisfaction, a map of River Hall and the country and town thereunto adjoining. Then he had a great fire lighted in the library, and spent the afternoon tapping the walls, trying the floors, and trying to obtain enlightenment from the passage which led from the library direct to the door opening into the lane.

After dinner, he asked me to lend him the shorthand report

I had made of the evidence given at the inquest. He made no comment upon it when he finished reading, but sat, for a few minutes, with one hand shading his eyes, and the other busily engaged in making some sort of a sketch on the back of an old letter.

"What are you doing, Munro?" I asked, at last.

"You shall see presently," he answered, without looking up, or pausing in his occupation.

At the expiration of a few minutes, he handed me over the paper, saying:

"Do you know anyone that resembles?"

I took the sketch, looked at it, and cried out incoherently in my surprise.

"Well," he went on, "who is it?"

"The man who follows me! The man I saw in this lane!"

"And what is his name?"

"That is precisely what I desire to find out," I answered. "When did you see him? How did you identify him? Why did—"

"I have something to tell you, if you will only be quiet, and let me speak," he interrupted. "It was, as you know, late last night before I left here, and for that reason, and also because I was perplexed and troubled, I walked fast—faster than even is my wont. The road was very lonely; I scarcely met a creature along the road, flooded with the moonlight. I never was out on a lovelier night; I had never, even in the country, felt I had it so entirely to myself.

"Every here and there I came within sight of the river, and it seemed, on each occasion, as though a great mirror had been put up to make every object on land—every house, every tree, bush, fern, more clearly visible than it had been before. I am coming to my story, Hal, so don't look so impatient.

"At last, as I came once again in view of the Thames, with the moon reflected in the water, and the dark arches of the bridge looking black and solemn contrasted against the silvery stream, I saw before me, a long way before me, a man whose figure stood out in relief against the white road—a man walking wearily and with evident difficulty—a man, too, slightly deformed.

"I walked on rapidly, till within about a score yards of him, then I slackened my speed, and taking care that my leisurely footsteps should be heard, overtook him by degrees, and then, when I was quite abreast, asked if he could oblige me with a light.

"He looked up in my face, and said, with a forced, painful smile and studied courtesy of manner:

"'I am sorry, sir, to say that I do not smoke.'

"I do not know exactly what reply I made. I know his countenance struck me so forcibly, it was with difficulty I could utter some commonplace remark concerning the beauty of the night.

"'I do not like moonlight,' he said, and as he said it, something, a connection of ideas, or a momentary speculation, came upon me so suddenly, that once again I failed to reply coherently, but asked if he could tell me the shortest way to the Brompton Road.

"'To which end?' he inquired.

"'That nearest Hyde Park Corner,' I answered.

"As it turned out, no question could have served my purpose better.

"'I am going part of the way there,' he said, 'and will show you the nearest route—that is,' he added, 'if you can accommodate your pace to mine,' and he pointed, as he spoke, to his right foot, which evidently was causing him considerable pain.

"Now, that was something quite in my way, and by degrees I got him to tell me about the accident which had caused his slight deformity. I told him I was a doctor, and had been to see a patient, and so led him on to talk about sickness and disease, till at length he touched upon diseases of a morbid character; asking me if it were true that in some special maladies the patient was haunted by an apparition which appeared at a particular hour.

"I told him it was quite true, and that such cases were peculiarly distressing, and generally proved most difficult to cure— mentioning several well-authenticated instances, which I do not mean to detail to you, Patterson, as I know you have an aversion to anything savouring of medical shop.

"'You doctors do not believe in the actual existence of any such apparitions, of course?' he remarked, after a pause.

"I told him we did not; that we knew they had their rise and origin solely in the malady of the patient.

"'And yet,' he said, 'some ghost stories—I am not now speaking of those associated with disease, are very extraordinary, unaccountable—'

"'Very extraordinary, no doubt,' I answered; 'but I should hesitate before saying unaccountable. Now, there is that River Hall place up the river. There must be some rational way of explaining the appearances in that house, though no one has yet found any clue to that enigma.'

"'River Hall—where is that?' he asked; then suddenly added, 'Oh! I remember now: you mean the Uninhabited House, as it is called. Yes, there is a curious story, if you like. May I ask if you are interested in any way in that matter?'

"'Not in any way, except that I have been spending the evening there with a friend of mine.'

"'Has he seen anything of the reputed ghost?' asked my companion, eagerly. 'Is he able to throw any light on the dark subject?'

"'I don't think he can,' I replied. 'He has seen the usual appearances which I believe it is correct to see at River Hall; but so far, they have added nothing to his previous knowledge.'

"'He has seen, you say?'

"'Yes; all the orthodox lions of that cheerful house.'

"'And still he is not daunted—he is not afraid?'

"'He is not afraid. Honestly, putting ghosts entirely on one side, I should not care to be in his shoes, all alone in a lonely house.'

"'And you would be right, sir,' was the answer. 'A man must be mad to run such a risk.'

"'So I told him,' I agreed.

"'Why, I would not stay in that house alone for any money

which could be offered to me,' he went on, eagerly.

"'I cannot go so far as that,' I said; 'but still it must be a very large sum which could induce me to do so.'

"'It ought to be pulled down, sir,' he continued; 'the walls ought to be razed to the ground.'

"'I suppose they will,' I answered, 'when Miss Elmsdale, the owner, comes of age; unless, indeed, our modern Don Quixote runs the ghost to earth before that time.'

"'Did you say the young man was ill?' asked my companion.

"'He has got a cold,' I answered.

"'And colds are nasty things to get rid of,' he commented, 'particularly in those low-lying localities. That is a most unhealthy part; you ought to order your patient a thorough change of air.'

"'I have, but he won't take advice,' was my reply. 'He has nailed his colours to the mast, and means, I believe, to stay in River Hall till he kills the ghost, or the ghost kills him.'

"'What a foolish youth!'

"'Undoubtedly; but, then, youth is generally foolish, and we have all our crotchets.'

"We had reached the other side of the bridge by this time, and saying his road lay in an opposite direction to mine, the gentleman I have sketched told me the nearest way to take, and bade me a civil good night, adding, 'I suppose I ought to say good morning.'"

"And is that all?" I asked, as Munro paused.

"*Bide a wee*, as the Scotch say, my son. I strode off along the road he indicated, and then, instead of making the detour he had kindly sketched out for my benefit, chose the first turning to my left, and, quite convinced he would soon pass that way, took up my position in the *portico* of a house which lay well in shadow. It stood a little back from the side-path, and a poor little Arab sleeping on the stone step proved to me the policeman was not over and above vigilant in that neighbourhood.

"I waited, Heaven only knows how long, thinking all the time I must be mistaken, and that his home did lie in the direction he took; but at last, looking out between the pillars and the concealing shrubs, I saw him. He was looking eagerly into the distance, with such a drawn, worn, painful expression, that for a moment my heart relented, and I thought I would let the poor devil go in peace.

"It was only for a moment, however; touching the sleeping boy, I bade him awake, if he wanted to earn a shilling. 'Keep that gentleman in sight, and get to know for me where he lives, and come back here, and I will give you a shilling, and perhaps two, for your pains.'

"With his eyes still heavy with slumber, and his perceptions for the moment dulled, he sped after the figure, limping wearily on. I saw him ask my late companion for charity, and follow the gentleman for a few steps, when the latter, threatening him with his stick, the boy dodged to escape a blow, and then, by way of showing how lightly his bosom's load sat upon him, began turning wheels down the middle of the street. He passed the place where I stood, and spun a hundred feet further on, then he gathered himself together, and seeing no one in sight, stealthily crept back to his porch again.

"'You young rascal,' I said, 'I told you to follow him home. I want to know his name and address particularly.'

"'Come along, then,' he answered, 'and I'll show you. Bless you, we all knows him—better than we do the police, or anybody hereabouts. He's a beak and a ward up at the church, whatever that is, and he has building-yards as big, oh! as big as two workhouses, and—'"

"His name, Munro—his name?" I gasped.

"Harringford."

I expected it. I knew then that for days and weeks my suspicions had been vaguely connecting Mr. Harringford with the mystery of the Uninhabited House.

This was the hiding figure in my dream, the link hitherto wanting in my reveries concerning River Hall. I had been looking for this—waiting for it; I understood at last; and yet, when Munro mentioned the name of the man who had thought it worth his while to watch my movements, I shrunk from the conclusion which forced itself upon me.

"Must we go on to the end with this affair?" I asked, after a pause, and my voice was so changed, it sounded like that of a stranger to me.

"We do not yet know what the end will prove," Munro answered; "but whatever it may be, we must not turn back now."

"How ought we to act, do you think?" I inquired.

"We ought not to act at all," he answered. "We had better wait and see what his next move will be. He is certain to take some step. He will try to get you out of this house by hook or by crook. He has already striven to effect his purpose through Miss Elmsdale, and failed. It will therefore be necessary for him to attempt some other scheme. It is not for me to decide on the course he is likely to pursue; but, if I were in your place, I should stay within doors at night. I should not sit in the dark near windows still unshuttered. I should not allow any strangers to enter the house, and I should have a couple of good dogs running loose about the premises. I have brought Brenda with me as a beginning, and I think I know where to lay my hand on a good old collie, who will stay near any house I am in, and let no one trespass about it with impunity."

"Good heavens! Munro, you don't mean to say you think the man would *murder* me!" I exclaimed.

"I don't know what he might, or might not do," he replied. "There is something about this house he is afraid may be found out, and he is afraid you will find it out. Unless I am greatly mistaken, a great deal depends upon the secret being preserved intact. At present we can only surmise its nature; but I mean, in the course of a few days, to know more of Mr. Harringford's antecedents than he might be willing to communicate to anyone. What is the matter with you, Hal? You look as white as a corpse."

"I was only thinking," I answered, "of one evening last week, when I fell asleep in the drawing-room, and woke in a fright, imagining I saw that horrid light streaming out from the library, and a face pressed up close to the glass of the window on my left hand peering into the room."

"I have no doubt the face was there," he said, gravely; "but I do not think it will come again, so long as Brenda is alive. Nevertheless, I should be careful. Desperate men are capable of desperate deeds."

The first post next morning brought me a letter from Mr. Craven, which proved Mr. Harringford entertained for the present no intention of proceeding to extremities with me.

He had been in Buckingham Street, so said my principal, and offered to buy the freehold of River Hall for twelve hundred pounds.

Mr. Craven thought he might be induced to increase his bid to fifteen hundred, and added: "Miss Blake has half consented to the arrangement, and Miss Elmsdale is eager for the matter to be pushed on, so that the transfer may take place directly she comes of age. I confess, now an actual offer has been made, I feel reluctant to sacrifice the property for such a sum, and doubt whether it might not be better to offer it for sale by auction—that is, if you think there is no chance of your discovering the reason why River Hall bears so bad a name. Have you obtained any clue to the mystery?"

To this I replied in a note, which Munro himself conveyed to the office.

"I have obtained an important clue; but that is all I can say for the present. Will you tell Mr. Harringford I am at River Hall, and that you think, being on the spot and knowing all about the place, I could negotiate the matter better than anyone else in the office? If he is desirous of purchasing, he will not object to calling some evening and discussing the matter with me. I have an idea that a large sum of money might be made out of this property by an enterprising man like Mr. Harringford; and it is just possible, after hearing what I have to say, he may find himself able to make a much better offer for the Uninhabited House than that mentioned in your note. At all events, the interview can do no harm. I am still suffering so much from cold that it would be imprudent for me to wait upon Mr. Harringford, which would otherwise be only courteous on my part."

"Capital!" said Munro, reading over my shoulder. "That will bring my gentleman to River Hall—. But what is wrong, Patterson? You are surely not going to turn chickenhearted now?"

"No," I answered; "but I wish it was over. I dread something, and I do not know what it is. Though nothing shall induce me to waver, I am afraid, Munro. I am not ashamed to say it: I am afraid, as I was the first night I stayed in this house. I am not a coward, but I am afraid."

He did not reply for a moment. He walked to the window and looked out over the Thames; then he came back, and, wringing my hand, said, in tones that tried unsuccessfully to be cheerful:

"I know what it is, old fellow. Do you think I have not had the feeling myself, since I came here? But remember, it has to be done, and I will stand by you. I will see you through it."

"It won't do for you to be in the room, though," I suggested.

"No; but I will stay within earshot," he answered.

We did not talk much more about the matter. Men rarely do talk much about anything which seems to them very serious, and I may candidly say that I had never felt anything in my life to be much more serious than that impending interview with Mr. Harringford.

That he would come we never doubted for a moment, and we were right. As soon as it was possible for him to appoint an interview, Mr. Harringford did so.

"Nine o'clock on tomorrow (Thursday) evening," was the hour he named, apologizing at the same time for being unable to call at an earlier period of the day.

"Humph!" said Munro, turning the note over. "You will receive him in the library, of course, Hal?"

I replied such was my intention.

"And that will be a move for which he is in no way prepared," commented my friend.

From the night when Munro walked and talked with Mr.

Harringford, no person came spying round and about the Un-inhabited House. Of this fact we were satisfied, for Brenda, who gave tongue at the slightest murmur wafted over the river from the barges lying waiting for the tide, never barked as though she were on the track of living being; whilst the collie—a tawny-black, unkempt, ill-conditioned, savage-natured, but yet most true and faithful brute, which Munro insisted on keeping within doors, never raised his voice from the day he arrived at River Hall, till the night Mr. Harringford rang the visitor's-bell, when the animal, who had been sleeping with his nose resting on his paws, lifted his head and indulged in a prolonged howl.

Not a nice beginning to an interview which I dreaded.

CHAPTER 14

A TERRIBLE INTERVIEW

I was in the library, waiting to receive Mr. Harringford. A bright fire blazed on the hearth, the table was strewn with pa-pers Munro had brought to me from the office, the gas was all ablaze, and the room looked bright and cheerful—as bright and as cheerful as if no ghost had been ever heard of in connection with it.

At a few minutes past nine my visitor arrived. Mrs. Stott ushered him into the library, and he entered the room evidently intending to shake hands with me, which civility I affected not to notice.

After the first words of greeting were exchanged, I asked if he would have tea, or coffee, or wine; and finding he rejected all offers of refreshment, I rang the bell and told Mrs. Stott I could dispense with her attendance for the night.

"Do you mean to tell me you stay in this house entirely alone?" asked my visitor.

"Until Mrs. Stott came I was quite alone," I answered.

"I would not have done it for any consideration," he re-marked.

"Possibly not," I replied. "People are differently constituted."

It was not long before we got to business. His offer of twelve hundred pounds I pooh-poohed as ridiculous.

"Well," he said—by this time I knew I had a keen man of business to deal with—"put the place up to auction, and see whether you will get as much."

"There are two, or rather, three ways of dealing with the property, which have occurred to me, Mr. Harringford," I explained. "One is letting or selling this house for a reformatory, or school. Ghosts in that case won't trouble the inmates, we may be quite certain; another is utilizing the buildings for a manufactory; and the third is laying the ground out for building purposes, thus—"

As I spoke, I laid before him a plan for a tri-sided square of building, the south side being formed by the river. I had taken great pains with the drawing of this plan: the future houses, the future square, the future river-walk with seats at intervals, were all to be found in the roll which I unfolded and laid before him, and the effect my sketch produced surprised me.

"In Heaven's name, Mr. Patterson," he asked, "where did you get this? You never drew it out of your own head!"

I hastened to assure him I had certainly not got it out of any other person's head; but he smiled incredulously.

"Probably," he suggested, "Mr. Elmsdale left some such sketch behind him—something, at all events, which suggested the idea to you."

"If he did, I never saw nor heard of it," I answered.

"You may have forgotten the circumstance," he persisted; "but I feel confident you must have seen something like this before. Perhaps amongst the papers in Mr. Craven's office."

"May I inquire why you have formed such an opinion?" I said, a little stiffly.

"Simply because this tri-sided square was a favourite project of the late owner of River Hall," he replied. "After the death of his wife, the place grew distasteful to him, and I have often heard him say he would convert the ground into one of the handsomest squares in the neighbourhood of London. All he wanted was a piece of additional land lying to the west, which piece is, I believe, now to be had at a price—"

I sat like one stricken dumb. By no mental process, for which I could ever account, had that idea been evolved. It sprang into life at a bound. It came to me in my sleep, and I wakened at once with the whole plan clear and distinct before my mind's eye, as it now lay clear and distinct before Mr. Harringford.

"It is very extraordinary," I managed at last to stammer out; "for I can honestly say I never heard even a suggestion of Mr. Elmsdale's design; indeed, I did not know he had ever thought of building upon the ground."

"Such was the fact, however," replied my visitor. "He was a speculative man in many ways. Yes, very speculative, and full of plans and projects. However, Mr. Patterson," he proceeded, "all this only proves the truth of the old remark, that 'great wits and little wits sometimes jump together.'"

There was a ring of sarcasm in his voice, as in his words, but I did not give much heed to it. The design, then, was not mine. It had come to me in sleep, it had been forced upon me, it had been explained to me in a word, and as I asked myself, By whom? I was unable to repress a shudder.

"You are not well, I fear," said Mr. Harringford; "this place seems to have affected your health. Surely you have acted imprudently in risking so much to gain so little."

"I do not agree with you," I replied. "However, time will show whether I have been right or wrong in coming here. I have learned many things of which I was previously in ignorance, and I think I hold a clue in my hands which, properly followed, may lead me to the hidden mystery of River Hall."

"Indeed!" he exclaimed. "May I ask the nature of that clue?"

"It would be premature for me to say more than this, that I am inclined to doubt whether Mr. Elmsdale committed suicide."

"Do you think his death was the result of accident, then?" he inquired, his face blanching to a ghastly whiteness.

"No, I do not," I answered, bluntly. "But my thoughts can have little interest for anyone, at present. What we want to talk about is the sale and purchase of this place. The offer you made to Mr. Craven, I consider ridiculous. Let on building lease, the land alone would bring in a handsome income, and the house ought to sell for about as much as you offer for the whole property."

"Perhaps it might, if you could find a purchaser," he answered; "and the land might return an income, if you could let it as you suggest; but, in the meantime, while the grass grows, the steed starves; and while you are waiting for your buyer and your speculative builder, Miss Blake and Miss Elmsdale will have to walk barefoot, waiting for shoes you may never be able to provide for them."

There was truth in this, but only a half-truth, I felt, so I said:

"When examined at the inquest, Mr. Harringford, you stated, I think, that you were under considerable obligations to Mr. Elmsdale?"

"Did I?" he remarked. "Possibly, he had given me a helping-hand once or twice, and probably I mentioned the fact. It is a long time ago, though."

"Not so very long," I answered; "not long enough, I should imagine, to enable you to forget any benefits you may have received from Mr. Elmsdale."

"Mr. Patterson," he interrupted, "are we talking business or sentiment? If the former, please understand I have my own interests to attend to, and that I mean to attend to them. If the latter, I am willing, if you say Miss Elmsdale has pressing need for the money, to send her my cheque for fifty or a hundred pounds. Charity is one thing, trade another, and I do not care to mix them. I should never have attained to my present position, had I allowed fine feelings to interfere with the driving of a bargain. I don't want River Hall. I would not give that," and he snapped his fingers, "to have the title-deeds in my hands tomorrow; but as Miss Elmsdale wishes to sell, and as no one else will buy, I offer what I consider a fair price for the place. If you think you can do better, well and good. If—"

He stopped suddenly in his sentence, then rising, he cried, "It is a trick—a vile, infamous, disgraceful trick!" while his utterance grew thick, and his face began to work like that of a person in convulsions.

"What do you mean?" I asked, rising also, and turning to look in the direction he indicated with outstretched arm and dilated eyes.

Then I saw—no need for him to answer. Standing in the entrance to the strong room was Robert Elmsdale himself, darkness for a background, the light of the gas falling full upon his face.

Slowly, sternly, he came forward, step by step. With footfalls that fell noiselessly, he advanced across the carpet, moving steadily forward towards Mr. Harringford, who, beating the air with his hands, screamed, "Keep him off! don't let him touch me!" and fell full length on the floor.

Next instant, Munro was in the room. "Hullo, what is the matter?" he asked. "What have you done to him—what has he been doing to you?"

I could not answer. Looking in my face, I think Munro understood we had both seen that which no man can behold unappalled.

"Come, Hal," he said, "bestir yourself. Whatever has happened, don't sink under it like a woman. Help me to lift him. Merciful Heaven!" he added, as he raised the prostrate figure. "He is dead!"

To this hour, I do not know how we managed to carry him into the drawing-room. I cannot imagine how our trembling hands bore that inert body out of the library and across the hall. It seems like a dream to me calling up Mrs. Stott, and then tearing away from the house in quest of further medical help, haunted, every step I took, by the memory of that awful presence, the mere sight of which had stricken down one of us in the midst of his buying, and bargaining, and boasting.

I had done it—I had raised that ghost—I had brought the man to his death; and as I fled through the night, innocent as I had been of the thought of such a catastrophe, I understood what Cain must have felt when he went out to live his life with the brand of murderer upon him.

But the man was not dead; though he lay for hours like one from whom life had departed, he did not die then. We had all the genius, and knowledge, and skill of London at his service. If doctors could have saved him, he had lived. If nursing could have availed him, he had recovered, for I never left him.

When the end came I was almost worn out myself.

And the end came very soon.

"No more doctors," whispered the sick man; "they cannot cure me. Send for a clergyman, and a lawyer, Mr. Craven as well as any other. It is all over now; and better so; life is but a long fever. Perhaps he will sleep now, and let me sleep too. Yes, I killed him. Why, I will tell you. Give me some wine.

"What I said at the inquest about owing my worldly prosperity to him was true. I trace my pecuniary success to Mr. Elmsdale; but I trace also hours, months, and years of anguish to his agency. My God! the nights that man has made me spend when he was living, the nights I have spent in consequence of his death—"

He stopped; he had mentally gone back over a long journey. He was retracing the road he had travelled, from youth to old age. For he was old, if not in years, in sorrow. Lying on his death-bed, he understood for what a game he had burnt his candle to the socket; comprehended how the agony, and the suspense, and the suffering, and the long, long fever of life, which with him never knew a remittent moment, had robbed him of that which every man has a right to expect, some pleasure in the course of his existence.

"When I first met Elmsdale," he went on, "I was a young man, and an ambitious one. I was a clerk in the City. I had been married a couple of years to a wife I loved dearly. She was possessed of only a small dot; and after furnishing our house, and paying for all the expenses incident on the coming of a first child, we thought ourselves fortunate in knowing there was still a deposit standing in our name at the Joint-Stock Bank, for something over two hundred pounds.

"Nevertheless, I was anxious. So far, we had lived within our income; but with an annual advance of salary only amounting to ten pounds, or thereabouts, I did not see how we were to manage when more children came, particularly as the cost of living increased day by day. It was a dear year that of which I am speaking.

"I do not precisely remember on what occasion it was I first saw Mr. Elmsdale; but I knew afterwards he picked me out as a person likely to be useful to him.

"He was on good terms with my employers, and asked them to allow me to bid for some houses he wanted to purchase at a sale.

"To this hour I do not know why he did not bid for them himself. He gave me a five-pound note for my services; and that was the beginning of our connection. Off and on, I did many things for him of one sort or another, and made rather a nice addition to my salary out of doing them, till the devil, or he, or both, put it into my head to start as builder and speculator on my own account.

"I had two hundred pounds and my furniture: that was the whole of my capital; but Elmsdale found me money. I thought my fortune was made, the day he advanced me my first five hundred pounds. If I had known—if I had known—"

"Don't talk anymore," I entreated. "What can it avail to speak of such matters now?"

He turned towards me impatiently.

"Not talk," he repeated, "when I have for years been as one dumb, and at length the string of my tongue is loosened! Not talk, when, if I keep silence now, he will haunt me in eternity, as he has haunted me in time!"

I did not answer, I only moistened his parched lips, and bathed his burning forehead as tenderly as my unaccustomed hands understood how to perform such offices.

"Lift me up a little, please," he said; and I put the pillows in position as deftly as I could.

"You are not a bad fellow," he remarked, "but I am not going to leave you anything."

"God forbid!" I exclaimed, involuntarily.

"Are not you in want of money?" he asked.

"Not of yours," I answered.

"Mine," he said; "it is not mine, it is his. He thought a great deal of money, and he has come back for it. He can't rest, and he won't let me rest till I have paid him principal and interest—compound interest. Yes—well, I am able to do even that."

We sat silent for a few minutes, then he spoke again.

"When I first went into business with my borrowed capital, nothing I touched really succeeded. I found myself going back—back. Far better was my position as clerk; then at least I slept sound at nights, and relished my meals. But I had tasted of so-called independence, and I could not go back to be at the beck and call of an employer. Ah! no employer ever made me work so hard as Mr. Elmsdale; no beck and call were ever so imperative as his.

"I pass over a long time of anxiety, struggle, and hardship. The world thought me a prosperous man; probably no human being, save Mr. Elmsdale, understood my real position, and he made my position almost unendurable.

"How I came first to bet on races, would be a long story, longer than I have time to tell; but my betting began upon a very small scale, and I always won—always in the beginning. I won so certainly and so continuously, that finally I began to hope for deliverance from Mr. Elmsdale's clutches.

"I don't know how"—the narrative was not recited straight on as I am writing it, but by starts, as strength served him—"Mr. Elmsdale ascertained I was devoting myself to the turf: all I can say is, he did ascertain the fact, and followed me down to Ascot to make sure there was no mistake in his information.

"At the previous Derby my luck had begun to turn. I had lost then—lost heavily for me, and he taxed me with having done so.

"In equity, and at law, he had then the power of foreclosing on every house and rood of ground I owned. I was in his power—in the power of Robert Elmsdale. Think of it—. But

263

you never knew him. Young man, you ought to kneel down and thank God you were never so placed as to be in the power of such a devil—

"If ever you should get into the power of a man like Robert Elmsdale, don't offend him. It is bad enough to owe him money; but it is worse for him to owe you a grudge. I had offended him. He was always worrying me about his wife—lamenting her ill-health, extolling her beauty, glorifying himself on having married a woman of birth and breeding; just as if his were the only wife in the world, as if other men had not at home women twice as good, if not as handsome as Miss Blake's sister.

"Under Miss Blake's insolence I had writhed; and once, when my usual prudence deserted me, I told Mr. Elmsdale I had been in Ireland and seen the paternal Blake's ancestral cabin, and ascertained none of the family had ever mixed amongst the upper thousand, or whatever the number may be which goes to make up society in the Isle of Saints.

"It was foolish, and it was wrong; but I could not help saying what I did, and from that hour he was my enemy. Hitherto, he had merely been my creditor. My own imprudent speech transformed him into a man lying in wait to ruin me.

"He bided his time. He was a man who could wait for years before he struck, but who would never strike till he could make sure of inflicting a mortal wound. He drew me into his power more and more, and then he told me he did not intend to continue trusting anyone who betted—that he must have his money. If he had not it by a certain date, which he named, he would foreclose.

"That meant he would beggar me, and I with an ailing wife and a large family!

"I appealed to him. I don't remember now what I said, but I do recollect I might as well have talked to stone.

"What I endured during the time which followed, I could not describe, were I to talk for ever. Till a man in extremity tries to raise money, he never understands the difficulty of doing so. I had been short of money every hour since I first engaged in business, and yet I never comprehended the meaning of a dead-lock till then.

"One day, in the City, when I was almost mad with anxiety, I met Mr. Elmsdale.

"'Shall you be ready for me, Harringford?' he asked.

"'I do not know—I hope so,' I answered.

"'Well, remember, if you are not prepared with the money, I shall be prepared to act,' he said, with an evil smile.

"As I walked home that evening, an idea flashed into my mind. I had tried all honest means of raising the money; I would try dishonest. My credit was good. I had large transactions with first-rate houses. I was in the habit of discounting largely, and I—well, I signed names to paper that I ought not to have done. I had the bills put through. I had four months and three days in which to turn round, and I might, by that time, be able to raise sufficient to retire the acceptances.

"In the meantime, I could face Mr. Elmsdale, and so I wrote, appointing an evening when I would call with the money, and take his release for all claims upon me.

"When I arrived at River Hall he had all the necessary documents ready, but refused to give them up in exchange for my cheque.

"He could not trust me, he said, and he had, moreover, no banking account. If I liked to bring the amount in notes, well and good; if not, he would instruct his solicitors.

"The next day I had important business to attend to, so a stormy interview ended in my writing 'pay cash' on the cheque, and his consenting to take it to my bankers himself.

"My business on the following day, which happened to be out of town, detained me much longer than I anticipated, and it was late before I could reach River Hall. Late though it was, however, I determined to go after my papers. I held Mr. Elmsdale's receipt for the cheque, certainly; but I knew I had not an hour to lose in putting matters in train for another loan, if I was to retire the forged acceptances. By experience, I knew how the months slipped away when money had to be provided at the end of them, and I was feverishly anxious to hold my leases and title-deeds once more.

"I arrived at the door leading to the library. Mr. Elmsdale opened it as wide as the chain would permit, and asked who was there. I told him, and, grumbling a little at the unconscionable hour at which I had elected to pay my visit, he admitted me.

"He was out of temper. He had hoped and expected, I knew, to find payment of the cheque refused, and he could not submit with equanimity to seeing me slip out of his hands.

"Evidently, he did not expect me to come that night, for his table was strewed with deeds and notes, which he had been reckoning up, no doubt, as a miser counts his gold.

"A pair of pistols lay beside his desk—close to my hand, as I took the seat he indicated.

"We talked long and bitterly. It does not matter now what he said or I said. We fenced round and about a quarrel during the whole interview. I was meek, because I wanted him to let me have part of the money at all events on loan again; and he was blatant and insolent because he fancied I cringed to him—and I did cringe.

"I prayed for help that night from Man as I have never since prayed for help from God.

"You are still young, Mr. Patterson, and life, as yet, is new to you, or else I would ask whether, in going into an entirely strange office, you have not, if agitated in mind, picked up from the table a letter or card, and kept twisting it about, utterly unconscious for the time being of the social solecism you were committing.

"In precisely the same spirit—God is my witness, as I am a dying man, with no object to serve in speaking falsehoods—while we talked, I took up one of the pistols and commenced handling it.

"'Take care,' he said; 'that is loaded'; hearing which I laid it down again.

"For a time we went on talking; he trying to ascertain how I had obtained the money, I striving to mislead him.

"'Come, Mr. Elmsdale,' I remarked at last, 'you see I have

been able to raise the money; now be friendly, and consent to advance me a few thousands, at a fair rate, on a property I am negotiating for. There is no occasion, surely, for us to quarrel, after all the years we have done business together. Say you will give me a helping-hand once more, and—'

"Then he interrupted me, and swore, with a great oath, he would never have another transaction with me.

"'Though you have paid *me*,' he said, 'I know you are hopelessly insolvent. I cannot tell where or how you have managed to raise that money, but certain am I it has been by deceiving someone; and so sure as I stand here I will know all about the transaction within a month.'

"While we talked, he had been, at intervals, passing to and from his strong room, putting away the notes and papers previously lying about on the table; and, as he made this last observation, he was standing just within the door, placing something on the shelf.

"'It is of no use talking to me anymore,' he went on. 'If you talked from now to eternity you could not alter my decision. There are your deeds; take them, and never let me see you in my house again.'

"He came out of the darkness into the light at that moment, looking burly, and insolent, and braggart, as was his wont.

"Something in his face, in the tone of his voice, in the vulgar assumption of his manner, maddened me. I do not know, I have never been able to tell, what made me long at that moment to kill him—but I did long. With an impulse I could not resist, I rose as he returned towards the table, and snatching a pistol from the table—fired.

"Before he could realize my intention, the bullet was in his brain. He was dead, and I a murderer.

"You can understand pretty well what followed. I ran into the passage and opened the door; then, finding no one seemed to have heard the report of the pistol, my senses came back to me. I was not sorry for what I had done. All I cared for was to avert suspicion from myself, and to secure some advantage from his death.

"Stealing back into the room, I took all the money I could find, as well as deeds and other securities. These last I destroyed next day, and in doing so I felt a savage satisfaction.

"He would have served them the same as me,' I thought. All the rest you know pretty well.

"From the hour I left him lying dead in the library every worldly plan prospered with me. If I invested in land, it trebled in value. Did I speculate in houses, they were sought after as investments. I grew rich, respected, a man of standing. I had sold my soul to the devil, and he paid me even higher wages than those for which I engaged—but there was a balance.

"One after another, wife and children died; and while my heart was breaking by reason of my home left desolate, there came to me the first rumour of this place being haunted.

"I would not believe it—I did not—I fought against the truth as men fight with despair.

"I used to come here at night and wander as near to the house as I safely could. The place dogged me, sleeping and waking. That library was an ever-present memory. I have sat in my lonely rooms till I could endure the horrors of imagination no longer, and been forced to come from London that I might look at this terrible house, with the silent river flowing sullenly past its desolate gardens.

"Life seemed ebbing away from me. I saw that day by day the blood left my cheeks. I looked at my hands, and beheld they were becoming like those of some one very aged. My lameness grew perceptible to others as well as to me, and I could distinguish, as I walked in the sunshine, the shadow my figure threw was that of one deformed. I grew weak, and worn, and tired, yet I never thoroughly lost heart till I knew you had come here to unravel the secret.

"'And it will be revealed to him,' I thought, 'if I do not kill him too.'

"You have been within an ace of death often and often since you set yourself this task, but at the last instant my heart always failed me.

"Well, you are to live, and I to die. It was to be so, I suppose; but you will never be nearer your last moment, till you lie a corpse, than you have been twice, at any rate."

Then I understood how accurately Munro had judged when he warned me to be on my guard against this man—now harmless and dying, but so recently desperate and all-powerful for evil; and as I recalled the nights I had spent in that desolate house, I shivered.

Even now, though the years have come and the years have gone since I kept my lonely watch in River Hall, I start sometimes from sleep with a great horror of darkness upon me, and a feeling that stealthily someone is creeping through the silence to take my life!

Chapter 15

Conclusion

I can remember the day and the hour as if it had all happened yesterday. I can recall the view from the windows distinctly, as though time had stood still ever since. There are no gardens under our windows in Buckingham Street. Buckingham Gate stands the entrance to a desert of mud, on which the young Arabs—shoeless, stockingless—are disporting themselves. It is low water, and the river steamers keep towards the middle arches of Waterloo. Up aloft the Hungerford Suspension rears itself in mid air, and that spick-and-span new bridge, across which trains run now ceaselessly, has not yet been projected. It is a bright spring day. The sunshine falls upon the buildings on the Surrey side, and lights them with a picturesque beauty to which they have not the slightest title. A barge, laden with hay, is lying almost motionless in the middle of the Thames.

There is, even in London, a great promise and hope about that pleasant spring day, but for me life has held no promise, and the future no hope, since that night when the mystery of River Hall was solved in my presence, and out of his own mouth the murderer uttered his condemnation.

How the weeks and the months had passed with me is soon

told. Ill when I left River Hall, shortly after my return home I fell sick unto death, and lay like one who had already entered the Valley of the Shadow.

I was too weak to move; I was too faint to think; and when at length I was brought slowly back to the recollection of life and its cares, of all I had experienced and suffered in the Uninhabited House, the time spent in it seemed to me like the memory of some frightful dream.

I had lost my health there, and my love too. Helena was now further removed from me than ever. She was a great heiress. Mr. Harringford had left her all his money absolutely, and already Miss Blake was considering which of the suitors, who now came rushing to woo, it would be best for her niece to wed.

As for me, Taylor repeated, by way of a good joke, that her aunt referred to me as a "decent sort of young man" who "seemed to be but weakly," and, ignoring the fact of ever having stated "she would not mind giving fifty pounds," remarked to Mr. Craven, that, if I was in poor circumstances, he might pay me five or ten sovereigns, and charge the amount to her account.

Of all this Mr. Craven said nothing to me. He only came perpetually to my sick-bed, and told my mother that whenever I was able to leave town I must get away, drawing upon him for whatever sums I might require. I did not need to encroach on his kindness, however, for my uncle, hearing of my illness, sent me a cordial invitation to spend some time with him.

In his cottage, far away from London, strength at last returned to me, and by the autumn my old place in Mr. Craven's office was no longer vacant. I sat in my accustomed corner, pursuing former avocations, a changed man.

I was hard-working as ever, but hope lightened my road no longer.

To a penny I knew the amount of my lady's fortune, and understood Mr. Harringford's bequest had set her as far above me as the stars are above the earth.

I had the conduct of most of Miss Elmsdale's business. As a compliment, perhaps, Mr. Craven entrusted all the work connected with Mr. Harringford's estate to me, and I accepted that trust as I should have done any other which he might choose to place in my hands.

But I could have dispensed with his well-meant kindness. Every visit I paid to Miss Blake filled my soul with bitterness. Had I been a porter, a crossing-sweeper, or a potman, she might, I suppose, have treated me with some sort of courtesy; but, as matters stood, her every tone, word, and look, said, plainly as possible, "If you do not know your station, I will teach it to you."

As for Helena, she was always the same—sweet, and kind, and grateful, and gracious; but she had her friends about her: new lovers waiting for her smiles. And, after a time, the shadow cast across her youth would, I understood, be altogether removed, and leave her free to begin a new and beautiful life, unalloyed by that hideous, haunting memory of suicide, which had changed into melancholy the gay cheerfulness of her lovely girlhood.

Yes; it was the old story of the streamlet and the snow, of the rose and the wind. To others my love might not have seemed hopeless, but to me it was dead as the flowers I had seen blooming a year before.

Not for any earthly consideration would I have made a claim upon her affection.

What I had done had been done freely and loyally. I gave it all to her as utterly as I had previously given my heart, and now I could make no bargain with my dear. I never for a moment thought she owed me anything for my pains and trouble. Her kindly glances, her sweet words, her little, thoughtful turns of manner, were free gifts of her goodness, but in no sense payment for my services.

She understood I could not presume upon them, and was, perhaps, better satisfied it should be so.

But nothing satisfied Miss Blake, and at length between her and Mr. Craven there ensued a serious disagreement. She insisted he should not "send that clerk of his" to the house again, and suggested if Mr. Craven were too high and mighty to attend to the concerns of Miss Elmsdale himself, Miss Blake must look out for another solicitor.

"The sooner the better, madam," said Mr. Craven, with great state; and Miss Blake left in a huff, and actually did go off to a rival attorney, who, however, firmly declined to undertake her business.

Then Helena came as peacemaker. She smoothed down Mr. Craven's ruffled feathers and talked him into a good temper, and effected a reconciliation with her aunt, and then nearly spoilt everything by adding:

"But indeed I think Mr. Patterson had better not come to see us for the present, at all events."

"You ungrateful girl!" exclaimed Mr. Craven; but she answered, with a little sob, that she was not ungrateful, only—only she thought it would be better if I stayed away.

And so Taylor took my duties on him, and, as a natural consequence, some very pretty disputes between him and Miss Blake had to be arranged by Mr. Craven.

Thus the winter passed, and it was spring again—that spring day of which I have spoken. Mr. Craven and I were alone in the office. He had come late into town and was reading his letters; whilst I, seated by a window overlooking the Thames, gave about equal attention to the river outside and a tedious document lying on my table.

We had not spoken a word, I think, for ten minutes, when a slip of paper was brought in, on which was written a name.

"Ask her to walk in," said Mr. Craven, and, going to the door, he greeted the visitor, and led Miss Elmsdale into the room.

I rose, irresolute; but she came forward, and, with a charming blush, held out her hand, and asked me some commonplace question about my health.

Then I was going, but she entreated me not to leave the room on her account.

"This is my birthday, Mr. Craven," she went on, "and I have come to ask you to wish me many happy returns of the day, and to do something for me—will you?"

"I wish you every happiness, my dear," he answered, with

a tenderness born, perhaps, of olden memories and of loving-kindness towards one so sweet, and beautiful, and lonely. "And if there is anything I can do for you on your birthday, why, it is done, that is all I can say."

She clasped her dear hands round his arm, and led him towards a further window. I could see her downcast eyes—the long lashes lying on her cheeks, the soft colour flitting and coming, making her alternately pale and rosy, and I was jealous. Heaven forgive me! If she had hung so trustfully about one of the patriarchs, I should have been jealous, though he reckoned his years by centuries.

What she had to say was said quickly. She spoke in a whisper, bringing her lips close to his ear, and lifting her eyes imploringly to his when she had finished.

"Upon my word, miss," he exclaimed, aloud, and he held her from him and looked at her till the colour rushed in beautiful blushes even to her temples, and her lashes were wet with tears, and her cheeks dimpled with smiles. "Upon my word—and you make such a request to me—to me, who have a character to maintain, and who have daughters of my own to whom I am bound to set a good example! Patterson, come here. Can you imagine what this young lady wants me to do for her now? She is twenty-one to-day, she tells me, and she wants me to ask you to marry her. She says she will never marry anyone else." Then, as I hung back a little, dazed, fearful, and unable to credit the evidence of my senses, he added:

"Take her; she means it every word, and you deserve to have her. If she had chosen anybody else I would never have drawn out her settlements."

But I would not take her, not then. Standing there with the spring landscape blurred for the moment before me, I tried to tell them both what I felt. At first, my words were low and broken, for the change from misery to happiness affected me almost as though I had been suddenly plunged from happiness into despair. But by degrees I recovered my senses, and told my darling and Mr. Craven it was not fit she should, out of very generosity, give herself to me—a man utterly destitute of fortune—a man who, though he loved her better than life, was only a clerk at a clerk's salary.

"If I were a duke," I went on, breaking ground at last, "with a duke's revenue and a duke's rank, I should only value what I had for her sake. I would carry my money, and my birth, and my position to her, and ask her to take all, if she would only take me with them; but, as matters stand, Mr. Craven—"

"I owe everything worth having in life to you," she said, impetuously, taking my hand in hers. "I should not like you at all if you were a duke, and had a ducal revenue."

"I think you are too strait-laced, Patterson," agreed Mr. Craven. "She does owe everything she has to your determination, remember."

"But I undertook to solve the mystery for fifty pounds," I remarked, smiling in spite of myself.

"Which has never been paid," remarked my employer. "But," he went on, "you young people come here and sit down, and let us talk the affair over all together." And so he put us in chairs as if we had been clients, while he took his professional seat, and, after a pause, began:

"My dear Helena, I think the young man has reason. A woman should marry her equal. He will, in a worldly sense, be more than your equal some day; but that is nothing. A man should be head of the household.

"It is good, and nice, and loving of you, my child, to wish to endow your husband with all your worldly goods; but your husband ought, before he takes you, to have goods of his own wherewith to endow you. Now, now, now, don't purse up your pretty mouth, and try to controvert a lawyer's wisdom. You are both young: you have plenty of time before you.

"He ought to be given an opportunity of showing what he can do, and you ought to mix in society and see whether you meet anyone you think you can like better. There is no worse time for finding out a mistake of that sort, than after marriage." And so the kind soul prosed on, and would, possibly, have gone on prosing for a few hours more, had I not interrupted one of his sentences by saying I would not have Miss Elmsdale bound by any engagement, or consider herself other than free as air.

"Well, well," he answered, testily, "we understand that thoroughly. But I suppose you do not intend to cast the young lady's affections from you as if they were of no value?"

At this juncture her eyes and mine met. She smiled, and I could not help smiling too.

"Suppose we leave it in this way," Mr. Craven said, addressing apparently some independent stranger. "If, at the end of a year, Miss Elmsdale is of the same mind, let her write to me and say so. That course will leave her free enough, and it will give us twelve months in which to turn round, and see what we can do in the way of making his fortune. I do not imagine he will ever be able to count down guineas against her guineas, or that he wants to do anything so absurd. But he is right in saying an heiress should not marry a struggling clerk. He ought to be earning a good income before he is much older, and he shall, or my name is not William Craven."

I got up and shook his hand, and Helena kissed him.

"Tut, tut! fie, fie! what's all this?" he exclaimed, searching sedulously for his double eyeglass—which all the while he held between his finger and thumb. "Now, young people, you must not occupy my time any longer. Harry, see this self-willed little lady into a cab; and you need not return until the afternoon. If you are in time to find me before I leave, that will do quite well. Goodbye, Miss Helena."

I did not take his hint, though. Failing to find a cab—perhaps for want of looking for one—I ventured to walk with my beautiful companion up Regent Street as far as Oxford Circus.

Through what enchanted ground we passed in that short distance, how can I ever hope to tell! It was all like a story of fairyland, with Helena for Queen of Unreality. But it was real enough. Ah! my dear, you knew your own mind, as I, after years and years of wedded happiness, can testify.

Next day, Mr. Craven started off to the west of England. He

did not tell me where he was going; indeed, I never knew he had been to see my uncle until long afterwards.

What he told that gentleman, what he said of me and Helena, of my poor talents and her beauty, may be gathered from the fact that the old admiral agreed first to buy me a partnership in some established firm, and then swore a mighty oath, that if the heiress was, at the end of twelve months, willing to marry his nephew, he would make him his heir.

"I should like to have you with me, Patterson," said Mr. Craven, when we were discussing my uncle's proposal, which a few weeks after took me greatly by surprise; "but, if you remain here, Miss Blake will always regard you as a clerk. I know of a good opening; trust me to arrange everything satisfactorily for you."

Whether Miss Blake, even with my altered fortunes, would ever have become reconciled to the match, is extremely doubtful, had the *beau monde* not turned a very decided cold-shoulder to the Irish patriot.

Helena, of course, everyone wanted, but Miss Blake no one wanted; and the fact was made very patent to that lady.

"They'll be for parting you and me, my dear," said the poor creature one day, when society had proved more than usually cruel. "If ever I am let see you after your marriage, I suppose I shall have to creep in at the area-door, and make believe I am some faithful old nurse wanting to have a look at my dear child's sweet face."

"No one shall ever separate me from you, dear, silly aunt," said my charmer, kissing first one of her relative's high cheekbones, and then the other.

"We'll have to jog on, two old spinsters together, then, I am thinking," replied Miss Blake.

"No," was the answer, very distinctly spoken. "I am going to marry Mr. Henry Patterson, and he will not ask me to part from my ridiculous, foolish aunt."

"Patterson! that conceited clerk of William Craven's? Why, he has not darkened our doors for fifteen months and more."

"Quite true," agreed her niece; "but, nevertheless, I am going to marry him. I asked him to marry me a year ago."

"You don't mean that, Helena!" said poor Miss Blake. "You should not talk like an infant in arms."

"We are only waiting for your consent," went on my lady fair.

"Then that you will never have. While I retain my powers of speech you shall not marry a pauper who has only asked you for the sake of your money."

"He did not ask me; I asked him," said Helena, mischievously; "and he is not a beggar. His uncle has bought him a partnership, and is going to leave him his money; and he will be here himself tomorrow, to tell you all about his prospects."

At first, Miss Blake refused to see me; but after a time she relented, and, thankful, perhaps, to have once again anyone over whom she could tyrannise, treated her niece's future husband— as Helena declared—most shamefully.

"But you two must learn to agree, for there shall be no quarrelling in our house," added the pretty autocrat.

"You needn't trouble yourself about that, Helena," said her aunt.

"He'll be just like all the rest. If he's civil to me before marriage, he won't be after. He will soon find out there is no place in the house, or, for that matter, in the world, for Susan Blake"; and my enemy, for the first time in my memory, fairly broke down and began to whimper.

"Miss Blake," I said, "how can I convince you that I never dreamt, never could dream of asking you and Helena to separate?"

"See that, now, and he calls you Helena already," said the lady, reproachfully.

"Well, he must begin sometime. And that reminds me the sooner he begins to call you aunt, the better."

I did not begin to do so then, of that the reader may be quite certain; but there came a day when the word fell quite naturally from my lips. For a long period ours was a hollow truce, but, as time passed on, and I resolutely refused to quarrel with Miss Blake, she gradually ceased trying to pick quarrels with me.

Our home is very dear to her. All the household management Helena from the first hour took into her own hands; but in the nursery Miss Blake reigns supreme. She has always a grievance, but she is thoroughly happy. She dresses now like other people, and wears over her gray hair caps of Helena's selection.

Time has softened some of her prejudices, and age renders her eccentricities less noticeable; but she is still, after her fashion, unique, and we feel in our home, as we used to feel in the office—that we could better spare a better man.

The old house was pulled down, and not a square, but a fine terrace occupied its site. Munro lives in one of those desirable tenements, and is growing rich and famous day by day. Mr. Craven has retired from practice, and taken a place in the country, where he is bored to death though he professes himself charmed with the quiet.

Helena and I have always been town-dwellers. Though the Uninhabited House is never mentioned by either of us, she knows I have still a shuddering horror of lonely places.

My experiences in the Uninhabited House have made me somewhat nervous. Why, it was only the other night—

"What are you doing, making all that spluttering on your paper?" says an interrupting voice at this juncture, and, looking up, I see Miss Blake seated by the window, clothed and in her right mind.

"You had better put by that writing," she proceeds, with the manner of one having authority, and I am so amazed, when I contrast Miss Blake as she is, with what she was, that I at once obey!

Diarmid Chittock's Story

Since the beginning of this century civilisation has advanced by such leaps and bounds that we may well ask how much further it can go.

In less than a hundred years we have on the sea learnt how to dispense with sails, and on land to travel at a speed which would have appalled our forefathers. Like Ariel, we have put a girdle round the world, so that messages can be flashed from earth's remotest corner in a few hours. All the luxuries of the East are brought to our doors. The cottager now possesses a more comfortable house than kings in the old days dreamt of. And yet the curious outcome of all this civilisation, all this luxury, all this comfort, is that the natural man—the strongest, bravest, staunchest, most masculine man, the man to whom one's heart turns instinctively—seems continually trying to escape from their trammels.

In the earlier stages of civilisation he liked to dance and attend mild parties, to don gorgeous dress, and, with a similarly minded friend, to lounge up and down Bond Street; but now all these things are to him pain and weariness.

By preference he wears a tweed suit and a pot hat, he shirks afternoon tea, and hostesses are at their wits' end to find a sufficient number of partners for their 'pretty girls'.

Girls themselves have for the most part now to do the love-making, and often fail to do it successfully, while the 'natural' man is considering how he can best get away to tempt the ocean, to shoot big game, to explore strange lands where civilisation was never so much as heard of, and camp out, and eat rough food, and lead as wild and savage a life as possible.

It is rare, on the other hand, for women to seek seclusion from the world nowadays.

When they do, it is, as a rule, in company with their fellows, especially their fellows of the male persuasion. With them they will for a time gladly chase the wild deer and follow the roe, climb cliffs, and scale mountains; but they have no fancy for the lonely days and nights men not merely endure but love, which is probably only another proof that Mohammedans are right when they say women are not possessed of souls.

It is perhaps the terrible thoughts that dwell in many a male soul which drive modern men out into desolate lands, as the unimaginable terrors of morbid or stricken consciences drove of old both saints and sinners into hermits' cells and awful fastnesses, such as we can at this time of the world only faintly realise.

However this may be, and perhaps a mere teller of stories has no right even to conjecture, it is certain that in the year of our Lord 1883, Mr Cyril Danson, well known in London society, felt a consuming desire to change his surroundings.

He was sick of them—sick of the men, more sick of the women; sick of the talk, sick of the streets, sick of the newspapers, sick of everything!

In modern society he was one of those individuals who seem to hang between heaven and hell. He was not rich enough to hunt with the hounds or poor enough to run with the hare. He came of good people, and was possessed of an independent income, which he lacked the business ability necessary to increase; he was not a director on the board of any company; it had never occurred to him to speculate; he did not feel inclined to go in for mines, or horses, or gambling, or concessions, or politics—in a word, he was only an honest English gentleman who held strictly by his own notions of honour and had grown tired of everything, merely because the one flower he fancied in that garden of beauty, 'London in the season,' was plucked by a newly-made lord with a fabulous rent-roll.

He had known and loved her a long time, and thought she loved him.

In the slang of today he was 'hit very hard'—hit so hard that at first his brain reeled under the blow.

After the lapse of a few weeks, however, he was able to see things in their true proportions and to feel the lady had been a very happy loss; but 'going out into the wilderness' was a fancy which nevertheless came to him and stayed with him, and, unlike his faithful love, refused to leave him.

Yes, he would go into the wilderness—he quite made up his mind on that point—but then a very pertinent question arose, *viz.* 'Into what wilderness should he go?'

It was impossible for him to seek his desert in Africa, or India, or even America.

He had enough money to live at home quietly like a gentleman, but he did not possess such means as would enable him to start as a modern apostle. Things have changed a good deal since St Paul's time, besides which the Apostle of the Gentiles throughout his Epistles merely indicates that his expenses were not extravagant, and never tells us the amount to which they totted up.

Mr Danson could have wished to go round the world—to visit stray groups of almost unknown islands, to spend a summer at the South Pole, to make his way across the interior of Africa, to see Siberia; but as it was necessary to stint his desires and keep them low like a weaned child, he decided to shake the London dust off his feet, and, taking only his soul for companion, talk confidentially with that too long neglected friend, conscience, when they reached some 'void place' situated in Wales, Scotland, or Blackstone Castle, Chittock's place. Ah! a capital thought. Chittock's house was no doubt vacant, for Chittock nearly three years before, very hard hit himself, had tried whether the wilderness of London could not minister to a mind diseased as well as any other desert.

Mr Danson knew Blackstone Castle well. In the days of his

early youth he had spent a month there so pleasantly that the memory remained with him like some sweet tune heard of yore.

No lonelier or lovelier place than Blackstone Castle could well be imagined. It stood on a cliff from which, to the nearest continent, stretched straight as a crow could fly a thousand miles of sea.

There was excellent shooting in the neighbourhood, to say nothing of lake and river fishing, a sandy beach, great stretches of bog land, mountains covered with purple heather, and deep wide valleys, where Fin M'Coul and his children might have been playing 'bowls' for centuries with huge fragments of granite for balls.

Yes, Blackstone Castle, situated almost at the world's end, was, if still lacking a tenant, precisely the hermit's cell he desired to find, and, having made up his mind on this point, he repaired to the Cashel Club, where he thought he should probably meet his man.

As it happened, he did meet him on the threshold, and they walked into St James's Park together, Mr Danson, though 'down', looking much as usual, but Mr Chittock, after nearly three years' experience of the great city, appearing so little the better for such a decided change, his companion felt shocked to notice the alteration a comparatively short time had wrought.

Formerly he had been a fine, handsome, jovial fellow, with a hearty ring in his cheerful voice and a kind word for everyone.

Now he was thin, haggard, dull, with a far-off sad expression in his blue eyes, seemingly twenty years older than his actual age.

Love serves her votaries many a strange trick. She strips the flesh off one, and plumps another up like a Christmas turkey!

In a very few words Mr Danson explained what he wanted, and in an even shorter sentence Mr Chittock told him the house had only been let one season for the shooting, and was at that moment empty, and quite at his service.

'Of course,' he went on after an instant's pause, 'I shall be charmed if you will take the place, but it is desolation made visible. It is twelve miles from anywhere. Personally, I would not go back again and live in my old house for any consideration. Had you not better think twice about the matter?'

Mr Danson would not think twice. He was done up; he craved for quiet; he was tired of people; he desired utter solitude.

'Cannot you compass that in London?' asked Mr Chittock, with a grave, curious smile.

'No—I must get quite away,' was the answer.

'Is it so bad as that?'

'So bad as that! Just as you, Chittock, found it necessary to leave Ireland, so I feel I cannot stop in London. It is not that I am heartbroken,' he added, moved by some impulse he was unable to resist, 'but I want to get to some out-of-the-way place where people won't look as if they saw "JILTED" printed in big type all over me.'

Mr Chittock nodded. Though he had not been jilted, he understood.

'I want to change my life, too,' went on Mr Danson, a little ashamed of his outburst. 'I could wish to be of a little use in the world—to know I had made a few persons the happier. If I were to die tomorrow not a creature, except perhaps my man, would be sorry. Did I only possess an estate like yours, even! But such good things are not for poor men.'

Mr Chittock walked on for about a dozen paces as though he did not hear—or, hearing, failed to understand. Then he said in those slow, melancholy tones, which contrasted so forcibly with his former utterances—'Things are changed as well as myself, and you might have Blackstone at a very low figure. I do not intend, however, to take any man in, unless indeed a millionaire, such as your lost love's lord,' he added, with a forced laugh. 'Go and try how you like living in my old barrack all alone; then if, after a fair trial, you still desire to buy, I will meet you more than half-way.'

Something he could not comprehend in Mr Chittock's voice and manner struck Mr Danson with a strange surprise, but he only answered—'All right, old fellow, state your figure. Let the lawyers put all shipshape, and if I can be your man I will—anyhow, I'll take the place for a twelvemonth. By-the-bye—'

'By-the-bye what?'

'Did your young woman marry a lord?'

'Certainly not.'

'Did she marry anybody, then, or what is she doing?'

'She never married at all, and is governessing I believe.'

'She preferred governessing?'

'Not very complimentary to me,' returned Mr Chittock, 'but a fact. And I loved her, Danson. She had no fortune; I wanted none, I only wanted her, and her father and mother wished her to marry me, but she wouldn't,' he added with a sort of gasp. 'There is something about me women don't like, I suppose. Anyhow, she would have nothing to do with me—not at any price.'

'Poor old chap! Was she very pretty?'

'I think not—I do not know. She was pretty enough for me, and I loved her. Do not let us talk about it anymore.'

Mr Danson asked no further questions. Here was a trouble deeper than any he had felt—a trouble he failed exactly to understand, and one with which he knew he lacked all right to intermeddle.

'My dear Chittock, I wish I could bring you balm of Gilead,' he said earnestly.

'If you could I am sure you would,' was the answer, 'but not a man living can do that—there is no balm for me anywhere.'

CHAPTER TWO

Despite its pretentious name, Blackstone Castle was really a rather modest mansion. A few crumbling walls and a ruined tower adjacent to the house bore picturesque testimony to the fact that some sort of fortress had in old, old days occupied its site; but the modern Blackstone Castle was merely a square, roomy country mansion, big enough to hold a large family of small sons and daughters when young, and welcome plenty of high-spirited, laughing, joyous guests when the little people grew old enough to think of love-making—of marriage and giving in marriage!

It was in his 'calf days'—which are, after all, the sweetest, pleasantest, most innocent days man can ever know, full of the fresh immaturity of morning and the happy, half-conscious expectation of a glorious noon to come—that Mr Danson had been made 'free' of Blackstone Castle, where he accompanied Diarmid Chittock when both of the young fellows were leaving school.

Forever the recollection of old Mr Chittock standing on the great doorstep and welcoming first his grandson's friend and then, well-nigh with tears, his grandson, remained in Mr Danson's memory.

Stalwart fellow as he was, his own eyes filled when he beheld once again the well-remembered place where that gracious, old-world man could never welcome friend nor grandson more.

A splendid old man—one of the best breed of gentry this world ever saw, and which it is unlikely the world will ever see again, belonging as it did to an impossible-to-return, long gone-by—a gone-by it is well never can return, but which was a magnificent painting nevertheless, full of gorgeous colouring and soft tender tints, deep shadows, and wrongs, alas! unimaginable.

As he entered the spacious hall—architectural grandeur was at one time a thing no good house in Ireland ever wanted—Mr Danson felt himself to be a very fortunate hermit, for while seeking solitude it was borne in upon him he need be no anchorite. His own man stood there to wait on him, just as if he had only stepped across Pall Mall; his horses were in the stables; his servants in the kitchen; certainly the rooms lacked all modern aesthetic refinement, but Mr Danson was weary of aesthetic refinement as well as of many other things.

He knew he was not in the van of civilisation, and he did not wish to be; nevertheless, on the other hand, he had not dropped quite to the rear. It was early summer; and while he smoked a quiet cigar after dinner he looked out over thousands of miles of ocean, and felt as if some soft hand were being laid on his heart and drawing something of its bitterness away.

That night, wearied with his journey, and believing he had

reached a desired goal, he slept, lulled by the gentle murmur of Atlantic waves, the deep restful sleep of youth.

Next day the rector called, next day the priest, the third the doctor.

The wilderness was not so absolutely desolate as he had intended, but still three visitors in seventy-two hours could not be regarded as exactly a 'rush' of society. Besides they were, each in his way, all interesting men, who had something to tell and were willing to hear.

Before the week was over, Mr Danson had quite settled down to the routine of a dull country life. He who had squirmed at afternoon teas, and garden parties, and days up the river, and four-in-hand expeditions to whatever race might be on; who had objected to assist at the laying of foundation-stones, to hearing of speeches, to receptions to dinners, to balls; who had grown to detest with a deadly detestation London gossip and even London itself—found himself taking an interest in the post, and walking down to the village each morning for his daily paper, returning the mail-car driver's salute with ceremonious civility and chattering to the local shopkeeper in the most affable manner possible.

So far as we have ever been told, saints and sinners who in the early days went out into the wilderness of this wicked world did none of these things; but, then, history is silent on many of those subjects about which we should all, no doubt, like to hear a great deal. Distance probably lends a considerable amount of enchantment to the holy men of old. Near at hand they were presumably much like their descendants. They could not have been considering their shortcomings, and contemplating the mysteries of life and death, day and night for forty years. Possibly, among those of the number who were sincere, their voluntary withdrawal from the world was only an attempt to coax back the mental strength of which a too-long sojourn in it had temporarily bereft them—just as Nature taught Mr Danson he ought to leave London and talk quietly with the wise old mother of us all if he wished ever again to have a sane mind located in a sound body. Her remedies are of the simplest; and quite unconsciously this man, who had been turning night into day, burning his candle at both ends, working harder than any horse in a mill, was taking them regularly.

The solitude could not be considered perfect; but though, properly speaking, it was out of character for him to take an interest in the rector's college reminiscences, in the priest's stories, or the doctor's recollections of Ballyragshanan dispensary, the hermit's cell he had chosen answered its purpose admirably, and

He ate and drank and slept—what then?
He ate and drank and slept again.

And there were times when he actually wondered why he had come to the 'back of beyond', and fancied it must have been for pleasure!

The face of his false lady-love and her wealthy lord soon grew faded and blurred like shadowy old photographs. He could read their names in the *Times* and never turn a hair. That great stretch of sand, that vast expanse of ocean, became pleasanter day by day, and he began to like his 'constitutional' beside the Atlantic as he had once never thought to like anything except the 'sweet shady side of Pall Mall.'

'Each morning when returning home with my paper' (posted to him regularly from London), Mr Danson said one day to the constabulary officer, with whom he was on particularly good terms. 'I meet a girl—not tall, not pretty, not striking-looking, but yet a girl who attracts me, because she has the quietest, saddest expression I ever saw on a woman's face. You can tell me who she is, no doubt?'

'Dressed in black? Steps out, too?'

'Yes, and walks well.'

'That is Miss Oona Rosterne.'

'Miss—?' suggested Cyril Danson, puzzled.

'Oona Rosterne,' repeated Mr Melsham, 'the daughter of my predecessor, who disappeared.'

'Good heavens! I thought that poor lady was a governess

somewhere.'

'So she is—daily governess at Fort Cloyne. Walks three miles out and three miles in—hail, shine, or snow—five times a week. If she would leave her mother she might get a large salary, for she can teach everything. As it is, the Mustos pay her fifty pounds a year, which is thought unbounded wealth hereabouts.'

'Was any trace of her father ever discovered?'

'Not a trace.'

'How very strange!'

'Why strange? There are bogs enough about here to engulf a whole army, let alone one inspector.'

'Do you mean that he lost his way?'

'Lost his way on a starlight night! Why, he knew every inch of the country,' scoffed Mr Melsham. 'No; someone knocked him over quietly and put him where he will, maybe, be dug up a couple of hundred years hence.'

'I thought people imagined he had left the country.'

'People over the Channel might, but not a soul about here did. He was over head and ears in debt, to be sure; but a man needs money when starting on foreign travel, and Rosterne never had any. Then he loved both wife and daughter after his fashion, and nobody was pressing for payment, because it was well known Miss Oona had but to say "Yes", and Chittock would have found every penny that was needed to rid her father of debt. No; the whole business is a mystery. One day, perhaps, when the fellow who did away with him is dying, or someone who knows gets tired of keeping the secret, we may hear more about the matter; but the likelihood is, not a soul now living will ever learn what it was happened between seven p.m., when he left Letterpass to walk home, and the next morning, when he had not got home. He was seen about two miles from Letterpass striking down to the shore, but never after by anyone we can trace.' A blank ensues. 'That is the whole story.'

'It is a terrible story. If his body had been found, dead or alive—'

'But it was not, you see. No wonder Miss Oona looks as

she does. Yes'—reflectively—'she walks three Irish miles out and three Irish miles in, five days a week, hail, rain, or shine, and her grandmother was an O'Considine, too!'

'Oh! was she?' said Mr Danson, who had not the faintest idea the O'Considines had ever been reckoned grand people—in fact, had never even heard of them till that moment.

'Indeed she was,' replied Mr Melsham, who received the remark as a tribute of respect to the great house mentioned. 'Her grandfather was about the last of the race—the last, that is, who could and did stick to the estate—drove his four-in-hand, kept open house, and never wanted for anything as long as there was a shot in the locker or an acre of land to be mortgaged.'

Though Mr Danson as yet knew but little of the 'first gem of the sea,' it seemed to him this had been the practice of many excellent Irish gentleman, and one apparently that had secured for them the esteem of their contemporaries and even the admiration of posterity. Right royally they had lived on their capital while it lasted.

And for those who came after?

Why, those who came after have ever since been paying for the piper's merry tune, to which men and women danced such joyous measures in the old days departed.

It was less, however, with those old days Mr Danson occupied his mind the while he strolled leisurely towards Blackstone Castle than with that girl who walked thirty miles each week and toiled all day, instructing, probably, many young ideas how to shoot, in order to add fifty pounds a year to her mother's income.

And all the while there was a man in London breaking his heart because this sad-faced governess would have nothing to do with him; and Blackstone Castle remained without a mistress, who would have lacked no manner of good things had she married its owner. Mr Danson's soul yearned over the pair; he longed to bring them together and make them happy—ay, even in spite of themselves.

Certainly a remarkable-looking girl, not strictly pretty, perhaps, but a girl not easily to be forgotten for all that. Though Mr Danson had not spoken to her, he knew those dark grey eyes, that curious melancholy expression, that sensitive, troubled mouth, would never pass quite out of his recollection.

Of course it was the knowledge that she ought to become Chittock's wife which attracted and riveted his attention.

Without some interest, he told himself, he would never have looked at her twice, and it was a long time before he remembered he had looked at her more than twice before he learned she was *the* woman of Chittock's life.

It would be an excellent work, he decided, to make the divided pair one, to bridge the river of their unhappiness, and bring about a happy reconciliation.

He could do this, he felt confident, and then he remembered that Mr Musto had called a week previously, while the new tenant of Blackstone Castle was exploring the Blackstone caves, and that his visit ought to be returned.

When people have an object in view they can take very prompt action. Accordingly Mr Danson, having an end to gain, decided to ride over to Fort Cloyne that very afternoon.

Only to meet with a check, however. Mr and Mrs Musto, he was informed, had left the same morning for Switzerland, and would be absent for two months, or perhaps longer.

Two months! For the second time that year life stretched before Mr Danson as a perfect blank. Foiled both in love and friendship, what could he do? Why, get acquainted with Mrs Rosterne. How stupid not to have thought sooner of that simple plan!

'Gorey,' he said, pulling up his horse to a walk, and beckoning the man so called, who was at once his own groom and Mr Chittock's foster-brother, to come beside him, 'I was talking to Mr Melsham this morning about Captain Rosterne's extraordinary disappearance.'

An English servant, had such a piece of information been vouchsafed to him, would have answered vaguely and discreetly, 'Yes, sir;' but Gorey replied after a different fashion—'Mr

Melsham was not here then, sir. He only came when Inspector Hume left.'

'And who was Inspector Hume?' asked Mr Danson, as utterly ignorant of the whole affair as anyone could be.

'Just about as sharp and clever a gentleman as any poor fellow in trouble would wish *not* to meet.'

'Meaning, I suppose, anyone who had stolen a sheep or killed a landlord?'

'Or done anything else your honour pleases to think of.'

This was a nice way of putting things! As if his honour was pleased with or had a love for people who stole sheep, or shot a landlord, or did 'anything else'.

And yet Mr Danson felt convinced Gorey could only be considered a willing, faithful, honest, capable servant, and a law-abiding man. Such was the character Mr Chittock had given him, and such, it may at once be said, was the character he deserved, with higher praise to the back of it.

'I suppose Mr Hume enquired into the whole matter?'

'He did, sir. He was at it day and night, after a manner of speaking. I don't think he had right rest all the time he was there, or the master either, for Mr Hume was forever at the castle.'

'And he never got a clue?'

'Not a one of any good at all. He went here and went there, but the end was the same as the beginning.'

'And what is your own notion, Gorey? Come, now, what do you think became of Captain Rosterne—where did he go? Or if he did not go, where was he taken?'

The afternoon sun was blazing into Mr Danson's eyes while he asked this question, and he might, he thought, have been in error. Nevertheless, he could not shake off the impression that just for one moment the guard of Gorey's impassive face changed, that his eyes flickered, as one may say, and the muscles of his mouth twitched.

The whole thing was instantaneous and perfectly incapable of description—a little transformation scene Mr Danson felt rather than saw—for the sun, as has been said, was in his eyes and blinding him, and when Gorey spoke his voice was calm and natural.

'Indeed, sir, I couldn't say. I don't know where he would want to go away from wife and child; and though he wasn't too well liked, I am very sure nobody ever wished him enough ill to put a bullet in his heart.'

'Oh! he wasn't well liked, then,' said Mr Danson, who felt at the moment as if he were a second Columbus.

'He wasn't hated, sir, if that is what you are thinking about,' returned Gorey in a moment, taking all the wind out of Mr Danson's sails; 'for he never did any man a serious wrong, so far as I heard. He was just, and often stood up for the poor when they had no other to speak for them. But still and for all that he wasn't liked. He had come from nothing, yet still took a heap on him. Many a one such as him does that.'

'He was bumptious, in fact?' suggested Mr Danson.

'People about here said he was an arbitrary gentleman,' said Gorey, substituting what he considered, and what was, a better word. 'No man had a keener notion of justice, no man was civiller. If a beggar touched his hat to him, up went his stick or umbrella or finger in return. He had the best of manners, sir; but yet there are those that feel good manners and the height of justice are not a patch on the love of God. And he had no love of God or of God's creatures.'

'That is a hard saying, Gorey,' remarked Mr Danson, impressed in spite of himself.

'It's true, your honour, for all that. Now I'll tell you. Supposing he was driving on his car and he saw a string of loaden carts on the wrong side of the road, where it was not metalled, he'd whistle them all to get out of the way—ay, and if they didn't, summon them. And all the same, I've seen her Grace the Duchess when she was driving her pair of cobs sign to the men to make no shift and walk her own horses over the stones, and was there a soul in the barony did not say, God bless her!'

'Still, in Captain Rosterne's position he might have thought it his duty to see that the rule of the road was observed.'

'Maybe, sir; but the Almighty is much easier with those who go a bit wrong than he was. Still, though nobody much cared for him, I never heard a man, woman, or child that hadn't the soft word for him when he forgot to come back—ay, and the wet eye too for the wife and child he left lamenting.'

'And what did chance to the unhappy man, Gorey?'

'Not a one was able to say, sir—not a one. Pat Harrigan met him on the shore road walking home, but he never got home, poor gentleman.'

'He did not drink?'

'No, sir, not to say drink; he took his glass like anybody else, but it was never said that he took a glass too much.'

'Or gamble?'

'He might a little, but not beyond the common.'

Mr Danson wondered what 'the common' might be, but held his tongue. So far he had not made a single point. Of course, if Gorey knew nothing, there could be nothing to tell. If, on the other hand, he suspected foul play, it was quite evident he did not intend to share that suspicion with anyone.

Moreover, the man had been questioned and cross-questioned, and no doubt Mr Chittock and he had talked the matter over exhaustively. The probability was he really had not a word to say, and yet Mr Danson could not feel satisfied concerning that strange flicker.

'Mr Chittock must have taken the affair terribly to heart,' he observed at last.

'He did so, sir; he never to say has been the same man since—and small wonder. There was no one in these parts he was as intimate with as the captain; he'd have been his son if all had gone as it might have done.'

It was all very well to speak to Gorey about Captain Rosterne's disappearance, but Mr Danson felt he could not let a servant talk concerning Captain Rosterne's daughter.

It seemed to him dreadful that such a girl should be the subject of common gossip. He would have set her on a pedestal high above the reach of vulgar tongues, which looked very much as if Mr Danson had conceived a marvellously high opinion of his friend's wife that was, he hoped, to be.

Very possibly he thought Captain Rosterne had for reasons of his own left the country. Some painful scandal, some terrible misfortune, might be at the bottom of the mystery, which he had better not try to search out further.

But it could do no harm to try and bring the divided pair together again, and, full of this intention, he proceeded at a good round trot to Blackstone Castle, followed by Gorey, who had dropped behind to a respectful distance.

Chapter Three

Mr Danson did not owe the rector a visit, but he thought he would walk down to the village and call on the rector's sister, a lady of uncertain age, though certainly not under fifty, who always amused Mr Danson immensely. Her one great desire, poor soul, was to see London; her one great regret that her brother's lines had been cast in such a primitive parish as Lisnabeg.

'Ah, if he were only in or near London now,' she said, 'where he could mix with men of his own calibre!'

It had never occurred to Mr Danson that the rector's intellectual capacities were so great he could hope only to meet with one equally mighty among the most cultured classes in a great city; but it would have needed a much harder heart than that which beat in the Englishman's breast even to hint that Miss Heath perhaps overrated her brother's abilities. He contented himself with remarking, therefore—'Sometimes London proves a little disappointing.'

'But why? How can it? Is not all the *Thought* of the world there?'

'Much of it, certainly; but a person may live a long time in London without meeting with a vast amount of thought, or any indeed,' he added.

'I scarcely understand how that can be at the fountain-head of everything.'

'True; but if you consider the fountain-head has a population almost equal to that of Ireland, you will understand many of the inhabitants have to remain at a considerable distance from the well.'

'Ah! that wouldn't be the case with Phil; he could make his way to the centre at once.'

'I am sure he would, whenever he was known,' answered Mr Danson heartily.

And then Miss Heath went on to tell him how he could not conceive—he who had so recently left 'the thought of the whole world, and still felt its invigorating breeze fanning his cheek'—how deadly dull their village really was.

'You have not to *live* in it, Mr Danson,' she went on; 'you can leave it whenever you like—run over to London or Paris, or New York, for that matter; but we who, fettered by pecuniary trammels, are compelled to tread the same monotonous round week after week and year after year, alone understand its weariness.'

Mr Danson thought he had felt the full weariness of fashionable London's monotonous round; but that was a subject on which he did not care to enter, so he seized the opportunity presented of saying—'The Mustos have taken wing, I find. I rode over today, only to hear they left this morning for Switzerland.'

'Oh, yes,' answered Miss Heath, 'and will be away for two months. They always start in this sudden fashion, just as the whim seizes them. We shall miss them very much, because, though they are not exactly—well, you know they are not of the old gentry—'

'I suppose the old gentry were new once also. Everything must have a beginning,' suggested Mr Danson.

'Quite so; and, as I was about to add, the Mustos are kindness itself—hospitable, charitable, and considerate. Why, the very carriage that took them to the station called on its way back for Mrs Rosterne.'

'Why for Mrs Rosterne?' asked Mr Danson.

'Because she and her daughter always stay at Fort Cloyne

when Mr and Mrs Musto are absent. They are quite members of the family, I assure you. Mrs Musto says she has never an anxious thought concerning the children when Oona Rosterne is in the house with them.'

'Miss Rosterne must be a very exceptional young lady,' Mr Danson forced himself to say, though he felt that day had been but a series of disappointments.

'Indeed she is. My brother says another girl like her could not be found in the three kingdoms, and he ought to know, because he prepared her for confirmation. Still I feel myself I never can forgive Oona the way in which she treated poor Mr Chittock.'

'But I always understood—and remember, no one can feel more sorry for Chittock than I—that she was straightforward from the first—told him plainly she had no love to give him,' answered Mr Danson, eagerly.

'And what right had a chit like Oona to set herself up against those older and wiser than she was?' asked Miss Heath. 'Look what a match it would have been for her—the salvation, after a fashion, of her heartbroken, overworked father; a husband she could have led about with a string; a home for her mother; the best of marriages any girl need have desired. But no; my lady had her own fancies, and would pay heed neither to father nor mother, lover nor friend. When I was young, Mr Danson, girls took advice; Oona would take none, and you see the result.'

'But still, if she could not care for Chittock—' pleaded Mr Danson.

'Could not care, indeed!' repeated Miss Heath. 'I have no patience with such nonsense. What was there about the dear kind fellow to dislike?'

'I cannot tell you, Miss Heath. I always liked him, and my dearest wish is to see him married to Miss Rosterne.'

'Then you may give it up, Mr Danson. So long as the sea ebbs and flows she will have nothing to do with him. Sorrow has not taught her; poverty has not changed her. Since her father's death—for no one believes the poor man is alive—she has been more set against Mr Chittock than ever. Would you believe it?—he wanted to allow Mrs Rosterne an annuity, and the foolish girl wouldn't let her mother take a penny. What do you think of that in one so young? For Oona can't be reckoned old even now, though she is nearly three and twenty. I call that young even for a governess.'

'If she did not care for Chittock, I think she was right.'

'But why did not she care for him? A man who was, as one may say, a specimen man—quiet and well-living, good to look at, and pleasant to listen to—a man who could not drink if he wished, because a glass of punch got into his head at once. Mrs Rosterne told me the only reason Oona ever gave for saying "no" was that she felt afraid of his temper; but, then, what is a husband who has no temper? And his was just a flash and over. It's a saint, I suppose, she's expecting to get, and I wish she may succeed.'

'Is there some suitor, then, Miss Rosterne favours?'

'I'd like to have seen the man except Diarmid Chittock dare look at, much less speak to her, when her father was alive. And who do you think she'd take up with would throw a thought her way now? No, she's let her chance slip—a grand chance, too. She'll never get another, so she'll just have to go on drudging through life. I am sorry for her, but she wouldn't take advice. You are not going yet, though, Mr Danson, surely? You would stop till my brother comes in? He won't be long.'

No, Mr Danson was much obliged, but he must get home; in fact, he had only called to bid a short goodbye. He intended to walk through Connemara. He wished to see that part of Ireland particularly, and might probably include in his programme Killarney and the Golden Mountains.

'Tired of Blackstone Castle already,' decided Miss Heath, as she watched him walking fast towards that desirable residence. 'Well, it's natural—no one can say it is not.'

Chapter Four

Fashions change, but not to such extent as many people imagine. A stout pair of walking-shoes now represents the picturesque sandal of old, and a well-made knapsack serves the pedestrian's purpose much better than any wallet ever did that of pilgrim; while the modern tourist is, seen from an artistic point of view, most distinctly merely an improved copy of the long-bearded, not over-clean, very often extremely lazy, peripatetic gentleman who formerly made a living by piously doing nothing.

The same restlessness that drove the devotee into void places and caused him to make his home among the graves now sends his smart, well-set-up, well-dressed, but much happier nineteenth-century prototype to scale mountains, to stem rivers, to cross oceans, and to live in unfamiliar countries.

There is, to put the matter in a sentence, as much human nature running loose about the world now as there was nineteen hundred years since, or, for the matter of that, as when, nearly forty centuries ago, Abraham 'sat in the tent door in the heat of the day'.

It was the human nature in Mr Danson that made him tell Miss Heath he intended to walk through Connemara—an idea which had never entered his mind till the rector's sister drove him to the verge of desperation by speaking with the voice of the world concerning Oona Rosterne.

He felt he could not endure to hear Chittock's dear love gossiped about in such fashion, and that he could still less endure waiting two long months before it would be possible to make Mrs Rosterne's acquaintance.

Therefore he resolved to go away, and he did; clad in a serviceable suit of frieze, well shod, admirably financed, he tramped from Castle-bar to Galway by zigzag routes, which enabled him to see every place of interest in the county; then he took train to Dublin, and returned to Blackstone Castle. He only remained there, however, long enough to find matters were going on as usual, and that likewise, as usual, Time was sitting on the cliff with folded wings brooding over Mr Rosterne's disappearance perhaps, but more possibly brooding over nothing.

Having satisfied himself on these points, he went away again, first to Dublin, where, chancing to pick up Le Fanu's *The House by the Churchyard,* he explored Chapelizod reverently and with a deep feeling of sadness, thinking all the while Chittock's future wife ought to be a second Lilian. Then through the too-little-known County Wicklow, and afterwards to beautiful Killarney. From thence he bent his vagrant steps to the Golden Mountains, and finally made his way back to Blackstone Castle, firmly convinced Ireland was the loveliest country on earth.

Nature seemed a pleasant change to this man, who had lived so much in society and been disappointed by it. Perhaps if he had lived is long with Nature she would have disappointed him also cruelly. Who can say?

When he last left Blackstone Castle, sea and land and sky lay bathed in mellow sunshine. It was the 'Green Isle's' golden season, when grain, ready for the sickle, and bound by the reaper into sheaves, was to be seen on every hillside; when the mountains looked purple, clad as they were with heather in full flower; and the Atlantic rippled in over a shell-strewn shore, quietly, as though storms and tempests had never ruffled its peace.

When he returned, the whole landscape was changed. Stern mountains looked darkly away to a swelling sea trying in vain to calm itself after wild Equinoctial gales. Afar out the white sea-horses were chasing each other like living things, while on the sunken rocks nearer at hand wild billows expended their fury by dashing over them in showers of spray; black and green, crested as if with snow, they rushed to their doom, succeeding each other with the solemn regularity of an advancing army.

Above, a grey sky kept mournful watch over the scene of desolation.

'Could anything be grander?' thought Mr Danson, as he walked along the cliffs and surveyed the mighty panorama spread below. 'What a magnificent country, what a glorious land!'

He was in excellent spirits—in such spirits as would have caused him to look favourably on even a much humbler picture.

The Mustos were at Fort Cloyne, and Mr Musto at once hastened to Blackstone Castle, and gratified the new tenant by asking him to join their house-party before it broke up.

'Just a few crack shots,' he said; 'men who enjoy a country like this, and never mind how long or how far they have to tramp after their game. Do come. We shall be so glad, though we have no inducement to offer beyond good sport. There are only four lady guests—two old friends of my wife, and Mrs and Miss Rosterne. You have heard of the latter, I dare say?—Yes. Poor Chittock—such a pity! We may expect you, then, tomorrow?'

Mr Danson said yes, saw his guest off, and then in a state of great exultation took his way along that high path which commanded so fine a prospect.

All things seemed possible to him then. He could see, he could talk to the girl Chittock loved so well. He would be his friend's ambassador, find out where the trouble lay, and put everything that was wrong right.

As a rule, people who essay meddling in the affairs of others make great mistakes. Perhaps the mere fact of adventuring on such delicate ground proves their unfitness for the self-imposed task. But Mr Danson knew no fear. The cause was so good, his own intentions so excellent, that success must ensue; and it was, therefore, with a light heart he sat down to dinner next evening, having on his right hand Mrs Musto and on his left Mrs Rosterne. Obliquely across the table he saw Miss Rosterne, who looked as though she would have been much happier anywhere else.

The dinner was rather a success. People talked freely, and when the ladies left the room and the gentleman drew closer together, Mr Danson felt he had assisted at many far more stupid entertainments when the London season was in full swing, in the days before he determined to give up this world's pomps and adopt the *role* of hermit.

Later on in the drawing-room, after some of the elder ladies had played and sung, a veteran colonel entreating Miss Oona, whom he seemed to know very well indeed, for one Irish ballad, 'if it must be only one, my dear,' Mr Chittock's obstinate fair, after a few preliminary notes of introduction, began—'An!

'tis all but a dream at the best;' and immediately a hush fell on everyone present, which lasted till the spell of Miss Rosterne's voice was broken by—utter silence.

The song itself is not specially pathetic, and yet the listeners did not at first seem inclined to speak.

'Isn't she wonderful?' at last Mrs Musto asked Cyril Danson almost in a whisper; but the gentleman could only look an answer, because the charm of the girl's rare voice held him dumb.

When at length he sought his room, he did it with the feeling that Chittock's infatuation was justified. Nevertheless he fell asleep while endeavouring to discover wherein the secret of Miss Rosterne's curious fascination lay. She was not handsome or beautiful, or even strictly pretty. She had no becks and nods and wreathed smiles for the outside world; she spread no lures to attract; her singing even lacked the little artifices with which quite legitimately many a woman tries to win admiration. No; he could not tell how or why it was she touched all the hidden fountains of his heart and drew virtue from them, only he knew her voice haunted his dreams, that he heard it during the course of an exhaustive conversation with her concerning Mr Chittock—a conversation that removed all misapprehensions, put all mistakes right!

When he awoke he could not, however, at all remember the arguments he had used, the misconceptions he had explained away. He only knew he had seen those strangely pathetic eyes uplifting to his, and heard that low rich voice assuring him, 'I always loved Diarmid—always, from the time I was a little girl.'

Which was well enough as a dream. In waking life, however, Mr Danson found at the end of seven pleasant days he had not advanced one step. With the other ladies he soon became on terms of friendly intimacy, but with Oona his progress was absolutely *nil*.

She did not repulse or snub him, it is true, but the masterly inactivity she displayed repelled his advances more effectually than any open antagonism could have done.

'I am afraid Miss Rosterne dislikes me,' said Mr Chittock's

friend to Mrs Musto on the day when his visit was to terminate.

'Do you think so?' returned the lady.

'Yes, I do—or rather I am sure she does,' he answered, 'and I cannot imagine the reason, for I have always endeavoured to conciliate her.'

'Yes,' said Mrs Musto.

'Cannot you help me to solve the enigma?' he asked. 'Ladies understand each other so much better than we do. I most earnestly wish to be on friendly terms with her, for poor Chittock's sake.'

'I imagine that is where the trouble lies.'

'I beg your pardon—I fear I am very dense.'

'You are thoroughly kind. Still, if you will forgive me for saying so, you made a mistake when you took Miss Heath into your confidence.'

'Miss Heath!' Mr Danson repeated, mystified; 'when did I take her into confidence?'

'You told her the dearest wish of your heart was to see Mr Chittock and Miss Rosterne man and wife.'

'Did I? Very possibly. I do not remember using such a phrase, but the matter has lain very close to my heart, and Miss Heath and I talked about the trouble once.'

'Precisely, and poor dear Miss Heath is a sad gossip. She does not mean to make mischief, but she is always repeating things that vex people, and I have no doubt what you said in such good faith has been told to Miss Rosterne with the inevitable additions, so that it hurt her very much.'

'I am extremely sorry. What can I do to repair my blunder?'

'Nothing much, I fear; but I should certainly refrain from speaking of Mr Chittock's rejected suit to anyone except myself. I except myself,' she added, with a pleasant little laugh, 'because I am quite on Oona's side. I consider she was right; everyone else believes she was wrong.'

'But why do you consider she was right, Mrs Musto?'

'Because she did not love the man.'

'And why did she not love him?'

'That is a question I am unable to answer positively, but I think because she knew him too well, and also because he wooed her after a somewhat masterful fashion—took too much for granted, in fact. Till she refused his hand, not once or twice or thrice, Mr Chittock's opinion of himself was exactly the opinion of everyone about here—namely, that he had but to ask and have. Now, to a girl brought up in the way Oona Rosterne was, that seemed utterly intolerable. Perhaps you do not know how she was brought up, Mr Danson?'

'I do not,' he answered humbly.

'Well, I will tell you. It seems to me a strangely pathetic story. Up to her ninth year she was just Oona Rosterne, which meant she was Oona anybody. Then Sir Thomas Glanmyre died in India, and his widow, an O'Considine, returned to Ireland and bethought her of the relative who had married Mr, or, as the people hereabouts always called him, Captain Rosterne. She came down here, took a fancy to the little girl, and adopted her. From that day, for seven years Oona lived amid luxury, saw only people moving in good society, was taught by the best masters and mistresses, and grew to be, to all intents and purposes, a child of the upper ten thousand.'

'Naturally.'

'Lady Glanmyre resided for the most part in Paris,' continued Mrs Musto, 'and only occasionally came to Ireland. It was always understood she would provide for Oona, but a short time before her death the bank in which her husband had invested his money failed, with the result that everything went except Lady Glanmyre's pension.

'The shock killed her. She left her young relative what she could—her jewellery, plate, furniture—but after the debts were paid only a mere trifle remained, which Captain Rosterne promptly spent.

'Then Mr Chittock appeared on the scene, and the girl would have none of him. Between her and her father there were several disagreements. Oona felt he was wanting to sell her, and Mr Chittock's very kindness about money estranged her more from him.

'After Mr Rosterne's death or disappearance, over head and ears in debt, very angry letters from Mr Chittock, written evidently under great irritation, were found among the missing man's papers, refusing to lend any more money, and asking why he should be expected to do so. They were disagreeable letters—letters which Mr Rosterne ought to have burnt at once, but which he did not, and Oona saw them, and the iron entered into her very soul, so Mrs Rosterne told me.

'I have only given you a mere sketch. You can fill in the details for yourself, and when you have done so, you will understand why the way to make Miss Rosterne dislike you is to plead Mr Chittock's cause.'

Mr Danson remained silent for a minute.

'Still I believe, if she could see poor Chittock now,' he began at last.

'It would make no difference whatever,' interrupted Mrs Musto. 'I spoke to her once—only once—on the subject, and gathered nothing-could reconcile her to the idea of marrying him. "And believe me, Mrs Musto," she said, "no one wishes less to marry me now than Mr Chittock; we quite understand each other." What she meant I do not know; but I suppose even a devoted lover may weary of a hopeless pursuit. At all events, what I have told you—in strict confidence—is absolutely correct. If you want Miss Rosterne to treat you more graciously, you must try to be less Mr Chittock's friend.'

'I can't be that,' said Mr Danson.

'Ah well, then, I am afraid the case is hopeless,' answered Mrs Musto.

But when she came to think matters over, she did not feel quite certain on that point.

Like a wise woman, however, she said nothing.

Chapter Five

Finding his scheme for making Mr Chittock happy was impracticable, Cyril Danson began to consider that a winter enlivened only by an occasional visit to Fort Cloyne and a continual prospect of the Atlantic might, to use Miss Heath's expression, prove 'monotonous', and accordingly, following Mr Musto's excellent example, he wrote to a few men he knew would enjoy the wild sport, the desolate country, and the utter liberty of the life he could offer—for a time.

He was right—each and all, they accepted his invitation. At the moment they were unfortunately engaged; but the moment they had, to quote one Curled Darling's expression, 'done their time,' he might depend on receiving a wire.

'It will be very jolly. Thank you, old fellow. It is good of you, who are off the treadmill, to remember those who are less lucky. We shall like to see your bogs and climb your mountains.'

So said the Curled Darling afore mentioned, and so in effect said the others.

Then, for the first time, Mr Danson took an exhaustive survey of Blackstone Castle, and considered its capabilities.

'I will change my quarters, and sleep in the oak room as soon as it can be got ready, Chenery,' he said.

'Yes, sir,' answered Chenery, who was that servant Mr Danson had referred to as the only person likely to miss him. Then, after an almost imperceptible pause, 'Gorey says the oak chamber is very cold indeed.'

'Possibly—but I like cold. And, Chenery, you had better have the dining-room put in order.'

'Yes, sir.' And Chenery turned, as if to commence operations forthwith.

If such were ever his intention, he must have changed his mind very speedily, for ere reaching the door he stopped to observe—'Beg pardon, sir, but Gorey says the wind is amazing blusterous in the dining-room, which is like a barrack in the winter-time.'

'Can you remember anything else Gorey has been pleased to remark?' asked Mr Danson.

'Well, no, sir, not at the moment, except that the library and the bedroom you occupy at present are the only two comfortable apartments in the house when stormy weather prevails, as it generally does in these parts from September to April.'

In spite of himself Mr Danson could not help smiling, even while he said—'You are becoming demoralised, Chenery, I am afraid. Do precisely what I have ordered, without any further reference to Gorey's opinions.'

'Yes, sir,' replied Chenery meekly, and departed.

But for the fact that he had so peremptorily signified his determination to be master in Blackstone Castle while he rented it, Mr Danson might within a week have returned to his former sleeping apartment.

Each room in a house, whether the house chance to lie in a town or country, has its own peculiar set of noises; and Mr Danson, who had occupied as many rooms in different houses as most men, was perfectly aware of this fact. Nevertheless, all previous experience proved quite insufficient to account for the sounds appertaining to the oak chamber.

They were always varying, yet scarcely with the variation which might well belong to the same family. Such unaccountable noises he had never heard before anywhere; but then he recollected he had never previously slept on the top of a rock within sound of an ocean's roar.

At last, unable longer to refrain from speech, he said to Gorey one morning—'I did not know there was any right of way up those steps from the beach.'

'No more there is, sir; but maybe once in a while some poor fellow does make so free as to take them as a short cut. It was done in the old gentleman's time now and again, and neither he nor Mr Diarmid made any disturbance more than a shake of the head or "I can't let this go on."'

'Oh!' returned Mr Danson, drawing a long breath. 'And when all that is settled,' he went on, as if talking to himself, 'what I should like to know is why anyone thinks fit to tramp up those steps in the dead of night.'

'Indeed it would be hard to tell, your honour, for the way is none too safe, even in the daytime,' Gorey made answer, though the quesion had not been addressed to him.

'I wonder sometimes,' observed Mr Danson, looking specu-latively in the man's face, 'whether you are very simple or very wise?'

'It would not be becoming in me, sir, to say,' replied the groom modestly, 'though there have been some thought I knew as much about horses as any man in the country. Colonel Je-rome, that took Blackstone Castle after the master went away, was that well pleased with my handling of his mare—who had, saving your presence, a devil of a temper—he wanted me to go with him to Worcestershire, and offered me good wages too.'

'Why did you not take his offer, then?' asked Mr Danson.

'I can give you no better reason, sir, than that I thought I would rather stay here.'

'Which, I suppose, was reason enough for you?'

'It was, your honour, and that's why I didn't go.'

There ensued a short pause, during the continuance of which Mr Danson considered the position, and Mr Chittock's foster-brother stood at ease.

'Gorey,' began his latest employer at length.

'Yes, sir!'

'I wish very much you would answer me one question straightforwardly—if you can?'

'You may depend I'll do my uttermost, your honour,' an-swered the man, unconscious, apparently, of the slur cast on his veracity.

'Then tell me who you suppose would wish to come up those steps after dark, to say nothing of midnight.'

'If I was never to speak another word, I don't know sir. At this time of the year there is hardly a man, unless among the gentry, out of his bed after nine o'clock, unless it might be a constable or a gauger.'

'Why, there's no smuggling here?'

'Not this many a year; but then there would be, the gaugers say, if it wasn't for them.'

'And do you mean to tell me any exciseman would risk his

neck up those steps in such pitch dark nights as we have been treated to of late?'

'Indeed, it is hard to say where they wouldn't go, for they are just like cats, and have as many lives. You see, sir, it is not so much smuggling they are keen on now as illicit stills. They got up a story once about there being a still in the dungeons of the old castle.'

'And was there?'

'They never found one, or any dungeons either. All the same, everybody round these parts believes the ruins are like a rabbit warren, and just burrowed with secret passages.'

'And what is your notion, Gorey?'

'I have none, sir; strange things were done in the old times, Mr Diarmid always did say. But I know I've heard old people sit and tell a parcel of nonsense over the fire till young girls, and boys for that matter, were afraid to turn their heads for fear of what might be standing behind them.'

'But not merely do I hear the sounds mentioned on the steps, but there are the strangest noises in the dining room.'

'It is all according to the wind, sir, as I made bold to tell Chenery. The east side of Blackstone Castle isn't fit to live in the whole winter through. Colonel Jerome said he'd as soon try to sleep on the seashore; and indeed, Mr Danson, if you'd take the lower path any evening after dusk, when the wind sets from the north-east, not even blowing a gale, but just a moderate breeze, you would wonder what could be going on out in the Atlantic. My old grandmother used to say it was the dead—drowned people, I mean—talking to each other, and making ready for the company the coming storm would send them. I'll take your honour down any night you like, and you can hear for yourself.'

'Thank you; I hear quite enough above,' returned Mr Danson, coldly. And he went away feeling very doubtful concerning Mr Daniel Gorey's strict adherence to truth.

When once a man gives imagination the rein, whether in the matter of love, hope, suspicion, jealousy, or any other master passion, it would be difficult to say where that artful sprite will take him. He may only pause to look at a glorious sunset, and behold, before the pomp of gold and crimson is chased away by clouds of darkness, fancy will have taken him round the world, and shown him such marvels as in his sober moments he never could have so much as thought of.

It was thus with Mr Danson; from the moment when he saw, or believed he saw, that flicker in Gorey's expression, he began to mistrust the man, and every word he spoke subsequently seemed confirmation that the truth was not in him.

His answers to questions were always shifty, Mr Danson considered, and hitherto that gentleman could not understand the reason. Now a light broke upon him—Gorey was engaged in some unlawful enterprise. Gorey wished to keep Blackstone Castle empty. The presence of any stranger interfered with his illegal operations. Possibly the excise officers were not far wrong when they suspected the existence of an illicit still on the premises, and who would be better able to baffle all search for it than a man who had known from childhood the house, the ruins, the caves, the coast, and every inch of country? Imagination had already taken Mr Danson on a wild chase, but it was inevitable but that fancy should lead him still further. Evidently, Gorey knew something about Captain Rosterne's disappearance. What more likely than that the unfortunate inspector had come across the potheen manufacturers and been done to death lest his revelations should stop their trade?

From all he, Mr Danson, had heard, Captain Rosterne was a man who would have died sooner than make terms with such people, and very probably—nay, very certainly—Gorey knew the whole of the circumstances.

So far, Mr Chittock's tenant did not suppose that Gorey assisted at Captain Rosterne's murder, or was even present at it, but who could tell the length to which imagination might yet take him? Once a man lets that jade get the bit between her teeth, he might as well be mounted on the *Phoul-a-Phooka*.

Three mornings later, Gorey asked his employer if he could 'spare a minute', and Mr Danson reluctantly intimating it might be possible for him to do so, the groom led him to the top of that rude flight of steps which gave access to the beach.

'I know now,' said Gorey, 'what it was your honour heard. It was that'—and he pointed to an upright piece of iron, to which was fitted a sort of broken wheel, which revolved when caught by the wind, and gave forth a sound as if of many feet hurrying up a stone staircase.

'D'ye hear, sir? Wait a minute, and the wind'll be on it again.'

'Oh!' exclaimed Mr Danson, thereby freezing the glow of Gorey's enthusiasm. 'And how did that invention come there?'

'No man now living could tell, I am thinking,' was the reply. 'It's bedded in the solid rock, and that is all time has left of it, but I said to myself I'll never rest till I find out the English for those steps, for I couldn't make head nor tail of the constant running up and down you said you heard.'

'Oh!' exclaimed Mr Danson, again giving the iron wheel, which would have served well to frighten birds, a careless touch with his stick, when *clatter, clatter, clatter, clang* it went as it a dozen men in hobnailed boots were running post-haste over the stones.

'Bring round the dog-cart in half an hour; I shall want you to go with me to Letterpass,' he said, in that peremptory-courteous, pleasant English way Gorey had learnt to know and dread.

It was disappointing, the groom felt; but, then, he knew Mr Danson had long lost confidence in him.

And he was quite right. Since the hour when he, in the dazzling sunlight, first fancied Gorey's face changed for an instant, the Englishman had not felt at ease concerning Mr Chittock's foster-brother.

To use a lovely phrase, he 'misdoubted' him, which involves a hard ordeal for the misdoubted man or woman to pass through.

The conclusion Mr Danson had come to was this: 'When first one sees the Irish, they seem quite open and above board; they charm by their apparent frankness, and are cheerful to a fault, if cheerfulness ever can be called a fault. As day after day passes, however, the reverse of the shield presents itself, and they show themselves in their true colours—shifty, plausible, false, unreliable, but pleasant—'to a certain point,' he mentally finished, 'though there is no more reliance to be placed on them than in their climate.'

Poor climate! Poor Ireland! Poor Irish! Poor Gorey!

And yet Mr Danson's feelings were natural enough. He had come to Ireland carrying his heart in his hand, and that hand open.

He had come prepared to like, prepared to give, wishful to make those he came in contact with happy, desirous most of all to remove a load of care from Mr Chittock; and of the two persons he thought could best have helped him to compass the last wish, one coldly thwarted his endeavours, while the other evaded his most simple question.

Often he marvelled why he remained amid such unsatisfactory surroundings. But Mrs Musto did not wonder; *she knew!*

There is no truer saying than that '*it never rains but it pours*,' and accordingly the post-bag one morning rained such a number of coming guests that Mr Danson for the moment felt appalled.

Not merely did the three men he had invited herald their early arrival, but two out of the number proposed to bring a friend with them. 'Adson wants to see your cell so awfully,' said one; 'may I bring him?' 'Mayford, who is the best fellow on earth, has never been in Ireland; can you take him in? If not, wire at once.'

Mr Danson telegraphed that he would be glad to see them all, and then set Chenery to work to make things ready for the expected guests. Immediately the whole economy of Blackstone Castle underwent a change—fires blazed in hitherto unoccupied apartments, the housemaid looked up her stores of linen, and asked for assistance. The cook told Chenery she must have more pots and pans, and a woman in to help. Chenery himself had to report an absence of sufficient glass and crockery ware. Gorey spent his time scouring the country in order to bespeak provisions and 'making ready' for the moment when he should receive orders to 'meet the train' at Letterpass, while to Mr Danson the bustle and excitement proved delightful after six months' absence from the hurly-burly, and diverted his attention completely from the noise of mysterious footsteps and the strange wailing sounds that rendered the dining-room well-nigh uninhabitable.

The dining-room at that time really was in the possession of Chenery, who served his master's meals in the library, and was making many changes which cost little more than a good deal of personal trouble, in the apartments devoted to the reception of company.

Chenery was in his element. His master gave him *carte blanche,* and he had men up from the village to shake, and clean, and hammer, and tack, as well as arrange goods ordered down from Dublin; and, in short, as the cook joyously expressed herself, 'It is like the good old times come again, God bless them!' while Gorey said, though not audibly, 'He'll have something now to take his mind off Captain Rosterne and the din there is about the place sometimes. Lord send these gentleman may entice him back with them to where he came from!'

Charlie Langley, the curled darling, dreaded by fashionable mothers, beloved of daughters, a sad, unscrupulous detrimental who danced like an angel and was a very bad boy without a bit of harm in him, was the first to arrive at Blackstone Castle.

He appeared one afternoon carrying a modest portmanteau, which, he explained, had, with himself, been 'tooled over from Letterpass by a delightful old Presbyterian minister who might have drawn up the Westminster Confession of Faith. He travelled in the compartment with me from Rathstewart, and we got into friendly relations immediately. I told him where I was going, and he told me the distance.

"'Which I must tramp, I suppose?" I said, "for Mr Danson doesn't know I am coming by this train."

"'You needn't do that," replied Martin Luther, "for if you don't object to an old-fashioned gig, I can give you a lift."

'I told him if there were one conveyance I loved more than another it was a gig of the pre-Adamite build; and then he said he liked young people with no nonsense about them, and that he knew you very well.'

'I am afraid I have not the honour of the gentleman's acquaintance,' interposed Mr Danson.

'By sight, by sight, my arrogant friend,' exclaimed Mr Langley. 'He lives at Cloyne Vale, and has seen you riding over to Fort Cloyne; pray, observe how pat I have your heathenish names already. My divine proceeded to say you were a fine-looking man; "would make three of you", he remarked so disparagingly that I felt constrained to answer, "I know I am very small, but indeed I am very good."

'He shook his head as if he did not believe my assurance, but only looked at me as a father might at a naughty child, more in sorrow than in anger, and we parted on the best terms. I said I would do myself the honour of calling on him, and I want you to ask him up here.'

'Very well,' agreed Mr Danson; 'only, Langley, there is one warning I must give you—the Irish do not like chaff.'

'I don't know about chaff,' returned Mr Langley, gaily, 'but they will like *me*.'

Chapter Six

The fulfilment justified Mr Langley's prediction. Before the week was out he had conquered the village. No one could be said to have a chance beside him. All the children, and they were many; all the dogs, likewise numerous; all the beggars, *ditto*, adored the lively young Englishman. Old women rose up and called him blessed. Men would have risked breaking their necks at his bidding. He knew everyone—the rector and the baker, the publican and the sinner, the doctor and his patient. Miss Heath was his sworn ally. Mr Danson discovered him on one knee holding her worsted while she wound. Mr and Mrs Musto and the little Mustos were enchanted with the newcomer, while he walked in and out of Mrs Rosterne's cottage as though an inmate of the house, and Miss Rosterne, whom he dubbed the 'blessed *damosel*,' was actually seen to laugh at one of what Mr Danson in his inmost heart called Langley's senseless sallies.

It was then a sword pierced Mr Danson's soul; then for the first time he asked himself a very serious question; then he began to understand what his feelings had always been towards the girl who held him at such a distance! 'And who now encourages that mountebank?' he reflected most unjustly, for Miss Rosterne did not encourage, only laughed, and that but once, as she might at the gambols of a frolicsome child. Then her face grew grave again as was its wont.

How tired Mr Danson soon felt of his visitors it would be difficult to tell. Their talk, their jokes, their liveliness, jarred upon him like merriment in church. What a roystering set they were to bring to a hermit's cell! How could he ever return to a world of which they were rather favourable representatives?

For they all could but be considered kindly, honourable men, who were doing nothing wrong except enjoying themselves thoroughly; who would have been quite as ready to condole with the sorrowful as they were to rejoice in their own youth.

'Jolly companions every one', they tramped across bogs and over heather; they walked long miles; they never grumbled if rain swept down upon their devoted heads; they were charmed with the scenery, delighted with the people; vowed they would ask nothing better than to spend years in Blackstone Castle, and voted their host by acclamation the best fellow living!

They sat up late and rose early; walked and rode when the weather proved propitious; lounged, chatted, and played billiards when it was wet; after dinner they amused themselves with cards, smoked cigars, and drank punch, which the doctor brewed scientifically; they made themselves as contented and happy as children; they declared they would never have such a good time again; and who could say they were mistaken? Christmas—a green Christmas—came and passed; and then one night the storm-fiends, which had been laid to rest for a long time, were let loose in their power and might. Through all the hours of darkness there raged a furious gale from the north-east, and when morning came Mr Danson saw 'what he had never seen'.

'The wild waves tossing their foam to the stormy sky'—earth

and heaven seeming to meet, giant billows madly chasing each other and rushing in-shore as if steadily purposed to sweep over and destroy the land.

He stood looking out on the magnificent spectacle in absorbed admiration till he suddenly remembered this was the wind which, according to Gorey, rendered the dining-room as well as his own sleeping apartment unfit for human habitation.

Well, he knew what the night had been to him, and he regretted not having told Chenery to lay breakfast in the library.

'Danson,' shouted Mr Langley up the wide staircase as soon as his host appeared, 'have you a cell underneath the dining-room where you keep all the winds that blow? I never heard such a din. Do make haste; the noise is glorious—better by far than anything I ever heard at sea. Just listen;' and he held his friend on the threshold while what one of the others called 'an infernal row' broke on his ears and fairly appalled him.

'No one could stand this,' Mr Danson said at last; 'let us go into the library.'

'No, no, I wouldn't miss the fun for anything,' declared Mr Langley; 'all the powers of hell seem to be warring against us. Talk of the Swine's Gun! Not to be compared with the concerted music at Blackstone Castle!'

'But what in the name of everything wonderful is it?' asked Mr Tankerton.

'The cry of the wind,' answered Mr Danson, feebly.

'Have you heard anything like this before?'

'No, but Gorey warned me this room was unfit for occupation during the winter.'

'I am going to occupy it, for one,' said Mr Langley, seating himself at the table. 'Here, who will have toast?'

'I will have potato cake—a good thing, and one I shall probably never taste again,' answered Mr Adson.

'The strangest part of the affair to me is that, spite of the saturnalia somebody is holding, the house still stands. It does not even rock,' contributed Mr Mayford to the conversation.

'I do not profess to understand or explain the noises about

Blackstone Castle,' said Mr Danson. 'They seem to have been here before I came.'

'After breakfast I shall make it my business to understand them,' declared Mr Langley, attacking a huge sirloin.

'Gorey knows more about Blackstone than anyone else,' remarked Mr Danson, not without a feeling of grim satisfaction at the idea of pitting the wits of his guest and his groom against each other.

'Then Gorey shall share his knowledge with me,' was the confident reply.

Mr Danson went to the sideboard and helped himself to fried cod.

The luncheon hour arrived and found Mr Langley comparatively silent. Yes, he had talked to Gorey. 'Yes,' in answer to pressing questions, Gorey had personally conducted him to that unsafe, rocky staircase leading to the beach, where his hat was blown off instantly, and he had to hold his hair tight lest that should follow also.

Gorey seemed favourably impressed with the devil's own triangles, which were making the most awful clatter he, the Curled Darling, ever heard.

Gorey had offered to take him that evening, after dark, to a place where he would be able to hear quite distinctly the dead talking to the dead, but Mr Langley had refused the charming invitation.

He did not care for great sensations. He told Gorey, he said, he was young and easily frightened, and liked his bed; so if Gorey of his kindness, instead of dragging him miles along the seashore, would come in and tuck him up and sing him to sleep, and remain beside him during the night lest he should wake up and be terrified at finding himself '*all his lone*'—a delightful Hibernian phrase—he would feel much more grateful than if taken to the grandest ghost-party ever given by the Atlantic.

'Gorey tells me he knows a lot of ballads,' finished Mr Langley, 'so I intend to make arrangements for a musical evening when next Danson and his rough team are invited to Fort Cloyne.'

'Of which I will give you due notice, and hope you may enjoy your sing-song,' said Mr Danson.

'I only wish the blessed *damosel* would come up and assist,' remarked Mr Langley.

'I should love to hear her rare voice mingling with Gorey's in "Fight on, ye brave heroes, fight on,"' said Munro. 'I can just fancy how she would give that line.'

'Miss Rosterne has endured a great trial, and I think we ought to respect her sorrow,' remarked Mr Danson, severely.

'I respect Miss Rosterne. She seems to me the pluckiest girl I ever met.' answered Mr Langley. 'But concerning her "trial" I am not quite so sure. At one *coup* it rid her of an unwelcome lover and a father who, if all accounts be true, was the most undesirable of "stern parents."'

No one replied. Mr Danson did not care to do so, and the other men were not sufficiently interested.

'One thing I do like about Gorey,' resumed Mr Langley, 'is that he has the most loyal regard for my "dear *damosel*". He says if she and the master, meaning Mr Chittock, could have "sorted matters", it would have been the making of Blackstone Castle and all these parts.'

'Very likely,' assented Mr Danson. 'Judging from appearances, Blackstone Castle as well as poor Chittock want someone badly to "make them."'

'The whole business seems to me so unaccountable!' observed Mr Tankerton. 'I always thought any girl would marry any man if only he were rich enough.'

Mr Danson winced, but said nothing. Mr Tankerton remembered and stopped—too late.

Mr Langley hummed 'I am a loyal subject, brave as any in this nation,' and remarked calmly, 'Gorey has certainly a great repertory.'

Chapter Seven

The storm had sobbed itself to rest. Worn out, the Atlantic lay almost calm under a cold winter sky; the dead were quiet in their ocean graves, or at least no sound of their terrible discourse broke the evening stillness; while Peace seemed for a time at least to have taken up her abode among the headlands of that iron-bound coast.

'But this weather is a delusion,' said the doctor, who, at the earnest desire of Mr Charles Langley, had, with the priest and Mr Melsham, been invited to relieve the monotony of Blackstone Castle, and was in the act as he spoke of mixing that famous brew which was known and esteemed within a circuit of fifteen miles—'a complete delusion; it is not going to last. I saw three gulls today on the Cronan Bog, and we know what that means. Eh, Father John?'

'It means mischief,' answered the other; 'are you sure they were gulls?'

'Quite; I was close to them, and I thought to myself, "There is a line storm brewing up at the North Pole, and it'll be here before Mr Langley bids us goodbye."'

'How jolly!' exclaimed that gentleman.

'You would not think it jolly if you were out on the Atlantic with only a plank between you and eternity,' observed the priest, gravely.

'Pooh!' was the reply; 'what is between us and eternity sitting in this room? After all, by land or by water, it is but a step from the world we know to the world we don't know.'

'It is a very serious one, my young friend.'

Mr Langley did not answer, and as no other person spoke for a few seconds, there ensued a brief silence, which was at last broken by the irrepressible Charlie.

'I am sorely vexed that duty calls,' he began. 'I don't remember ever being so sorry to leave a place in my life. When I am back in London I shall always be thinking of this grim old spot—the lonely mountains, the stretch of sad seashore, and the "wild waves raging high." And one was able to enjoy it in peace and comfort,' he added, throwing up his arms and laying his head on his hands, clasped lazily behind, 'because there were no women to spoil the fun.'

'Hear him!' exclaimed Mr Tankerton. 'Why, the fellow is never happy unless he is making love to half a dozen girls.'

'I don't like the sport, though—I don't, upon my word. When a man gets to my age—there is nothing to laugh at,' he added, as his friends grinned in mockery—'when a man gets to my age he begins to tire of all that sort of thing. Wherever I went since the 1st August last there were women, women, women—women, old and young, plain and pretty, women who rode, women who drove, shot, fished, stalked, swam, handled an oar, danced, dressed, spouted on platforms—and never left one a moment in peace. I don't know what the world is coming to—petticoats here, petticoats there, petticoats everywhere. Enough to make a man go hang himself!'

The last word was barely spoken before there echoed through the room a long, wailing sigh—a sigh as if someone's suffering heart were being literally rent in twain.

'Heaven preserve us!' said the priest.

'What the——is that!' exclaimed the doctor, with such an excess of profane expression that Father John crossed himself, the while Mr Melsham sprang to his feet—an example followed, indeed, by every person present.

'Was anyone in the room trying to play a bad practical joke?' asked Mr Adson, sternly. 'Good Lord! the house must be coming down,' he suddenly added, as a tremendous crash, followed by the sound of bitter gasping sobs, struck consternation into all present. Mr Langley was the first to recover his composure.

'Faith, Danson,' he said, 'all the winds of heaven were bad enough, but this is worse. There must be something very wrong somewhere, and you ought to see about it.'

'Gorey warned me this room was uninhabitable during the winter,' said Mr Danson, trying to speak calmly, though a terrible idea had come into his mind—*viz*. that Captain Rosterne still lived, and was dragging out a miserable existence in some dungeon known only to his captors.

It was an absurd idea—one he would have felt ashamed to mention. Yet the mystery of the inspector's disappearance, the crumbling ruins of the old castle, the utter desolation of the new building, the unearthly sounds, the weird stories he had listened to concerning the unquiet dead, had prepared his mind to receive any impression, no matter how wild and impossible.

'It must have grown uninhabitable very lately, then,' said the doctor, in answer to Mr Danson's remark, 'for many a pleasant evening I have spent here, both in storm and shine, and never heard a sound except of the wind or the rain beating against the glass.'

'If I had not gone into the cellars and found them as quiet as family vaults, I'd have sworn there must be one beneath this room, where Mr Danson kept a few Atlantic tempests for his own especial benefit,' remarked Mr Langley. 'Just hark! Can Gorey's drowned have come on shore to hold their revel?'

The party had not resumed their chairs, and stood looking stupidly at each other and into the dark corners which the fire and lamplight failed to penetrate.

'I think there is something very suspicious about all this,' said Mr Melsham, speaking for the first time.

The priest's lips moved, though no word was audible. The doctor's glance wandered along the east wall with a curious intentness.

'I wonder—' he began at last.

'What do you wonder?' asked Mr Melsham.

'Well, there used to be a door behind where that sideboard now stands. It has been papered over, and I was wondering—but that is all nonsense. Old Mr Chittock was in the habit of opening it often enough, and I never heard an uncanny sound.'

'Where did the door lead to?'

'To the island of Madeira—in other words, to a small cellar where the old gentleman kept some marvellous wine he produced on special occasions only.'

'We will find that door,' said Mr Langley. 'Tankerton, Adson, Mayford, bear a hand. Here you are,' he cried, tapping the wall, from which a heavy sideboard had been dragged. 'Has anybody a knife?' And, one being forthcoming, in a trice the canvas over which the paper had been hung was cut away, and some light boarding stood revealed.

'That covers the door,' said the doctor, oracularly.

'We will soon get to that,' declared Mr Melsham, ripping off a length of the match-boarding. 'There it is, right enough. We must have the rest of this woodwork down, though.'

'I was here for a month when a lad,' observed Mr Danson, puzzled, 'but I never remember noticing that door.'

'A screen always stood in front of it,' said the doctor; 'besides, you were not a wine-bibber in those days, I suppose, and if you had been, Mr Chittock would scarcely have produced his old Madeira for a boy's benefit.'

'Here we are then,' interrupted Mr Langley, 'face to face with a locked door, and a deuce of a wind blowing through the key-hole. How it moans, like a lost soul in torment! Who keeps the key?'

'Gorey, I conclude. Let us have him in.'

And Gorey accordingly was summoned.

As he saluted the company, his eye caught the gaping rent in the paper, and his attitude instantly stiffened.

'Where is the key of that door, Gorey?' asked Mr Danson.

'I never had it, sir.'

'Fetch an axe, then.'

'What for, your honour—if I may make so free?'

'To get into the cellar beyond.'

'Begging your pardon, I can't do that, sir.'

'Why not?'

'Because I am Mr Chittock's servant before I am yours, and I dursn't break any lock in this house without his authority.'

'There is something in that,' muttered Mr Melsham.

'Of course, if you take that line, Gorey, there is nothing more to be said,' returned Mr Danson.

'But I am sure Mr Chittock would not object,' urged Mr Langley. 'Now, seriously, Gorey, do you believe he would wish any gentleman to sit over a cauldron bubbling such infernal noises as we have been listening to for the last half-hour?'

'I do not suppose he would, sir; but, all the same, there are plenty of other rooms in the house, and it is not likely he would be best pleased to see his property wrecked this way. If Mr Danson will get my master's leave, I'll try to knock down the castle, if that is all.'

'You need say no more; you can go,' remarked Mr Danson, coldly.

'Might I speak one word, sir, first?' pleaded the man. 'It doesn't take long for a letter to travel from here to London, and maybe you'd be glad afterwards to think you hadn't destroyed the place.'

'You had better leave the room,' repeated Mr Danson, more than ever determined not to be thwarted, and Gorey reluctantly departed.

What did Mr Chittock's friend expect?

If the truth must be told, he had been straining his ears to catch a cry for help, a word of thankfulness, passionate entreaties for release, and instead there came at intervals only that strange sobbing, that pathetic, long-drawn sigh.

'It is just the wind that's rising,' said the doctor, 'but where it comes from is beyond me. The house was as tight as a drum in the old days.'

'What are we going to do now?' asked Mr Danson, though indeed he knew perfectly what he meant to do. 'What should you advise, Mr Melsham?'

'I can scarcely advise,' was the reply. 'The way that fellow put the matter seems to me right enough. You are not the owner of this house, and it is a risky thing to burst open any place the rightful possessor has locked up. There may be wine in that cellar, or whisky, or—or anything, and indeed I think if I were in your place—'

'You'd see the matter through,' finished Mr Langley.

'No, nothing of the sort. I should communicate with Mr Chittock.'

'Well, it is of no use writing till tomorrow, so meantime I vote we have some punch,' cried the young misogamist. 'Let me carry the flowing bowl, Danson; the doctor's brew will taste better in the library. Follow, gentleman all, please. We are going to make a night of it.'

Despite this assurance, however, the village guests were walking sedately home when the church clock struck eleven, and gravely opining something had given way in the cellar which ought to be seen to. But it could only be considered right and proper in the first instance to communicate with Mr Chittock, who would probably come over.

'It is a deuced awkward thing to tamper with locks and bolts,' declared Mr Melsham. 'No, it would not have done to break in that door. Put it to yourself, Father John.'

'I should not stand anything in my house being meddled with,' declared that worthy.

'And I am sure you wouldn't, doctor?'

'No. All the same, I'd like to see the inside of that old cellar. It is built with slabs, which formed part of the original castle, and which look on the outside just like rough pieces of rock flung together anyhow.'

'I suppose there is some foundation for that legend about a secret passage?' said Mr Melsham, tentatively.

'There may be. Listen to the "sea's trouble," as the poor people about here call it, which always seems to me the saddest, most impressive sound on earth,' and the doctor stood still while he spoke. 'It is like a deep grief which no words could tell; a lost soul might make such a lament.'

'Well I know it,' capped the priest. 'Many a night when I have been coming home from some far-away cabin where my help was needed I have wondered what sore trouble the great deep was trying to express, for hers is an awful wail!'

'Let us get on,' said Mr Melsham impatiently, 'and leave the ocean to manage its own affairs. What a chilly night!'

Whether Mr Danson found the night chilly or not has never been recorded. One thing only is certain—it seemed very long.

Disturbed by doubt, distracted by conjecture, he sought rest and did not find it. When, utterly exhausted, he fell into an uneasy slumber, it was but to go over all the old weary ground again.

Ceaselessly Mr Chittock, Captain Rosterne, Gorey, and Blackstone Castle, with its mysterious noises and various unknown passages, flitted across the field of his dream-seeing eyes.

The real and the imaginary mingled together in such awful fashion that he felt glad when the first faint streak of dawn declared that the time of dreams was over, and the period for action close at hand.

More than once during the passage of an apparently endless night he had, moved by some impulse he could not analyse, risen and bent his steps to that room which, he felt assured, held the key to his perplexity.

Well, if it did contain anything in the shape of a mystery, ere many hours passed the doubts which had taken his mind captive would be either justified or laid to rest.

After the departure of Doctor Gage, and his friends, it had been decided at a council composed of the Blackstone Castle house-party at all hazards to force an entrance into what Mr Langley styled the 'mysterious cave'. 'And I will go down to the village quite early tomorrow morning,' proceeded that young gentleman, 'and get a couple of stalwart fellows, armed with picks and crowbars,' which promise he fulfilled so admirably that even before Mr Danson left his sleeping apartment he heard sounds in the dining-room betokening preparations were being made for the siege.

On the landing he came face to face with Gorey, who looked as if he had not slept for a month.

'I beg pardon, sir, for making so free to ask,' began the groom, 'but is it true you are going to batter in the cellar door without writing to Mr Chittock?'

'Quite true,' answered Mr Danson.

'I suppose, then, it is no use my saying a word more?'

'Of no use whatever, unless you give me some good reason for staying my hand. What is the secret you are trying to keep, Gorey?'

'What secret could there be, your honour?'

'That is precisely what I want to know.'

'If you were away on a journey, sir, you would not be best pleased to find when you came home we had picked the lock of your dressing-box.'

'I will account to Mr Chittock for my present action, but not to anyone else,' replied Mr Chittock's friend, passing Gorey with a gesture of dismissal.

'I hope you'll never rue this morning's work, sir,' said Gorey, in a voice which struck Mr Danson unpleasantly even while he replied—

'I must take my chance of that.'

'What am I to do? What am I to do at all?' muttered the groom, as he turned despairingly to leave.

Mr Danson could not catch the words, but he heard the pitiful sorrow in their tone, and saw the blank hopelessness written on the man's face.

'Gorey,' he said, retracing his steps so as to speak without being overheard.

'Yes, sir.'

'Is there any place you would like to go—never mind where—but should you like to go?'

'What for would I want to go away from Blackstone Castle?'

'You alone can tell that. Understand, however, if you do, I will give you ten pounds. That would take you a long distance.'

'It would, and thank you kindly; but I have no conceit to leave Blackstone Castle. There is only one thing,' he added, 'that your honour could do for me this morning, and that is, send word to my master about what you have in your mind.'

'Unless you give me some better reason than I have yet heard I need not trouble your master.'

For a moment Gorey hesitated—then, 'I can't do that, sir,' he said.

'Very well;' and Mr Danson walked into the dining-room and closed the door.

Already the men had turned back the carpet prior to commencing operations.

'It will be a tough job,' remarked Mr Langley. 'Hillo! where is Gorey off to in such a hurry?'

Mr Danson turned to one of the windows in time to see Mr Chittock's foster-brother running down the castle slope as fast as his legs would take him.

'He has gone,' thought the Englishman, relieved.

But Gorey had not gone far. Ere he reached the village he slackened his speed, and walked sedately enough up to the door of Mrs Rostern's cottage, where he asked if he could see Miss Oona for a minute, and then, when she came into her narrow hall, if he could speak a word with her alone.

'Certainly,' said the girl, taking him into a little drawing-room not much larger than a band-box.

'Are you in trouble? Is there anything I can do for you?' she asked.

'Yes, miss, in sore trouble, and I want you to write a line of a telegraphed message for me.'

'Of course,' producing a slip of paper and a pencil. 'What am I to say?'

'It is for Mr Chittock, miss.'

'Oh! And what am I to write?'

'Mr Danson is breaking open the door that was papered up in the dining-room—the door leading into the old cellar.'

Gorey stopped. Miss Rosterne was looking at him with a sort of questioning horror—not writing, but resting her elbows on the table and holding the pencil between her fingers.

'For the Lord's sake, put down what I tell you,' gasped Gorey.

She did not answer. She sat like one deaf, slowly twirling the pencil round and round, round and round.

'You never were hard, Miss Oona. Write, and God'll reward you. *It's a man's life,'* he added hoarsely.

Still she did not speak or move, save to twirl that pencil slowly, slowly round.

'I thought you'd have done it; I never deemed you would deny me; but I can't be wasting my time here,' he went on in an access of passionate disappointment. 'I'll go to the church minister or the doctor. I'll find somebody that'll do that much for me;' and he was rushing out of the room, when the girl said—'Stop, Dan, I will do what you ask. It was not that—no, it was not that.'

'I spoke too sudden, but there's no time to spare,' Gorey was beginning, with a quick revulsion of feeling, when she made a sign for him to remain silent, while she wrote rapidly without waiting for any dictation.

'Will this do?' she asked, when she had finished reading the message aloud.

'Yes.'

'Then go back to the castle and I will send the telegram from Terrig. Leave all to me. *I promise you,*' she finished, seeing his hesitation.

And Gorey went out and made his way back to Blackstone by various lonely paths, crying like a child.

Nothing had happened during his absence. When he returned, the lock was still intact, Chenery told him, and the hinges had not given. Sitting on some trusses of straw, he trembled in his stable, as even there he heard the thud of the pickaxe, the grind of the crowbar. A mist lay over the Atlantic. The morning was warm and lowering, the gulls were flying inland, and the ocean's lament sounded mournful as some wild death keen; but Gorey did not see shore or sea or sky, or aught save the interior of that vault, which, during the passage of the last few years, he had often longed to enter.

Suddenly there came one tremendous crash and then silence. He knew what had happened, and instinctively rose to his feet, placing a hand on one of the stalls to steady himself.

'Why, Gorey, I thought you were out,' cried Mr Langley, jubilantly rushing in. 'We are through, and I have come for the stable lantern.'

'I will bring it in, your honour,' answered the man in a dull, slow voice.

'Come along then. Never mind stopping to light it; we can do that ourselves.'

Like one walking in some horrible nightmare, Gorey followed the lively young fellow across the yard, through the back passages, into the front hall and the dining-room beyond, where they were met by a rush of strangely chill air, and a sound as of the wash and sob of many waters against the rocks.

In a moment Mr Langley had taken the lantern out of his hand, lighted it, and disappeared through the gaping doorway into the cavernous darkness beyond.

Every man present followed him save Gorey, who stood by the threshold waiting.

There was a noise as if of the crunching of glass underfoot, then ensued a pause while one stopped apparently to pick up something.

'Why, it is a spoon,' said Mr Tankerton, which remark caused a laugh that awoke every unearthly echo in the place.

Still, with Mr Langley as leader, the search-party went forward, squeezing into a passage beyond the cellar, the door opening into which stood ajar.

No one spoke. The darkness and the mystery seemed to daunt even Mr Langley. Gorey strained his ears to listen. All at once a voice said, 'What is this?' then, 'My God!'

The long strain was over. The worst had come. Sight and hearing deserted Gorey, and for the first time in his life he fell back in a dead faint.

When he came to himself he was lying on a sofa in the dining-room, where many people were standing around.

Mr Langley chafed his left hand, while Dr Burke felt his right pulse, and as from a great distance came the sound of Mr Melsham's voice speaking earnestly to Mr Danson.

'Quiet, gentleman, if you please,' said the doctor. 'He is regaining consciousness.'

Immediately a dead silence ensued, a silence broken at last by Gorey, who, struggling to a sitting position, exclaimed—'*I done it. Take me where you please.*'

About the time he made this statement a gentleman resident in London sat in a pleasant room overlooking Holland Park busily engaged in finishing his correspondence for the day.

For more than an hour he wrote on steadily, but at length he laid down his pen, closed and sealed the last envelope, then placed that letter with others in a conspicuous position. He seemed weary. A glass of water stood beside him. Into this he poured a few drops of something which diffused a strange yet not un-pleasant odour through the room, and immediately drained the tumbler. After doing so he laid his head back and died. The man was Diarmid Chittock, and the liquid poison.

Conclusion

Nearly twenty years have come and gone since that grey morning on which the house-party at Blackstone Castle passed gaily into the mysterious darkness of Madeira Island to find a corpse. Yet the story of Mr Chittock's crime, and of his foster-brother's loyal attempt to take the burden and the punishment on his own shoulders, remains fresh in the memory of Lisnabeg as the green grass growing on Captain Rosterne's grave.

Mr Chittock's heir-at-law now resides at the castle. He has blocked up the passage leading from the caves to the cellar. He and his friends have drunk all the old Madeira. There are boys and girls in the familiar rooms, young men and maidens tread the cliffs and uneven steps, but the tale of their relative's sin and sorrow means nothing to them save that it gave to their father a property he might never otherwise have owned.

On a fair estate in Hampshire Cyril Danson lives the quiet, happy life of an English country gentleman.

Not alone, however. After long and patient wooing he won for his wife the girl who 'walked three miles Irish out, and three in, five days a week, and she an O'Considine', and is the angel of the fair home.

Gorey says there 'never was her like for goodness', and de-clares the master is not far behind. Yet, though he is happy enough and well-to-do, his heart clings with fond faithfulness to the memory of that poor sinner who received his death-warrant when the telegram carried by Oona Rosterne to Terrig reached its destination.

And yet she had hoped to save him—she did all she could to save him!

Walnut-Tree House

THE NEW OWNER

Many years ago there stood at the corner of a street leading out of Upper Kennington Lane a great red-brick house, covering a goodly area of ground, and surrounded by gardens magnificent in their proportions when considered in relation to the populous neighbourhood mentioned.

Originally a place of considerable pretension; a gentleman's seat in the country probably when Lambeth Marsh had not a shop in the whole of it; when Vauxhall Gardens were still *in nubibus;* when no South-Western Railway was planned or thought of; when London was comparatively a very small place, and its present suburbs were mere country villages—hamlets lying quite remote from the heart of the city.

Once, the house in question had been surrounded by a small park, and at that time there were fish-ponds in the grounds, and quite a stretch of meadow-land within the walls. Bit by bit, however, the park had been cut up into building ground and let off on building leases; the meadows were covered with bricks and mortar, shops were run up where cows once chewed the cud, and the roar and rumble of London traffic sounded about the old house and the deserted garden, formerly quiet and silent as though situated in some remote part of the country.

Many a time in the course of the generations that had come and gone, been born and buried, since the old house was built, the freehold it covered changed hands. On most estates of this kind round London there generally is a residence which passes like a horse from buyer to buyer. When it has served one man's need it is put up for sale and bid for by another. When rows and rows of houses, and line after line of streets, have obliterated all the familiar marks, it is impossible to cultivate a sentiment as regards property; and it is unlikely that the descendants of the first possessors of Walnut-Tree House who had grown to be country folk and lived in great state, oblivious of business people, and entertaining a great contempt for trade, knew that in a very undesirable part of London there still stood the residence where the first successful man of their family went home each day from his counting-house over against St Mildred's Church, in The Poultry.

One very wet evening, in an autumn the leaves of which have been dead and gone this many a year, Walnut-Tree House, standing grim and lonely in the mournful twilight, looked more than ordinarily desolate and deserted.

There was not a sign of life about it; the shutters were closed —the rusty iron gates were fast locked—the approach was choked up with grass and weeds—through no chink did the light of a single candle flicker. For seven years it had been given over to rats and mice and blackbeetles; for seven years no one had been found to live in it; for seven years it had remained empty, while its owner wore out existence in fits of moody dejection or of wild frenzy in the madhouse close at hand; and now that owner was dead and buried and forgotten, and the new owner was returning to take possession. This new owner had written to his lawyers, or rather he had written to the lawyers of his late relative, begging them to request the person in charge of the house to have rooms prepared for his arrival; and, when the train drew into the station at Waterloo, he was met by one of the clerks in Messrs Timpson and Co.'s office, who, picking out Mr Stainton, delivered to that gentleman a letter from the firm, and said he would wait and hear if there were any message in reply.

Mr Stainton read the letter—looked at the blank flyleaf- and then, turning back to the first words, read what his solicitors had to say all through once again, this time aloud.

'The house has stood empty for more than seven years,' he said, half addressing the clerk and half speaking to himself. 'Must be damp and uninhabitable; there is no one living on the premises. Under these circumstances we have been unable to comply with your directions, and can only recommend you to go to an hotel till we are able personally to discuss future arrangements.'

'Humph,' said the new owner, after he had finished. 'I'll go and take a look at the place, anyhow. Is it far from here, do you know?' he asked, turning to the young man. from Timpsons'.

'No, sir; not very far.'

'Can you spare time to come over there with me?' continued Mr Stainton.

The young man believed that he could, adding, 'If you want to go into the house we had better call for the key. It is at an estate agent's in the Westminster Bridge Road.'

'I cannot say I have any great passion for hotels,' remarked the new owner, as he took his seat in the cab.

'Indeed, sir?'

'No; either they don't suit me, or I don't suit them. I have led a wild sort of life: not much civilisation in the bush, or at the gold-fields, I can tell you. Rooms full of furniture, houses where a fellow must keep to the one little corner he has hired, seem to choke me. Then I have not been well, and I can't stand noise and the trampling of feet. I had enough of that on board ship; and I used to lie awake at nights and think how pleasant it would be to have a big house all to myself, to do as I liked in.'

'Yes, sir,' agreed the clerk.

'You see, I have been used to roughing it, and I can get along very well for a night without servants.'

'No doubt, sir.'

'I suppose the house is in substantial repair—roof tight, and all that sort of thing?'

'I can't say, I am sure, sir.'

'Well, if there is a dry corner where I can spread a rug, I shall sleep there tonight.'

The clerk coughed. He looked out of the window, and then he looked at Messrs Timpsons' client.

'I do not think—' he began, apologetically, and then stopped.

'You don't think what?' asked the other.

'You'll excuse me, sir, but I don't think—I really do not think, if I were you, I'd go to that house tonight.'

'Why not?'

'Well, it has not been slept in for nearly seven years, and it must be blue mouldy with damp; and if you have been ill, that is all the more reason you should not run such a risk. And, besides—'

'Besides?' suggested Mr Stainton. 'Out with it! Like a postscript, no doubt, that "besides" holds the marrow of the argument.'

'The house has stood empty for years, sir, because—there is no use in making any secret of it—the place has a bad name.'

'What sort of a bad name—unhealthy?'

'Oh, no!'

'Haunted?'

The clerk inclined his head. 'You have hit it, sir,' he said.

'And that is the reason no one has lived there?'

'We have been quite unable to let the house on that account.'

'The sooner it gets unhaunted, then, the better,' retorted Mr Stainton. 'I shall certainly stop there tonight. You are not disposed to stay and keep me company, I suppose?'

With a little gesture of dismay the clerk drew back. Certainly, this was one of the most unconventional of clients. The young man from Timpsons' did not at all know what to make of him.

'A rough sort of fellow,' he said afterwards, when describing the new owner; 'boorish; never mixed with good society, that sort of thing.'

He did not in the least understand this rich man, who treated him as an equal, who objected to hotels, who didn't mind taking up his abode in a house where not even a drunken charwoman could be induced to stop, and who calmly asked a stranger on whom he had never set eyes before—a clerk in the respectable office of Timpson and Co., a young fellow anxious to rise in the world, careful as to his associates, particular about the whiteness of his shirts and the sit of his collar and the cut of his coats—to 'rough' things with him in that dreadful old dungeon, where, perhaps, he might even be expected to light a fire.

Still, he did not wish to offend the new owner. Messrs Timpson expected him to be a profitable client; and to that impartial firm the money of a boor would, he knew, seem as good as the money of a count.

'I am very sorry,' he stammered; 'should only have felt too much honoured; but the fact is—previous engagement—'

Mr Stainton laughed.

'I understand,' he said. 'Adventures are quite as much out of your line as ghosts. And now tell me about this apparition. Does the "old man" walk?'

'Not that I ever heard of,' answered the other.

'Is it, then, the miserable beggar who tried to do for himself?'

'It is not the late Mr Stainton, I believe,' said the young man, in a tone which mildly suggested that reference to a client of Timpsons' as a 'miserable beggar' might be considered bad taste.

'Then who on earth is it?' persisted Mr Stainton.

'If you must know, sir, it is a child—a child who has driven every tenant in succession out of the house.'

The new owner burst into a hearty laugh—a laugh which gave serious offence to Timpsons' clerk.

'That is too good a joke,' said Mr Stainton. 'I do not know when I heard anything so delicious.'

'It is a fact, whether it be delicious or not,' retorted the young man, driven out of all his former propriety of voice and demeanour by the contemptuous ridicule this 'digger' thought fit to cast on his story; 'and I, for one, would not, after all I have heard about your house, pass a night in it—no, not if anybody offered me fifty pounds down.'

'Make your mind easy, my friend,' said the new owner, quietly. 'I am not going to bid for your company. The child and I can manage, I'll be bound, to get on very comfortably by ourselves.'

CHAPTER TWO

THE CHILD

It was later on in the same evening; Mr Stainton had an hour previously taken possession of Walnut-Tree House, dismissed his cab, bidden Timpsons' clerk good evening, and, having ordered in wood and coals from the nearest greengrocer, besides various other necessary articles from various other tradesmen, he now stood by the front gate waiting the coming of the goods purchased.

As he waited, he looked up at the house, which in the uncertain light of the street lamps appeared gloomier and darker than had been the case even in the gathering twilight.

The long rows of shuttered windows, the silent solemnity of the great trees, remnants of a once goodly avenue that had served to give its name to Walnut-Tree House; the appalling silence of everything within the place, when contrasted with the noise of passing cabs and whistling street boys, and men trudging home with unfurled umbrellas and women scudding along with draggled petticoats, might well have impressed even an unimpressionable man, and Edgar Stainton, spite of his hard life and rough exterior, was impressionable and imaginative.

'It has an "uncanny" look, certainly,' he considered; 'but it is not so cheerless for a lonely man as the "bush;" and though I am not overtired, I fancy I shall sleep more soundly in my new home than I did many a night at the goldfields. When once I can get a good fire up I shall be all right. Now, I wonder when those coals are coming!'

As he turned once again towards the road, he beheld on its way the sack of fuel with which the nearest greengrocer said he thought he could—indeed, said he would—'oblige' him. A ton—half a ton—quarter of a ton, the greengrocer affirmed would be impossible until the next day; but a sack—yes—he would promise that. Bill should bring it round; and Bill was told to put his burden on the truck, and twelve bundles of wood, 'and we'll make up the rest tomorrow,' added Bill's master, with the air of one who has conferred a favour.

In the distance Mr Stainton descried a very grimy Bill, and a very small boy, coming along with the truck leisurely, as though the load had been Herculean.

Through the rain he watched the pair advancing and greeted Bill with a glad voice of welcome.

'So you've come at last; that's right. Better late than never. Bring them this way. I'll have this small lot shot in the kitchen for the night.'

'Begging your pardon, sir,' answered Bill, 'I don't think you will—that is to say, not by me. As I told our governor, I'll take 'em to the house as you've sold 'em to the house, but I won't set a foot inside it.'

'Do you mean to say you are going to leave them out on the pavement?' asked Mr Stainton.

'Well, sir, I don't mind taking them to the front door if it'll be a convenience.'

'That will do. You are a brave lot of people in these parts I must say.'

'As for that,' retorted Bill, with sack on back and head bent forward, 'I dare say we're as brave about here as where you come from.'

'It is not impossible,' retorted Mr Stainton; 'there are plenty of cowards over there too.'

With a feint of being very much afraid, Bill, after he had shot his coals on the margin of the steps, retreated from the door, which stood partly open, and when the boy who brought up the wood was again out with the truck, said, putting his knuckles to his eyebrows:

'Beg pardon, sir, but I suppose you couldn't give us a drop of beer? Very wet night, sir.'

'No, I could not,' answered Mr Stainton, very decidedly. 'I shall have to shovel these coals into the house myself; and, as for the night, it is as wet for me as it is for you.'

Nevertheless, as Bill shuffled along the short drive—shuffling wearily—like a man who, having nearly finished one day's hard work, was looking forward to beginning another hard day in the morning, the new owner relented.

'Here,' he said, picking out a sixpence to give him, 'it isn't your fault, I suppose, that you believe in old women's tales.'

'Thank you kindly, sir,' Bill answered; 'I am sure I am extremely obliged; but if I was in your shoes I wouldn't stop in that house—you'll excuse me, sir, meaning no offence—but I wouldn't; indeed I wouldn't.'

'It seems to have got a good name, at any rate,' thought Mr Stainton, while retracing his steps to the banned tenement. 'Let us see what effect a fire will have in routing the shadows.'

He entered the house, and, striking a match, lighted some candles he had brought in with him from a neighbouring oil-shop.

Years previously the gas company, weary of receiving no profit from the house, had taken away their meter and cut off their connections. The water supply was in the same case, as Mr Stainton, going round the premises before it grew quite dark, had discovered. Of almost all small articles of furniture easily broken by careless tenants, easily removed by charwomen, the place was perfectly bare; and as there were no portable candlesticks in which to place the lights the new tenant was forced to make his illumination by the help of some dingy mirrors provided with sconces, and to seek such articles as he needed by the help of a guttering mould candle stuck in the neck of a broken bottle. After an inspection of the ground-floor rooms he decided to take up his quarters for the night in one which had evidently served as a library.

In the centre of the apartment there was the table covered with leather. Around the walls were bookcases, still well filled with volumes, too uninviting to borrow, too valueless in the opinion of the ignorant to steal. In one corner stood a bureau, where the man who for so many years had been dead even while living, kept his letters and papers.

The floor was bare. Once a Turkey carpet had been spread over the centre of the polished oak boards, but it lay in its wonted place no longer; between the windows hung a convex mirror, in which the face of any human being looked horrible and distorted; whilst over the mantle-shelf, indeed, forming a portion of it, was a long, narrow glass, bordered by a frame ornamented with a tracery of leaves and flowers. The ceiling was richly decorated, and, spite of the dust and dirt and neglect of years, all the appointments of the apartment he had selected gave Edgar Stainton the impression that it was a good thing to be the owner of such a mansion, even though it did chance to be situated as much out of the way of fashionable London as the diggings whence he had come.

'And there is not a creature but myself left to enjoy it all,' he mused, as he sat looking into the blazing coals. 'My poor mother, how she would have rejoiced tonight, had she lived to be the mistress of so large a place! And my father, what a harbour this would have seemed after the storms that buffeted him! Well, they are better off, I know; and yet I cannot help thinking how strange it all is—that I, who went away a mere beggar, should come home rich, to be made richer, and yet stand so utterly alone that in the length and breadth of England I have not a relative to welcome me or to say I wish you joy of your inheritance.'

He had eaten his frugal supper, and now, pushing aside the table on which the remains of his repast were spread, he began walking slowly up and down the room, thinking over the past and forming plans for the future.

As he was buried in reflection, the fire began to die down without his noticing the fact; but a sudden feeling of chilliness at length causing him instinctively to look towards the hearth, he threw some wood into the grate, and, while the flames went blazing up the wide chimney, piled on coals as though he desired to set the house alight.

While he was so engaged there came a knock at the door of the room—a feeble, hesitating knock, which was repeated more than once before it attracted Mr Stainton's attention.

When it did, being still busy with the fire, and forgetting he was alone in the house, he called out, 'Come in.'

Along the panels there stole a rustling sort of touch, as if someone were feeling uncertainly for the handle—a curious noise, as of a weak hand fumbling about the door in the dark; then, in a similar manner, the person seeking admittance tried to turn the lock.

'Come in, can't you?' repeated Mr Stainton; but even as he spoke he remembered he was, or ought to be, the sole occupant of the mansion.

He was not alarmed; he was too much accustomed to solitude and danger for that; but he rose from his stooping position and instinctively seized his revolver, which he had chanced, while unpacking some of his effects, to place on the top of the bureau.

'Come in, whoever you are,' he cried; but seeing the door remained closed, though the intruder was evidently making futile efforts to open it, he strode halfway across the room, and then stopped, amazed.

For suddenly the door opened, and there entered, shyly and timidly, a little child—a child with the saddest face mortal ever beheld; a child with wistful eyes and long, ill-kept hair; a child poorly dressed, wasted and worn, and with the mournfullest expression on its countenance that face of a child ever wore.

'What a hungry little beggar,' thought Mr Stainton. 'Well, young one, and what do you want here?' he added, aloud.

The boy never answered, never took the slightest notice of his questioner, but simply walked slowly round the room, peering into all the corners, as if looking for something. Searching the embrasures of the windows, examining the recesses beside the fireplace, pausing on the hearth to glance under the library table, and finally, when the doorway was reached once more, turning to survey the contents of the apartment with an eager and yet hopeless scrutiny.

'What *is* it you want, my boy?' asked Mr Stainton, glancing as he spoke at the child's poor thin legs, and short, shabby frock, and shoes well-nigh worn out, and arms bare and lean and unbeautiful. 'Is it anything I can get for you?'

Not a word—not a whisper; only for reply a glance of the wistful brown eyes.

'Where do you come from, and who do you belong to?' persisted Mr Stainton

The child turned slowly away.

'Come, you shall not get off so easily as you seem to imagine,' persisted the new owner, advancing towards his visitor. 'You have no business to be here at all; and before you go you must tell me how you chance to be in this house, and what you expected to find in this room.'

He was close to the doorway by this time, and the child stood on the threshold, with its back towards him.

Mr Stainton could see every detail of the boy's attire—his little plaid frock, which he had outgrown, the hooks which fastened it; the pinafore, soiled and crumpled, tied behind with strings broken and knotted; in one place the skirt had given from the body, and a piece of thin, poor flannel showed that the child's under habiliments matched in shabbiness his exterior garments.

'Poor little chap,' thought Mr Stainton. 'I wonder if he would like something to eat. Are you hungry, my lad?'

The child turned and looked at him earnestly, but answered never a word.

'I wonder if he is dumb,' marvelled Mr Stainton; and, seeing he was moving away, put out a hand to detain him. But the child eluded his touch, and flitted out into the hall and up the wide staircase with swift, noiseless feet.

Only waiting to snatch a candle from one of the sconces, Mr Stainton pursued as fast as he could follow.

Up the easy steps he ran at the top of his speed; but, fast as he went, the child went faster. Higher and higher he beheld the tiny creature mounting, then, still keeping the same distance between them, it turned when it reached the top storey and trotted along a narrow corridor with rooms opening off to right and left. At the extreme end of this passage a door stood ajar. Through this the child passed, Mr Stainton still following.

'I have run you to earth at last,' he said, entering and closing the door. 'Why, where has the boy gone?' he added, holding the candle above his head and gazing round the dingy garret in which he found himself.

The room was quite empty. He examined it closely, but could find no possible outlet save the door, and a skylight which had evidently not been opened for years.

There was no furniture in the apartment, except a truckle bedstead, a rush-bottomed chair, and a rickety washstand. No wardrobe, or box or press where even a kitten might have lain concealed.

'It is very strange,' muttered Mr Stainton, as he turned away baffled. 'Very strange!' he repeated, while he walked along the corridor. 'I don't understand it at all,' he decided, proceeding slowly down the topmost flight of stairs; but then all at once he stopped.

'*It is the child!*' he exclaimed aloud, and the sound of his own voice woke strange echoes through the silence of that desolate house. '*It is the child!*' And he descended the principal staircase very slowly, with bowed head, and his grave, thoughtful face graver and more thoughtful than ever.

CHAPTER THREE

SEEKING FOR INFORMATION

It was enough to make any man look grave; and as time went on the new owner of Walnut-Tree House found himself pondering continually as to what the mystery could be which attached to the child he had found in possession of his property, and who had already driven tenant after tenant out of the premises. Inclined at first to regard the clerk's story as a joke, and his own experience on the night of his arrival a delusion, it was impossible for him to continue incredulous when he found, even in broad daylight, that terrible child stealing down the staircase and entering the rooms, looking—looking, for something it never found.

Never after the first horror was over did Mr Stainton think

342

of leaving the house in consequence of that haunting presence which had kept the house tenantless. It would have been worse than useless, he felt. With the ocean stretching between, his spirit would still be in the old mansion at Lambeth—his mental vision would always be watching the child engaged in the weary search to which there seemed no end—that never appeared to produce any result.

At bed and at board he had company, or the expectation of it. No apartment in the building was secure from intrusion. It did not matter where he lay; it did not matter where he ate; between sleeping and waking, between breakfast and dinner, whenever the notion seized it, the child came gliding in, looking, looking, looking, and never finding; not lingering longer than was necessary to be certain the object of its search was absent, but wandering hither and thither, from garret to kitchen, from parlour to bedchamber, in that quest which still seemed fresh as when first begun.

Mr Stainton went to his solicitors as the most likely persons from whom to obtain information on the subject, and plunged at once into the matter.

'Who is the child supposed to be, Mr Timpson?' he asked, making no secret that he had seen it.

'Well, that is really very difficult to say,' answered Mr Timpson.

'There *was* a child once, I suppose—a real child—flesh and blood?'

Mr Timpson took off his spectacles and wiped them.

'There were two; yes, certainly, in the time of Mr Felix Stainton—a boy and a girl.'

'In that house?'

'In that house. They survived him.'

'And what became of them?'

'The girl was adopted by a relation of her father's, and the—boy—died.'

'Oh! the boy died, did he? Do you happen to know what he died of?'

'No; I really do not. There was nothing wrong about the affair, however, if that is what you are thinking of. There never was a hint of that sort.' Mr Stainton sat silent for a minute; then he said: 'Mr Timpson, I can't shake off the idea that somehow there has been foul play with regard to those children. Who were they?'

'Felix Stainton's grandchildren. His daughter made a low marriage, and he cast her adrift. After her death the two children were received at Walnut-Tree House on sufferance—fed and clothed, I believe, that was all; and when the old man died the heir-at-law permitted them to remain.'

'Alfred Stainton?'

'Yes; the unhappy man who became insane. His uncle died intestate, and he consequently succeeded to everything but the personalty, which was very small, and of which these children had a share.'

'There was never any suspicion, you say, of foul play on the part of the late owner?'

'Dear, dear! No; quite the contrary.'

'Then can you throw the least light on the mystery?'

'Not the least; I wish I could.'

For all that, Mr Stainton carried away an impression Mr Timpson knew more of the matter than he cared to tell; and was confirmed in this opinion by a chance remark from Mr Timpson's partner, whom he met in the street almost immediately after.

'Why can't you let the matter rest, Mr Stainton?' asked the Co. with some irritation of manner when he heard the object of their client's visit. 'What is the use of troubling your head about a child who has been lying in Lambeth Churchyard these dozen years? Take my advice, have the house pulled down and let or sell the ground for building. You ought to get a pot of money for it in that neighbourhood. If there were a wrong done it is too late to set it right now.'

'What wrong do you refer to?' asked Mr Stainton eagerly, thinking he had caught Timpson's partner napping. But that gentleman was too sharp for him.

'I remarked *if* there were a wrong done—not that there had been one,' he answered; and then, without a pause, added, 'We shall hope to hear from you that you have decided to follow our advice.' But Mr Stainton shook his head.

'I will not pull down the old house just yet,' he said, and walked slowly away.

'There is a mystery behind it all,' he considered. 'I must learn more about these children. Perhaps some of the local tradespeople may recollect them.'

But the local tradespeople for the most part were newcomers—or else had not supplied 'the house'.

'So far as ever I could understand,' said one 'family butcher', irascibly sharpening his knife as he spoke, 'there was not much to supply. *That* custom was not worth speaking of. I hadn't it, so what I am saying is not said on my own account. A scrag end of neck of mutton—a bit of gravy beef—two pennyworth of sheep's liver—that was the sort of thing. Misers, sir, misers; the old gentleman bad, and the nephew worse. A bad business, first and last. But what else could be expected? When people as can afford to live on the fat of the land never have a sirloin inside their doors, why, worse must come of it. No, sir, I never set eyes on the children to my knowledge; I only knew there were children by hearing one of them was dead, and that it was the poorest funeral ever crossed a decent threshold.'

'Poor little chap,' thought Mr Stainton, looking straight out into the street for a moment; then added, 'lest the family misfortunes should descend to me, you had better send round a joint to Walnut-Tree House.'

'Lor', sir, are you the gentleman as is living there? I beg your pardon, I am sure, but I have been so bothered with questions in regard of that house and those children that I forget my manners when 1 talk about them. A joint, sir—what would you please to have?' The new owner told him; and while he counted out the money to pay for it Mr Parker remarked: 'There is only one person I can think of, sir, likely to be able to give any information about the matter.'

'And that is?'

'Mr Hennings, at the Pedlar's Dog. He had some acquaintances with the old lady as was housekeeper both to Mr Felix Stainton and the gentleman that went out of his mind.'

Following the advice, the new owner repaired to the Pedlar's Dog, where (having on his first arrival at Walnut-Tree House ordered some creature comforts from that well-known public) he experienced a better reception than had been accorded to him by Mr Parker.

'Do I know Walnut-Tree House, sir?' said Mr Hennings, repeating his visitor's question. 'Well, yes, rather. Why, you might as well ask me, do I know the Pedlar's Dog. As boy and man I can remember the old house for close on five-and-fifty years. I remember Mr George Stainton; he used to wear a skull-cap and knee-breeches. There was an orchard then where Stainton Street is now, and his whole time was taken up in keeping the boys out of it. Many a time I have run from him.'

'Did you ever see anything of the boy and girl who were there, after Mr Alfred succeeded to the property—Felix Stainton's grandchildren, I mean?' asked the new owner, when a pause in Mr Henning's reminiscences enabled him to take his part in the conversation.

'Well, sir, I may have seen the girl, but I can't bring it to my recollection; the boy I do remember, however. He came over here two or three times with Mrs Toplis, who kept house for both Mr Staintons, and I took notice of him, both because he looked so peaky and old-fashioned, and also on account of the talk about him.'

'There was talk about him, then?'

'Bless you, yes, sir; as much talk while he was living as since he died. Everybody thought he ought to have been the heir.'

'Why?' enquired the new owner.

'Because there was a will made leaving the place to him.'

Here was information. Mr Stainton's heart seemed to stand still for a second and then leap on with excitement.

'Who made the will?'

'The grandfather, Felix Stainton, to be sure; who else should make it?'

'I did not mean that. Was it not drawn out by a solicitor?'

'Oh! Yes—now I understand you, sir. The will was drawn right enough by Mr Quinance, in the Lambeth Road, a very clever lawyer.'

'Not by Timpson, then? How was that?'

'The old man took the notion of making it late one night, and so Mrs Toplis sent to the nearest lawyer she knew of.'

'Yes; and then?'

'Well, the will was made and signed and witnessed, and everything regular; and from that day to this no one knows what has become of it.'

'How very strange.'

'Yes, sir, it is more than strange—unaccountable. At first Mr Quinance was suspected of having given it up to Mr Alfred; but Mrs Toplis and Quinance's clerk—he has succeeded to the business now—say that old Felix insisted upon keeping it himself. So, whether he destroyed it or the nephew got hold of it, Heaven only knows; for no man living does, I think.'

'And the child—the boy, I mean?'

'If you want to hear all about him, sir, Mrs Toplis is the one to tell you. If you have a mind to give a shilling to a poor old lady who always did try to keep herself respectable, and who, I will say, paid her way honourable as long as she had a sixpence to pay it honourable with, you cannot do better than go and see Mrs Toplis, who will talk to you for hours about the time she lived at Walnut-Tree House.'

And with this delicate hint that his minutes were more valuable than the hours of Mrs Toplis, Mr Hennings would have closed the interview, but that his visitor asked where he should be able to find the housekeeper.

'A thousand pardons!' he answered, with an air; 'forgetting the very cream and marrow of it, wasn't I? Mrs Toplis, sir, is to be found in Lambeth Workhouse—and a pity, too.'

Edgar Stainton turned away, heart-sick. Was this all wealth had done for his people and those connected with them?

No man seemed to care to waste a moment in speaking about their affairs; no one had a good word for or kindly memory of them. The poorest creature he met in the streets might have been of more use in the world then they. The house they had lived in mentioned as if a curse rested on the place; themselves only recollected as leaving everything undone which it befitted their station to do. An old servant allowed to end her days in the workhouse!

'Heaven helping me,' he thought, 'I will not so misuse the wealth which has been given me.'

The slight put upon his family tortured and made him wince, and the face of the dead boy who ought to have been the heir seemed, as he hurried along the streets, to pursue and look on him with a wistful reproach.

'If I cannot lay that child I shall go mad,' he said, almost audibly, 'as mad, perhaps, as Alfred Stainton.' And then a terrible fear took possession of him. The horror of that which is worse than any death made for the moment this brave, bold man more timid than a woman.

'God preserve my senses,' he prayed, and then, determinedly putting that phantom behind him, he went on to the Workhouse.

Chapter Four

Brother and Sister

Mr Stainton had expected to find Mrs Toplis a decrepit crone, bowed with age and racked with rheumatism, and it was therefore like a gleam of sunshine streaming across his path to behold a woman, elderly, certainly, but carrying her years with ease, ruddy-cheeked, clear-eyed, upright as a dart, who welcomed him with respectful enthusiasm.

'And so you are Mr Edgar, the son of the dear old captain,' she said, after the first greetings and explanations were over, after she had wiped her eyes and uttered many ejaculations of astonishment and expressions of delight. 'Eh! I remember him coming to the house just after he was married, and telling me about the sweet lady his wife. I never heard a gentleman so proud; he never seemed tired of saying the words, "My wife".'

'She was a sweet lady,' answered the new owner.

'And so the house has come to you, sir? Well, I wish you joy. I hope you may have peace, and health, and happiness, and prosperity in it. And I don't see why you should not—no, indeed, sir.'

Edgar Stainton sat silent for a minute, thinking how he should best approach his subject.

'Mrs Toplis,' he began at last, plunging into the very middle of the difficulty, 'I want you to tell me about it. I have come here on purpose to ask you what it all means.'

The old woman covered her face with her hands, and he could see that she trembled violently.

'You need not be afraid to speak openly to me,' he went on. 'I am quite satisfied there was some great wrong done in the house, and I want to put it right, if it lies in my power to do so. I am a rich man. I was rich when the news of this inheritance reached me, and I would gladly give up the property tomorrow if I could only undo whatever may have been done amiss.'

Mrs Toplis shook her head.

'Ah, sir; you can't do that,' she said. 'Money can't bring back the dead to life; and, if it could, I doubt if even you could prove as good a friend to the poor child sleeping in the churchyard yonder as his Maker did when He took him out of this troublesome world. It was just soul-rending to see the boy the last few months of his life. I can't bear to think of it, sir! Often at night I wake in a fright, fancying I still hear the patter, patter of his poor little feet upon the stair.'

'Do you know, it is a curious thing, but he doesn't frighten me,' said Mr Stainton; 'that is, when I am in the house; although when I am away from it the recollection seems to dog every step I take.'

'What?' cried Mrs Toplis. *'Have you, then, seen him too?* There! What am I talking about? I hope, sir, you will forgive my foolishness.'

'I see him constantly,' was the calm reply.

'I wonder what it means!—I wonder what it can mean!' exclaimed the housekeeper, wringing her hands in dire perplexity and dismay.

'I do not know,' answered the new owner, philosophically; 'but I want you to help me to find out. I suppose you remember the children coming there at first?'

'Well, sir—well, they were poor Miss Mary's son and daughter. She ran away, you know, with a Mr Fenton—made a very poor match; but I believe he was kind to her. When they were brought to us, a shivering little pair, my master was for sending them here. Ay, and he would have done it, too, if somebody had not said he could be made to pay for their keep. You never saw brother and sister so fond of one another—never. They were twins. But, Lor'! the boy was more like a father to the little girl than aught else. He'd have kept an apple a month rather than eat it unless she had half; and the same with everything.

'I think it was seeing that—watching the love they had, he for her and she for him, coming upon them unsuspected, with their little arms round one another's necks, made the old gentleman alter his mind about leaving the place to Mr Alfred; for he said to me, one day, thoughtful like, pointing to them, "Wonderful fond, Toplis!" and I answered, "Yes, sir; for all the world like the Babes in the Wood;" not thinking of how lonely that meant—

'Shortly afterwards he took to his bed; and while he was lying-there, no doubt, better thoughts came to him, for he used to talk about his wife and Miss Mary, and the captain, your father, sir, and ask if the children were gone to bed, and such-like—things he never used to mention before.

'So when he made the will Mr Quinance drew out I was not surprised—no, not a bit. Though before that time he always spoke of Mr Alfred as his heir, and treated him as such.'

'That will never was found,' suggested Mr Stainton, anxious to get at another portion of the narrative.

'Never, sir; we hunted for it high and low. Perhaps I wronged him, but I always thought Mr Alfred knew what became of it. After the old gentleman's death the children were treated shameful—shameful. I don't mean beaten, or that like; but half-starved and neglected. He would not buy them proper clothes, and he would not suffer them to wear decent things if anybody else bought them. It was just the same with their food. I durs'n't give them even a bit of bread and butter unless it was on the sly; and, indeed, there was not much to give in that house. He turned regular miser. Hoarding came into the family with Mrs Lancelot Stainton, Mr Alfred's great grandmother, and they went on from bad to worse, each one closer and nearer than the last, begging your pardon for saying so, sir; but it is the truth.'

'I fear so, Mrs Toplis,' agreed the man, who certainly was neither close nor near.

'Well, sir, at last, when the little girl was about six years old, she fell sick, and we didn't think she would get over the illness. While she was about at her worst, Mrs May, her father's sister, chanced to be stopping up in London, and, as Mr Alfred refused to let a doctor inside his doors, she made no more ado but wrapped the child up in blankets, sent for a cab, and carried her off to her own lodgings. Mr Alfred made no objection to that. All he said as she went through the hall was: "If you take her now, remember, you must keep her."

'"Very well," she replied, "I will keep her."'

'And the boy? the boy?' cried Mr Stainton, in an agony of impatience.

'I am coming to him, sir, if you please. He just dwindled away after his sister and he were parted, and died in December, as she was taken away in the July.'

'What did he die of?'

'A broken heart, sir. It seems a queer thing to say about a child; but if ever a heart was broken his was. At first he was always wandering about the house looking for her, but towards the end he used to go up to his room and stay there all by himself. At last I wrote to Mrs May, but she was ill when the letter got to her, and when she did come up he was dead. My word, she talked to Mr Alfred! I never heard any one person say so much to another. She declared he had first cheated the boy of his inheritance, and then starved him to death; but that was not true, the child broke his heart fretting after his sister.'

'Yes; and when he was dead—'

'Sir, I don't like to speak of it, but as true as I am sitting here, the night he was put in his coffin he came pattering down just as usual, looking, looking for his sister. I went straight upstairs, and if I had not seen the little wasted body lying there still and quiet, I must have thought he had come back to life. We were never without him afterwards, never; that, and nothing else, drove Mr Alfred mad. He used to think he was fighting the child and killing it. When the worst fits were on him he tried to trample it under foot or crush it up in a corner, and then he would sob and cry, and pray for *it* to be taken away. I have heard he recovered a little before he died, and said his uncle told him there was a will leaving all to the boy, but he never saw such a paper. Perhaps it was all talk, though, or that he was still raving.'

'You are quite positive there was no foul play as regards the child?' asked Mr Stainton, sticking to that question pertinaciously.

'Certain, sir; I don't say but Mr Alfred wished him dead. That is not murder, though.'

'I am not clear about that,' answered Mr Stainton.

Chapter Five

The Next Afternoon

Mr Stainton was trying to work off some portion of his perplexities by pruning the grimy evergreens in front of Walnut-Tree House, and chopping away at the undergrowth of weeds and couch grass which had in the course of years matted together beneath the shrubs, when his attention was attracted to two ladies who stood outside the great iron gate looking up at the house.

'It seems to be occupied now,' remarked the elder, turning to her companion. 'I suppose the new owner is going to live here.

It looks just as dingy as ever; but you do not remember it, Mary.'

'I think I do,' was the answer. 'As I look the place grows familiar to me. I do recollect some of the rooms, I am sure just like a dream, as I remember Georgie. What I would give to have a peep inside.'

At this juncture the new owner emerged from amongst the bushes, and, opening the gate, asked if the ladies would like to look over the place.

The elder hesitated; whilst the younger whispered, 'oh, aunt, pray do!'

'Thank you,' said Mrs May to the stranger, whom she believed to be a gardener; 'but perhaps Mr Stainton might object.'

'No; he wouldn't, I know,' declared the new owner. 'You can go through the house if you wish. There is no one in it. Nobody lives there except myself.'

'Taking charge, I suppose?' suggested Mrs May blandly.

'Something of that sort,' he answered.

'I do not think he is a caretaker,' said the girl, as she and her relative passed into the old house together.

'What do you suppose he is, then?' asked her aunt.

'Mr Stainton himself.'

'Nonsense, child!' exclaimed Mrs May, turning, nevertheless, to one of the windows, and casting a curious glance towards the new owner, who was now, his hands thrust deep in his pockets, walking idly up and down the drive.

After they had been all over the place, from hall to garret, with a peep into this room and a glance into that, Mrs May found the man who puzzled her leaning against one of the pillars of the porch, waiting, apparently, for their reappearance.

'I am sure we are very much obliged to you,' she began, with a certain hesitation in her manner.

'Pray do not mention it,' he said.

'This young lady has sad associations connected with the house,' Mrs May proceeded, still doubtfully feeling her way.

He turned his eyes towards the girl for a moment, and though her veil was down, saw she had been weeping. 'I surmised as much,' he replied. 'She is Miss Fenton, is she not?'

'Yes, certainly,' was the answer; 'and you are—'

'Edgar Stainton,' said the new owner, holding out his hand. 'I am all alone here,' he went on, after the first explanations were over. 'But I can manage to give you a cup of tea. Pray do come in, and let me feel I am not entirely alone in England.'

Only too well pleased, Mrs May complied, and ten minutes later the three were sitting round a fire, the blaze of which leapt and flickered upon the walls and over the ceiling, casting bright lights on the dingy mirrors and the dark oak shelves.

'It is all coming back to me now,' said the girl softly, addressing her aunt. 'Many an hour Georgie and I have sat on that hearth seeing pictures in the fire.'

But she did not see something which was even then standing close beside her, and which the new owner had witnessed approach with a feeling of terror that precluded speech.

It was the child! The child searching about no longer for something it failed to find, but standing at the girl's side still and motionless, with its eyes fixed upon her face, and its poor, wasted figure nestling amongst the folds of her dress.

'Thank Heaven she does not see it!' he thought, and drew his breath, relieved.

No; she did not see it—though its wan cheek touched her shoulder, though its thin hand rested on her arm, though through the long conversation which followed it never moved from her side, nor turned its wistful eyes from her face.

When she went away—when she took her fresh young beauty out of the house it seemed to gladden and light up—the child followed her to the threshold; and then in an instant it vanished, and Mr Stainton watched for its flitting up the staircase all in vain.

But later on in the evening, when he was sitting alone beside the fire, with his eyes bent on the glowing coals, and perhaps seeing pictures there, as Mary said she and her brother had done in their lonely childhood, he felt conscious, even without looking round, that the boy was there once again.

And when he fell to thinking of the long, long years during

which the dead child had kept faithful and weary watch for his sister, searching through the empty rooms for one who never came, and then bethought him of the sister to whom her dead brother had become but the vaguest of memories, of the summers and winters during the course of which she had probably forgotten him altogether, he sighed deeply; and heard his sigh echoed behind him in the merest faintest whisper.

More, when he, thinking deeply about his newly found relative and trying to recall each feature in her face, each tone of her voice, found it impossible to dissociate the girl grown to womanhood from the child he had pictured to himself as wandering about the old house in company with her twin brother, their arms twined together, their thoughts one, their sorrows one, their poor pleasures one—he felt a touch on his hand, and knew the boy was beside him, looking with wistful eyes into the firelight, too.

But when he turned he saw that sadness clouded those eyes no longer. She was found; the lost had come again to meet a living friend on the once desolate hearth, and up and down the wide, desolate staircase those weary little feet pattered no longer.

The quest was over, the search ended; into the darksome corners of that dreary house the child's glance peered no longer.

She was come! Through years he had kept faithful watch for her, but the waiting was ended now.

That night Edgar Stainton slept soundly; and yet when morning dawned he knew that once in the darkness he wakened suddenly and was conscious of a small, childish hand smoothing his pillow and touching his brow.

Sweet were the dreams which visited his rest subsequently; sweet as ought to be the dreams of a man who had said to his own soul—and meant to hold fast by words he had spoken:

'As I deal by that orphan girl, so may God deal with me!'

Chapter Six

The Missing Will

Ere long there were changes in the old house. Once again

Mrs Toplis reigned there, but this time with servants under her—with maids she could scold and lads she could harass.

The larder was well plenished, the cellars sufficiently stocked; windows formerly closely shuttered now stood open to admit the air; and on the drive grass grew no longer—too many footsteps passed that way for weeds to flourish.

It was Christmas-time. The joints in the butchers' shops were gay with ribbons; the grocers' windows were tricked out to delight the eyes of the children, young and old, who passed along. In Mr May's house up the Clapham Road all was excitement, for the whole of the family—father, mother, grown-up sons and daughters—girls still in short frocks and boys in round jackets—were going to spend Christmas Eve with their newly-found cousin, whom they had adopted as a relation with a unanimity as rare as charming.

Cousin Mary also was going—Cousin Mary had got a new dress for the occasion, and was having her hair done up in a specially effective manner by Cissie May, when the *toilette* proceedings were interrupted by half a dozen young voices announcing: 'A gentleman in the parlour wants to see you, Mary. Pa says you are to make haste and come down immediately.'

Obediently Mary made haste as bidden and descended to the parlour, to find there the clerk from Timpsons' who met Mr Stainton on his arrival in London.

His business was simple, but important. Once again he was the bearer of a letter from Timpson and Co., this time announcing to Miss Fenton that the will of Mr Felix Stainton had been found, and that under it she was entitled to the interest of ten thousand pounds, secured upon the houses in Stainton Street.

'Oh! aunt, Oh! uncle, how rich we shall be,' cried the girl, running off to tell her cousins; but the uncle and aunt looked grave. They were wondering how this will might effect Edgar Stainton.

While they were still talking it over—after Timpsons' young man had taken his departure, Mr Edgar Stainton himself arrived.

'Oh, it's all right!' he said, in answer to their questions. 'I found the will in the room where Felix Stainton died. Walnut-Tree House and all the freeholds were left to the poor little chap who died, chargeable with Mary's ten thousand pounds, five hundred to Mrs Toplis, and a few other legacies. Failing George, the property was to come to me. I have been to Quinance's successor, and found out the old man and Alfred had a grievous quarrel, and that in consequence he determined to cut him out altogether. Where is Mary? I want to wish her joy.'

Mary was in the little conservatory, searching for a rose to put in her pretty brown hair.

He went straight up to her, and said:

'Mary, dear, you have had one Christmas gift tonight, and I want you to take another with it.'

'What is it, Cousin Edgar?' she asked; but when she looked in his face she must have guessed his meaning, for she drooped her head, and began pulling her sweet rose to pieces.

He took the flower, and with it her fingers.

'Will you have me, dear?' he asked. 'I am but a rough fellow, I know; but I am true, and I love you dearly.'

Somehow, she answered him as he wished, and all spent a very happy evening in the old house.

Once, when he was standing close beside her in the familiar room, hand clasped in hand, Edgar Stainton saw the child looking at them.

There was no sorrow or yearning in his eyes as he gazed— only a great peace, a calm which seemed to fill and light them with an exquisite beauty.

The Last of Squire Ennismore

'Did I see it myself? No, sir; I did not see it: and my father before me did not see it; or his father before him, and he was Phil Regan, just the same as myself. But it is true, for all that; just as true as that you are looking at the very place where the whole thing happened. My great-grandfather (and he did not die till he was ninety-eight) used to tell, many and many's the time, how he met the stranger, night after night, walking lonesome-like about the sands where most of the wreckage came ashore.'

'And the old house, then, stood behind that belt of Scotch firs?'

'Yes; a fine house it was, too. Hearing so much talk about it when a boy, my father said, made him often feel as if he knew every room in the building, though it had all fallen to ruin before he was born. None of the family ever lived in it after the squire went away. Nobody else could be got to stop in the place. There used to be awful noises, as if something was being pitched from the top of the great staircase down into the hall; and then there would be a sound as if a hundred people were clinking glasses and talking all together at once. And then it seemed as if barrels were rolling in the cellars; and there would be screeches, and howls, and laughing, fit to make your blood run cold. They say there is gold hid away in those cellars; but not one has ever ventured to find it. The very children won't come here to play; and when the men are ploughing the field behind, nothing will make them stay in it, once the day begins to change. When the night is coming on, and the tide creeps in on the sand, more than one thinks he has seen mighty queer things on the shore there.'

'But what is it really they think they see? When I asked my landlord to tell me the story from beginning to end, he said he could not remember it; and, at any rate, the whole rigmarole was nonsense, put together to please strangers.'

'And what is he but a stranger himself? And how should he know about the doings of real quality like the Ennismores? For they were gentry, every one of them—good old stock; and as for wickedness, you might have searched Ireland through and not found their match. It is a sure thing, though, that if Riley can't tell you the story, I can; for, as I said, my own people were in it, of a manner of speaking. So, if your honour will rest yourself off your feet, on that bit of a bank, I'll set down my creel and give you the whole pedigree of how Squire Ennismore went away from Ardwinsagh.

'It was a lovely day, in the early part of June; and, as the Englishman cast himself on a low ridge of sand, he looked over Ardwinsagh Bay with a feeling of ineffable content. To his left lay the Purple Headland; to his right, a long range of breakers, that went straight out into the Atlantic till they were lost from sight; in front lay the Bay of Ardwinsagh, with its bluish-green water sparkling in the summer sunlight, and here and there breaking over some sunken rock, against which the waves spent themselves in foam.

'You see how the currents set, sir? That is what makes it dangerous, for them as doesn't know the coast, to bathe here at any time, or walk when the tide is flowing. Look how the sea is creeping in now, like a race-horse at the finish. It leaves that tongue of sand bare to the last, and then, before you could look round, it has you up to the middle. That is why I made bold to speak to you; for it is not alone on the account of Squire Ennismore the bay has a bad name. But it is about him and the old house you want to hear. The last mortal being that tried to live in it, my great-grandfather said, was a creature, by name Molly Leary; and she had neither kith nor kin, and begged for her bite and sup, sheltering herself at night in a turf cabin she had built at the back of a ditch. You may be sure she thought herself a made woman when the agent said, "Yes: she might try if she could stop in the house; there was peat and bog-wood," he told her, "and half-a-crown a week for the winter, and a golden guinea once Easter came," when the house was to be put in order for the family; and his wife gave Molly some warm clothes and a blanket or two; and she was well set up.

'You may be sure she didn't choose the worst room to sleep in; and for a while all went quiet, till one night she was wakened by feeling the bedstead lifted by the four corners, and shaken like a carpet. It was a heavy four-post bedstead, with a solid top: and her life seemed to go out of her with the fear. If it had been a ship in a storm off the Headland, it couldn't have pitched worse; and then, all of a sudden, it was dropped with such a bang as nearly drove the heart into her mouth.

'But that, she said, was nothing to the screaming and laughing, and hustling and rushing that filled the house. If a hundred people had been running hard along the passages and tumbling downstairs, they could not have made a greater noise.

'Molly never was able to tell how she got clear of the place; but a man coming late home from Ballycloyne Fair found the creature crouched under the old thorn there, with very little on her—saving your honour's presence. She had a bad fever, and talked about strange things, and never was the same woman after.'

'But what was the beginning of all this? When did the house first get the name of being haunted?'

'After the old squire went away: that was what I purposed telling you. He did not come here to live regularly till he had got well on in years. He was near seventy at the time I am talking about; but he held himself as upright as ever, and rode as hard as the youngest; and could have drunk a whole roomful under the table, and walked up to bed as unconcerned as you please at the end of the night.

'He was a terrible man. You couldn't lay your tongue to a

wickedness he had not been in the fore-front of—drinking, du-elling, gambling—all manner of sins had been meat and drink to him since he was a boy almost. But at last he did something in London so bad, so beyond the beyonds, that he thought he had best come home and live among people who did not know so much about his goings on as the English. It was said he wanted to try and stay in this world for ever; and that he had got some secret drops that kept him well and hearty. There was something wonderful queer about him, anyhow.

'He could hold foot with the youngest; and he was strong, and had a fine fresh colour in his face; and his eyes were like a hawk's; and there was not a break in his voice—and him near upon threescore and ten!

'At long and at last it came to be the March before he was seventy—the worst March ever known in all these parts—such blowing, sleeting, snowing, had not been experienced in the memory of man; when one blusterous night some foreign vessel went to bits on the Purple Hleadland. They say it was an awful sound to hear the death-cry that went up high above the noise of the wind; and it was as bad a sight to see the shore there strewed with corpses of all sorts and sizes, from the little cabin boy to the grizzled seaman.

'They never knew who they were or where they came from, but some of the men had crosses, and beads, and such like, so the priest said they belonged to him, and they were all buried decently in the chapel graveyard.

'There was not much wreckage of value drifted on shore. Most of what is lost about the Head stays there; but one thing did come into the bay—a queer thing—a puncheon of brandy.

'The squire claimed it; it was his right to have all that came on his land, and he owned this sea-shore from the Head to the breakers—every foot—so, in course, he had the brandy; and there was sore ill-will because he gave his men nothing—not even a glass of whiskey.

'Well, to make a long story short, that was the most won-derful liquor anybody ever tasted. The gentry came from far and near to take share, and it was cards and dice, and drinking and story-telling night after night—week in, week out. Even on Sundays, God forgive them! the officers would drive over from Ballyclone, and sit emptying tumbler after tumbler till Monday morning came, for it made beautiful punch.

'But all at once people quit coming—a word went round that the liquor was not all it ought to be. Nobody could say what ailed it, but it got about that in some way men found it did not suit them.

'For one thing, they were losing money very fast.

'They could not make head against the squire's luck, and a hint was dropped the puncheon ought to have been towed out to sea, and sunk in fifty fathoms of water.

'It was getting to the end of April, and fine, warm weather for the time of year, when first one, and then another, and then another still, began to take notice of a stranger who walked the shore alone at night. He was a dark man, the same colour as the drowned crew lying in the chapel graveyard, and had rings in his ears, and wore a strange kind of hat, and cut wonderful antics as he walked, and had an ambling sort of gait, curious to look at. Many tried to talk to him, but he only shook his head; so, as nobody could make out where he came from or what he wanted, they felt sure he was the spirit of some poor wretch who was tossing about the Head, longing for a snug corner in holy ground.

'The priest went and tried to get some sense out of him.

'"Is it Christian burial you're wanting?" asked his reverence; but the creature only shook his head.

'"Is it word sent to the wives and daughters you've left orphans and widows, you'd like?" but no; it wasn't that.

'"Is it for sin committed you're doomed to walk this way? Would masses comfort ye? There's a heathen," said his reverence; "did you ever hear tell of a Christian that shook his head when masses were mentioned?"

'"Perhaps he doesn't understand English, Father," says one of the officers who was there; "try him with Latin."

'No sooner said than done. The priest started off with such a string of *aves* and *paters* that the stranger fairly took to his heels and ran.

'"He is an evil spirit," explained the priest, when he had stopped, tired out, "and I have exorcised him."

'But the next night my gentleman was back again, as unconcerned as ever.

'"And he'll just have to stay." said his reverence, "for I've got lumbago in the small of my back, and pains in all my joints— never to speak of a hoarseness with standing there shouting; and I don't believe he understood a sentence I said."

'Well, this went on for a while, and people got that frightened of the man, or appearance of a man, they would not go near the sands; till in the end Squire Ennismore, who had always scoffed at the talk, took it into his head he would go down one night, and see into the rights of the matter himself. He, maybe, was feeling lonesome, because, as I told your honour before, people had left off coming to the house, and there was nobody for him to drink with.

'Out he goes, then, as bold as brass; and there were a few followed him. The man came forward at sight of the squire and took off his hat with a foreign flourish, Not to be behind in civility, the squire lifted his.

'"I have come, sir," he said, speaking very loud, to try to make him understand, "to know if you are looking for anything, and whether I can assist you to find it."

'The man looked at the squire as if he had taken the greatest liking to him, and took off his hat again.

'"Is it the vessel that was wrecked you are distressed about?"

'There came no answer, only a forbye mournful shake of the head.

'"Well, *I* haven't your ship, you know; it went all to bits months ago; and as for the sailors, they are snug and sound enough in consecrated ground."

'The man stood and looked at the squire with a queer sort of smile on his face.

"What *do* you want?" asked Mr Ennismore, in a bit of a passion. "If anything belonging to you went down with the vessel it's about the Head you ought to be looking for it, not here—unless, indeed, it's after the brandy you're fretting."

'Now, the squire had tried him in English and French, and was now speaking a language you'd have thought nobody could understand; but, faith, it seemed natural as kissing to the stranger.

'"Oh! that's where you are from, is it?" said the squire. "Why couldn't you have told me so at once. I can't give you the brandy, because it's mostly drunk; but come along, and you shall have as stiff a glass of punch as ever crossed your lips." And without more to-do off they went, as sociable as you please, jabbering together in some outlandish tongue that made moderate folks' jaws ache to hear.

'That was the first night they conversed together, but it wasn't the last. The stranger must have been the height of good company, for the squire never tired of him. Every evening, regularly, he came up to the house, always dressed the same, always smiling and polite, and then the squire called for brandy and hot water, and they drank and played cards till cock-crow, talking and laughing into the small hours.

'This went on for weeks and weeks, nobody knowing where the man came from, or where he went; only two things the old housekeeper did know—that the puncheon was nearly empty, and that the squire's flesh was wasting off him; and she felt so uneasy she went to the priest, but he could give her no manner of comfort.

'She got so concerned at last that she felt bound to listen at the dining-room door; but they always talked in that foreign gibberish, and whether it was blessing or cursing they were at she couldn't tell.

'Well, the upshot of it came one night in July—on the eve of the squire's birthday—there wasn't a drop of spirit left in the puncheon—no, not as much as would drown a fly. They had drunk the whole lot clean up—and the old woman stood trembling, expecting every minute to hear the bell ring for more brandy, for where was she to get more if they wanted any?

'All at once the squire and the stranger came out into the hall. It was a full moon, and light as day.

"I'll go home with you tonight by way of a change," says the squire.

'"Will you so?" asked the other.

'"That I will," answered the squire.

'"It is your own choice, you know."

'"Yes; it is my own choice: let us go."

'So they went. And the housekeeper ran up to the window on the great staircase and watched the way they took. Her niece lived there as housemaid, and she came and watched too; and, after a while, the butler as well. They all turned their faces this way, and looked after their master walking beside the strange man along these very sands. Well, they saw them walk out and out to the very ebb-line—but they didn't stop there—they went on, and on, and on, and on, till the water took them to their knees, and then to their waists, and then to their armpits, and then to their heads; but long before that the women and the butler were running out on the shore as fast as they could, shouting for help.'

'Well?' said the Englishman.

'Living or dead, Squire Ennismore never came back again. Next morning, when the tide ebbed again, one walking over the sand saw the print of a cloven foot—that he tracked to the water's edge. Then everybody knew where the squire had gone, and with whom.'

'And no more search was made?'

'Where would have been the use searching?'

'Not much, I suppose. It's a strange story, anyhow.'

'But true, your honour—every word of it.'

'Oh! I have no doubt of that,' was the satisfactory reply.

The Open Door

Some people do not believe in ghosts. For that matter, some people do not believe in anything. There are persons who even affect incredulity concerning that open door at Ladlow Hall. They say it did not stand wide open—that they could have shut it; that the whole affair was a delusion; that they are sure it must have been a conspiracy; that they are doubtful whether there is such a place as Ladlow on the face of the earth; that the first time they are in Meadowshire they will look it up.

That is the manner in which this story, hitherto unpublished, has been greeted by my acquaintances. How it will be received by strangers is quite another matter. I am going to tell what happened to me exactly as it happened, and readers can credit or scoff at the tale as it pleases them. It is not necessary for me to find faith and comprehension in addition to a ghost story, for the world at large. If such were the case, I should lay down my pen.

Perhaps, before going further, I ought to premise there was a time when I did not believe in ghosts either. If you had asked me one summer's morning years ago when you met me on London Bridge if I held such appearances to be probable or possible, you would have received an emphatic 'No' for answer.

But, at this rate, the story of the Open Door will never be told; so we will, with your permission, plunge into it immediately.

★★★★★★

'Sandy!'

'What do you want?'

'Should you like to earn a sovereign?'

'Of course I should.'

A somewhat curt dialogue, but we were given to curtness in the office of Messrs Frimpton, Frampton and Fryer, auctioneers and estate agents, St Benet's Hill, City.

(My name is not Sandy or anything like it, but the other clerks so styled me because of a real or fancied likeness to some character, an ill-looking Scotchman, they had seen at the theatre. From this it may be inferred I was not handsome. Far from it. The only ugly specimen in my family, I knew I was very plain; and it chanced to be no secret to me either that I felt grievously discontented with my lot. I did not like the occupation of clerk in an auctioneer's office, and I did not like my employers. We are all of us inconsistent, I suppose, for it was a shock to me to find they entertained a most cordial antipathy to me.)

'Because,' went on Parton, a fellow, my senior by many years—a fellow who delighted in chaffing me, 'I can tell you how to lay hands on one.'

'How?' I asked, sulkily enough, for I felt he was having what he called his fun.

'You know that place we let to Carrison, the tea-dealer?'

Carrison was a merchant in the China trade, possessed of fleets of vessels and towns of warehouses; but I did not correct Parton's expression, I simply nodded.

'He took it on a long lease, and he can't live in it; and our governor said this morning he wouldn't mind giving anybody who could find out what the deuce is the matter, a couple of sovereigns and his travelling expenses.'

'Where is the place?' I asked, without turning my head; for the convenience of listening I had put my elbows on the desk and propped up my face with both hands.

'Away down in Meadowshire, in the heart of the grazing country.'

'And what is the matter?' I further enquired.

'A door that won't keep shut.'

'What?'

'A door that will keep open, if you prefer that way of putting it,' said Parton.

'You are jesting.'

'If I am, Carrison is not, or Fryer either. Carrison came here in a nice passion, and Fryer was in a fine rage; I could see he was, though he kept his temper outwardly. They have had an active correspondence it appears, and Carrison went away to talk to his lawyer. Won't make much by that move, I fancy.'

'But tell me,' I entreated, 'why the door won't keep shut?'

'They say the place is haunted.'

'What nonsense!' I exclaimed.

'Then you are just the person to take the ghost in hand. I thought so while old Fryer was speaking.'

'If the door won't keep shut,' I remarked, pursuing my own train of thought, 'why can't they let it stay open?'

'I have not the slightest idea. I only know there are two sovereigns to be made, and that I give you a present of the information.'

And having thus spoken, Parton took down his hat and went out, either upon his own business or that of his employers.

There was one thing I can truly say about our office, we were never serious in it. I fancy that is the case in most offices nowadays; at all events, it was the case in ours. We were always chaffing each other, playing practical jokes, telling stupid stories, scamping our work, looking at the clock, counting the weeks to next St Lubbock's Day, counting the hours to Saturday.

For all that we were all very earnest in our desire to have our salaries raised, and unanimous in the opinion no fellows ever before received such wretched pay. I had twenty pounds a year, which I was aware did not half provide for what I ate at home. My mother and sisters left me in no doubt on the point, and when new clothes were wanted I always hated to mention the fact to my poor worried father.

We had been better off once, I believe, though I never remember the time. My father owned a small property in the country, but owing to the failure of some bank, I never could understand what bank, it had to be mortgaged; then the interest was not paid, and the mortgages foreclosed, and we had nothing left save the half-pay of a major, and about a hundred a year which my mother brought to the common fund.

We might have managed on our income, I think, if we had not been so painfully genteel; but we were always trying to do something quite beyond our means, and consequently debts accumulated, and creditors ruled us with rods of iron.

Before the final smash came, one of my sisters married the younger son of a distinguished family, and even if they had been disposed to live comfortably and sensibly she would have kept her sisters up to the mark. My only brother, too, was an officer, and of course the family thought it necessary he should see we preserved appearances.

It was all a great trial to my father, I think, who had to bear the brunt of the dunning and harass, and eternal shortness of money; and it would have driven me crazy if I had not found a happy refuge when matters were going wrong at home at my aunt's. She was my father's sister, and had married so 'dreadfully below her' that my mother refused to acknowledge the relationship at all.

For these reasons and others, Parton's careless words about the two sovereigns stayed in my memory.

I wanted money badly—I may say I never had sixpence in the world of my own—and I thought if I could earn two sovereigns I might buy some trifles I needed for myself, and present my father with a new umbrella. Fancy is a dangerous little jade to flirt with, as I soon discovered.

She led me on and on. First I thought of the two sovereigns; then I recalled the amount of the rent Mr Carrison agreed to pay for Ladlow Hall; then I decided he would gladly give more than two sovereigns if he could only have the ghost turned out of possession. I fancied I might get ten pounds—twenty pounds. I considered the matter all day, and I dreamed of it all night, and when I dressed myself next morning I was determined to speak to Mr Fryer on the subject.

I did so—I told that gentleman Parton had mentioned the matter to me, and that if Mr Fryer had no objection, I should like to try whether I could not solve the mystery. I told him I had been accustomed to lonely houses, and that I should not feel at all nervous; that I did not believe in ghosts, and as for burglars, I was not afraid of them.

'I don't mind your trying,' he said at last. 'Of course you understand it is no cure, no pay. Stay in the house for a week; if at the end of that time you can keep the door shut, locked, bolted, or nailed up, telegraph for me, and I will go down—if not, come back. If you like to take a companion there is no objection.'

I thanked him, but said I would rather not have a companion.

'There is only one thing, sir, I should like,' I ventured.

'And that—?' he interrupted.

'Is a little more money. If I lay the ghost, or find out the ghost, I think I ought to have more than two sovereigns.'

'How much more do you think you ought to have?' he asked.

His tone quite threw me off my guard, it was so civil and conciliatory, and I answered boldly:

'Well, if Mr Carrison cannot now live in the place perhaps he wouldn't mind giving me a ten-pound note.'

Mr Fryer turned, and opened one of the books lying on his desk. He did not look at or refer to it in any way—I saw that.

'You have been with us how long, Edlyd?' he said.

'Eleven months tomorrow,' I replied.

'And our arrangement was, I think, quarterly payments, and one month's notice on either side?'

'Yes, sir.' I heard my voice tremble, though I could not have said what frightened me.

'Then you will please to take your notice now. Come in before you leave this evening, and I'll pay you three months' salary, and then we shall be quits.'

'I don't think I quite understand,' I was beginning, when he broke in:

'But I understand, and that's enough. I have had enough of you and your airs, and your indifference, and your insolence here. I never had a clerk I disliked as I do you. Coming and dictating terms, forsooth! No, you shan't go to Ladlow. Many a poor chap'—(he said 'devil')—'would have been glad to earn half a guinea, let alone two sovereigns; and perhaps you may be before you are much older.'

'Do you mean that you won't keep me here any longer, sir?' I asked in despair. I had no intention of offending you. I—'

'Now you need not say another word,' he interrupted, 'for I won't bandy words with you.

Since you have been in this place you have never known your position, and you don't seem able to realize it. When I was foolish enough to take you, I did it on the strength of your connections, but your connections have done nothing for me. I have never had a penny out of any one of your friends—if you have any. You'll not do any good in business for yourself or anybody else, and the sooner you go to Australia'—(here he was very emphatic)—'and get off these premises, the better I shall be pleased.'

I did not answer him—I could not. He had worked himself to a white heat by this time, and evidently intended I should leave his premises then and there. He counted five pounds out of his cash-box, and, writing a receipt, pushed it and the money across the table, and bade me sign and be off at once.

My hand trembled so I could scarcely hold the pen, but I had presence of mind enough left to return one pound ten in gold, and three shillings and fourpence I had, quite by the merest good fortune, in my waistcoat pocket.

'I can't take wages for work I haven't done,' I said, as well as sorrow and passion would let me. 'Good-morning,' and I left his office and passed out among the clerks.

I took from my desk the few articles belonging to me, left the papers it contained in order, and then, locking it, asked Parton if he would be so good as to give the key to Mr Fryer.

'What's up?' he asked 'Are you going?'

I said, 'Yes, I am going'.

'Got the sack?'

'That is exactly what has happened.'

'Well, I'm—!' exclaimed Mr Parton.

I did not stop to hear any further commentary on the matter, but bidding my fellow-clerks goodbye, shook the dust of Frimpton's Estate and Agency Office from off my feet.

I did not like to go home and say I was discharged, so I walked about aimlessly, and at length found myself in Regent Street. There I met my father, looking more worried than usual.

'Do you think, Phil,' he said (my name is Theophilus), 'you could get two or three pounds from your employers?'

Maintaining a discreet silence regarding what had passed, I answered:

'No doubt I could.'

'I shall be glad if you will then, my boy,' he went on, 'for we are badly in want of it.'

I did not ask him what was the special trouble. Where would have been the use? There was always something—gas, or water, or poor-rates, or the butcher, or the baker, or the bootmaker. Well, it did not much matter, for we were well accustomed to the life; but, I thought, 'if ever I marry, we will keep within our means'. And then there rose up before me a vision of Patty, my cousin—the blithest, prettiest, most useful, most sensible girl that ever made sunshine in poor man's house.

My father and I had parted by this time, and I was still walking aimlessly on, when all at once an idea occurred to me. Mr Fryer had not treated me well or fairly. I would hoist him on his own petard. I would go to headquarters, and try to make terms with Mr Carrison direct.

No sooner thought than done. I hailed a passing omnibus, and was ere long in the heart of the city. Like other great men, Mr Carrison was difficult of access—indeed, so difficult of access, that the clerk to whom I applied for an audience told me plainly I could not see him at all. I might send in my message if I liked, he was good enough to add, and no doubt it would be attended to. I said I should not send in a message, and was then asked what I would do. My answer was simple. I meant to wait till I did see him. I was told they could not have people waiting about the office in this way.

I said I supposed I might stay in the street. 'Carrison didn't own that,' I suggested.

The clerk advised me not to try that game, or I might get locked up.

I said I would take my chance of it.

After that we went on arguing the question at some length, and we were in the middle of a heated argument, in which several of Carrison's 'young gentlemen', as they called themselves, were good enough to join, when we were all suddenly silenced by a grave-looking individual, who authoritatively enquired:

'What is all this noise about?'

Before anyone could answer I spoke up:

'I want to see Mr Carrison, and they won't let me.'

'What do you want with Mr Carrison?'

'I will tell that to himself only.'

'Very well, say on—I am Mr Carrison.'

For a moment I felt abashed and almost ashamed of my persistency; next instant, however, what Mr Fryer would have called my 'native audacity' came to the rescue, and I said, drawing a step or two nearer to him, and taking off my hat:

'I wanted to speak to you about Ladlow Hall, if you please, sir.'

In an instant the fashion of his face changed, a look of irritation succeeded to that of immobility; an angry contraction of the eyebrows disfigured the expression of his countenance.

'Ladlow Hall!' he repeated; 'and what have you got to say about Ladlow Hall?'

'That is what I wanted to tell you, sir,' I answered, and a dead hush seemed to fall on the office as I spoke.

The silence seemed to attract his attention, for he looked sternly at the clerks, who were not using a pen or moving a finger.

'Come this way, then,' he said abruptly; and next minute I was in his private office.

'Now, what is it?' he asked, flinging himself into a chair, and addressing me, who stood hat in hand beside the great table in the middle of the room.

I began—I will say he was a patient listener—at the very beginning, and told my story straight through. I concealed nothing. I enlarged on nothing. A discharged clerk I stood before him, and in the capacity of a discharged clerk I said what I had to say. He heard me to the end, then he sat silent, thinking.

At last he spoke.

'You have heard a great deal of conversation about Ladlow, I suppose?' he remarked.

'No sir; I have heard nothing except what I have told you.'

'And why do you desire to strive to solve such a mystery?'

'If there is any money to be made, I should like to make it, sir.'

'How old are you?'

'Two-and-twenty last January.'

'And how much salary had you at Frimpton's?'

'Twenty pounds a year.'

'Humph! More than you are worth, I should say.'

'Mr Fryer seemed to imagine so, sir, at any rate,' I agreed, sorrowfully.

'But what do you think?' he asked, smiling in spite of himself.

'I think I did quite as much work as the other clerks,' I answered.

'That is not saying much, perhaps,' he observed. I was of his opinion, but I held my peace.

'You will never make much of a clerk, I am afraid,' Mr Carrison proceeded, fitting his disparaging remarks upon me as he might on a lay figure. 'You don't like desk work?'

'Not much, sir.'

'I should judge the best thing you could do would be to emigrate,' he went on, eyeing me critically.

'Mr Fryer said I had better go to Australia or—' I stopped, remembering the alternative that gentleman had presented.

'Or where?' asked Mr Carrison.

'The ——, sir' I explained, softly and apologetically.

He laughed—he lay back in his chair and laughed—and I laughed myself, though ruefully.

After all, twenty pounds was twenty pounds, though I had not thought much of the salary till I lost it.

We went on talking for a long time after that; he asked me all about my father and my early life, and how we lived, and where we lived, and the people we knew; and, in fact, put more questions than I can well remember.

'It seems a crazy thing to do,' he said at last; 'and yet I feel disposed to trust you. The house is standing perfectly empty. I can't live in it, and I can't get rid of it; all my own furniture I have removed, and there is nothing in the place except a few old-fashioned articles belonging to Lord Ladlow. The place is a loss to me. It is of no use trying to let it, and thus, in fact, matters are at a deadlock. You won't be able to find out anything, I know, because, of course, others have tried to solve the mystery ere now; still, if you like to try you may. I will make this bargain with you. If you like to go down, I will pay your reasonable expenses for a fortnight; and if you do any good for me, I will give you a ten-pound note for yourself. Of course I must be satisfied that what you have told me is true and that you are what you represent. Do you know anybody in the city who would speak for you?'

I could think of no one but my uncle. I hinted to Mr Carrison he was not grand enough or rich enough, perhaps, but I knew nobody else to whom I could refer him.

'What!' he said, 'Robert Dorland, of Cullum Street. He does business with us. If he will go bail for your good behaviour I shan't want any further guarantee. Come along.' And to my intense amazement, he rose, put on his hat, walked me across the outer office and along the pavements till we came to Cullum Street.

'Do you know this youth, Mr Dorland?' he said, standing in front of my uncle's desk, and laying a hand on my shoulder.

'Of course I do, Mr Carrison,' answered my uncle, a little apprehensively; for, as he told me afterwards, he could not imagine what mischief I had been up to. 'He is my nephew.'

'And what is your opinion of him—do you think he is a young fellow I may safely trust?'

My uncle smiled, and answered, 'That depends on what you wish to trust him with.'

'A long column of addition, for instance.'

'It would be safer to give that task to somebody else.'

'Oh, uncle!' I remonstrated; for I had really striven to conquer my natural antipathy to figures—worked hard, and every bit of it against the collar.

My uncle got off his stool, and said, standing with his back to the empty fire-grate. 'Tell me what you wish the boy to do, Mr Carrison, and I will tell you whether he will suit your purpose or not. I know him, I believe, better than he knows himself.'

In an easy, affable way, for so rich a man, Mr Carrison took possession of the vacant stool, and nursing his right leg over his left knee, answered:

'He wants to go and shut the open door at Ladlow for me. Do you think he can do that?'

My uncle looked steadily back at the speaker, and said, 'I thought, Mr Carrison, it was quite settled no one could shut it?'

Mr Carrison shifted a little uneasily on his seat, and replied: 'I did not set your nephew the task he fancies he would like to undertake.'

'Have nothing to do with it, Phil,' advised my uncle, shortly.

'You don't believe in ghosts, do you, Mr Dorland?' asked Mr Carrison, with a slight sneer.

'Don't you, Mr Carrison?' retorted my uncle.

There was a pause—an uncomfortable pause—during the course of which I felt the ten pounds, which, in imagination, I had really spent, trembling in the scale. I was not afraid. For ten pounds, or half the money, I would have faced all the inhabitants of spirit land. I longed to tell them so; but something in the way those two men looked at each other stayed my tongue.

'If you ask me the question here in the heart of the city, Mr Dorland,' said Mr Carrison, at length, slowly and carefully,

377

'I answer "No"; but it you were to put it to me on a dark night at Ladlow, I should beg time to consider. I do not believe in supernatural phenomena myself, and yet—the door at Ladlow is as much beyond my comprehension as the ebbing and flowing of the sea.'

And you can't live at Ladlow?' remarked my uncle.

'I can't live at Ladlow, and what is more, I can't get anyone else to live at Ladlow.'

'And you want to get rid of your lease?'

'I want so much to get rid of my lease that I told Fryer I would give him a handsome sum if he could induce anyone to solve the mystery. Is there any other information you desire, Mr Dorland? Because if here is, you have only to ask and have. I feel I am not here in a prosaic office in the city of London, but in the Palace of Truth.'

My uncle took no notice of the implied compliment. When wine is good it needs no bush. If a man is habitually honest in his speech and in his thoughts, he desires no recognition of the fact.

'I don't think so,' he answered; 'it is for the boy to say what he will do. If he be advised by me he will stick to his ordinary work in his employers' office, and leave ghost-hunting and spirit-laying alone.'

Mr Carrison shot a rapid glance in my direction, a glance which, implying a secret understanding, might have influenced my uncle could I have stooped to deceive my uncle.

'I can't stick to my work there any longer,' I said. 'I got my marching orders today.'

'What *had* you been doing, Phil?' asked my uncle.

'I wanted ten pounds to go and lay the ghost!' I answered, so dejectedly, that both Mr Carrison and my uncle broke out laughing.

'Ten pounds!' cried my uncle, almost between laughing and crying. 'Why, Phil boy, I had rather, poor man though I am, have given thee ten pounds than that thou should'st go ghost-hunting or ghostlaying.'

When he was very much in earnest my uncle went back to thee and thou of his native dialect. I liked the vulgarism, as my mother called it, and I knew my aunt loved to hear him use the caressing words to her. He had risen, not quite from the ranks it is true, but if ever a gentleman came ready born into the world it was Robert Dorland, upon whom at our home every-one seemed to look down.

'What will you do, Edlyd?' asked Mr Carrison; 'you hear what your uncle says, "Give up the enterprise", and what I say; I do not want either to bribe or force your inclinations.'

'I will go, sir,' I answered quite steadily. I am not afraid, and I should like to show you—' I stopped. I had been going to say, 'I should like to show you I am not such a fool as you all take me for,' but I felt such an address would be too familiar, and refrained.

Mr Carrison looked at me curiously. I think he supplied the end of the sentence for himself, but he only answered:

'I should like you to show me that door fast shut; at any rate, if you can stay in the place alone for a fortnight, you shall have your money.'

'I don't like it, Phil,' said my uncle: 'I don't like this freak at all.'

'I am sorry for that, uncle,' I answered, 'for I mean to go.

'When?' asked Mr Carrison.

'Tomorrow morning,' I replied.

'Give him five pounds, Dorland, please, and I will send you my cheque. You will account to me for that sum, you under-stand,' added Mr Carrison, turning to where I stood.

'A sovereign will be quite enough,' I said.

'You will take five pounds, and account to me for it,' repeated Mr Carrison, firmly; 'also, you will write to me every day, to my private address, and if at any moment you feel the thing too much for you, throw it up. Good afternoon,' and without more formal leave-taking he departed.

'It is of no use talking to you, Phil, I suppose?' said my uncle.

'I don't think it is,' I replied; 'you won't say anything to them at home, will you?'

'I am not very likely to meet any of them, am I?' he answered, without a shade of bitterness—merely stating a fact.

'I suppose I shall not see you again before I start,' I said, 'so I will bid you goodbye now.'

'Goodbye, my lad; I wish I could see you a bit wiser and steadier.'

I did not answer him; my heart was very full, and my eyes too. I had tried, but office-work was not in me, and I felt it was just as vain to ask me to sit on a stool and pore over writing and figures as to think a person born destitute of musical ability could compose an opera.

Of course I went straight to Patty; though we were not then married, though sometimes it seemed to me as if we never should be married, she was my better half then as she is my better half now.

She did not throw cold water on the project; she did not discourage me. What she said, with her dear face aglow with excitement, was, 'I only wish, Phil, I was going with you.' Heaven knows, so did I.

Next morning I was up before the milkman. I had told my people overnight I should be going out of town on business. Patty and I settled the whole plan in detail. I was to breakfast and dress there, for I meant to go down to Ladlow in my volunteer garments. That was a subject upon which my poor father and I never could agree; he called volunteering child's play, and other things equally hard to bear; whilst my brother, a very carpet warrior to my mind, was never weary of ridiculing the force, and chaffing me for imagining I was 'a soldier'.

Patty and I had talked matters over, and settled, as I have said, that I should dress at her father's.

A young fellow I knew had won a revolver at a raffle, and willingly lent it to me. With that and my rifle I felt I could conquer an army.

It was a lovely afternoon when I found myself walking through leafy lanes in the heart of Meadowshire. With every vein of my heart I loved the country, and the country was look-ing its best just then: grass ripe for the mower, grain forming in the ear, rippling streams, dreamy rivers, old orchards, quaint cottages.

'Oh that I had never to go back to London,' I thought, for I am one of the few people left on earth who love the country and hate cities. I walked on, I walked a long way, and being un-certain as to my road, asked a gentleman who was slowly riding a powerful roan horse under arching trees—a gentleman ac-companied by a young lady mounted on a stiff white pony—my way to Ladlow Hall.

'That is Ladlow Hall,' he answered, pointing with his whip over the fence to my left hand. I thanked him and was going on, when he said:

'No one is living there now.'

'I am aware of that,' I answered.

He did not say anything more, only courteously bade me good-day, and rode off. The young lady inclined her head in acknowledgement of my uplifted cap, and smiled kindly. Alto-gether I felt pleased, little things always did please me. It was a good beginning—halfway to a good ending!

When I got to the Lodge I showed Mr Carrison's letter to the woman, and received the key.

'You are not going to stop up at the Hall alone, are you, sir?' she asked.

'Yes, I am,' I answered, uncompromisingly, so uncompromis-ingly that she said no more.

The avenue led straight to the house; it was uphill all the way, and bordered by rows of the most magnificent limes I ever beheld. A light iron fence divided the avenue from the park, and between the trunks of the trees I could see the deer browsing and cattle grazing. Ever and *anon* there came likewise to my ear the sound of a sheep-bell.

It was a long avenue, but at length I stood in front of the Hall—a square, solid-looking, old-fashioned house, three storeys high, with no basement; a flight of steps up to the principal entrance; four windows to the right of the door, four windows to the left; the whole building flanked and backed with trees; all the blinds pulled down, a dead silence brooding over the place: the sun westering behind the great trees studding the park. I took all this in as I approached, and afterwards as I stood for a moment under the ample porch; then, remembering the business which had brought me so far, I fitted the great key in the lock, turned the handle, and entered Ladlow Hall.

For a minute—stepping out of the bright sunlight—the place looked to me so dark that I could scarcely distinguish the objects by which I was surrounded; but my eyes soon grew accustomed to the comparative darkness, and I found I was in an immense hall, lighted from the roof, a magnificent old oak staircase conducted to the upper rooms.

The floor was of black and white marble. There were two fireplaces, fitted with dogs for burning wood; around the walls hung pictures, antlers, and horns, and in odd niches and corners stood groups of statues, and the figures of men in complete suits of armour.

To look at the place outside, no one would have expected to find such a hall. I stood lost in amazement and admiration, and then I began to glance more particularly around.

Mr Carrison had not given me any instructions by which to identify the ghostly chamber—which I concluded would most probably be found on the first floor.

I knew nothing of the story connected with it—if there were a story. On that point I had left London as badly provided with mental as with actual luggage—worse provided, indeed, for a hamper, packed by Patty, and a small bag were coming over from the station; but regarding the mystery I was perfectly unencumbered. I had not the faintest idea in which apartment it resided.

Well, I should discover that, no doubt, for myself ere long.

I looked around me—doors—doors—doors I had never before seen so many doors together all at once. Two of them stood open—one wide, the other slightly ajar.

'I'll just shut them as a beginning,' I thought, 'before I go

382

upstairs.'

The doors were of oak, heavy, well-fitting, furnished with good locks and sound handles. After I had closed I tried them. Yes, they were quite secure. I ascended the great staircase feeling curiously like an intruder, paced the corridors, entered the many bedchambers—some quite bare of furniture, others containing articles of an ancient fashion, and no doubt of considerable value—chairs, antique dressing-tables, curious wardrobes, and such like. For the most part the doors were closed, and I shut those that stood open before making my way into the attics.

I was greatly delighted with the attics. The windows lighting them did not, as a rule, overlook the front of the Hall, but commanded wide views over wood, and valley, and meadow. Leaning out of one, I could see, that to the right of the Hall the ground, thickly planted, shelved down to a stream, which came out into the daylight a little distance beyond the plantation, and meandered through the deer park. At the back of the Hall the windows looked out on nothing save a dense wood and a portion of the stable-yard, whilst on the side nearest the point from whence I had come there were spreading gardens surrounded by thick yew hedges, and kitchen-gardens protected by high walls; and further on a farmyard, where I could perceive cows and oxen, and, further still, luxuriant meadows, and fields glad with waving corn.

'What a beautiful place!' I said. 'Carrison must have been a duffer to leave it.' And then I thought what a great ramshackle house it was for anyone to be in all alone.

Getting heated with my long walk, I suppose, made me feel chilly, for I shivered as I drew my head in from the last dormer window, and prepared to go downstairs again.

In the attics, as in the other parts of the house I had as yet explored, I closed the doors, when there were keys locking them; when there were not, trying them, and in all cases, leaving them securely fastened.

When I reached the ground floor the evening was drawing on apace, and I felt that if I wanted to explore the whole house before dusk I must hurry my proceedings.

'I'll take the kitchens next,' I decided, and so made my way to a wilderness of domestic offices lying to the rear of the great hall. Stone passages, great kitchens, an immense servants'-hall, larders, pantries, coal-cellars, beer-cellars, laundries, brewhouses, housekeeper's room—it was not of any use lingering over these details. The mystery that troubled Mr Carrison could scarcely lodge amongst cinders and empty bottles, and there did not seem much else left in this part of the building.

I would go through the living-rooms, and then decide as to the apartments I should occupy myself.

The evening shadows were drawing on apace, so I hurried back into the hall, feeling it was a weird position to be there all alone with those ghostly hollow figures of men in armour, and the statues on which the moon's beams must fall so coldly. I would just look through the lower apartments and then kindle a fire. I had seen quantities of wood in a cupboard close at hand, and felt that beside a blazing hearth, and after a good cup of tea, I should not feel the solitary sensation which was oppressing me.

The sun had sunk below the horizon by this time, for to reach Ladlow I had been obliged to travel by cross lines of railway, and wait besides for such trains as condescended to carry third-class passengers; but there was still light enough in the hall to see all objects distinctly. With my own eyes I saw that one of the doors I had shut with my own hands was standing wide!

I turned to the door on the other side of the hall. It was as I had left it—closed. This, then, was the room—this with the open door For a second I stood appalled; I think I was fairly frightened.

That did not last long, however. There lay the work I had desired to undertake, the foe I had offered to fight; so without more ado I shut the door and tried it.

'Now I will walk to the end of the hall and see what happens,' I considered. I did so. I walked to the foot of the grand staircase and back again, and looked.

The door stood wide open.

I went into the room, after just a spasm of irresolution—went in and pulled up the blinds: a good-sized room, twenty by twenty (I knew, because I paced it afterwards), lighted by two long windows.

The floor, of polished oak, was partially covered with a Turkey carpet. There were two recesses beside the fireplace, one fitted up as a bookcase, the other with an old and elaborately caned cabinet. I was astonished also to find a bedstead in an apartment so little retired from the traffic of the house; and there were also some chairs of an obsolete make, covered, so far as I could make out, with faded tapestry. Beside the bedstead, which stood against the wall opposite to the door, I perceived another door. It was fast locked, the only locked door I had as yet met with in the interior of the house. It was a dreary, gloomy room: the dark panelled walls; the black, shining floor; the windows high from the ground; the antique furniture; the dull four-poster bedstead, with dingy velvet curtains; the gaping chimney; the silk counterpane that looked like a pall.

'Any crime might have been committed in such a room,' I thought pettishly; and then I looked at the door critically.

Someone had been at the trouble of fitting bolts upon it, for when I passed out I not merely shut the door securely, but bolted it as well.

'I will go and get some wood, and then look at it again,' I soliloquized. When I came back it stood wide open once more.

'Stay open, then!' I cried in a fury. 'I won't trouble myself any more with you tonight!'

Almost as I spoke the words, there came a ring at the front door. Echoing through the desolate house, the peal in the then state of my nerves startled me beyond expression.

It was only the man who had agreed to bring over my traps. I bade him lay them down in the hall, and, while looking out some small silver, asked where the nearest post-office was to be found. Not far from the park gates, he said; if I wanted any letter sent, he would drop it in the box for me; the mail-cart picked up the bag at ten o'clock.

I had nothing ready to post then, and told him so. Perhaps the money I gave was more than he expected, or perhaps the dreariness of my position impressed him as it had impressed me, for he paused with his hand on the lock, and asked:

'Are you going to stop here all alone, master?'

'All alone,' I answered, with such cheerfulness as was possible under the circumstances.

'That's the room, you know,' he said, nodding in the direction of the open door, and dropping his voice to a whisper.

'Yes, I know,' I replied.

'What you've been trying to shut it already, have you? Well, you are a game one!' And with this complementary if not very respectful comment he hastened out of the house. Evidently he had no intention of proffering his services towards the solution of the mystery.

I cast one glance at the door—it stood wide open. Through the windows I had left bare to the night, moonlight was beginning to stream cold and silvery. Before I did aught else I felt I must write to Mr Carrison and Patty, so straightway I hurried to one of the great tables in the hall, and lighting a candle my thoughtful link girl had provided, with many other things, sat down and dashed off the two epistles.

Then down the long avenue, with its mysterious lights and shades, with the moonbeams glinting here and there, playing at hide-and-seek round the boles of the trees and through the tracery of quivering leaf and stem, I walked as fast as if I were doing a match against time.

It was delicious, the scent of the summer odours, the smell of the earth; if it had not been for the door I should have felt too happy. As it was—

'Look here, Phil,' I said, all of a sudden; 'life's not child's play, as uncle truly remarks. That door is just the trouble you have now to face, and you must face it! But for that door you would never have been here. I hope you are not going to turn coward the very first night. Courage!—that is your enemy—conquer it.'

'I will try,' my other self answered back. 'I can but try. I can

386

but fail.'

The post-office was at Ladlow Hollow, a little hamlet through which the stream I had remarked dawdling on its way across the park flowed swiftly, spanned by an ancient bridge.

As I stood by the door of the little shop, asking some questions of the postmistress, the same gentleman I had met in the afternoon mounted on his roan horse, passed on foot. He wished me goodnight as he went by, and nodded familiarly to my companion, who curtseyed her acknowledgements.

'His lordship ages fast,' she remarked, following the retreating figure with her eyes.

'His lordship,' I repeated. 'Of whom are you speaking?'

'Of Lord Ladlow,' she said.

'Oh! I have never seen him,' I answered, puzzled.

'Why, *that* was Lord Ladlow!' she exclaimed.

You may be sure I had something to think about as I walked back to the Hall—something beside the moonlight and the sweet night-scents, and the rustle of beast and bird and leaf, that make silence seem more eloquent than noise away down in the heart of the country.

Lord Ladlow! my word, I thought he was hundreds, thousands of miles away; and here I find him—he walking in the opposite direction from his own home—I an inmate of his desolate abode. Hi!—what was that? I heard a noise in a shrubbery close at hand, and in an instant I was in the thick of the underwood. Something shot out and darted into the cover of the further plantation. I followed, but I could catch never a glimpse of it. I did not know the lie of the ground sufficiently to course with success, and I had at length to give up the hunt—heated, baffled, and annoyed.

When I got into the house the moon's beams were streaming down upon the hall; I could see every statue, every square of marble, every piece of armour. For all the world it seemed to me like something in a dream; but I was tired and sleepy, and decided I would not trouble about fire or food, or the open door, till the next morning: I would go to sleep.

With this intention I picked up some of my traps and carried them to a room on the first floor I had selected as small and habitable. I went down for the rest, and this time chanced to lay my hand on my rifle.

It was wet. I touched the floor—it was wet likewise.

I never felt anything like the thrill of delight which shot through me. I had to deal with flesh and blood, and I would deal with it, heaven helping me.

The next morning broke clear and bright. I was up with the lark—had washed, dressed, breakfasted, explored the house before the postman came with my letters.

One from Mr Carrison, one from Patty, and one from my uncle: I gave the man half a crown, I was so delighted, and said I was afraid my being at the Hall would cause him some additional trouble.

'No, sir,' he answered, profuse in his expressions of gratitude; 'I pass here every morning on my way to her ladyship's.'

'Who is her ladyship?' I asked.

'The Dowager Lady Ladlow,' he answered—'the old lord's widow.'

'And where is her place?' I persisted.

'If you keep on through the shrubbery and across the waterfall, you come to the house about a quarter of a mile further up the stream.'

He departed, after telling me there was only one post a day; and I hurried back to the room in which I had breakfasted, carrying my letters with me.

I opened Mr Carrison's first. The gist of it was, 'Spare no expense; if you run short of money telegraph for it.'

I opened my uncle's next. He implored me to return; he had always thought me hair-brained, but he felt a deep interest in and affection for me, and thought he could get me a good berth if I would only try to settle down and promise to stick to my work. The last was from Patty. O Patty, God bless you! Such women, I fancy, the men who fight best in battle, who stick last to a sinking ship, who are firm in life's struggles, who are brave to resist temptation, must have known and loved. I can't tell you more about the letter, except that it gave me strength to go on to the end.

I spent the forenoon considering that door. I looked at it from within and from without. I eyed it critically. I tried whether there was any reason why it should fly open, and I found that so long as I remained on the threshold it remained closed; if I walked even so far away as the opposite side of the hall, it swung wide.

Do what I would, it burst from latch and bolt. I could not lock it because there was no key.

Well, before two o'clock I confess I was baffled.

At two there came a visitor—none other than Lord Ladlow himself. Sorely I wanted to take his horse round to the stables, but he would not hear of it.

'Walk beside me across the park, if you will be so kind,' he said; 'I want to speak to you.'

We went together across the park, and before we parted I felt I could have gone through fire and water for this simple-spoken nobleman.

'You must not stay here ignorant of the rumours which are afloat,' he said. 'Of course, when I let the place to Mr Carrison I knew nothing of the open door.'

'Did you not, sir?—my lord, I mean,' I stammered.

He smiled. 'Do not trouble yourself about my title, which, indeed, carries a very empty state with it, but talk to me as you might to a friend. I had no idea there was any ghost story connected with the Hall, or I should have kept the place empty.'

I did not exactly know what to answer, so I remained silent.

'How did you chance to be sent here?' he asked, after a pause.

I told him. When the first shock was over, a lord did not seem very different from anybody else. If an emperor had taken a morning canter across the park, I might, supposing him equally affable, have spoken as familiarly to him as to Lord Ladlow. My mother always said I entirely lacked the bump of veneration!

Beginning at the beginning, I repeated the whole story, from

Parton's remark about the sovereign to Mr Carrison's conversation with my uncle. When I had left London behind in the narrative, however, and arrived at the Hall, I became somewhat more reticent. After all, it was *his* Hall people could not live in—*his* door that would not keep shut; and it seemed to me these were facts he might dislike being forced upon his attention.

But he would have it. What had *I* seen? What did *I* think of the matter? Very honestly I told him I did not know what to say. The door certainly would not remain shut, and there seemed no human agency to account for its persistent opening; but then, on the other hand, ghosts generally did not tamper with firearms, and my rifle, though not loaded, had been tampered with—I was sure of that.

My companion listened attentively. 'You are not frightened, are you?' he enquired at length.

'Not now,' I answered. 'The door did give me a start last evening, but I am not afraid of that since I find someone else is afraid of a bullet.'

He did not answer for a minute; then he said:

'The theory people have set up about the open door is this: As in that room my uncle was murdered, they say the door will never remain shut till the murderer is discovered.'

'Murdered!' I did not like the word at all; it made me feel chill and uncomfortable.

'Yes—he was murdered sitting in his chair, and the assassin has never been discovered. At first many persons inclined to the belief that I killed him; indeed, many are of that opinion still.'

'But you did not, sir—there is not a word of truth in that story, is there?'

He laid his hand on my shoulder as he said:

'No, my lad; not a word. I loved the old man tenderly. Even when he disinherited me for the sake of his young wife, I was sorry, but not angry; and when he sent for me and assured me he had resolved to repair that wrong, I tried to induce him to leave the lady a handsome sum in addition to her jointure. "If you do not, people may think she has not been the source of happiness you expected," I added.

"'Thank you, Hal," he said. "You are a good fellow; we will talk further about this tomorrow."

'And then he bade me goodnight.

'Before morning broke—it was in the summer two years ago—the household was aroused by a fearful scream. It was his death-cry. He had been stabbed from behind in the neck. He was seated in his chair writing—writing a letter to me. But for that I might have found it harder to clear myself than was in the case; for his solicitors came forward and said he had signed a will leaving all his personalty to me—he was very rich—unconditionally, only three days previously. That, of course, supplied the motive, as my lady's lawyer put it. She was very vindictive, spared no expense in trying to prove my guilt, and said openly she would never rest till she saw justice done, if it cost her the whole of her fortune.

'The letter lying before the dead man, over which blood had spurted, she declared must have been placed on his table by me; but the coroner saw there was an animus in this, for the few opening lines stated my uncle's desire to confide in me his reasons for changing his will—reasons, he said, that involved his honour, as they had destroyed his peace. "In the statement you will find sealed up with my will in—" At that point he was dealt his death-blow. The papers were never found, and the will was never proved. My lady put in the former will, leaving her everything. Ill as I could afford to go to law, I was obliged to dispute the matter, and the lawyers are at it still, and very likely will continue at it for years.

'When I lost my good name, I lost my good health, and had to go abroad; and while I was away Mr Carrison took the Hall. Till I returned, I never heard a word about the open door. My solicitor said Mr Carrison was behaving badly; but I think now I must see them or him, and consider what can be done in the affair. As for yourself, it is of vital importance to me that this mystery should be cleared up, and if you are really not timid, stay on. I am too poor to make rash promises, but you won't find me ungrateful.'

'Oh, my lord!' I cried—the address slipped quite easily and naturally off my tongue—'I don't want any more money or anything, if I can only show Patty's father I am good for something—'

'Who is Patty?' he asked.

He read the answer in my face, for he said no more.

'Should you like to have a good dog for company?' he enquired after a pause.

I hesitated; then I said:

'No, thank you. I would rather watch and hunt for myself.'

And as I spoke, the remembrance of that 'something' in the shrubbery recurred to me, and I told him I thought there had been someone about the place the previous evening.

'Poachers,' he suggested; but I shook my head.

'A girl or a woman I imagine. However, I think a dog might hamper me.'

He went away, and I returned to the house. I never left it all day. I did not go into the garden, or the stable-yard, or the shrubbery, or anywhere; I devoted myself solely and exclusively to that door.

If I shut it once, I shut it a hundred times, and always with the same result. Do what I would, it swung wide. Never, however, when I was looking at it. So long as I could endure to remain, it stayed shut—the instant I turned my back, it stood open.

About four o'clock I had another visitor; no other than Lord Ladlow's daughter—the Honourable Beatrice, riding her funny little white pony.

She was a beautiful girl of fifteen or thereabouts, and she had the sweetest smile you ever saw.

'Papa sent me with this,' she said; 'he would not trust any other messenger,' and she put a piece of paper in my hand.

Keep your food under lock and key; buy what you require yourself. Get your water from the pump in the stable-yard. I am going from home; but if you want anything, go or send to my daughter.

'Any answer?' she asked, patting her pony's neck.

'Tell his lordship, if you please, I will "keep my powder dry"!' I replied.

'You have made papa look so happy,' she said, still patting that fortunate pony.

'If it is in my power, I will make him look happier still, Miss —' and I hesitated, not knowing how to address her.

'Call me Beatrice,' she said, with an enchanting grace; then added, slily, 'Papa promises me I shall be introduced to Patty ere long,' and before I could recover from my astonishment, she had tightened the bit and was turning across the park.

'One moment, please,' I cried. 'You can do something for me.'

'What is it?' and she came back, trotting over the great sweep in front of the house.

'Lend me your pony for a minute.'

She was off before I could even offer to help her alight—off, and gathering up her habit dexterously with one hand, led the docile old sheep forward with the other.

I took the bridle—when I was with horses I felt amongst my own kind—stroked the pony, pulled his ears, and let him thrust his nose into my hand.

Miss Beatrice is a countess now, and a happy wife and mother; but I sometimes see her, and the other night she took me carefully into a conservatory and asked:

'Do you remember Toddy, Mr Edlyd?'

'Remember him!' I exclaimed; 'I can never forget him!'

'He is dead!' she told me, and there were tears in her beautiful eyes as she spoke the words.

'Mr Edlyd, I *loved* Toddy!'

Well, I took Toddy up to the house, and under the third window to the right hand. He was a docile creature, and let me stand on the saddle while I looked into the only room in Ladlow Hall I had been unable to enter.

It was perfectly bare of furniture, there was not a thing in it—not a chair or table, not a picture on the walls, or ornament on the chimney-piece.

'That is where my grand-uncle's valet slept,' said Miss Beatrice. 'It was he who first ran in to help him the night he was murdered.'

'Where is the valet?' I asked.

'Dead,' she answered. 'The shock killed him. He loved his master more than he loved himself.'

I had seen all I wished, so I jumped off the saddle, which I had carefully dusted with a branch plucked from a lilac tree; between jest and earnest pressed the hem of Miss Beatrice's habit to my lips as I arranged its folds; saw her wave her hand as she went at a hand-gallop across the park; and then turned back once again into the lonely house, with the determination to solve the mystery attached to it or die in the attempt.

Why, I cannot explain, but before I went to bed that night I drove a gimlet I found in the stables hard into the floor, and said to the door:

'Now *I* am keeping you open.'

When I went down in the morning the door was close shut, and the handle of the gimlet, broken off short, lying in the hall.

I put my hand to wipe my forehead; it was dripping with perspiration. I did not know what to make of the place at all! I went out into the open air for a few minutes; when I returned the door again stood wide.

If I were to pursue in detail the days and nights that followed, I should weary my readers. I can only say they changed my life. The solitude, the solemnity, the mystery, produced an effect I do not profess to understand, but that I cannot regret.

I have hesitated about writing of the end, but it must come, so let me hasten to it.

Though feeling convinced that no human agency did or could keep the door open, I was certain that some living person had means of access to the house which I could not discover, This was made apparent in trifles which might well have escaped unnoticed had several, or even two people occupied the mansion, but that in my solitary position it was impossible to overlook. A chair would be misplaced, for instance; a path would be visible over a dusty floor; my papers I found were moved; my clothes touched—letters I carried about with me, and kept under my pillow at night; still, the fact remained that when I went to the post-office, and while I was asleep, someone did wander over the house.

On Lord Ladlow's return I meant to ask him for some further particulars of his uncle's death, and I was about to write to Mr Carrison and beg permission to have the door where the valet had slept broken open, when one morning, very early indeed, I spied a hairpin lying close beside it.

What an idiot I had been! If I wanted to solve the mystery of the open door, of course I must keep watch in the room itself. The door would not stay wide unless there was a reason for it, and most certainly a hairpin could not have got into the house without assistance.

I made up my mind what I should do—that I would go to the post early, and take up my position about the hour I had hitherto started for Ladlow Hollow. I felt on the eve of a discovery, and longed for the day to pass, that the night might come.

It was a lovely morning; the weather had been exquisite during the whole week, and I flung the hall-door wide to let in the sunshine and the breeze. As I did so, I saw there was a basket on the top step—a basket filled with rare and beautiful fruit and flowers.

Mr Carrison had let off the gardens attached to Ladlow Hall for the season—he thought he might as well save something out of the fire, he said, so my fare had not been varied with delicacies of that kind. I was very fond of fruit in those days, and seeing a card addressed to me, I instantly selected a tempting peach, and ate it a little greedily perhaps.

I might say I had barely swallowed the last morsel, when Lord Ladlow's caution recurred to me. The fruit had a curious flavour—there was a strange taste hanging about my palate. For a moment, sky, trees and park swam before my eyes; then I made up my mind what to do.

I smelt the fruit—it had all the same faint odour; then I put some in my pocket—took the basket and locked it away—walked round to the farmyard—asked for the loan of a horse that was generally driven in a light cart, and in less than half an hour was asking in Ladlow to be directed to a doctor.

Rather cross at being disturbed so early, he was at first inclined to pooh-pooh my idea; but I made him cut open a pear and satisfy himself the fruit had been tampered with.

'It is fortunate you stopped at the first peach,' he remarked, after giving me a draught, and some medicine to take back, and advising me to keep in the open air as much as possible. 'I should like to retain this fruit and see you again tomorrow.'

We did not think then on how many morrows we should see each other!

Riding across to Ladlow, the postman had given me three letters, but I did not read them till I was seated under a great tree in the park, with a basin of milk and a piece of bread beside me.

Hitherto, there had been nothing exciting in my correspondence. Patty's epistles were always delightful, but they could not be regarded as sensational; and about Mr Carrison's there was a monotony I had begun to find tedious. On this occasion, however, no fault could be found on that score. The contents of his letter greatly surprised me. He said Lord Ladlow had released him from his bargain—that I could, therefore, leave the Hall at once. He enclosed me ten pounds, and said he would consider how he could best advance my interests; and that I had better call upon him at his private house when I returned to London.

'I do not think I shall leave Ladlow yet awhile,' I considered, as I replaced his letter in its envelope. 'Before I go I should like to make it hot for whoever sent me that fruit; so unless Lord Ladlow turns me out I'll stay a little longer.'

Lord Ladlow did not wish me to leave. The third letter was from him. He wrote:

I shall return home tomorrow night, and see you on Wednesday. I have arranged satisfactorily with Mr Carrison, and as the Hall is my own again, I mean to try to solve the mystery it contains myself. If you choose to stop and help me to do so, you would confer a favour, and I will try to make it worth your while.

'I will keep watch tonight, and see if I cannot give you some news tomorrow,' I thought. And then I opened Patty's letter—the best, dearest, sweetest letter any postman in all the world could have brought me.

If it had not been for what Lord Ladlow said about his sharing my undertaking, I should not have chosen that night for my vigil. I felt ill and languid—fancy, no doubt, to a great degree inducing these sensations. I had lost energy in a most unaccountable manner. The long, lonely days had told upon my spirits—the fidgety feeling which took me a hundred times in the twelve hours to look upon the open door, to close it, and to count how many steps I could take before it opened again, had tried my mental strength as a perpetual blister might have worn away my physical. In no sense was I fit for the task I had set myself, and yet I determined to go through with it. Why had I never before decided to watch in that mysterious chamber? Had I been at the bottom of my heart afraid? In the bravest of us there are depths of cowardice that lurk unsuspected till they engulf our courage.

The day wore on—the long, dreary day; evening approached—the night shadows closed over the Hall. The moon would not rise for a couple of hours more. Everything was still as death. The house had never before seemed to me so silent and so deserted.

I took a light, and went up to my accustomed room, moving about for a time as though preparing for bed; then I extinguished the candle, softly opened the door, turned the key, and put it in my pocket, slipped softly downstairs, across the hall, through the open door. Then I knew I had been afraid, for I felt a thrill of terror as in the dark I stepped over the threshold. I paused and listened—there was not a sound—the night was still and sultry, as though a storm were brewing.

Not a leaf seemed moving—the very mice remained in their holes! Noiselessly I made my way to the other side of the room. There was an old-fashioned easy-chair between the bookshelves and the bed; I sat down in it, shrouded by the heavy curtain.

The hours passed—were ever hours so long? The moon rose, came and looked in at the windows, and then sailed away to the west; but not a sound, no, not even the cry of a bird. I seemed to myself a mere collection of nerves. Every part of my body appeared twitching. It was agony to remain still; the desire to move became a form of torture. Ah! a streak in the sky; morning at last, Heaven be praised! Had ever anyone before so welcomed the dawn? A thrush began to sing—was there ever heard such delightful music? It was the morning twilight, soon the sun would rise; soon that awful vigil would be over, and yet I was no nearer the mystery than before. Hush! what was that? *It had come.* After the hours of watching and waiting; after the long night and the long suspense, it came in a moment.

The locked door opened—so suddenly, so silently, that I had barely time to draw back behind the curtain, before I saw a woman in the room. She went straight across to the other door and closed it, securing it as I saw with bolt and lock. Then just glancing around, she made her way to the cabinet, and with a key she produced shot back the wards. I did not stir, I scarcely breathed, and yet she seemed uneasy. Whatever she wanted to do she evidently was in haste to finish, for she took out the drawers one by one, and placed them on the floor; then, as the light grew better, I saw her first kneel on the floor, and peer into every aperture, and subsequently repeat the same process, standing on a chair she drew forward for the purpose. A slight, lithe woman, not a lady, clad all in black—not a bit of white about her. What on earth could she want? In a moment it flashed upon me—*The will and the letter! She is searching for them.*

I sprang from my concealment—I had her in my grasp; but she tore herself out of my hands, fighting like a wild-cat: she hit, scratched, kicked, shifting her body as though she had not a bone in it, and at last slipped herself free, and ran wildly towards the door by which she had entered.

If she reached it, she would escape me. I rushed across the room and just caught her dress as she was on the threshold. My blood was up, and I dragged her back: she had the strength of twenty devils, I think, and struggled as surely no woman ever did before.

'I do not want to kill you,' I managed to say in gasps, 'but I will if you do not keep quiet.'

'Bah!' she cried; and before I knew what she was doing she had the revolver out of my pocket and fired.

She missed: the ball just glanced off my sleeve. I fell upon her—I can use no other expression, for it had become a fight for life, and no man can tell the ferocity there is in him till he is placed as I was then—fell upon her, and seized the weapon. She would not let it go, but I held her so tight she could not use it. She bit my face; with her disengaged hand she tore my hair. She turned and twisted and slipped about like a snake, but I did not feel pain or anything except a deadly horror lest my strength should give out.

Could I hold out much longer? She made one desperate plunge, I felt the grasp with which I held her slackening; she felt it too, and seizing her advantage tore herself free, and at the same instant fired again blindly, and again missed.

Suddenly there came a look of horror into her eyes—a frozen expression of fear.

'See!' she cried; and flinging the revolver at me, fled.

I saw, as in a momentary flash, that the door I had beheld locked stood wide—that there stood beside the table an awful figure, with uplifted hand—and then I saw no more. I was struck at last; as she threw the revolver at me she must have pulled the trigger, for I felt something like red-hot iron enter my shoulder, and I could but rush from the room before I fell senseless on the marble pavement of the ball.

When the postman came that morning, finding no one stirring, be looked through one of the long windows that flanked the door; then he ran to the farmyard and called for help.

'There is something wrong inside,' he cried. 'That young gentleman is lying on the floor in a pool of blood.'

As they rushed round to the front of the house they saw Lord

Ladlow riding up the avenue, and breathlessly told him what had happened.

'Smash in one of the windows,' he said; 'and go instantly for a doctor.'

They laid me on the bed in that terrible room, and telegraphed for my father. For long I hovered between life and death, but at length I recovered sufficiently to be removed to the house Lord Ladlow owned on the other side of the Hollow.

Before that time I had told him all I knew, and begged him to make instant search for the will.

'Break up the cabinet if necessary,' I entreated, 'I am sure the papers are there.'

And they were. His lordship got his own, and as to the scandal and the crime, one was hushed up and the other remained unpunished. The dowager and her maid went abroad the very morning I lay on the marble pavement at Ladlow Hall—they never returned.

My lord made that one condition of his silence.

Not in Meadowshire, but in a fairer county still, I have a farm which I manage, and make both ends meet comfortably.

Patty is the best wife any man ever possessed—and I—well, I am just as happy if a trifle more serious than of old; but there are times when a great horror of darkness seems to fall upon me, and at such periods I cannot endure to be left alone.

Why Dr Cray Left Southam

'You want to know why I left Southam?' said the doctor, meditatively knocking the ashes out of his pipe, preparatory to refilling it—he had just come back from the diggings with a nugget big enough to make him rich and, if he pleased, an idle man for life; and he was sitting in Jacob Graham's chambers in Gray's Inn, opposite to his old friend and schoolfellow, the same unkempt, untrimmed, unconventional Jack Cray Jacob could remember ever since they went—a pair of graceless lads—to Todmarsh Grammar School. 'You want to know why I left Southam? Well, I don't mind telling you; in fact, now I am strong enough to stand an action for libel, I don't mind telling anybody.'

'There was a scandal, then?'

'Not that ever became public, except about myself; but you shall hear. It was in the spring of 1850 that, investing the small amount of money my old grandmother left me, I became partner to Dr Montrose, of Southam. It was the sweetest place I ever beheld. Green, sloping meadows, clear streams, wooded heights, picturesque cottages covered with roses and clematis, old-fashioned houses—where old-fashioned people lived within their incomes, and saved fortunes for their pretty daughters—great mansions affected by the nobility and gentry, good boating, good fishing, good shooting; the very *beau ideal* of a neighbourhood. No wonder Montrose, who was getting into the autumn of existence, wanted a partner to keep his connection together, to prevent any outsider taking the cream of a practice which must have grown of itself, for he could never have made it. I may say, at once, he did not get that partner in me. We had not been trying to run in harness together for three months before he told me, as plainly as long habits of beating about the bush would permit, that either we must separate, or get in a third partner.

'"The *suaviter in modo,* my good Cray," he said, "we want, and we must have a little more of that. You see what my patients are—now, don't you?"

'I did. So we got a third partner—a man who knew even less of his profession than Dr Montrose himself, but who was pronounced by the ladies, charming. The way he placed two fingers on their wrists was in itself a study, and the reverie into which he fell, when the delicate creatures complained of a pain "just here", persuaded the patients themselves, and every relation they had in the world, the case was very serious.

'Why,' went on Dr Cray, waxing indignant, 'I have known that fellow keep a girl lying on her back for six months, who had no more the matter with her than I have—and yet he was liked, and I was not! To put the matter in plain language, except in desperate cases, there was a beautiful unanimity in preferring my absence to my presence. It was hard, I felt it to be so; for with all my heart and soul loved my profession, and sympathised with those who really needed such help as I could give them. What I failed to do was, to treat a fair lady's finger-ache as though she had broken every bone in her body; and prescribe for an idle man's imaginary ailments, as if I were not perfectly aware nothing on earth was the matter with him save the lack of some real trouble to occupy his mind—always supposing he had any.

'But when there was anything dangerous in the shape of accident, sickness, or epidemic, Montrose always sent me to the scene of action.

'"Ah! Cray," he said, "if you had only a little tact, you might carry all before you."

'That was after a railway smash, when our list of wounded would not have shamed a battlefield. We did very well out of that, one way or another; but, somehow, though I had all the work, Dr Montrose got all the credit—and really, and seriously, upon my honour, Graham, he knew no more about medicine than your clerk.'

'I want to know why you left Southam,' Mr Graham said; this disparaging reference to his clerk reminding him of his own profession. Why should Dr Cray suppose Cripps ignorant of medicine? For aught he knew Cripps might have attended all the lectures at St Bartholomew's!

'I am coming to that, my friend,' the Doctor answered. 'Only first I must tell you it was after the railway accident he allowed me and Clara to become engaged. She was a dear little thing. I am told she is most happily married, and that her husband is do-ing wonders as a homoeopathist. I was very fond of Clara, and, if it had not been for that little trouble of mine at Southam, I should, perhaps, ere now have moulded myself on the Montrose pattern and become as genial a practitioner as her father.'

'For heaven's sake,' his friend entreated, 'get on.'

'What is the hurry?' asked Dr Cray. 'The night is still young, and already I imagine you must feel yourself in possession of the routine of my life at Southam.

'Was the squire's coachman thrown off the box of the brougham, I attended his broken leg, which was duly charged to the Manor in our bill. Was there fever at the Hall, I, with the help of God, pulled the patients through. When the rector was stricken with cholera, I never left him till I could give good hope to his weeping wife. When my lord put out his shoulder I reduced the dislocation. When—'

'Jack,' solemnly interrupted Mr Graham, 'if you do not tell me, and at once, why you left Southam, I shall get up and put your pipe out.'

He laughed. Jack Cray was always, except upon some few points, the most good-natured fellow in all the world.

'Well,' he said, 'to cut a long story short, my worthy father-in-law who was to be had a good patient at a place called The Chase; a lady, of course—a married lady. Whenever married la-dies took to be chronically invalid, we, I speak now in the partnership sense, found them the best patients of all. The name of the lady was Glenalbyn, *née* Frottiss. She was about thirty years of age—old looking for that—plain, not clever, extremely slight and lean, feeble, I should have said, of intellect, but Dr Montrose maintained, "a most superior person".

'Anyhow, she "enjoyed" bad health; from some cause or other she was eternally wanting the doctor. "A poor, fragile creature," said my worthy partner. I would have made her walk five miles a day, when I warrant, she would have been well enough. Glenalbyn (Lord! what a name; I would have split it had I been he, and taken either half) seemed wrapped up in her.

'"Such devotion," said Dr Montrose, "I never witnessed. I never saw a couple so attached, and my experience, Cray," he added, with tears in his old eyes, "has been large."

'As far as the Glenalbyns were concerned I had not the smallest reason to doubt my partner's assertion—neither did I. All I thought was, there could not, judging from the medicine made up, be much of consequence the matter with Mrs Glenalbyn. Every preparation sent was of the mildest and most rose-water description.

'Digestion out of order, nerves unstrung-nerves unstrung, digestion out of order—that was the way his patient swung backwards and forwards. These symptoms were occasionally varied with a slight cold, earache, pain under her right shoulder; and all the other trivial ailments that afflict the path of those who have nothing in the world to do except get ill, and send for the doctor.

'Montrose was always being sent for to The Chase, and, you may be very sure, he never, when at home or within possible reach, had to be sent for twice. Mrs Glenalbyn liked him greatly, and Mr Glenalbyn was wont to say, he did not know what in the world he should do if Dr Montrose were to leave Southam.

'"He understands my wife's constitution to a nicety," he generally finished; it being a peculiarity of many persons that they think the constitutions of themselves and families are a sort of special creation.

'However, to sum up the position of affairs in our happy village in the June of 1852, there were three persons resident there perfectly satisfied with each other—Mrs and Mr Glenalbyn, and Dr Montrose.

'Summer outings, which have since then come to be considered an absolute necessity, were not at that time generally common. People who had friends went to visit them; persons who possessed business to see to went and saw to it. Perhaps the same craze for gadding existed, but it was called by another name; the difference might be that families then scattered instead of migrating.

'Anyhow, Dr Montrose went off to stay with a nephew in Scotland, while his family remained behind. Clara had been away earlier in the year, Mrs Montrose was going later. Southam was fuller than ever, by reason of the many friends who were stopping on visits at the mansions and old-fashioned houses, but still it seemed to our senior that Perry and I could manage all there was to be done, and he said "he wanted a change"—I am sure, I did.'

'Even though Clara remained?' suggested Mr Graham.

'Yes. I did not see much of her, and whenever I did, Mrs Montrose was at our elbow. However, Clara has nothing to do with my story, nothing whatever.

'When Dr Montrose left, the Glenalbyns were away; but shortly after his departure they returned. Mrs Glenalbyn had not found the air of the place where they were stopping suit her. Mrs Glenalbyn "did not find the air of any place suit her so well as Southam"—Mr Glenalbyn felt sure "no air could suit her as well as the air of The Chase." It is needless to say Southam repeated and approved this opinion. After all, contentment is a virtue!

'The lady had not, however, been long back at The Chase before her nerves and her digestion commenced their old pranks. Montrose was sent for, and being absent, Perry went.

'"A great pity Mrs Glenalbyn is so delicate," he said to me. "Delightful woman!" And the mild prescriptions, the pills at night, the draught in the morning, the mixture three times a day, began again, and were duly sent till Mrs Glenalbyn was pronounced convalescent.

'Just at this time Perry had the misfortune to poison his hand. His was not a constitution to bear anything of the sort with impunity, and though I did my best for, and instead of him, he was at last obliged to knock off work, and go to his mother, who lived in Kent. He sent Southam, in his stead, a raw stripling, just fresh from the examiners, but, upon the whole, I do not think this callow bird did much more harm than Perry himself.

'As a matter of course, I could not trust such a mere child with the care of an important patient like Mrs Glenalbyn, for, although she had no disease, Dr Montrose chose to believe her delicate, and I did not want the practice to suffer during his absence. In the chapter of accidents, it was thus it chanced that on the next occasion when Dr Montrose was sent for I repaired to The Chase.'

'It is a nice name,' observed Mr Graham.

'Yes, and it is a beautiful place. As I rode up the avenue—bordered by a double row of the most magnificent lime-trees I ever beheld—I could not help thinking about the apparent injustice of conditions in the world—I had stopped to speak a word with poor old Mrs Jones, suffering from heart complaint, who was labouring away at the washtub, and now I was going to prescribe for a fine lady who had nothing on earth the matter with her. Of course we doctors know—'

'Cray, do please proceed with your story, and defer all reflections till after it is finished,' entreated Mr Graham. 'How did you find Mrs Glenalbyn?'

'As I expected—well enough if she could only have been induced to think so. I had always considered her a plain woman, but she was far plainer than I imagined. When I saw her near, in a good light and without a bonnet, I wondered what in the world Glenalbyn, who was a handsome fellow, could have beheld in her to make him propose.

'If she had been the loveliest creature on the face of the earth, however, he could not have been more attentive to, or seemed more anxious about her.

"'My angel,'" he said, leaning over the back of her chair.

"'Darling,'" she murmured, rapturously turning a face which might have belonged to a black monkey of an inferior sort, up to his.

"'I shall be in the next room, love, if you want me,'" he said.

"'How good you are, dearest!'"

'After a little more of this sort of thing he left me alone with my patient. As I knew nothing of her constitution, or, to speak more correctly, of what might be wrong with it, I asked several questions, which she answered satisfactorily. She was not a bad sort of woman, I soon discovered—weak, undoubtedly, and crazily fond of her husband, but not selfish or affected. She had no disease, that I could make out, no real ailment. She was sound in mind and limb, but no one could have pronounced her strong. Upon the whole I felt more charitably disposed towards Mrs Glenalbyn than I could have believed possible, seeing she had only about a quarter of an inch of forehead, and might have been mistaken for the "missing link." She was certainly a gentlewoman, and seemed amiable and sympathetic. She promised to help poor Mrs Jones, and begged me not to hesitate to mention any deserving case that came under my notice. As wives go, Glenalbyn might have done worse.

'When I was passing out he intercepted my exit, and insisted I should go into the dining-room and take a glass of wine. Whilst this was in progress he asked anxiously what I thought of his wife. In reply I could but echo Dr Montrose's words of wisdom—she was not strong, but I could detect no sign of disease; her nervous system was poor, and her digestion weak. I would send something round, and trusted in a few days to find her much better.

'Very courteously Mr Glenalbyn thanked me, adding some gracious words of compliment concerning my known skill. Altogether I left the house feeling gratified with the manners of its owners. For almost the first time Dr Montrose and I were at one in our opinions. Husband and wife were undeniably pleasant people.'

'Well?' said Mr Graham, interrogatively, as Dr Cray paused.

'It was not exactly well,' answered the doctor; 'Mrs Glenalbyn failed to recover under my treatment as rapidly as she had done when Montrose attended her. I wish to conceal nothing, so I must tell you at once I had altered the medicine. I thought that by strengthening her general system I might get her nerves and digestion into such a state that our services could be to a great extent dispensed with, but I soon found that some way or other I had made a mistake in my diagnosis. To be brief the lady got no better.

'"Are you quite sure that you understand my wife's constitution?" asked Mr Glenalbyn one day, when, meeting him in the avenue, after an unsatisfactory interview with Mrs Glenalbyn, I was bound to confess the "improvement slower than I had expected." "You must forgive my seeming rudeness in putting the question, Dr Cray; a husband's anxiety, you know, will supersede politeness—and Dr Montrose comprehends so perfectly the cause of her slightest ailment."

'A medical man has to bear a great deal, but though I felt Mr Glenalbyn had hit me very hard indeed on my most sensitive point, I was forced to confess I did not seem to be so successful in my treatment of the lady as my partner.

'"Do not you think it might be well to call in a further opinion?" suggested Mr Glenalbyn blandly.

'I answered I should like a further opinion very much indeed, if he was not afraid of causing unnecessary alarm to the patient.

'"Oh! I can manage that," he answered. "And I believe, Dr Cray, there can be no doubt that in any case where there seems the slightest perplexity it is, even in the interest of a medical man himself, better to take a second opinion. Two heads, you know," he added pleasantly, as if, by an old saw of that kind, he thought to rob his meaning of its sting.

'Dr Montrose always insisted one of my faults was a conviction I knew my profession more thoroughly than any other person living. If this were so I had now got a nasty fall; and what made it the more aggravating was I had met with it in such a road. It was like a man who after having hunted a bad county gets thrown in a park, through his horse stumbling over a mole-hill.'

'Poor Cray!' ejaculated his friend with suspicious gravity; for Graham well remembered how at school Jack had believed no one knew anything except himself.

'Thank heaven, however,' went on Dr Cray, with a visible increase of animation, 'I was in no worse case than the London bigwig I met in consultation. That no mistake might be made this time through any hankering after new ideas, when Mr Glenalbyn asked the name of the physician I considered it would be best to meet, I unhesitatingly mentioned a gentleman in whom Dr Montrose placed the greatest confidence; by whom, were a stronger expression applicable as regarded my partner, I should say he swore.

'He altered my medicine a little, accommodating it more to the good old Montrose pattern; was most courteous to the lady, encouraging to the gentleman, friendly to myself, and left on good terms with everybody, carrying away with him golden reasons for thinking well of Southam.

'He agreed with me Mrs Glenalbyn had no disease, and yet, perhaps for that very reason, I began to suspect she must have. If only her nerves and her digestion were out of order, why the deuce should she not get better under treatment that ought to have put her to rights at once? I could discern no disease, yet for all that, there might be one in progress, one yet not sufficiently developed for science to detect its presence. What could it be? I thought over every possible complaint. I studied my patient's appearance. I troubled myself about her; on my honour, Graham, Mrs Glenalbyn's case began to haunt me. I never had been so puzzled before in all my life.

'As delicately as I could hint such a thing, I asked her husband if he knew of any secret trouble. He assured me she was as happy as possible. Her mind is a "clear pool", he added, "I know every pebble at the bottom of it."

'I then tried to ascertain if there were any hereditary disease; but apparently no member of the Frottiss family had ever died from anything save "accident or old age".

'"You are vexing yourself too much over what I am sure is really a very simple ailment," said Mr Glenalbyn. "*I* am not uneasy now; when Dr Montrose comes back he will set everything to rights."

'If such a speech were not enough to drive Montrose's partner to frenzy, I should like to know what you would consider sufficient cause to do so!

'That same afternoon I had to visit a patient residing at some distance from Southam, and, as I returned, the fancy took me to make a slight detour through the woods that rose dark and dense at the back of The Chase. They were no part of that property, and the Southam public was free to wander through them at will; possibly that was the reason the Southam public seemed determined to eschew them altogether. They were the loneliest, loveliest portion of the neighbourhood, and I always chose their green glades when time and opportunity permitted.

'I was walking leisurely along the velvety turf, with my horse's bridle thrown over my arm, when, just before I came to a bridge under which the river meandered gently on its way, I met a Mrs Coulton—without exception the greatest gossip in England.

'I tried to pass her with a bow, but she would not let me. She forced me to stop while she stood chattering over the affairs of the village.

"What did I think of the rector's sermon on Sunday? How was Mr Perry? When would Dr Montrose be back? Why did not Mrs Montrose and Miss Clara accompany him? Had I heard Miss Mowbray was going to be married—yes, to that tall, dark-looking gentleman who sat at the right-hand corner of the family pew on the previous Sunday."

'I had nearly cut my way through this barrier of talk, and was on the very point of escape, when she said: "And so I hear poor Mrs Glenalbyn is worse."

"'I am not aware that she is worse," I answered.

"'Oh, indeed! I was told you met a great London physician there the other day, and that his opinion was she would require the most extreme care."

"'If he made any remark of that sort, he did not make it to me," was my somewhat incautious reply.

"'Dear, dear! What a place Southam is for magnifying every little bit of news! But then, Dr Cray, you see people would naturally say if Mrs Glenalbyn is no worse, why have a great London doctor to see her? Dr Montrose never needed any other opinion than his own. For my own part I shouldn't wonder if she died; and then all the Southam ladies will be pulling caps for that fine handsome husband of hers. As they walk up the aisle together, sometimes I think, what a contrast!"

'I broke away at last, but after I had crossed the bridge I still heard Mrs Coulton's stream of talk maundering peaceably along. The river did not ripple more ceaselessly between its banks than Mrs Coulton's tongue wagged about business with which she had no concern. What was Mrs Glenalbyn's life or death to her? What right had she to institute comparison between me and Montrose?

'It was late—late for Southam I mean, before I went to bed that night. The day had been hot, and my work heavy, and I was tired, for all of which reasons I fell asleep directly. At the end of about a couple of hours, however, I was awakened suddenly by someone saying in my ear, distinctly, in quite a matter of fact voice,—"*Mrs Glenalbyn is dead.*"

'I started up and looked about me. There was not a soul near. The moon was shining broad and clear into the room, and I could see no creature in it save myself. Nevertheless, I felt quite satisfied someone must have spoken. I was so sure of this I jumped on the floor, and putting my head out of the open window, looked if any messenger were standing on the broad step. No; in the length and breadth of that quiet street there was no living creature, not even a dog. The moonlight lay mellow on the sandy horse-road. The white houses gleamed whiter in its beams. But, look which way I would, not a human being was in sight.

'"What a fool I am," I thought, and went back to bed again. Still, tired though I was, I could not immediately settle myself to sleep. Mrs Glenalbyn's case would persist in obtruding itself. Mrs Glenalbyn's lack of vital power troubled me to such a degree that at last I thought of getting up and dressing myself, and probably I should have done so but that while I was considering the *pros* and *cons* of such a course my eyes closed, and without effort I dropped off into dreamland.

'What I dreamt about I have not the slightest recollection. I must have slept and dreamt a long time, for when I again woke, which I did in a state of terrified alarm, the sounds of labour and of life were commencing. It was broad daylight, and a lovely morning.

'But just then I did not notice the beauty of the morning. I was differently engaged. I was wondering who it was that had said in my ear and startled me, *"Look at his eyes! Look at his eyes!"* Whose eyes? Why, I knew, I *had* looked at them more than once.

'I could not shake off the influence of this second fright as I had done the first. I dressed, went downstairs, and I took a long solitary walk.

'What did it all mean. In my sleep I knew I could only have been following out to its legitimate end some course of thought I had been pursuing when awake. Hitherto there was a point where I invariably stopped short, where the actual ended, and the vague and unintelligible began. Now I knew where my doubts had all hitherto been tending. I was suspicious of Mr Glenalbyn—I had felt suspicious of him for weeks.

'Sitting down beside the river, I tried to recall everything I had ever heard concerning that gentleman. There was not much, but I recollected enough to show there might be some ground for my suspicion. Good Heavens! Whither was I drifting? Did I really believe the man wanted to be rid of his wife? Did I feel sure he was murdering her before my eyes? I went home and shut myself up. I looked out every book I could find bearing on the points in the case which puzzled me. I suffered nothing to escape my attention likely to elucidate the mystery. I paced my room till I was tired; I thought till I was weary; and at length, when I received an important summons forcing me to go out, I had still to confess myself baffled.'

'Did you imagine he was poisoning her, then?' asked Mr Graham, his interest finally aroused.

'Yes—felt sure of it, though there was no poison I was acquainted with that exhibited the symptoms which so puzzled and perplexed me. Needless to say, I went that morning as soon as I could to The Chase. Mrs Glenalbyn seemed neither better nor worse; but she complained of having passed a bad night, and Mr Glenalbyn, who was present, asked if I could not give her something to induce sleep.

'I shook my head, and said, perhaps a little foolishly, that what we wanted to get rid of was the cause which prevented her sleeping.

'"It strikes me, doctor," he answered, "you are a little too fond of searching for causes—don't you think that, till you can find them, it might be wiser to deal with effects."

'"I will send some sedative if you wish me to do so," I replied, taking no notice of his taunt; but as I walked away from The Chase, I determined I would not send a sedative, and secondly, that before twelve hours had passed I would try to get to know something more of Mr Glenalbyn's game.

'I could only think of one man in London likely even to be able to help me. If he were alive, I knew I should find him at home, for the simple reason that from year's end to year's end he never went out. He had just enough money to keep a little old-fashioned house, in Westminster, over his head. It was situated near the Horseferry Road. He let off the ground floor to a man who had been forty years clerk in some old bank in the city; he himself occupied the two floors above. He had spent his prime of existence and all his spare cash in purchasing old books, and now in his old age he shut himself up to enjoy their possession.

'I had not seen him for a long time, but I remembered, quite suddenly, he had at one period made poisons his study. He even talked of publishing a book, entitled *The Poisons of All Times and All Nations.* It had not appeared, however, and I did not think it was likely to appear.'

'Why, the title alone,' Mr Graham was beginning, when doctor Cray stopped him—

'I am coming to the gist of my story now—let me finish. The same day I ran up to London and found Mr Ordford in cap, slippers and dressing gown. The place might have been cleaner, and so might he for that matter, but I gave little heed at the moment to externals. Time was of value to me. If things at The Chase were as I suspected, not an hour ought to be lost. He was very glad to see me, and offered, in an old-fashioned way, "such hospitality as his poor house boasted," but I told him I could not stop—that I had come to him for help. In ten minutes I had told my story, described the symptoms, and asked if in his researches he had come on any poison in use amongst the Hindoos or North American Indians likely to reduce the vital power as I had seen. Ordford had studied medicine, and though some reason—laziness, I suspect—prevented his following it as a profession, he was as well able to follow what I said as the first doctor in London might have been.

'When I had done he rose, and, unlocking a cupboard, produced a manuscript book covered only with brown paper. There were about a hundred such on the shelf piled one above the other. On the outside of each was pasted a piece of white paper. That he first brought out was labelled—*Poisons in Use amongst the Natives of India.*

'Opening the folio and running his finger down the index, which was singularly clear and copious he asked, "What reason have you for thinking your man has resorted to India for his materials?"

'I had no better reason to give than that his father was long stationed in India, he himself was born there, and I vaguely recollected hearing something about when he was "amongst the Indians".

"'Ah! that would not be the Hindoos," said Mr Ordford. "There is nothing in this volume to help us. Let us try another," and he produced a second manuscript book labelled—*Poisons in Use amongst the Different Tribes of North American Indians.*

'I never saw anything so full as that old man's repertory. I will not say every poison on earth was to be found mentioned there; but it seemed to me an almost exhaustive analysis of a subject which has never yet received sufficient attention. The symptoms—the result—the antidote, if any—the mode of use—everything you could speak of almost, was written down in a clerkly hand, with a conciseness and brevity that seemed to me amazing.

"'There is nothing to help us here either," he said, after he had referred to several books and examined many papers. "Shall we try Italy?"

'We tried Italy with the same result.

"'What shall we do now?" he asked. "We are just about as wise as when we started."

'I felt woefully disappointed. "Have you no recollection at all," I enquired, "of hearing anything or reading of some simple subtle poison chemistry cannot trace, medicine cannot combat?"

'He smiled, and laid his hand on his manuscript treasures, as he answered, "Why, these are full of such. Chemistry as a rule could not detect them—as yet science cannot combat them. In most cases the antidote, provided by nature for the bane she provides likewise, is known to man, but not to civilised man. Why, our own fields and hedgerows produce the most dangerous poisons, and to how many of them can we point the antidote? And yet there can be no question they grow almost side by side. If you see a nettle, be sure a dock is not far distant, and if we only were wise enough to know, we should be able to place our hand as instantly on the herb from which virtue may be distilled, as on that containing the deadliest poison."

"'Look here," he added, and producing another book he placed it before me. "This contains a list of poisonous plants growing in the three kingdoms—plants fatal to man or cattle, or

415

both. Here is a harmless-looking weed,[1] which did a good deal of mischief in the middle ages. Ah!—"

'He pushed back his cap, he drew a long breath, he turned towards me, and then with his forefinger pointed to the manuscript.

'"There you have it," he said, "there you have your mysterious illness, your 'symptoms which baffle the most skilful leeches', your method of preparation, your mode of administration, the time it takes to kill by almost imperceptible degrees, and the antidote," and Mr Ordford folded up his spectacles, put them in their case, took out his box, refreshed himself with a pinch of snuff, and felt like Sir Christopher Wren when he saw from London Bridge that the lantern spire of St Dunstan's in the East defied the fury of the gale, and that his faith was justified.

'"My dear Ordford!" was all I could say for a minute.

'"What are you going to do now?" he asked.

'"I don't know," I answered. "First tell me where I can get this herb—this antidote—I do not know it even by name."

'"It was freely grown in English gardens in the time of Gerard," he replied; "now it has fallen almost out of cultivation, but it can still, no doubt, be procured."

'"Where, for Heaven's sake?" I asked.

'"In Covent Garden, I dare say."

'I could not get it in Covent Garden, however, but was there told where it might be kept, and being fortunate enough to secure a small portion I hastened back to Southam.

'Already I had matured a plan of action—already I was taking the first step in a course which compelled me to leave my partner, my promised wife, give up my professional prospects, and start for the diggings. In wild haste I decocted the antidote, scented it with poppies, labelled it "Sedative draught", and rode over myself with it to The Chase. Mr Glenalbyn was absent, and not expected back till late. So much the better.

'Next morning found me again at The Chase. Mrs Glenalbyn

---

1. For obvious reasons the author refrains from giving either the common or botanical name.

had slept a little, and said she thought the draught had done her good.

"'I know you do not like opiates, Doctor," said Mr Glenalbyn, who came into the room at this juncture, "but you see I was right. If you think well, she might have another draught tonight—a little stronger."

'I saw what his drift was, but only answered, "I should like to leave one night between."

'After I had said "Good morning" to my patient, Mr Glenalbyn, as usual, came down the staircase with me. Instead of going to the hall-door, as he expected, I asked if I could speak to him for a minute.

"'Certainly," he answered, looking a little surprised; "you don't think my wife worse, do you, Doctor?"

"'I do not consider her worse this morning," I replied, "but, looking back over a week, I cannot blind myself to the fact that she is not making the progress she ought. Has she any friends, that in case of—of—"

"'Good Heavens!" he cried, "you don't mean to imply that there is *danger!*"

"'I am not at all satisfied," I said. "I have never clearly understood what was the matter; I only see that, from whatever cause, Mrs Glenalbyn is losing strength daily; and, though the end may be long deferred, still if some change does not soon—"

'I stopped. I had been looking him straight in the face, and saw his eyes flash with a momentary delight, which brought again the sleeping horror to my mind. I felt I turned colour—I felt the expression of my face change—but evidently he misunderstood the cause of my emotion, for he exclaimed, "Well, rest assured of one thing, Dr Cray. *Whatever* may happen I shall not blame you. So far as you could, you have done your best—"

"'God knows I have!" I interrupted.

"'And though I may foolishly have imagined Dr Montrose, had he been here at first, might have done more—"

"'He could not," I interposed.

"'However that may be, you have done your utmost to save

her. Do I understand you to say—I am so stunned with the suddenness of the blow—there is *no* hope?"

"'While there is life there is hope,' I replied; "but still, unless some great alteration takes place—"

"'Quite so—quite so; I comprehend," and he turned his head aside as if struggling to conceal the agony of his feelings; then, after a pause, "Her poor father—and—mother, wrapped up in her—only daughter—only—child. Do you think I had better telegraph for them?"

"'There is no actual necessity for such haste as that, I should hope,' I answered, well on my guard to avoid exciting his suspicion.

"'Still it might be more satisfactory. And you do not think you will send her another sleeping draught?"

"'Not tonight. I mean to try altering the medicine a little, and may look in again this evening."

"'Do so—do so, by all means; and—Cray—if I have seemed at all to question your skill, forgive me; my anxiety has made me occasionally scarcely know what I have been saying."

"'All now depends on the father,' I thought, after I had left Mr Glenalbyn, his eyes a shade too near together, with a glitter in them which was not agreeable to contemplate.

'Alas! next morning when the father came I saw he was a degree more feeble mentally than his daughter. If anything depended on him she was a dead woman; but Mrs Frottiss was a different sort of person altogether—strong, sharp, brisk, decided—to her I determined to appeal.

'She took me apart from the others, and asked me many questions. She grew so earnest in her maternal trouble and anxiety, that at last she put her hand on my arm and led me through the open window.

"'I can't understand it at all, Doctor Cray," she said, and her voice never faltered, though her eyes were full of tears; "it seems so sudden—so inexplicable. What is my daughter dying of, doctor? Oh! pray, pray be frank!"

'Instantly I took my resolution. "Mrs Frottiss," I said, "I can't tell you here. I want to speak to you alone. Can you make any excuse to come into Southam this afternoon, and call on me. I have something to say which is most important, but—"

'She looked at me keenly, then "You don't want Glenalbyn to know."

'I inclined my head.

'She was a wise woman, but she had not grasped the truth, yet.

'Three hours later she was sitting in my room—Mr Glenalbyn's carriage waited outside my door, Mr Glenalbyn's horses were impatiently pawing the ground.

'"I will come direct to the point," I began. "Has Mr Glenalbyn any interest in your daughter's life?"

'"No more than in her death," answered the old lady. "She inherited a large fortune from her godmother—she ran away with her husband, there were no settlements; he has everything now, and when she dies he will have everything just the same."

'Then I told her. I began at the beginning, and traced every step of the way. I gave the antidote into her hands and begged her to see it was taken. I said I knew it was not too late to save her daughter's life, but unless she could remove her entirely from The Chase, I failed to see how Mrs Glenalbyn's safety was to be ensured.

'"Would she consult Mr Frottiss," I suggested.

'"Not of the slightest use," she answered. "See, Doctor Cray, are you willing to repeat what you have told me, in Mr Glenalbyn's presence?"

'For a moment I hesitated, but after that I said, "Yes, I am."

'"Then I shall telegraph for our solicitor as I return to The Chase."'

'What was the result,' enquired Mr Graham curiously.

'Such a scene as I trust I may never be present at again. I told my story, and I believe if Mr Glenalbyn could have killed me on the spot, I should not be talking to you now. He vowed and protested—he stormed and raved. He said I was an ignorant impostor, who desiring to escape the consequences of my own want of knowledge, had devised this vile plan of fixing guilt on a husband who only loved his wife too much.

'Like a rock the solicitor stood firm.

'"All we want," he said, "is to remove Mrs Glenalbyn; we shall take no further steps."

'"Because you cannot," interrupted Mr Glenalbyn.

'"We shall remove Mrs Glenalbyn to her father's, where I trust she may recover her health—we desire no scandal—we claim no portion of her fortune."'

'You got her away, I suppose, on those terms?' said Mr Graham. 'Did she recover?'

'Oh, yes, she recovered,' answered Doctor Cray, with a grim smile.

'And—'

'The first thing she did was to rejoin her husband! and her next to state publicly I had tried to sow disunion between them. Such is Woman's Devotion!'

'Husband and wife and Doctor Montrose and Perry all joined forces against me. A party was formed, I found it useless to resist, and that was the reason I left Southam.'

'And is Mrs Glenalbyn still living?'

'No; she died the victim of bronchitis—at least so it was reported. It is possible she succumbed to Montrose and the malady. I don't think Glenalbyn was to blame that time.'

'He got all her money, I suppose?'

'Every farthing. He is married again, and still lives at The Chase. He put up a monument, with a most touching inscription to his wife's memory, in Southam Church.'

'What is Ordford doing?'

'I do not know; for one thing—he is dead.'

'And his manuscripts?'

'He died without a will, and the heir-at-law sold them for waste paper.'

'And you, Jack, do you propose to take up doctoring again?'

'No—I mean to follow Ordford's example, and write a *History of Poisons*'

'Oh!' said Mr Graham, and it would have been difficult to add anything to the significance of that interjection as uttered by the barrister.

The Old House in Vauxhall Walk

'Houseless—homeless—hopeless!'

Many a one who had before him trodden that same street must have uttered the same words— the weary, the desolate, the hungry, the forsaken, the waifs and strays of struggling humanity that are always coming and going, cold, starving and miserable, over the pavements of Lambeth Parish; but it is open to question whether they were ever previously spoken with a more thorough conviction of their truth, or with a feeling of keener self-pity, than by the young man who hurried along Vauxhall Walk one rainy winter's night, with no overcoat on his shoulders and no hat on his head.

A strange sentence for one-and-twenty to give expression to—and it was stranger still to come from the lips of a person who looked like and who was a gentleman. He did not appear either to have sunk very far down in the good graces of Fortune. There was no sign or token which would have induced a passer-by to imagine he had been worsted after a long fight with calamity. His boots were not worn down at the heels or broken at the toes, as many, many boots were which dragged and shuffled and scraped along the pavement. His clothes were good and fashionably cut, and innocent of the rents and patches and tatters that slunk wretchedly by, crouched in doorways, and held out a hand mutely appealing for charity. His face was not pinched with famine or lined with wicked wrinkles, or brutalised by drink and debauchery, and yet he said and thought he was hopeless, and almost in his young despair spoke the words aloud.

It was a bad night to be about with such a feeling in one's heart. The rain was cold, pitiless and increasing. A damp, keen wind blew down the cross streets leading from the river. The fumes of the gas works seemed to fall with the rain. The road-way was muddy; the pavement greasy; the lamps burned dimly; and that dreary district of London looked its very gloomiest and worst.

Certainly not an evening to be abroad without a home to go to, or a sixpence in one's pocket, yet this was the position of the young gentleman who, without a hat, strode along Vauxhall Walk, the rain beating on his unprotected head.

Upon the houses, so large and good—once inhabited by well-to-do citizens, now let out for the most part in floors to weekly tenants—he looked enviously. He would have given much to have had a room, or even part of one. He had been walking for a long time, ever since dark in fact, and dark falls soon in December. He was tired and cold and hungry, and he saw no prospect save of pacing the streets all night.

As he passed one of the lamps, the light falling on his face re-vealed handsome young features, a mobile, sensitive mouth, and that particular formation of the eyebrows—not a frown exactly, but a certain draw of the brows—often considered to bespeak genius, but which more surely accompanies an impulsive organ-isation easily pleased, easily depressed, capable of suffering very keenly or of enjoying fully. In his short life he had not enjoyed much, and he had suffered a good deal. That night, when he walked bareheaded through the rain, affairs had come to a crisis.

So far as he in his despair felt able to see or reason, the best thing he could do was to die. The world did not want him; he would be better out of it.

The door of one of the houses stood open, and he could see in the dimly lighted hall some few articles of furniture waiting to be removed. A van stood beside the curb, and two men were lifting a table into it as he, for a second, paused.

'Ah,' he thought, 'even those poor people have some place to go to, some shelter provided, while I have not a roof to cover my head, or a shilling to get a night's lodging.' And he went on fast,, as if memory were spurring him, so fast that a man running after had some trouble to overtake him.

'Master Graham! Master Graham!' this man exclaimed, breathlessly; and, thus addressed, the young fellow stopped as if he had been shot.

'Who are you that know me?' he asked, facing round.

'I'm William; don't you remember William, Master Graham? And, Lord's sake, sir, what are you doing out a night like this without your hat?'

'I forgot it,' was the answer; 'and I did not care to go back and fetch it.'

'Then why don't you buy another, sir? You'll catch your death of cold; and besides, you'll excuse me, sir, but it does look odd.'

'I know that,' said Master Graham grimly; 'but I haven't a halfpenny in the world.'

'Have you and the master, then—' began the man, but there he hesitated and stopped.

'Had a quarrel? Yes, and one that will last us our lives,' finished the other, with a bitter laugh.

'And where are you going now?'

'Going! Nowhere, except to seek out the softest paving stone, or the shelter of an arch.'

'You are joking, sir.'

'I don't feel much in a mood for jesting either.'

'Will you come back with me, Master Graham? We are just at the last of our moving, but there is a spark of fire still in the grate, and it would be better talking out of this rain. Will you come, sir?'

'Come! Of course I will come,' said the young fellow, and, turning, they retraced their steps to the house he had looked into as he passed along.

An old, old house, with long, wide hall, stairs low, easy of ascent, with deep cornices to the ceilings, and oak floorings, and mahogany doors, which still spoke mutely of the wealth and stability of the original owner, who lived before the Tradescants and Ashmoles were thought of, and had been sleeping far longer than they, in St Mary's churchyard, hard by the archbishop's palace.

'Step upstairs, sir,' entreated the departing tenant; 'it's cold down here, with the door standing wide.'

'Had you the whole house, then, William?' asked Graham Coulton, in some surprise.

'The whole of it, and right sorry I, for one, am to leave it; but nothing else would serve my wife. This room, sir,' and with a little conscious pride, William, doing the honours of his late residence, asked his guest into a spacious apartment occupying the full width of the house on the first floor.

Tired though he was, the young man could not repress an exclamation of astonishment.

'Why, we have nothing so large as this at home, William,' he said.

'It's a fine house,' answered William, raking the embers together as he spoke and throwing some wood upon them; 'but, like many a good family, it has come down in the world.'

There were four windows in the room, shuttered close; they had deep, low seats, suggestive of pleasant days gone by; when, well-curtained and well-cushioned, they formed snug retreats for the children, and sometimes for adults also; there was no furniture left, unless an oaken settle beside the hearth, and a large mirror let into the panelling at the opposite end of the apartment, with a black marble console table beneath it, could be so considered; but the very absence of chairs and tables enabled the magnificent proportions of the chamber to be seen to full advantage, and there was nothing to distract the attention from the ornamented ceiling, the panelled walls, the old-world chimney-piece so quaintly carved, and the fireplace lined with tiles, each one of which contained a picture of some scriptural or allegorical subject.

'Had you been staying on here, William,' said Coulton, flinging himself wearily on the settle, 'I'd have asked you to let me stop where I am for the night.'

'If you can make shift, sir, there is nothing as I am aware of to prevent you stopping,' answered the man, fanning the wood into a flame. 'I shan't take the key back to the landlord till tomorrow, and this would be better for you than the cold streets at any rate.'

'Do you really mean what you say?' asked the other eagerly. 'I should be thankful to lie here; I feel dead beat.'

'Then stay, Master Graham, and welcome. I'll fetch a basket of coals I was going to put in the van, and make up a good fire, so that you can warm yourself then I must run round to the other house for a minute or two, but it's not far, and I'll be back as soon as ever I can.'

'Thank you, William; you were always good to me,' said the young man gratefully. 'This is delightful,' and he stretched his numbed hands over the blazing wood, and looked round the room with a satisfied smile.

'I did not expect to get into such quarters,' he remarked, as his friend in need reappeared, carrying a half-bushel basket full of coals, with which he proceeded to make up a roaring fire. 'I am sure the last thing I could have imagined was meeting with anyone I knew in Vauxhall Walk.'

'Where were you coming from, Master Graham?' asked William curiously.

'From old Melfield's. I was at his school once, you know, and he has now retired, and is living upon the proceeds of years of robbery in Kennington Oval. I thought, perhaps he would lend me a pound, or offer me a night's lodging, or even a glass of wine; but, oh dear, no. He took the moral tone, and observed he could have nothing to say to a son who defied his father's authority.

He gave me plenty of advice, but nothing else, and showed me out into the rain with a bland courtesy, for which I could have struck him.'

William muttered something under his breath which was not a blessing, and added aloud:

'You are better here, sir, I think, at any rate. I'll be back in less than half an hour.'

Left to himself, young Coulton took off his coat, and shifting the settle a little, hung it over the end to dry. With his handkerchief he rubbed some of the wet out of his hair; then, perfectly exhausted, he lay down before the fire and, pillowing his head on his arm, fell fast asleep.

He was awakened nearly an hour afterwards by the sound of someone gently stirring the fire and moving quietly about the room. Starting into a sitting posture, he looked around him, bewildered for a moment, and then, recognising his humble friend, said laughingly:

'I had lost myself; I could not imagine where I was.'

'I am sorry to see you here, sir,' was the reply; 'but still this is better than being out of doors. It has come on a nasty night. I brought a rug round with me that, perhaps, you would wrap yourself in.'

'I wish, at the same time, you had brought me something to eat,' said the young man, laughing.

'Are you hungry, then, sir?' asked William, in a tone of concern.

'Yes; I have had nothing to eat since breakfast. The governor and I commenced rowing the minute we sat down to luncheon, and I rose and left the table. But hunger does not signify; I am dry and warm, and can forget the other matter in sleep.'

'And it's too late now to buy anything,' soliloquised the man; 'the shops are all shut long ago.

Do you think, sir,' he added, brightening, 'you could manage some bread and cheese?'

'Do I think—I should call it a perfect feast,' answered Graham Coulton. 'But never mind about food tonight, William; you have had trouble enough, and to spare, already.'

William's only answer was to dart to the door and run downstairs. Presently he reappeared, carrying in one hand bread and cheese wrapped up in paper, and in the other a pewter measure full of beer.

'It's the best I could do, sir,' he said apologetically. 'I had to beg this from the landlady.'

'Here's to her good health!' exclaimed the young fellow gaily, taking a long pull at the tankard. 'That tastes better than champagne in my father's house.'

'Won't he be uneasy about you?' ventured William, who, having by this time emptied the coals, was now seated on the inverted basket, looking wistfully at the relish with which the son of the former master was eating his bread and cheese.

'No,' was the decided answer. 'When he hears it pouring cats and dogs he will only hope I am out in the deluge, and say a good drenching will cool my pride.'

'I do not think you are right there,' remarked the man.

'But I am sure I am. My father always hated me, as he hated my mother.'

'Begging your pardon, sir; he was over fond of your mother.'

'If you had heard what he said about her today, you might find reason to alter your opinion. He told me I resembled her in mind as well as body; that I was a coward, a simpleton, and a hypocrite.'

'He did not mean it, sir.'

'He did, every word. He does think I am a coward, because I—I—' And the young fellow broke into a passion of hysterical tears.

'I don't half like leaving you here alone,' said William, glancing round the room with a quick trouble in his eyes; 'but I have no place fit to ask you to stop, and I am forced to go myself, because I am night watchman, and must be on at twelve o'clock.'

'I shall be right enough,' was the answer. 'Only I mustn't talk any more of my father. Tell me about yourself, William. How did you manage to get such a big house, and why are you leaving it?'

'The landlord put me in charge, sir; and it was my wife's fancy not to like it.'

'Why did she not like it?'

'She felt desolate alone with the children at night,' answered William, turning away his head; then added, next minute: 'Now, sir, if you think I can do no more for you, I had best be off.

Time's getting on. I'll look round tomorrow morning.'

'Goodnight,' said the young fellow, stretching out his hand, which the other took as freely and frankly as it was offered. 'What should I have done this evening if I had not chanced to meet you?'

'I don't think there is much chance in the world, Master Graham,' was the quiet answer. 'I do hope you will rest well, and not be the worse for your wetting.'

'No fear of that,' was the rejoinder, and the next minute the young man found himself all alone in the Old House in Vauxhall Walk.

CHAPTER TWO

Lying on the settle, with the fire burnt out, and the room in total darkness, Graham Coulton dreamed a curious dream. He thought he awoke from deep slumber to find a log smouldering away upon the hearth, and the mirror at the end of the apartment reflecting fitful gleams of light.

He could not understand how it came to pass that, far away as he was from the glass, he was able to see everything in it; but he resigned himself to the difficulty without astonishment, as people generally do in dreams.

Neither did he feel surprised when he beheld the outline of a female figure seated beside the fire, engaged in picking something out of her lap and dropping it with a despairing gesture.

He heard the mellow sound of gold, and knew she was lifting and dropping sovereigns, he turned a little so as to see the person engaged in such a singular and meaningless manner, and found that, where there had been no chair on the previous night, there was a chair now, on which was seated an old, wrinkled hag, her clothes poor and ragged, a mob cap barely covering her scant white hair, her cheeks sunken, her nose hooked, her fingers more like talons than aught else as they dived down into the heap of gold, portions of which they lifted but to scatter mournfully.

'Oh! my lost life,' she moaned, in a voice of the bitterest anguish. 'Oh! my lost life—for one day, for one hour of it again!'

Out of the darkness—out of the corner of the room where the shadows lay deepest—out from the gloom abiding near the door—out from the dreary night, with their sodden feet and wet dripping from their heads, came the old men and the young children, the worn women and the weary hearts, whose misery that gold might have relieved, but whose wretchedness it mocked.

Round that miser, who once sat gloating as she now sat lamenting, they crowded—all those pale, sad shapes—the aged of days, the infant of hours, the sobbing outcast, honest poverty, repentant vice; but one low cry proceeded from those pale lips—a cry for help she might have given, but which she withheld.

They closed about her, all together, as they had done singly in life; they prayed, they sobbed, they entreated; with haggard eyes the figure regarded the poor she had repulsed, the children against whose cry she had closed her ears, the old people she had suffered to starve and die for want of what would have been the merest trifle to her; then, with a terrible scream, she raised her lean arms above her head, and sank down—down—the gold scattering as it fell out of her lap, and rolling along the floor, till its gleam was lost in the outer darkness beyond.

Then Graham Coulton awoke in good earnest, with the perspiration oozing from every pore, with a fear and an agony upon him such as he had never before felt in all his existence, and with the sound of the heart-rending cry—'Oh! my lost life'—still ringing in his ears.

Mingled with all, too, there seemed to have been some lesson for him which he had forgotten, that, try as he would, eluded his memory, and which, in the very act of waking, glided away.

He lay for a little thinking about all this, and then, still heavy with sleep, retraced his way into dreamland once more.

It was natural, perhaps, that, mingling with the strange fantasies which follow in the train of night and darkness, the former vision should recur, and the young man ere long found himself toiling through scene after scene wherein the figure of the woman he had seen seated beside a dying fire held principal place.

He saw her walking slowly across the floor munching a dry crust—she who could have purchased all the luxuries wealth can command; on the hearth, contemplating her, stood a man of commanding presence, dressed in the fashion of long ago. In his eyes there was a dark look of anger, on his lips a curling smile of disgust, and somehow, even in his sleep, the dreamer understood it was the ancestor to the descendant he beheld—that the house put to mean uses in which he lay had never so far descended from its high estate, as the woman possessed of so pitiful a soul, contaminated with the most despicable and insidious vice poor humanity knows, for all other vices seem to have connection with the flesh, but the greed of the miser eats into the very soul.

Filthy of person, repulsive to look at, hard of heart as she was, he yet beheld another phantom, which, coming into the room, met her almost on the threshold, taking her by the hand, and pleading, as it seemed, for assistance. He could not hear all that passed, but a word now and then fell upon his ear. Some talk of former days; some mention of a fair young mother—an appeal, as it seemed, to a time when they were tiny brother and sister, and the accursed greed for gold had not divided them.

All in vain; the hag only answered him as she had answered the children, and the young girls, and the old people in his former vision. Her heart was as invulnerable to natural affection as it had proved to human sympathy. He begged, as it appeared, for aid to avert some bitter misfortune or terrible disgrace, and adamant might have been found more yielding to his prayer. Then the figure standing on the hearth changed to an angel, which folded its wings mournfully over its face, and the man, with bowed head, slowly left the room.

Even as he did so the scene changed again; it was night once more, and the miser wended her way upstairs. From below, Graham Coulton fancied he watched her toiling wearily from step to step. She had aged strangely since the previous scenes. She moved with difficulty; it seemed the greatest exertion for her to creep from step to step, her skinny hand traversing the balusters with slow and painful deliberateness. Fascinated, the young man's eyes followed the progress of that feeble, decrepit woman. She was solitary in a desolate house, with a deeper blackness than the darkness of night waiting to engulf her.

It seemed to Graham Coulton that after that he lay for a time in a still, dreamless sleep, upon awaking from which he found himself entering a chamber as sordid and unclean in its appointments as the woman of his previous vision had been in her person. The poorest labourer's wife would have gathered more comforts around her than that room contained. A four-poster bedstead without hangings of any kind—a blind drawn up awry—an old carpet covered with dust, and dirt on the floor—a rickety washstand with all the paint worn off it—an ancient mahogany dressing-table, and a cracked glass spotted all over—were all the objects he could at first discern, looking at the room through that dim light which oftentimes obtains in dreams.

By degrees, however, he perceived the outline of someone lying huddled on the bed. Drawing nearer, he found it was that of the person whose dreadful presence seemed to pervade the house.

What a terrible sight she looked, with her thin white locks scattered over the pillow, with what were mere remnants of blankets gathered about her shoulders, with her claw-like fingers clutching the clothes, as though even in sleep she was guarding her gold!

An awful and a repulsive spectacle, but not with half the terror in it of that which followed.

Even as the young man looked he heard stealthy footsteps on the stairs. Then he saw first one man and then his fellow steal cautiously into the room. Another second, and the pair stood beside the bed, murder in their eyes.

Graham Coulton tried to shout—tried to move, but the deterrent power which exists in dreams only tied his tongue and paralysed his limbs. He could but hear and look, and what he heard and saw was this: aroused suddenly from sleep, the woman started, only to receive a blow from one of the ruffians, whose fellow followed his lead by plunging a knife into her breast.

Then, with a gurgling scream, she fell back on the bed, and at the same moment, with a cry, Graham Coulton again awoke, to thank heaven it was but an illusion.

CHAPTER THREE

'I hope you slept well, sir.' It was William, who, coming into the hall with the sunlight of a fine bright morning streaming after him, asked this question: 'Had you a good night's rest?'

Graham Coulton laughed, and answered:

'Why, faith, I was somewhat in the case of Paddy, "*who could not slape for dhraming*". I slept well enough, I suppose, but whether it was in consequence of the row with my dad, or the hard bed, or the cheese—most likely the bread and cheese so late at night—I dreamt all the night long, the most extraordinary dreams. Some old woman kept cropping up, and I saw her murdered.'

'You don't say that, sir?' said William nervously.

'I do, indeed,' was the reply. 'However, that is all gone and past. I have been down in the kitchen and had a good wash, and I am as fresh as a daisy, and as hungry as a hunter; and, oh, William, can you get me any breakfast?'

'Certainly, Master Graham. I have brought round a kettle, and I will make the water boil immediately. I suppose, sir'—this tentatively—'you'll be going home today?'

'Home!' repeated the young man. 'Decidedly not. I'll never go home again till I return with some medal hung to my coat, or a leg or arm cut off. I've thought it all out, William. I'll go and enlist. There's a talk of war; and, living or dead, my father shall have reason to retract his opinion about my being a coward.'

'I am sure the admiral never thought you anything of the sort, sir,' said William. 'Why, you have the pluck of ten!'

'Not before him,' answered the young fellow sadly.

'You'll do nothing rash, Master Graham; you won't go 'listing, or aught of that sort, in your anger?'

'If I do not, what is to become of me?' asked the other. 'I cannot dig—to beg I am ashamed. Why, but for you, I should not have had a roof over my head last night.'

'Not much of a roof, I am afraid, sir.'

'Not much of a roof!' repeated the young man. 'Why, who could desire a better? What a capital room this is,' he went on, looking around the apartment, where William was now kindling a fire; 'one might dine twenty people here easily!'

'If you think so well of the place, Master Graham, you might stay here for a while, till you have made up your mind what you are going to do. The landlord won't make any objection, I am very sure.'

'Oh! nonsense; he would want a long rent for a house like this.'

'I dare say; *if he could get it*,' was William's significant answer.

'What do you mean? Won't the place let?'

'No, sir. I did not tell you last night, but there was a murder done here, and people are shy of the house ever since.'

'A murder! What sort of a murder? Who was murdered?'

'A woman, Master Graham—the landlord's sister; she lived here all alone, and was supposed to have money. Whether she had or not, she was found dead from a stab in her breast, and if there ever was any money, it must have been taken at the same time, for none ever was found in the house from that day to this.'

'Was that the reason your wife would not stop here?' asked the young man, leaning against the mantelshelf, and looking thoughtfully down on William.

'Yes, sir. She could not stand it any longer; she got that thin and nervous one would have believed it possible; she never saw anything, but she said she heard footsteps and voices, and then when she walked through the hall, or up the staircase, someone always seemed to be following her. We put the children to sleep in that big room you had last night, and they declared they often saw an old woman sitting by the hearth. Nothing ever came my way, finished William, with a laugh; 'I was always ready to go to sleep the minute my head touched the pillow.'

'Were not the murderers discovered?' asked Graham Coulton.

'No, sir; the landlord, Miss Tynan's brother, had always lain under the suspicion of it—quite wrongfully, I am very sure—but he will never clear himself now. It was known he came and asked her for help a day or two before the murder, and it was also known he was able within a week or two to weather whatever trouble had been harassing him. Then, you see, the money was never found; and, altogether, people scarce knew what to think.'

'Humph!' ejaculated Graham Coulton, and he took a few turns up and down the apartment.

'Could I go and see this landlord?'

'Surely, sir, if you had a hat,' answered William, with such a serious decorum that the young man burst out laughing.

'That is an obstacle, certainly,' he remarked, 'and I must make a note do instead. I have a pencil in my pocket, so here goes.'

Within half an hour from the dispatch of that note William was back again with a sovereign; the landlord's compliments, and he would be much obliged if Mr Coulton could 'step round.'

'You'll do nothing rash, sir,' entreated William.

'Why, man,' answered the young fellow, 'one may as well be picked off by a ghost as a bullet. What is there to be afraid of?'

William only shook his head. He did not think his young master was made of the stuff likely to remain alone in a haunted house and solve the mystery it assuredly contained by dint of his own unassisted endeavours. And yet when Graham Coulton came out of the landlord's house he looked more bright and gay than usual, and walked up the Lambeth road to the place where William awaited his return, humming an air as he paced along.

'We have settled the matter,' he said. 'And now if the dad wants his son for Christmas, it will trouble him to find him.'

'Don't say that, Master Graham, don't,' entreated the man, with a shiver; 'maybe after all it would have been better if you had never happened to chance upon Vauxhall Walk.'

'Don't croak, William,' answered the young man; 'if it was not the best day's work I ever did for myself I'm a Dutchman.'

During the whole of that forenoon and afternoon, Graham Coulton searched diligently for the missing treasure Mr Tynan assured him had never been discovered. Youth is confident and self-opinionated, and this fresh explorer felt satisfied that, though others had failed, he would be successful. On the second floor he found one door locked, but he did not pay much attention to that at the moment, as he believed if there was anything concealed it was more likely to be found in the lower than the upper part of the house. Late into the evening he pursued his researches in the kitchen and cellars and old-fashioned cupboards, of which the basement had an abundance.

It was nearly eleven, when, engaged in poking about amongst the empty bins of a wine cellar as large as a family vault, he suddenly felt a rush of cold air at his back. Moving, his candle was instantly extinguished, and in the very moment of being left in darkness he saw, standing in the doorway, a woman, resembling her who had haunted his dreams overnight.

He rushed with outstretched hands to seize her, but clutched only air. He relit his candle, and closely examined the basement, shutting off communication with the ground floor ere doing so. All in vain. Not a trace could he find of living creature—not a window was open—not a door unbolted.

'It is very odd,' he thought, as, after securely fastening the door at the top of the staircase, he searched the whole upper portion of the house, with the exception of the one room mentioned.

'I must get the key of that tomorrow,' he decided, standing gloomily with his back to the fire and his eyes wandering about the drawing-room, where he had once again taken up his abode.

Even as the thought passed through his mind, he saw standing in the open doorway a woman with white dishevelled hair, clad in mean garments, ragged and dirty. She lifted her hand and shook it at him with a menacing gesture, and then, just as he was darting towards her, a wonderful thing occurred.

From behind the great mirror there glided a second female figure, at the sight of which the first turned and fled, littering piercing shrieks as the other followed her from storey to storey.

Sick almost with terror, Graham Coulton watched the dreadful pair as they fled upstairs past the locked room to the top of the house.

It was a few minutes before he recovered his self-possession. When he did so, and searched the upper apartments, he found them totally empty.

That night, ere lying down before the fire, he carefully locked and bolted the drawing-room door; before he did more he drew the heavy settle in front of it, so that if the lock were forced no entrance could be effected without considerable noise.

For some time he lay awake, then dropped into a deep sleep, from which he was awakened suddenly by a noise as if of something scuffling stealthily behind the wainscot. He raised himself on his elbow and listened, and, to his consternation, beheld seated at the opposite side of the hearth the same woman he had seen before in his dreams, lamenting over her gold.

The fire was not quite out, and at that moment shot up a last tongue of flame. By the light, transient as it was, he saw that the figure pressed a ghostly finger to its lips, and by the turn of its head and the attitude of its body seemed to be listening.

He listened also—indeed, he was too much frightened to do aught else; more and more distinct grew the sounds which had aroused him, a stealthy rustling coming nearer and nearer—up and up it seemed, behind the wainscot.

'It is rats,' thought the young man, though, indeed, his teeth were almost chattering in his head with fear. But then in a moment he saw what disabused him of that idea—*the gleam of a candle or lamp through a crack in the panelling.* He tried to rise, he strove to shout—all in vain; and, sinking down, remembered nothing more till he awoke to find the grey light of an early morning stealing through one of the shutters he had left partially unclosed.

For hours after his breakfast, which he scarcely touched, long after William had left him at mid-day, Graham Coulton, having in the morning made a long and close survey of the house, sat thinking before the fire, then, apparently having made up his mind, he put on the hat he had bought, and went out.

When he returned the evening shadows were darkening down, but the pavements were full of people going marketing, for it was Christmas Eve, and all who had money to spend seemed bent on shopping.

It was terribly dreary inside the old house that night. Through the deserted rooms Graham could feel that ghostly semblance was wandering mournfully. When he turned his back he knew she was flitting from the mirror to the fire, from the fire to the mirror; but he was not afraid of her now—he was far more afraid of another matter he had taken in hand that day.

The horror of the silent house grew and grew upon him. He could hear the beating of his own heart in the dead quietude which reigned from garret to cellar.

At last William came; but the young man said nothing to him of what was in his mind. He talked to him cheerfully and hopefully enough—wondered where his father would think he had got to, and hoped Mr Tynan might send him some Christmas pudding. Then the man said it was time for him to go, and, when Mr Coulton went downstairs to the hall-door, remarked the key was not in it.

'No,' was the answer, 'I took it out today, to oil it.'

'It wanted oiling,' agreed William, 'for it worked terribly stiff.' Having uttered which truism he departed.

Very slowly the young man retraced his way to the drawing-room, where he only paused to lock the door on the outside; then taking off his boots he went up to the top of the house, where, entering the front attic, he waited patiently in darkness and in silence.

It was a long time, or at least it seemed long to him, before he heard the same sound which had aroused him on the previous night—a stealthy rustling—then a rush of cold air—then cautious footsteps—then the quiet opening of a door below.

It did not take as long in action as it has required to tell. In a moment the young man was out on the landing and had closed a portion of the panelling on the wall which stood open; noiselessly he crept back to the attic window, unlatched it, and sprung a rattle, the sound of which echoed far and near through the deserted streets, then rushing down the stairs, he encountered a man who, darting past him, made for the landing above; but perceiving the way of escape closed, fled down again, to find Graham struggling desperately with his fellow.

'Give him the knife—come along,' he said savagely; and next instant Graham felt something like a hot iron through his shoulder, and then heard a thud, as one of the men, tripping in his rapid flight, fell from the top of the stairs to the bottom.

At the same moment there came a crash, as if the house was falling, and faint, sick, and bleeding, young Coulton lay insensible on the threshold of the room where Miss Tynan had been murdered.

When he recovered he was in the dining-room, and a doctor was examining his wound.

Near the door a policeman stiffly kept guard. The hall was full of people; all the misery and vagabondism the streets contain at that hour was crowding in to see what had happened.

Through the midst two men were being conveyed to the station-house; one, with his head dreadfully injured, on a stretcher, the other handcuffed, uttering frightful imprecations as he went.

After a time the house was cleared of the rabble, the police took possession of it, and Mr Tynan was sent for.

'What was that dreadful noise?' asked Graham feebly, now seated on the floor, with his back resting against the wall.

'I do not know. Was there a noise?' said Mr Tynan, humouring his fancy, as he thought.

'Yes, in the drawing-room, I think; the key is in my pocket.'

Still humouring the wounded lad, Mr Tynan took the key and ran upstairs.

When he unlocked the door, what a sight met his eyes! The mirror had fallen—it was lying all over the floor shivered into a thousand pieces; the console table had been borne down by its weight, and the marble slab was shattered as well. But this was not what chained his attention.

Hundreds, thousands of gold pieces were scattered about, and an aperture behind the glass contained boxes filled with securities amid deeds amid bonds, the possession of which had cost his sister her life.

★★★★★★

'Well, Graham, and what do you want?' asked Admiral Coulton that evening as his eldest born appeared before him, looking somewhat pale but otherwise unchanged.

'I want nothing,' was the answer, 'but to ask your forgiveness. William has told me all the story I never knew before; and, if you let me, I will try to make it up to you for the trouble you have had. I am provided for,' went on the young fellow, with a nervous laugh; 'I have made my fortune since I left you, and another man's fortune as well.'

'I think you are out of your senses,' said the admiral shortly.

'No, sir, I have found them,' was the answer; 'and I mean to strive and make a better thing of my life than I should ever have done had I not gone to the Old House in Vauxhall Walk.'

'Vauxhall Walk! What is the lad talking about?'

'I will tell you, sir, if I may sit down,' was Graham Coulton's answer, and then he told his story.

Conn Kilrea

CHAPTER ONE

Ever since morning, when the early post brought him a letter, Private Conway Kilray had been in low spirits; not by any means an unusual occurrence, for no man of his regiment could remember ever seeing him in good, but on the evening of the 14th December, 1892, he seemed to have sounded even a lower depth of depression than that wherein he usually dwelt.

He was young—not eight and twenty—fairly good looking, healthy, in full enjoyment of such faculties, bodily and mental, as God gives to most men, and yet possessed by a demon of melancholy, discontent, or unavailing repentance, that made him a mystery to his comrades and the dullest companion possible.

All the men among whom his lot was cast had tried to pierce the mail of his reserve, and retired worsted, feeling as though they had struck against something tougher than chain armour.

They could not make him out; he was always willing to help, always ready to do a good turn, always civil and quiet spoken, but always also grievously depressed, weighed down by some sin or wrong or trouble which lay heavy at his heart.

When, on the evening of that 14th December, he entered the barrack library at Weyport, the gloom of his expression so awed the few soldiers present that no one spoke while he passed to a desk, followed by a wiry Scotch terrier, who, being indeed nobody's dog, but only a poor stray, had conceived a fancy for the silent, lonely man.

Private Kilray seemed to have brought a blight into the room with him, which hushed the light chatter of those who were playing cards, and caused others who had selected reading as an amusing way of filling time, to glance constantly at the man who sat writing, cloaked with some strange gloom they could not understand, while the dog lay at his feet silent and self-contained also.

A few of those present winked at each other, or shook their heads gravely, but neither action was of any real import, for they knew nothing of what had put one life out of joint, whether murder, burglary, highway robbery, or forgery.

Some who had once been privileged to see Kilray in a passion held that the first-named crime had driven him into the army, but the most general belief, founded perhaps on his bold and dashing calliraphy, was that signing a name not his own would eventually be found sufficient to account for much that puzzled them.

'Depend upon it, he took to gambling, and then used his pen once too often,' said the oracle of 'The Light Bays,' when Kilray first joined. 'He is Irish, yet he enlisted in England, as if there were not always regiments enough stationed in his own country, any one of which might have served his turn. No; we'll hear more about him after a while, and then the whole thing will be plain as a pikestaff.'

At the end of eighteen months, however, things were as dark as at first. No enquiries had been made for Conway Kilray. No friend or foe had asked whether he were living or dead. A few letters arrived, which he answered and posted himself. When first he came among the Light Bays, a report soon got about that he knew more concerning horses than the riding master himself, who was asserted to have said he had nothing to teach the young recruit except how to trot.

Private Kilray had found that piece of learning difficult exceedingly, as most good riders do, but he set his teeth and curbed his temper, and ere very long could trot with the best. For the rest he groomed a horse excellently well; no one found any fault with him, no one said a word against him, but yet he was not popular. He walked a living enigma among his fellows, never making merry, never laughing nor joking, never taking part in any buffoonery nor more sober enjoyment. He was sufficient unto himself, which it may here be said is a peculiarity society— any society, whether high or low—cannot forgive, and naturally, since it is unpleasant to be continually getting figurative slaps in the face in return for well-meant civility,

On the evening when this story opens Private Kilray had not advanced at all in favour of his comrades, rather the reverse, as he had chosen to keep himself to himself. They, after some attempts at friendliness, held aloof, and looked at him as he sat at his desk with a certain amount of curiosity and dislike.

Never heeding them, he wrote on, filling sheet after sheet, which he blotted hastily, folded without once glancing over, and placed in a directed and stamped envelope. Then he pushed the letter from him, and, resting his elbow on the desk, leaned his head upon his hand as though tired.

He sat so long thus that a man who was reading close by suspended his occupation in order to watch him. While he was doing so he became aware of a singular change in Kilray's manner. At first while engaged in thinking out some evidently unpleasant subject he kept his eyes dreamily fixed on a corner of the room near at hand which lay in shadow.

After a time, however, he lifted his head and peered into the darkness, as though he saw something he could not quite understand.

Involuntarily the man who was watching turned to see what his comrade was looking at, but failed to discern any object.

He had withdrawn his attention only for a moment, yet when he glanced again at Kilray he perceived his attitude was totally changed.

Both his hands firmly clenched were on the desk, he was sitting bolt upright. His eyes, filled with an expression of incredulous horror, were fixed on something he perceived looming out of the darkness.

He was white as death—he who was never known to fear—

and a sort of grey shade came over his face, as with a shudder he rose and tried to pull himself together.

Then, for the first time, the other noticed that Kilray's terrier was looking into the corner also, the very hair on his body standing more upright than ever.

'Hillo! have you seen a ghost, old man?' asked a newcomer who had just lounged up to the little group.

Startled by the question, Kilray turned swiftly round as if to resent it. Instantly recollecting himself, however, he laconically answered 'yes,' picked up his letter, and strode out into the night, followed by his dog.

CHAPTER TWO

Instinctively choosing the least frequented road, Private Kilray, feeling like one in a nightmare, walked on till he reached the seashore, and heard the waves washing in over a sandy beach.

It was a dark night—lit not by moon or star—but none too dark for a man, whose whole mind was filled by thoughts of eternity, to wrestle with the terror of that awful warning which had so lately, as he believed, been delivered to him.

Before he began to write he would have told anyone, and according to his then belief truly, that he felt his life not worth living, that there was little pleasant in the past to look back upon, and nothing in the future to look forward to; but now, when it seemed his time was come, he could have prayed for more years to be given unto him—years, whether joyful or sorrowful, that he might live and not go to the grave while it was yet noon.

The love of life is a thanksgiving to God. Which amongst us, having some jewel of price received from some earthly friend, decries its value? If we met with such an ingrate, we should write him down accordingly, and what must we say of the man who fails in his heart of hearts to praise God for placing him in a land overflowing with beauty, rich with colour, fragrant with perfume? And why? Because he has to work for his day's wage of things good and fair and sweet, he is discontented because he wants to choose his wage rather than accept that his Maker bestows!

Standing by the seashore, with the night wind fanning his face, with the waves' sobbing music sounding in his ears, with heaven's canopy above him and the dear earth beneath his feet, some dim understanding came to Private Kilray that he had been a very churl—that he had not made the best of life; that like a child in a temper he had refused to smile when Nature was putting out her loveliest playthings for his delight, and turned his back on man's more clumsy efforts to please and befriend him.

Ah, if he could only have seen sooner—if sight had not come so late! And then and there he bared his soul before God, and talked with the Almighty as he might aforetime have talked with man.

He had thought in the first bitterness of his anguish, he who was done with life, to tear his letter to bits, and cast it to the winds; but his heart failed him now. That letter lay close to his bosom, close and warm like some throbbing human heart, and he could not fling it to the mercy of the elements as a thing of no account.

It is a sore trial to have to die, but it is a worse trial to die hard, with an angry and rebellious spirit, with a hand which refuses to take its loving Lord's as guide through the awful darkness of that valley which, willing or unwilling, our feet must tread!

Through the darkness the truth of this came home to one who felt himself standing on the very border of that unseen land whither he was journeying.

'Dear God,' he cried in his agony, where there was no one save God to hear, where the night winds alone stirred, and only sea birds and the waves broke the stillness, 'dear God, forgive my sins, and grant me courage when Thy appointed time comes, to give my soul into Thy holy keeping, bravely and without fear, for Christ's sake—Amen.' And he fell down beside a piece of rock, and covered his face, even though it was night, and dark, and arose comforted!

After a while, hearing some clock strike, he retraced his steps to the barracks, posting that letter by the way. His comrades, who were all acquainted with the fact that Kilray had actually seen a ghost, presumably of someone whose death he would ere long have to answer for, spoke to him with a strange reserve, which did not affect the young man at all.

He knew what they did not know. He was attended to the barrack-room by a face never seen since early childhood, which he had quite forgotten till it looked solemnly at him from out of the darkness of that unlighted corner.

The ghastly inheritance of an old family hovered over his bed, and caused foreboding dreams the while he slept uneasily, surrounded by the careless, the indifferent, the sorrowful, the struggling, the bad and the good till getting-up time came, and awoke with its noisy bustling, memories he would have fain forgotten for a little longer.

It was afternoon before he could snatch a minute in which to write another letter as short as the first had been long. He said:

Dearest Kathleen

I have bad news for you, love; and yet, perhaps, it is the best I could have to tell you, because it points to the cutting of many a difficulty—to the ending of all anxiety. *I have seen Lord Yiewsly. You know what that means,* so I need add no more. I will meet you when and where you appoint to say goodbye. Do not grieve, dear. Fate has settled matters better for us than we could have done for ourselves. God bless you, my faithful darling.

Ever in this world and in the next, your devoted lover,

Conn

If I wrote a word yesterday that caused you annoyance, forgive me. I hadn't seen *him* then, though the envelope was scarcely closed before he appeared. I thought at one time of tearing up the sheets, but could not—my last love letter! Oh, sweet! pardon all the pain I have given you—I, who would have died to save you sorrow.

As the day wore on, as the twilight faded and merged into the gloom of evening, the restlessness which had, nearly twenty-four hours previously, driven him out through the night to the sad seashore, returned with greater intensity. He could not sit still. He felt like one who, having received sudden marching orders, wants to utilise every moment of the brief time left at his command; who tries to pack, to purchase, to make arrangements, to go and bid farewell, to be at home when someone dear calls, to clasp hands in a parting that may be eternal, to read letters, to write them, to make his will, to speak the tender words which always sound so inadequate.

He felt all this; and over and above and beyond he longed for the touch of humanity, to hear the sound of a mortal voice bringing his trouble within the range of possibility. Death and dying in a natural way would have been bad enough, but to have to depart, he knew not how, at the beckoning of a ghostly finger, at the wordless bidding of one from out the world of spirits, added a new horror to the gruesome mandate. He must speak or he should go mad. So, as a sort of forlorn hope, he betook him to the chaplain, though, indeed, he knew rather less of that reverend gentleman than he did of his commanding officer.

At that moment, however, he was not thinking much of incongruities of rank or inequalities of station. He felt only intent on getting a straightforward answer to a question which was troubling him; therefore, when once he found himself in the clergyman's presence, and taken a chair, having been politely bidden to sit, he said—'I am distressed in mind, sir; so I thought I would come round to you.'

'It is my earnest desire that all who are distressed in mind or uneasy in conscience should bring their perplexities and burdensome sins to me, that I may tell them where to find relief,' was the answer.

'You are very kind;' and the pair looked at each other.

'Not at all; I am only doing my duty,' said the chaplain, graciously, though he did not quite like or understand his visitor.

If it be true that there is no bar to human progress like a theory, it is equally true that a foregone conclusion destroys human usefulness.

Mr Pellock had accepted the charge of military souls without the faintest idea of what those souls were like. All he felt sure about was that they were wrong in the lump, and he dealt with them accordingly. They were given to drunkenness, brawling, folly, and many other sins—that is, whole regiments, excepting here and there a picked saint, a brand plucked from the burning, who believed in Mr Pellock, in his sermons, his ministrations, his exhortations, his rebukes. If ever there was a square peg fitted painfully into a round hole, that peg was the Reverend Carus Pellock. Of the British soldier, save as a good fighting creature, he had not the smallest opinion. He said sadly that he knew poor Tommy Atkins too well, but there were officers, old and young, who inclined to the belief he knew him too little. However this might be, Mr Pellock did not think much either of the raw recruit or the finished warrior.

'A soldier disheartened him,' he was wont to declare in moments of sadness, when the result of all his efforts seemed about as satisfactory as making ropes from sea-sand. That he might be saved seemed to Mr Pellock possible, but only through a miracle. Nevertheless, the chaplain tried hard to do his duty, preached at, and to, and over the heads of his people, and was always courteous in a highly dignified sort of way.

He did not like anyone presuming on his affability though, and doubted whether Private Kilray had a proper appreciation of the gulf which yawned between a simple unit in Her Majesty's famous regiment, The Light Bays, and the man who had been good enough to undertake the charge of all the Light Bays' souls.

For this reason he answered 'not at all,' politely, yet with a certain frigid restraint, which failed to produce the desired effect.

'You remember, sir, perhaps, preaching a sermon about angels some little time since.'

Remember! As if the Rev. Carus Pellock ever forgot the matter of his sermons. 'Really,' he thought, 'this is very remarkable—very gratifying to find one of the rank and file so appreciative!

But he is Irish evidently from his accent, and the Irish are more open to impressions than the English. I must know more of this poor fellow', all of which pleasant music Mr Pellock played to himself the while he answered—'You are quite right. I rejoice to find you were so attentive.'

'In that sermon you said the angels were always with us.'

'Just so, just so,' purred the chaplain, feeling like a cat whose back is being stroked gently.

'And I suppose you believe what you said?'

Here was a question to be put to a clergyman wont to talk about angels and archangels familiarly, as though he had been brought up amongst them!

'I should certainly not preach anything I did not believe implicitly,' he answered in such a crushing tone that his visitor, humbly apologetic, replied—'No, sir, I feel certain of that; but it is hard to understand. That was all I meant, I assure you; I intended no offence.'

'It is very odd,' thought the chaplain, appeased, 'but this private speaks almost like a gentleman.' Then he said aloud—'Many things in which we believe most firmly are difficult to understand.'

'No one knows that better than I,' was the answer, so sadly spoken Mr Pellock felt constrained to reply—

'Only tell me your doubts, and I will try to help you to overcome them.'

'I don't doubt; I only wish I could,' was the unexpected rejoinder. 'You preached another sermon, sir, on All Saints' Eve,' continued Private Kilray, before the clergyman could interpose. 'I remember it particularly, because in certain districts in Ireland All Saints' Eve is kept with religious observance.'

'Very proper, very proper indeed,' said Mr Pellock, who had not the faintest idea what the observance was, and felt more convinced than ever the Irish must be a charming people to work among.

'And if I did not greatly misunderstand,' went on Private Kilray, as though he had not heard the chaplain's approving remark, 'you are of opinion it is not possible for departed spirits to return to earth.'

'I do not imagine I said impossible—only that such reappearances have never taken place,' answered the chaplain, immensely interested—so greatly interested that he scarcely noticed the wording of Private Kilray's criticism.

'Never taken place!' repeated that person; 'think a moment—only think.'

Mr Pellock did not need to think, and recovered his mistake by a clever flank movement.

'Nearly two thousand years have elapsed,' he said reverently, 'since the Divine reappearance, to which, no doubt, you allude. It was miraculous, and we have no right to quote it as a precedent. What I spoke against, and always shall consider my duty to speak against, are the legendary stories inspired by superstitious fear, and the wicked and pernicious falsehoods continually poured forth from the press, more especially at Christmas—Christmas of all times!'

'But if those legends and what you call falsehoods are true, or at least have a substratum of truth? Dead men did appear to living men once—take the case of Samuel, for instance—why should they not do so now?'

'Idle enquiries are always profitless,' was the reply. 'Surely it is enough for us to know, that though all things are possible, as a matter of fact the dead do *not* now return. Tell me the sin or sorrow that is troubling you, and I will do my best to advise and console, but I must decline to discuss abstract questions.'

'Then, if I were to tell you that no later than last night I saw one risen from the dead, what should you say?'

'I should say you need either a confessor or a doctor.'

'In other words, that I am either criminal or mad; but you mistake, sir; the man whom I saw was done to death more than a hundred years before I came into the world, and during the whole of that time he has appeared to every member of my family previous to his or her decease. He came to me because I have been thankless and foolish, and did not value the gift of life;

and now I want to live—I want to live!'

'You want a doctor, your hands twitch, your cheeks are flushed, your lips parched—you are in an overwrought and highly nervous condition. Go to a doctor, and repeat to him what you have told me. He will know how to deal with your complaint. You ought to see him soon, so I won't keep you longer now, but I should like on a future day to have some more talk with you.'

Hearing this broad hint, Private Kilray rose at once and said, in his best soldier manner—

'I thank you, sir, for your kindness; goodnight.' Then, after saluting, he went out.

'Clear case of mania,' thought Mr Pellock. 'Religious mania!—worst form of all. An interesting case.' After which, the conversation having suggested an idea to him, he turned to his desk and wrote—

'On the fleshy walls of our earthly tenements a mysterious hand is always writing the solemn warning, "This night thy soul shall be required of thee." Let us take heed that we do not neglect it', with which burst of eloquence he concluded a sermon on the following Sunday—a sermon no single person present understood, for Private Kilray, who might have hazarded a wide conjecture as to its meaning, was not amongst the audience.

CHAPTER THREE

No. Private Kilray, doubtless to his great disadvantage, did not hear Mr Pellock's famous sermon on the text, 'Now, the king's countenance changed, and his thoughts troubled him,' which was long remembered among the 'Light Bays' by reason of its utter irrelevance to any subject likely to touch or interest that gallant corps.

He was gone on leave. After his interview with the chaplain, he did not seek medical advice; rather, when the proper time came, went to bed feeling sorely depressed, not merely on account of the many things he had from boyhood left undone which he ought to have done, and the many more things he had done which he ought not to have done, but also by reason of the utter impossibility he had always experienced of getting anyone to understand him—except Kathleen. She was the one sweet exception in a bitter world, and he lay awake a long time, wondering whether there could be anywhere on earth so brave, so patient, so wise, so dear a girl as Kathleen Mawson, once in her little way an heiress, now a homeless orphan, companion to Mrs FitzDonnell, widow of Admiral Burke FitzDonnell, who wrote his name large on the naval history of England? Yes, she was living with that lady in Lowndes Square, and had told him no further back than the previous morning that Mrs FitzDonnell would not let a private soldier inside her door, not even if that private were her own son.

On reading which statement, Private Kilray waxed exceeding wroth, and, not waiting to consider whether there might not be some faint rhyme or reason, or sense, or expediency or anything save prejudice in the amiable old lady's objection to receive such a visitor, delivered his soul of a passionate tirade against a state of society which had compelled him to accept her Majesty's shilling, and Miss Mawson a salary.

This was the letter on which he had been engaged while Lord Yiewsley, dead and buried for a century and a half, or thereabouts, was stealing back from wherever he had gone to, in order that he might frighten one of his enemy's descendants almost out of his wits.

In this amiable intention he succeeded, for Private Kilray, who would have gone into battle with a light heart, was quite demoralised by the sight of that apparition which came he knew not whence, and went he knew not where.

When quite a child, living with his mother on a lonely seashore, he had one night sprung up out of his sleep uttering fearful shrieks and earnest entreaties for his nurse to 'take that man away,' which shrieks and entreaties were remembered when news arrived of his father's death.

Gossips then shook their heads, and observed, 'Ay, *he* has not forgotten; *he'll* come, as he promised he would, till there's not one of the stock left to die,' which, indeed, had been his lordship's threat. In local opinion this threat received remarkable confirmation from the fact that his enemy's family went on steadily disappearing from the face of the earth. In the ordinary course of events they ought to have multiplied exceedingly, whereas there were now left of an old family but three men and two women.

For which reason it seemed likely Lord Yiewsley's self-imposed task would soon be completed.

The morning's post following his interview with Mr Pellock might have brought an answer to Private Kilray's letter full of love for Kathleen, and brimful of anger against everyone else, but it did not, and the unhappy young man felt glad to think his darling, having received that despairing second epistle, would not now write to chide him for his first, but despatch instead a tender missive breathing forgiveness, sorrow, pity—

As it is always the unexpected which happens, however, the letter—one of two which reached him in the afternoon—proved quite different from what he had expected. Began his fair—

You silly, silly Conn, are you the only one of your name left? Is it because you consider yourself such a great personage that you imagine you must take precedence of the rest of your family? If you did see Lord Yiewsley, which I do not for a moment believe, having, as you know, always considered that story on all fours with the mourning coach, the drummer boy, the ghostly funeral procession, the white bird, the wailing banshees, and other cheerful omens proudly claimed by various families, you may live to be ninety notwithstanding. Do try to put away such silly fancies, dear boy. No, I will not meet you anywhere to say goodbye, but I am going to Weyport to bid you hope very much.

I took courage today, and told Mrs FitzDonnell our story, and what a foolish wrong-headed person my Conn is, prone to give way to little tempers, prone to spoiling his life because the moon won't come down to him, honourable darling living, for all that.

And she? Well, she said, 'I should like to see this strange creature, so we will take a train for Weyport one day before Christmas, and put up at the Sussex, which I know well, and your Conn shall come to us there, and we must think what can be done for him, the poor hot-headed young fellow.' There, Sir, is not that better than seeing a hundred Lord Yiewsleys? I feel wild with happiness, for Mrs FitzDonnell would not even half promise anything she was not able to fulfil.

Ever yours,

Kathleen

I do hope you will get this *soon*.

It was a well-meant, nice letter—Kathleen all *over*—affectionate, encouraging, sensible from beginning to end; but Private Kilray derived no comfort from it.

He knew that he had seen Lord Yiewsley, and though that defunct nobleman's visits could not be considered agreeable, still, had they ceased, every member of the young soldier's family would have felt as though some order had been taken from the Kilreas. People who have never owned a banshee, or a white bird, or a phantom drummer, or even a modest mouse, would probably fail to understand either the pride or the fear of possession, but the pride and the fear are both very strong for all that.

Had Miss Mawson been so fortunate as to be able to claim an ancestor who killed his man in the year 1640, she would have cherished his memory just as fondly as anybody else, and respected the family ghost his sin created very much indeed.

Still there was some truth in what she said. Though bad luck had pursued him through life, the summons might not have been specially meant for Private Kilray. His aunts now were getting on in years; one was nearly sixty; perhaps she would like to die; she always said she wished to do so; but, no, he would not think of such a thing; the lot had fallen on him, and he must meet his fate like a man.

While these thoughts and many more were passing through his mind, the second letter lay still unopened. It was disagreeably suggestive of a bill, and though Private Kilray was to die so soon—Lord Yiewsley's shade never gave his victims longer than a fortnight—he did not care to open that business-like envelope, on which one postmark (Dublin) stood out with painful distinctiveness. Others—London, for instance—were but faintly stamped, while Dublin blackly pointed its accusing finger at a young man never backward in the former days about getting into debt.

How had any creditor discovered his whereabouts? And he turned the letter over gingerly.

If a man were going to the scaffold it would give him a shock to be presented with 'my little bill, sir,' on the way. Humanity to its latest breath retains an insuperable objection to such ghastly reminders of happy times departed, and it was some little while before Private Kilray, taking his courage in his hand, tore open the well-gummed envelope, which he found to contain a letter, a memorandum, and a banker's draft. The memorandum said—

— Street, Dublin
15th December, 1892

Dear Sir

By request of Mrs Kilrea, we beg to enclose draft at sight for ten pounds, and remain your obedient servants,
            Kavanagh, Rutland & Co., Ltd.

There are few things capable of producing a more sudden transformation scene than a cheque or its equivalent. Who has not seen sunshine instantly take the place of shade on the receipt of a remittance; the life and joyousness of summer succeed to the cold dullness of winter when, after weeks of shortness, an empty purse is again relined with crisp bank notes? But as every rule has its exception, that ten-pound draft, which, after a fashion, was a fortune to one of Her Majesty's rank and file, caused, when he read the sealed letter which accompanied it, an expression of pained grief and anxiety to overspread his countenance. So ran the epistle—

Moyle Abbey, Moyle

My dear Grandson

Directly you receive this I want you, if possible, to come over here. Your grandfather is very ill, and *has asked for you,* and I do hope will not have to ask long in vain. Perhaps he was too hasty; but remember, Conn, you were hasty also when you ought to have remembered he was an old man who had been very kind to you. How could you leave us for eighteen months without knowledge of your whereabouts? But for Kathleen Mawson I should not even now know where to address this letter. With it Messrs Kavanagh will enclose ten pounds, as you may be without ready money. *Come at once.*

Your affectionate grandmother,

Mary Kilrea

The young man hardly read this letter—rather his eyes galloped over it.

'My God! It is he, then; the dear old man,' he muttered, as he glanced up at the clock. 'I shall have time to do it if I get leave,' he thought; 'and if I don't get leave I will take it.'

Having swiftly decided which point, he rushed off in search of his No. 1, who, yielding to the urgency of his entreaties, forthwith accompanied him to his section officer, who in turn took him into the presence of a commanding officer named Captain Dace.

Now, Captain Dace was just going out, and, not feeling pleased at the detention, sharply refused Private Kilray's request.

He felt that if he granted leave about Christmas time to every man whose father, or grandfather, or sisters, or uncles, or other relatives were ill, he would soon have no men left, and said so in remarkably terse and forcible language.

Everyone, however, knew that Captain Dace's bark was worse than his bite, and the section officer therefore ventured to remind him that Private Kilray had never asked for leave before.

'Well, he has made up for it now; a whole fortnight, no less!'

'I mightn't want so long,' said the applicant in a hoarse whisper.

'Such perpetual applications really cannot be entertained,' returned Captain Dace, brusquely, though touched by something in the private's tone. 'If it had been your father, now'—relenting—'but a grandfather!'

'He was a father to me when my own died. If you would just glance over this letter, captain, perhaps—'

It was all said in little jerks by one evidently striving hard not to break down while the letter got into the officer's hands, that gentleman himself scarcely knew how.

Much inclined to return it, he nevertheless looked at the written sheet, on the top of which was printed 'Moyle Abbey'.

Why, he knew Moyle Abbey—at least, where it was. He had once been staying with a friend who lived a few miles from it—about eight—and what are eight miles in one of the wildest parts of Ireland, where gentlemen's seats are few and far between, the roads perfect, the horses almost thoroughbred?

He had heard of Moyle Abbey, and the family that lived there, and thought of all this while he read, and the fashion of his face changed.

'Do you mean to say you are one of the Kilreas, of Moyle Abbey?'

'Yes,' answered the young man softly, as though confessing some sin.

'And enlisted under the name Kilray'—with the accent well on the first syllable, whereas the accent in Kilrea was, the speaker knew, laid on the last.

'No, I gave my right name, "Conn Kilrea", but the sergeant thought he knew better how to spell and pronounce the word than I—that is all.'

'But how the—'

Captain Dace got no further in that sentence, and his private, though he was perfectly aware of the nature of the question left unfinished, made no reply.

'I suppose you are the heir?' were the next words spoken.

'No—Major Kilrea, of the Rushers,' a regiment so called

because of the wild way in which officers and men had once charged and turned the fortunes of war when defeat seemed inevitable.

'The Rushers, eh?' commented Captain Dace. 'Well'—looking at his watch—'you have just an hour before the express for London. You can catch the mail train to Holyhead. I hope you will find your grandfather better,' with which words the interview ended, and Private Kilray left his chief, accompanied by the section officer, who felt deeply convinced men may, and often do, even nowadays entertain angels unawares.

CHAPTER FOUR

As the Irish mail sped across England, Conn Kilrea thought concerning his past and future as he had never done before, even while the dread of death lay sore upon him. His own death would have ended the business, written '*Finis*' to the uncompleted volume, once containing so many hopes, latterly only soiled and blotted by fears; but with the belief that the doom he had shrunk from was transferred to another, something for which he could find no name began to struggle within him, and fight with his worse self for mastery.

Looking back, he knew he had been his own most bitter foe—that it was his indifference, his indolence, his love of pleasure, his uncontrolled jealousy, his bursts of passion, which gave a handle to the enemy, while grieving the hearts and wounding the pride of those who loved him best.

He had been given his chance, and neglected it, he bitterly confessed. He thought of his schoolboy days, when he would not learn; of his college career, when he only laughed at opportunity, casting each as it came aside for the sake of some rowdy party or foolish escapade. He had taken life as a jest, and feasted and made merry till the hour of reckoning came, when, solemnly convinced the world was all wrong, or at least Conn Kilrea the only right person in it, he cast himself adrift from old ties, and took refuge amongst those who were but as his father's 'hired servants'.

Then, instead of making the best of a bad business, as even in the ranks a man may, he had allowed a very demon of sullenness to gain possession of him, and repelled the well-meant, though rough attempt at kindness of those who would have tried to make his life better. Voluntarily he had thrown himself out of the rank in which he had been born, and then he resented the fact that people did not know by intuition he was a prince in disguise.

'A prince', indeed! Nay, rather a humble dependant, who had not been grateful for the money spent, for the money given, for shelter, food, clothing; who had never earned a single penny till he enlisted in the 'Light Bays.'

He saw it all at last. While the train swept through the night he recalled the story of his life from youth to manhood, and found it wanting.

'God helping me, I'll try to mend my ways now,' he thought, 'but; it's too late to please the dear old man—too late, too late!'

At the very time all this passed through Conn Kilrea's mind, and he was inaudibly uttering his own heartfelt self-condemnation, another man, who had far more reason than his prodigal cousin to love the owner of Moyle Abbey, stood in a brilliant ballroom, waiting and watching for the arrival of one he believed was not indifferent to him.

At last she entered—his fair, his queen. The expectant lover's pulse beat a little faster as he advanced to meet a portly lady, magnificently dressed, glittering with jewels, handsome, self-possessed, a thorough woman of society, and one well able to hold her own in it.

'Ah, Major Kilrea,' she said, 'we did not expect to see you here tonight.'

'Why not?' he asked gallantly, in a tone addressed more to the daughter than the mother.

'Because I thought you would be in Ireland.'

'I go to Ireland by the early morning mail.'

'Oh!' she returned; and he knew instantly why her manner had changed.

'I was so grieved to hear of Mr Kilrea's illness,' Mrs Gerrard went on, after an almost imperceptible pause.

'Yes, but I trust it is not serious,' rejoined Mr Kilrea's grandson. 'He has had similar attacks before.' And then Mrs and Miss Gerard were swept away, and their friend the handsome major was left to his own reflections.

'Just my luck,' he thought, 'my cursed luck.'

Quite an hour elapsed before Miss Gerard could give him the waltz she had promised a week previously.

'You do not blame me for coming here tonight,' he said tenderly, as they stopped for a moment.

'Oh no,' she returned with a cool ease, which showed she would at some future time be as good a society woman as her mother; 'everyone must in such matters judge for himself.'

'You speak as though I ought to have gone'—reproachfully.

'I should have gone, but, as I said this moment, no one can judge for another.'

The game was up. He felt he had lost her and her fortune as certainly as though a thousand tongues had proclaimed the fact.

'Are you rested? Shall we take another turn?' he asked, and it was not till they paused again that Major Kilrea enquired, 'From whom did you hear of my grandfather's illness?'

'From Admiral Gerard, who was saying also how sorry he had been to learn his old comrade's son was in the Light Bays, and only a private. He thought something ought to be done for him.'

She spoke quite calmly and distinctly, as if talking about some common matter, but the officer felt there was a sting in every word.

'Conn is an odd fellow, and it is hard to know what to do for him. He has never written me a line since he enlisted.'

'Perhaps he expected a line from you,' she answered. 'I hope you will have a good passage, and find Mr Kilrea better,' she added, as another partner came forward. 'Goodbye,' and so left him to consider the irony of fate.

This was what was going on a few miles out of London while

the Irish express dashed through Wales. The wind had risen, and howled mournfully among the hills.

'Doesn't omen well,' said one of Conn's fellow-passengers, and the omen was fulfilled.

But after an awful passage the young man stepped ashore, hurried up to Dublin, and without stopping to eat or drink, crossed the city, and took train for Moyle.

A groom stood outside the station holding two horses. It was like a dream. Conn Kilray had not thought to come home thus or ever!

'How is my grandfather?' he asked the man.

'Very bad, sir; but he'll be better for the sight of you!'

They rode on fast, and in less than an hour Conn was pressing the sick man's hand, but could not speak because of tears which were choking him.

'I thought Leo would have been here by now,' said old Mr Kilrea, feebly.

'I am sure he will come as soon as he can get away,' answered the young man, stinting his grief.

'Can that be Conn who spoke?' thought Mrs Kilrea—Conn who for years had never uttered a word concerning his cousin without an accent of irritation.

Yes, it was Conn—Conn also who sat up with his grandfather, watched him as a mother might a child, raised him tenderly, and twenty-four hours later broke the news just received by telegram that the reason why Major Kilrea did not come was because he had met with an accident!

Before very long they were obliged to tell the old man that accident was death. He had been pitched from his dogcart while driving a friend home from the ball at Stanmore, and killed on the spot.

Said the friend before the coroner: 'He drove so recklessly, I wonder I am alive to tell the tale. The horse bolted; we ran into a market van, were both shot out; Major Kilrea was dead when picked up.'

The catastrophe affected Mr Kilrea less than might have been expected. He had heard something about his heir's proceedings, which, perhaps, reconciled him to that heir's premature death. Besides, he himself was old, and felt life very sweet.

'It was not for me then,' he muttered, 'not for me; poor Leo,' and forthwith began to get better.

But Conn took his cousin's fate greatly to heart, and won golden opinions by the humility with which he assumed his new honours, and his gentle forbearance and kindness to all with whom he came in contact.

'The Light Bays must be a gran' corps for training a man,' said the old butler to the old cook at Moyle when the spring had come and flowers were blooming, 'for it's not Conn Kilrea they've sent back to us, but a saint. He has never rapped out an oath, nor knocked down a single one, nor run over man or woman, child or pig, since he came home! Instead of the biggest divil ever stepped, anybody might think he'd been brought up in a convent—among the holy nuns. Milk is strong compared with him, and if he only holds on as he's doing he'll be the best Kilrea ever owned Moyle Abbey, and there never was to say a bad one yet!'

From which it would seem that Lord Yiewsley's visit had been productive of good, though neither Mrs Kilrea senior nor junior will permit that nobleman's name to be mentioned in the house.

LEONAUR

ALSO FROM LEONAUR
AVAILABLE IN SOFTCOVER OR HARDCOVER WITH DUST JACKET

THE COMPLETE FOUR JUST MEN: VOLUME 2 *by Edgar Wallace*—*The Law of the Four Just Men* & *The Three Just Men*—disillusioned with a world where the wicked and the abusers of power perpetually go unpunished, the Just Men set about to rectify matters according to their own standards, and retribution is dispensed on swift and deadly wings.

THE COMPLETE RAFFLES: 1 *by E. W. Hornung*—*The Amateur Cracksman* & *The Black Mask*—By turns urbane gentleman about town and accomplished cricketer, life is just too ordinary for Raffles and that sets him on a series of adventures that have long been treasured as a real antidote to the 'white knights' who are the usual heroes of the crime fiction of this period.

THE COMPLETE RAFFLES: 2 *by E. W. Hornung*—*A Thief in the Night* & *Mr Justice Raffles*—By turns urbane gentleman about town and accomplished cricketer, life is just too ordinary for Raffles and that sets him on a series of adventures that have long been treasured as a real antidote to the 'white knights' who are the usual heroes of the crime fiction of this period.

THE COLLECTED SUPERNATURAL AND WEIRD FICTION OF WILKIE COLLINS: VOLUME 1 *by Wilkie Collins*—Contains one novel 'The Haunted Hotel', one novella 'Mad Monkton', three novelettes 'Mr Percy and the Prophet', 'The Biter Bit' and 'The Dead Alive' and eight short stories to chill the blood.

THE COLLECTED SUPERNATURAL AND WEIRD FICTION OF WILKIE COLLINS: VOLUME 2 *by Wilkie Collins*—Contains one novel 'The Two Destinies', three novellas 'The Frozen deep', 'Sister Rose' and 'The Yellow Mask' and two short stories to chill the blood.

THE COLLECTED SUPERNATURAL AND WEIRD FICTION OF WILKIE COLLINS: VOLUME 3 *by Wilkie Collins*—Contains one novel 'Dead Secret,' two novelettes 'Mrs Zant and the Ghost' and 'The Nun's Story of Gabriel's Marriage' and five short stories to chill the blood.

FUNNY BONES *selected by Dorothy Scarborough*—An Anthology of Humorous Ghost Stories.

MONTEZUMA'S CASTLE AND OTHER WEIRD TALES *by Charles B. Cory*—Cory has written a superb collection of eighteen ghostly and weird stories to chill and thrill the avid enthusiast of supernatural fiction.

SUPERNATURAL BUCHAN *by John Buchan*—Stories of Ancient Spirits, Uncanny Places & Strange Creatures.

LEONAUR

ALSO FROM LEONAUR
AVAILABLE IN SOFTCOVER OR HARDCOVER WITH DUST JACKET

MR MUKERJI'S GHOSTS *by S. Mukerji*—Supernatural tales from the British Raj period by India's Ghost story collector.

KIPLINGS GHOSTS *by Rudyard Kipling*—Twelve stories of Ghosts, Hauntings, Curses, Werewolves & Magic.

THE COLLECTED SUPERNATURAL AND WEIRD FICTION OF WASHINGTON IRVING: VOLUME 1 *by Washington Irving*—Including one novel 'A History of New York', and nine short stories of the Strange and Unusual.

THE COLLECTED SUPERNATURAL AND WEIRD FICTION OF WASHINGTON IRVING: VOLUME 2 *by Washington Irving*—Including three novelettes 'The Legend of the Sleepy Hollow', 'Dolph Heyliger', 'The Adventure of the Black Fisherman' and thirty-two short stories of the Strange and Unusual.

THE COLLECTED SUPERNATURAL AND WEIRD FICTION OF JOHN KENDRICK BANGS: VOLUME 1 *by John Kendrick Bangs*—Including one novel 'Toppleton's Client or A Spirit in Exile', and ten short stories of the Strange and Unusual.

THE COLLECTED SUPERNATURAL AND WEIRD FICTION OF JOHN KENDRICK BANGS: VOLUME 2 *by John Kendrick Bangs*—Including four novellas 'A House-Boat on the Styx', 'The Pursuit of the House-Boat', 'The Enchanted Typewriter' and 'Mr. Munchausen' of the Strange and Unusual.

THE COLLECTED SUPERNATURAL AND WEIRD FICTION OF JOHN KENDRICK BANGS: VOLUME 3 *by John Kendrick Bangs*—Including twor novellas 'Olympian Nights', 'Roger Camerden: A Strange Story', and ten short stories of the Strange and Unusual.

THE COLLECTED SUPERNATURAL AND WEIRD FICTION OF MARY SHELLEY: VOLUME 1 *by Mary Shelley*—Including one novel 'Frankenstein or the Modern Prometheus', and fourteen short stories of the Strange and Unusual.

THE COLLECTED SUPERNATURAL AND WEIRD FICTION OF MARY SHELLEY: VOLUME 2 *by Mary Shelley*—Including one novel 'The Last Man', and three short stories of the Strange and Unusual.

THE COLLECTED SUPERNATURAL AND WEIRD FICTION OF AMELIA B. EDWARDS *by Amelia B. Edwards*—Contains two novelettes 'Monsieur Maurice', and 'The Discovery of the Treasure Isles', one ballad 'A Legend of Boisguilbert'and seventeen short stories to cill the blood.

Printed in the USA
CPSIA information can be obtained
at www.ICGtesting.com
CBHW030111090224
4188CB00007B/58